CHASERS

a novel

LORENZO CARCATERRA

WITHDRAWN

POCKET BOOKS

LONDON • SYDNEY • NEW YORK • TORONTO

First published in the United States of America
by the Random House Publishing Group, 2007
First published in Great Britain by Simon & Schuster UK Ltd, 2007
This edition first published by Pocket Books, 2008
An imprint of Simon & Schuster UK ltd
A CBS COMPANY

Copyright © 2007 by Lorenzo Carcaterra

This book is copyright under the Berne Convention.
No reproduction without permission.
All rights reserved.
Pocket Books & Design is a registered trademark of Simon & Schuster Inc.

The right of Lorenzo Carcaterra to be identified as the author
of this work has been asserted by him in accordance with sections
77 and 78 of the Copyright, Designs and Patents Act, 1988.

1 3 5 7 9 10 8 6 4 2

Simon & Schuster UK Ltd
Africa House
64-78 Kingsway
London WC2B 6AH

www.simonsays.co.uk

Simon & Schuster Australia
Sydney

A CIP catalogue record for this book is available from the British Library

ISBN 978-1-4165-1172-4

This book is a work of fiction. Names, characters, places and incidents
are either a product of the author's imagination or are used fictitiously.
Any resemblance to actual people living or dead, events or locales
is entirely coincidental.

Typeset by M Rules
Printed and bound in Great Britain by
Cox & Wyman Ltd, Reading, Berks

This one is for Mary Jane Miller Toepfer
April 22, 1920–February 3, 2006

1

Revenge is an act of passion.
Vengeance of justice.

— SAMUEL JOHNSON

1

CHAPTER

APRIL, 1985

It took her less than a minute to die.

Two bullets, both close-contact hits, sent her slumping to the black-and-white tiled floor, crystal-blue eyes glazed and watery, staring up at a blue ceiling dotted with red stars. Her long brown hair was heavy with sweat and blood and was forced to one side of what had been a face pretty enough to always earn a smile. During those last few seconds, she lay there whispering a silent prayer, the two plates of hot food she had been holding scattered, white cream sauce from the grilled Dover sole running down the right leg of her black slacks. Her left arm twitched and one of her shoes had somehow landed near her neck, a low-heeled pump resting on its side, black strap snapped off. She had bought the shoes with the money from her last paycheck, paying more than she could afford for a pair of Ferragamos she had always dreamed of owning. She closed her eyes and wondered if she would be buried wearing those shoes.

The main dining room of the large midtown restaurant was now a crime scene.

Men and women, police shields hanging on chain collars around their necks, walked and took notes of all that they saw. The forensics unit was busy snapping photos and bagging biologicals, moving with practiced ease from one body to the next. A medical examiner knelt over one of the dead, a middle-aged man in a designer suit, ensconced in a leather booth, head back, hands flat on a blood-splattered table, tailored white shirt now crimson but dry. Uniformed officers took statements from nerve-shattered waiters, waitresses, patrons, managers, and owners. Thick strips of police tape blocked off a large portion of the area. Outside, lights twirled and TV news crews set up position posts.

It was 2:35 P.M., a clear and warm Thursday afternoon in New York City.

The kind of spring day when the city felt clean, crisp. When couples rode bikes in the park or walked to work and office employees chose to eat their lunch outside.

A day when no one deserved to die.

"Get a chance to grab me some coffee?" the detective asked. He was young, neatly dressed: a light brown suit, tan loafers.

"Been pretty busy in here," the uniformed officer said. He was older, his blues begging for starch and a hot iron, his body a few years removed from giving up the ghost. "Haven't had a chance to take a run outside yet."

The detective turned away from the body and stared with dark eyes at the uniform. "You don't need to run or walk outside," he said. "Seeing as how we're in a restaurant, I'd put odds on better than good there's a hot pot of coffee in here somewhere. All you need to do is look."

The uniform nodded and headed toward a small workstation

tucked in behind one of the back booths, silver pots at rest beside warm burners, his dream of one day ditching the uniform for a detective's shield doing a slow fade. Nine years on the job and here he was still reduced to running errands, a civil servant in every sense. He reached under the counter for a white cup, and it was then that he noticed the man standing there, his eyes locked onto the crime scene. The man wasn't flashing a shield and he wasn't dressed in a suit, but he smelled of it all the same: cop.

"I help you with anything?" the uniform asked, his voice trying to stay casual but also to establish authority.

"Don't see how," the man said, not taking his eyes off the scene, his words sounding like the street. "Unless you pulled in early enough to eyeball the doers."

"You working this?" the uniform asked, resting the cup on the counter and easing in closer to the man.

"Guy in the blue jacket, gray slacks," the man said, ignoring the question. "One who sent you on the coffee run. He the primary?"

"Jenkins," the uniform said, turning away from the man to glare across the room at the detective. "If he isn't yet, he will be by the time the bodies are zippered and tagged. He makes it his business to catch all the multiples in the sector."

The man reached under the counter and pulled out a cup. He grabbed a silver dispenser and filled the cup halfway with lukewarm coffee. He turned away from the uniform and stepped deeper into the crime scene, the fingers of his right hand wrapped around the cup.

"You didn't answer my question," the uniform said as the man brushed past.

"And you didn't get Detective Jenkins his coffee," the man said.

Coffee in hand, Giovanni "Boomer" Frontieri stared down at the body of the young girl, his eyes hard, his mind racing back through the photo album of her years. He saw her behind thick hospital glass, less than a day old, a six-pound seven-ounce bundle, her skin the color of Sunday sauce. Even back then, Boomer knew this would be as close as he'd ever get to a child of his own—a niece he could dote on and help raise from a distance. He flipped forward to her Holy Communion, thin legs shaky as she made her way down the center aisle of Blessed Sacrament Church, smiling when she caught his eye, finding comfort and confidence in his presence. He remembered sitting at his sister's kitchen table, sipping a hot espresso, when she walked down the hall steps wearing a flowered dress he had bought her at a J. C. Penney half-price sale, ready to embark on her first formal date. Boomer closed his eyes, felt her head on his shoulder, tears running down her face and onto his leather jacket, minutes after he had told her of her father's death. Boomer opened his eyes again and this time heard her laughter, the little-girl giggle mixed in with the full-throated chuckle of a young woman, and he swallowed hard, not looking just now to share his own tears.

"You got business here?" Jenkins was next to him now.

"I have *family* here," Boomer said, handing Jenkins the now cold cup of coffee. "The waitress is my sister's kid. Only the start of her third week working here. She liked it enough. Gave her a chance to meet new people, and she was always eager to do that."

Jenkins rested the coffee on a table to his left. "You should be waiting down at the precinct," he said. "At some point, a uniform will find you and tell you all you need to know."

"The target was the one in the booth," Boomer said. "The three on the ground, my niece included, are collateral. The hit team couldn't have numbered more than four: two shooters, a lookout, and a driver. They're pros, but fudged it to make it look like they weren't. They used high-caliber bullets and cleared the casings. Picked a visible place at a crowded time. The vic was at the table alone, means his crew was in on the hit, cleared out soon as they spotted the gunners. They wanted this hit to be known, noticed."

Boomer turned and looked at Jenkins. "But why the hell am I telling you any of this? You must have figured all that soon as you walked in."

"How long you been off the job?" Jenkins asked.

"Five years, give or take," Boomer said. He gave a quick scan to the activity around them, nodding at several familiar faces, watching the scene develop. There's never a need to rush a sealed homicide crime scene. The evidence spread across the room as if on a buffet table, and everyone waits for a detective with a sharp eye to mull his choices before making any final selections. "You narrow your players down yet?"

"We really shouldn't be talking about this," Jenkins said.

"We're not," Boomer said. "And if anybody asks, we weren't."

Jenkins did a slow nod, hands thrust inside his Dockers, and dropped his voice two levels. "The Italians look to me to be clean on this," he said. "Not their play to do a hit in front of enough witnesses to fill a small theater. And the vic scans way too rich and too connected to be running into any gang-bang action. Besides which, this is not a part of town the brothers be allowed to play in."

"Which leaves your eyes where?"

"Off the top, at either the Russians or the Colombians," Jenkins said. "They both may still be toddlers in this town, but they're hands down the most dangerous. And they eat this kind of shit up with a knife and fork. They love nothing more than to leave behind a room filled with bodies, and us with nothing but theory to prove it was them that did the work."

"You connect the vic to any one crew?" Boomer asked, tossing a look at the man in the booth, surrounded by three members from the forensics unit.

"My guess is we will soon as we get a name from his prints and dentals," Jenkins said. "The doers walked out with his ID, including a watch, a ring, and an earring."

"Any families been notified yet?" Boomer asked.

"Way early for that, still," Jenkins said. "Then again, you just about beat me to the scene. How'd that come to happen?"

"I was looking for a cup of coffee," Boomer said, gazing at his niece one final time. "Same as you."

"The guys did this, they're not going to be on the loose for very long," Jenkins said, his manner confident. "Pros or not, they get sloppy, take a slip and tumble. More often than not, a gun and a badge will be right there, ready to lay down a cuff and convict."

Boomer took the young detective in. "That's no help to the dead," he said.

———

He walked outside the roped-off parameters, leaving behind the lab techs, uniforms, detectives, photo unit, medical-examiner personnel, and potential witnesses, each in the early stages of processing those who were killed for reasons to be determined. He walked with a slight limp, favoring his right leg, shredded years earlier in a gunfight with a drug dealer. He had his hands balled into tight fists and his upper body was tense and coiled, eyes looking toward the congested traffic outside. He never once glanced back. He didn't need to see her corpse as it was casually laid inside an open body bag, waiting for two attendants to ease her into the morgue van for the slow ride downtown. He didn't need any further reason to remember what he could never forget.

He eased past two detectives and stepped out onto a sidewalk crowded with the curious, determined to put his own brand on the justice that needed to be served.

2

The tall man sat on the top bleacher, staring out at the high school track and gazing at the array of students prepping for an afternoon's practice. He had a sweaty bottle of Corona beer wrapped inside a wet paper bag by his right foot and scratched at three days' stubble. As the day had stretched on, the weather had turned cool, the sun hiding behind a small battalion of clouds.

The man leaned a set of strong shoulders against a wooden rail. "Tell me what is on your mind, Roberto," he said to the young man sitting to his left. "And do it before the kids begin their runs."

"The way the hit went down today was not right," Roberto said. "It could have been and should have been a lot cleaner. How are we going to be respected by the other gangs in this city if the best we can do is botch a restaurant hit?"

The man picked up the paper bag and took a long swig of the Corona. He looked over at Roberto and smiled. "I don't want their *respect*," he said. "All that ever gets you is a sympathy card and fresh flowers at your funeral. I want them to *shiver* when they hear my name. I want them to think that I will do *anything* at *any time* to *anyone*. Who are we to fear? The police? You think they give a shit about a dead spic? To them, it's one less player they need to concern themselves over. This job was our first success, my young friend. And one of many more that will come our way."

"The police may give it only a shrug, but the Gonzalez brothers will care," Roberto said, holding tight to his concern. "They will care very much about that one dead spic."

"I expect nothing less," the man said. "It was one of their own we put down. So the first instinct will be to bite back. They'll call out their guns and aim them our way. And they will hold their own, at least for a while. But they, too, will meet their day. It's only a question of when."

Roberto stared out at the runners, a sprint team from Holy Angels High School, going through a series of warm-up exercises, a coach in a sweatshirt carrying a stopwatch, clocking their every move. "Do you miss it much?" he asked.

"It was my life," the man said, leaning forward, thin arms at rest on steady legs. "For thirty years all I knew, all I loved, was my religion and my sport. I began each day with a short prayer and ended it with a long run. I thought it would go that way until it was my time to die."

"Were you a good coach?" Roberto asked, knowing that he was stepping into the older man's comfort zone, an arena where he more closely resembled a saint than a stone killer.

"Some years, yes," the man said, throwing Roberto a relaxed smile. "Those years, we won many meets and took home trophies by the armful. Other years, when my squads lacked discipline, were not so kind."

"I came to one of your meets," Roberto said. "Went with my older brothers up to Mexico City to see their school race against yours. They were favored that day, a much faster group than the one you bused into town."

"And?" the man said, his eyes focused on a tall, lanky boy with a high-end leg kick. "Was their school better?"

"Maybe they were, but not on that day and not on that track," Roberto said. "They were run to the ground by Father Angel Cortez and his squad."

"Even back in those years I hated to lose," Angel said. "A bad trait, I suppose, in a priest, no matter how good the intentions. But one that has served me well in my second cycle."

Roberto nodded.

"I won over a hundred gold medals in the years I coached," Angel said. "If I put them all together, I couldn't buy my way into a minor-league ballpark. You reach my age and you come to realize the foolishness of a vow of poverty. It does nothing except help to line the pockets of other men."

Angel finished the last of his beer and leaned back, letting what was left of a setting sun illuminate his tanned face. He was a slight man, kept thin by a diet that consisted of one small meal a day, usually a mixture of steamed rice and carrots. Angel's vices were limited to cold Coronas and chilled rosé at the ready. He was sixty-one, the only son of a Colombian shepherd with a religious bent and a Mexican mother who taught him to say his first Mass in the small kitchen of their two-bedroom farm. At fourteen, he was signed over to the priesthood, destined to serve out a life devoted to God and little else. He took full advantage of the educational avenues open to him, earning top honors and entry to the best schools in South America. The Church was more than willing to fund his way, eager to nourish the passions of a young and zealous priest. And he took to his calling, earning degrees in English literature, music, and art history, passing his newfound knowledge down to his eager and attentive students at the high school where he was assigned to teach. The students of the small town, less than a fifteen-minute drive south of Bogotá, were poor, undernourished, and possessed of little hope for the future. The one road leading out of town, the one path promising something—anything—could be seen from the windows of their homes and classrooms day and night, and the poppy fields that dotted the landscape might as well have been layered with dollar bills, for they, more than books or sports, were the enticement that drove the young men and women of the town who were looking to line their pockets.

Father Angel Cortez knew the odds were bad, but he bet against the house.

He worked with the kids, preaching and teaching a better way. "I know more than my share of old doctors, lawyers, and teachers," he would tell his students. "But I don't know any old drug dealers. Most, if at all lucky, live only as long as an abandoned dog."

He fought against the encroachment of the drug cartels by keeping the children under his domain constantly busy. He helped to organize baseball and basketball tournaments, got some of the town businesses to kick in money and build a new track and grandstands for the school. He then took a handful of teenagers, used to running up and down the rugged mountain terrain surrounding the town, and turned them into one of the most élite track-and-field teams in South America. Before long, college recruiters and professional scouts from as far north as Detroit and Chicago ventured down, looking to offer fast and easy money along with full-ride four-year scholarships to the young padre's crew. Father Angel's dreams for a better world and a safer and more rewarding life for the students under his care seemed on the verge of a hard-fought victory.

Then reality intruded, and Father Angel's dreams were swallowed up by a whirlpool of deceit, corruption, and murder, leaving in its wake only the ruined and the ravaged. It began with a street shooting, a weekly occurrence in an area blighted by drug-related crimes. The victim was named Edgardo Vizcaino, a promising sixteen-year-old, four-hundred-meter track star. His older brother Alberto was a runner for the Diablos de Dios, a local drug gang on the payroll of the big guns in Bogotá. Alberto had grown weary of running drugs in and past an elaborate network of police blockades and federal sting setups, risking a long stretch in prison in return for the short end of the money train. He was looking to start his own shop, and let it be known that he would take down the leaders of the Diablos de Dios if the action called for it.

In the drug world, as in any criminal endeavor, the road to an early death is paved with indecision. Alberto spoke rather than acted, and that allowed the Diablos to pounce. And their way was a seek-and-destroy quest to rid themselves of any and all potential threats. Alberto's battered and torched body was left hanging from the low branch of an old tree. Then they pressed their agenda forward and set about murdering each member of the Vizcaino family, saving Edgardo, the youngest and most vulnerable, for last.

Angel was never sure exactly what it was about the murder of Edgardo Vizcaino, as opposed to any of the other horrible crimes he had seen perpetrated on people too weak or unwilling to fight back, that forced his hand. But that early morning, as the body of a boy he had grown to respect as much as to love was being prepped for burial, he decided that the time for reflection and prayer had ended. The Diablos were not interested in the words of a priest. They would respond only to action.

The war raged for three years.

In that time, Father Cortez morphed from a benevolent small-town priest into a man so deadly and ruthless that the local papers began to refer to him as the Black Angel. He still sought out the area's young and gifted, but instead of putting their skills to the test on a running track he ran them out into the line of fire armed with Mac .9s and turned them into dealers and killing machines.

By the late fall of 1982, Angel Cortez ruled over a criminal enterprise that stretched from the sandy streets of his small village to the high-rises of Bogotá and into the deep money of Mexico City and South Florida. There were 350 full-time dealers under his domain, 175 mules running cocaine packets across various state and national boundaries, and an army of 200 heavily armed hitters, each quick of trigger and Nike fast on the escape, making police detection close to an impossible task. His determined vow of poverty had now been replaced by a quest for riches, with a stream of offshore sheltered accounts totaling nearly $6 million. And all that gun power sitting on top of the small mountains of cold cash pointed the former priest in only one direction: an all-out takeover of the streets of New York. By the spring of 1985, Angel Cortez was ready to make his move to the big show.

"How soon you think before they bite us back?" Roberto asked.

"Not long. A week at the most," Angel said. "It won't be a heavy move. Not at first. Not their kind of play. They'll look to hit us at our softest spot and work their way up from there. It's how they have worked since they first hit the city, and there's no reason for them to change their ways now."

"Sí, but we have a soft spot?" Roberto asked, shrugging his shoulders.

"Everyone does," Angel said. "No matter how prepared they think they are or how much thought they put into their plans. We are no exception. Unless, of course, I choose to eliminate that soft spot myself, saving the Gonzalez brothers a handful of bullets."

"And what is ours?"

Angel Cortez stood, the empty beer bottle inside the paper bag dangling from the thin fingers of his right hand, and stared down at Roberto. "You are."

"I'm not looking to talk you out of anything you already set your mind to get into," Davis "Dead-Eye" Winthrop said. "I'm too old and still too angry to burn my time on getting nowhere. So let me put it out there for you nice and clean. I want in on this just as much as you do."

Boomer took a deep breath and raised his face to the late-afternoon sky, which featured a string of ominous clouds. They were standing in a tight and grease-free alley off the Fontana Brothers Funeral Parlor, backs pressed against a redbrick wall. Up the small hill and to their right, they could see the back door to the mourning room partially open, a chubby man in an ill-fitting jacket and tie shoving his head out, letting cigarette smoke filter through his nostrils. Inside, on the second floor, in the middle of three rooms, lay his niece's closed coffin, surrounded by an array of sobbing friends and family, large bouquets of flowers slowly wilting under the weight of a humid day.

"This one's different," Boomer said.

"Why?" Dead-Eye asked. "Because she's family? If that's the line, then you can sell that brand of shit on some other corner. That don't wash anywhere near me. That girl was as much blood to me as if she were my own kid."

"That's not it," Boomer said, letting his eyes roll across his oldest and most trusted friend. "Not even close."

"Then tell me what is close," Dead-Eye said.

"What's it been since that last job now, three years?" Boomer asked.

"Month or two, give or take," Dead-Eye said. "Depends more on how you count the time invested. Way I look at it, job was done when my last wound healed."

"And I still don't know if we won that tussle because we were lucky or because we were better," Boomer said.

"Little bit of both," Dead-Eye said.

"This time, the coin tosses might not all go our way," Boomer said. "Then, throw into the mix a new set of crews, colder and harder than what we've been up against before. Put it all together and we're not exactly staring at a Kodak moment."

"Bad is still bad no matter what end of the world they call home, Boom," Dead-Eye said. "And you're still going in, no matter what the scoreboard reads like."

Boomer nodded. "I don't have much to call my own," he said. "That's not a complaint, just a fact we both need to take a long look at. My family pictures are on the spare side, and the only one I ever really loved from that end, the one that owned my heart, is waiting to take a long ride to a small cemetery."

"That were my boy in there waiting to get buried instead of your niece, would you step aside even if I told you it was how I wanted it?" Dead-Eye asked.

"No," Boomer said.

"Then let's move on to the second part of the exam," Dead-Eye said. "You pick up any intel on the shooters, street or department?"

"It could be the Russians—the shooting has some of their tire tracks on it," Boomer said. "But the smart cash is riding on a crew from South America looking to impress the SAs working the coke-and-gun end of town. Now, the only new crew making any noise these last few months has been a kill-crazy band of white-line pistols cherried by a dealer who used to be a priest. My gut is to look their way, but it might be best to do a wash and rinse on both ends just so we lock down on the right target."

"A man of God gone to hell," Dead-Eye said. "I tell you straight, they don't give themselves much of a shake these days. Take your pick of evil, my man. They either popping caps in some innocent bystander in broad daylight or molesting kids under a white sheet at night."

"He didn't come into town alone," Boomer said. "Got at least two, maybe three hundred guns within reach, answer only to his words. And he's not the shy type of padre, kind who works best in the shadows. He's up front and personal and will put the drop down himself, the mood strikes."

"He might think, for now at least, he's holding a full tray of fresh cookies," Dead-Eye said. "But just wait until he gets wind of us—two shot-up, beat-up, crippled ex-cops putting a hunt party out on his SA ass. What, my friend, do you suppose the ole padre is going to do once that shit filters through his ears?"

"If luck is still running our way, he'll laugh until he dies," Boomer said.

4

CHAPTER

Stephanie Torres walked down the burnt-out hallway, the thick and familiar smell of burnt wood and rubber filling her nose and lungs as smoke smoldered off the walls. She moved with seasoned steps, her eyes scanning each crack in the wall, each hole in the floorboards, easing her way from one ruined apartment to the next. She was looking for the one piece of evidence that would allow her to label the fire, which only a few hours earlier was a cauldron that had taken a full New York fire battalion to combat, the work of an arsonist. It cost the lives of three civilians and put two veteran smoke-eaters in an ICU ward. She moved up the landing, stepping over a large, gaping hole and moving past the bodies of a half dozen rats smoldering in a corner. At the top of the steps, she bent down and ran her gloved fingers over a small mound of dust, picking out the burnt remains of a safety pin. She reached into the pocket of her fire coat, pulled out a small cellophane evidence bag, dropped it in, and sealed it shut. She stood up and walked deeper into the second-floor hallway.

She was an arson investigator assigned to the New York Police Department, working out of a set of precincts in the East Bronx. It was a neighborhood that she knew well, having grown up in a two-story house on Boyd Avenue, the only daughter of a Puerto Rican garage mechanic and a tough-willed mother one generation removed from the streets of San Juan. Back then, the neighborhood was a series of redbrick houses that served as first homes to a working-class enclave of Italian, Irish, and Hispanic immigrants, each of whom found a common ground in rearing children and vegetable gardens. Stephanie was at ease both at school, where she excelled in science and English lit, and on the street in front of her home, where she had mastered the intricate rules of bottle-cap baseball before she lost all her baby teeth. Her father, Hector, a proud and stubborn man and the first in his family to land a civil-service job with the Department of Sanitation, would sit behind the small white gate leading to the basement steps of the two-story house he owned, mortgage-free, and watch his little girl at play. He preferred to work the more demanding eight-to-four morning shift in order to be home to spend time with Stephanie. She was a frail girl, suited more to the leafy confines of suburban sprawl than to the daily give-and-take tumble of the Bronx streets, but he was also confident that what Stephanie lacked in brawn she more than made up for with grit and sheer force of will. Across many years of lazy spring and fall afternoons, Hector would sit in an old garden chair, a cup of iced tea resting next to the folded sports pages of the *New York Post,* and allow the gleeful sounds of laughing and shouting children to transport him back to the streets of his native land.

Those afternoons also transported him back to a life he missed and a woman he could never forget. Hector Torres first laid eyes on Maria Espinoza on a side street just off the crowded main drag in Old

San Juan. He was a week shy of sixteen and she couldn't have been any older than fifteen, but it took only a second for the full, blunt force of love to give them each a hard jolt. They married less than a year later and were bound for New York a month after the wedding, not in the pursuit of wealth and dreams but in search of a steady job and a good home and a good school for the daughter they would soon call their own.

Those early years in 1950s New York were not an easy time for a young and ambitious couple, the available jobs being menial and on the low end of the pay scale. But working-class dreams die a slow death and Hector and Maria struggled on, determined not to live their lives in a cold-water, third-story walk-up where the radiators stopped hissing heat at ten at night, causing the windows to crack by morning. In the summer, the unforgiving humidity of the stifling days and nights turned the rooms into saunas. Hector, who found work as a school custodian, a gas-station attendant, a member of a park cleanup crew, and a boiler duster, all of them off-the-book and temporary jobs with no upside, sought and found the mother lode of middle-class stability. A two-year stint in the military, followed by a civil-service exam, gave him safe passage to a new world, one filled with low-cost housing and better schools. This allowed them a final break from the shackles of cash-by-the-day employment and the fast-money lure of the dark side of the street.

Hector and Maria saved as much as they could from each paycheck, putting small chunks away for a down payment on a new home and for Stephanie's school, the rest going to meet both the daily demands and the pleasures of their new world order. They took their first vacation—a four-day stay in Bermuda—with Christmas-bonus and tip money Hector earned hauling and tossing garbage from the high-end, doormanned buildings along Park and Madison Avenues. And he doted on Stephanie, as did his Maria, the husband and wife eager to shower the bright young girl with all of their love and attention.

There were weekly ice-skating lessons in the fall months for Stephanie, dance lessons in the spring, and piano lessons year-round. She acted in school productions, helped to organize the annual church canned-food giveaway, and, along with her mother, worked one weekend a month as a volunteer, bringing meals and other necessities to those in the neighborhood who were either too poor or too infirm to provide for themselves.

Their life was a dream that was never meant to end, but it did, on a late-summer morning with a hint of fall in the crisp air. It was September, 1970.

Maria Espinoza, her arms filled with grocery bags, stepped into the dank basement vestibule of her grandfather's three-bedroom rent-controlled apartment on East 138th Street in the Bronx, the imposing shadows of the Cross Bronx Expressway noticeable in the distance. Grandpa Olmeda, eighty-four and still feisty, always refused any calls for him to move out of a building that had long ago dismissed any hopes of a return to glory days. Most of the other tenants had evacuated their apartments, goaded by a landlord desperate to sell to a consortium of city power brokers eager to put up a string of low-income houses on the street. On her last weekly visit, Grandpa Olmeda told Maria that the landlord had just left the apartment, having made what he had called his final offer. "The slick little bastard thinks he can get me out of my home with a check," Olmeda said, his words, as always, coming in a great rush just before a coughing fit, his decades-long bout with damaged lungs now entering its final rounds. "I chased his ass fast out the door. And, if I were a few years younger, would have kicked it out to boot."

"How much was the check for, Papi?" Maria asked. She never lost the warmth of her disposition, no matter how frustrating it was for her to see anyone suffer—especially the elderly man to whom she owed so much of the good in her early life.

"Does it make a nickel's worth of difference?" he asked. "Dirty money never turns clean, I don't care in whose hands it goes."

"Maybe you should move out," Maria told him. "All your friends are gone to live with family or are in better neighborhoods. No reason you couldn't do the same. It doesn't matter if you take the landlord's check or not, even though, whatever the amount, it would help with your move. Then you could come and live with us. We have plenty of room. Hector is the one who always brings it up to me, and Stephanie would be so happy to have her papi there for her every day."

"This is my home, Maria," Olmeda said, fighting back another urge to cough. "It was my home when I was young and had a family, and it will stay my home for as long as the good Lord wants me to keep taking a breath. And the house you and Hector and Steph have, that is your home. That is as it should be. The bastards want me out, they have to learn patience. Once I'm dead, and they carry my body out that front door, they can do whatever the hell they want. But not one second before that day."

Maria rested the grocery bags by her feet and searched her open purse for the key to the front door. She closed her eyes for a brief moment. The bus ride down from her home in the Wakefield section had taken longer than usual, the driver forced to make his way around a number of main streets under fresh repair; Con Ed and construction crews were hard at work coiling wires and cracking pavement. She had nodded off halfway through the stop-and-go twenty-minute ride as the bus snaked its way through the Bronx streets, crammed with the old and the weary, who were so content to reach their eventual destination in due time. Maria was wearing a blue jean jacket over a floral print dress. The dress was a two-year-old birthday gift from her grandfather, and she knew that wearing it was one of the few things she could do that would bring a smile to his face.

She got off two stops before her grandfather's building, under the El and across from the Met supermarket. She walked into the poorly stocked store, moving up and down the disheveled aisles, filling her cart with her grandfather's weekly list. It had taken three full months of pleading before he finally relented and allowed her to shop for his groceries. "You want the damn job so bad, it's yours to take," he told her, surrendering one more vestige of his freedom to the insatiable demands of old age. "But you come back in here with one thing that isn't right, just one is all, and I pull the job right out from under you."

He wasn't angry at her—never was, truth be told. He had simply turned sour on the life he was now locked into, knowing that death was his only escape route. His days and nights had evolved into routines chiseled in stone, always accompanied by the sounds of an old television blaring too loudly in the background. He fed the cat—an overweight and elderly animal he had named Roberto in honor of his favorite baseball player, Roberto Clemente of the Pittsburgh Pirates—and put on the morning coffee. He read a few select passages from the tattered pages of a Bible that had been in the family for two generations and then moved on to the few domestic chores he was still capable of completing. Summer afternoons and evenings were spent next to his old Philips radio, tuned in to either a Yankees or Mets game, eagerly rooting both teams home to victory. In winter, he followed the same pattern, listening to the

Knicks, the Jets, and the Giants. He never watched any of the games on his eighteen-inch television. "If I can't go to the games and see them with my own eyes," he once said to Hector, "then I'm a lot happier and better off seeing them play out in my head. Makes me feel like I used to feel when I took the train to the stadium or the Garden and watched them up close. Besides, you listen to those TV voices for too long, you're close to ready to reach for a knife and shove an end to your day. I tell you the Lord's truth, no lie, but they can be an annoying group of bastards."

Maria slid the key into the lock and turned it to the right, listening for the click of the deadbolt shifting loose. She turned the rust-stained doorknob and eased the thick and dented wood door open. A heavy odor of gas filtered through the foyer, causing her eyes to burn. She stepped deeper into the apartment, shades and curtains drawn tight, leaving the two grocery bags in the outside vestibule. "Grandpa," she said, her lungs aching from the smell. "Grandpa, are you in here?"

The walls on both sides were covered with family photos and framed childhood drawings. The furniture that filled each room was as familiar to her as the lyrics of an old song. It was as if she had entered a time capsule, one that transported her back to the night before her twelfth birthday, when she was allowed to stay up until the midnight hour, baking cake and cookies in the kitchen with her Grandma Elena. The same night she caught a peek at her new bike, red with a white basket and a blue bell, hidden in the hall closet, just off the living room. Maria would never forget that night and that very special birthday, and she always looked forward to a time when she could do something that would be as memorable for her own child.

The smell of gas grew stronger with each careful step Maria took. She moved quietly past the small dining room. The table, chairs, and overhead fixtures, not used during the passing decades, maintained their store-bought shine and glow, helped by her grand-father's weekly hand wax. Her eyes were tearing now, and her throat had an acid burn with each swallow as she turned into the large living room, where the radio was tuned to an all-news station. She stood in the center of the room, across from the three-seat couch that was still covered with her grandmother's hand-stitched embroi-dery, and stared at her grandfather. Olmeda was in his recliner, slippered feet stretched out, a copy of the *Post* half open across his thin chest. His head was tilted back, at rest against the soft green leather, his eyes open and glistening with tears, thin lines of spittle coursing down the right side of his mouth. Maria fell to her knees and cupped her hands to her mouth, swallowing a scream along with the bile. She didn't need to step any closer or check his vital signs to know the truth.

She shook her head, the room growing blurry, her vision dim-ming, her breath coming in gasps. Rising once again to her feet, she moved toward a shuttered window, anxious to bring fresh air into the rank apartment. Her hands reached for the thin brown cord that sealed shut the thick drapes. She wrapped two shaky fingers around the cord and pulled it down. That was when she saw the black fuse and heard the click of the timer snap into place. She turned her head to the right and caught a glimpse of her commun-ion photo, her rich black hair done up in curls, her white dress crisp and new, matching the folded-down socks and the short veil. Her hands were clasped together in prayer, black rosary beads wrapped around her fingers.

It was the last image she would ever see.

The massive blast shook the building down to the base of its shaky foundation, sending hunks of brick, shards of wood, and slices of glass flooding out into the busy Bronx street. A large mountain of dust billowed out of the basement like a derailed tornado and stretched its brown tentacles across the face of the tenements dotting the blighted avenue. A half dozen parked cars were lifted off the ground and tossed onto their sides, windows shattering and tires exploding from the heat. Three men and a child were knocked to the ground, and an elderly woman was slammed against a light pole, cutting her head and face. In the distance, car alarms and police sirens went off almost in unison, black-and-whites rushing to respond to the blast, called in by a dozen locals.

Inside the apartment, there was nothing but ruin. The bodies of Grandpa Olmeda and Maria lay mangled and destroyed—two innocent souls blinked out of existence at one end of the Bronx.

At the other end, three miles to the north, a young girl sat in a classroom listening with full attention to her English teacher dissecting Betty Smith's novel *A Tree Grows in Brooklyn*. She did not yet know it, but at that moment the life she had known had ended and a journey had begun. A journey that would lead her to the hard hands that planted the bomb that erased her mother and her grandfather from her world—and created in her a hurt and an ache that she could do nothing to ease.

From that day forward, Stephanie Torres would never again be able to refer to herself as innocent.

5

—— CHAPTER ——

The young man jogged down the empty sidewalk. He was looking to better his eight-minute mile and glanced occasionally at the stop-watch clutched in his right hand. It was a cool morning, light barely breaking across Washington Heights, the riot gates on the bodegas and the candy stores he passed lifted and morning newspapers taken in, the smell of fresh coffee filling the foggy air. Julio Aguilera was two months past his twenty-third birthday and had lived in the Heights for all of those years, venturing outside his neighborhood only once, for a weekend trip to Miami with his parents when he was six. He was a high school dropout and had held a series of one-way jobs before latching on to eyeball work for a Colombian crew new to the area, paying get-by cash for any street information he passed their way. The money he was given was more than enough to cover the expenses on the one-bedroom third-floor walk-up whose kitchen window faced out onto a thin alleyway where a dozen years earlier the body of his brother, Miguel, a low-end drug dealer, was found in his own blood. It was Julio who had identified the body for the police on the scene, gazing down at the gaping wounds that had torn open his brother's back and the top of his skull. Miguel had thrown the money he earned into a heroin habit he could ill afford, which marked him as an easy prey for a street-corner takeout. It was on that humid night, watching Miguel's body get bagged and tagged in an alley, that Julio vowed that any cash he took in from the lucrative Heights drug trade would be tossed deep into a bank account—not slipped into a bent needle with little give.

Which led him to his current position as a street stool, spying for the new set of cocaine cowboys in town, Father Angel's hard-dealing fresh-off-the-runway crew. They rolled into the city little more than six months ago, looking to break into the crowded upper tiers of the white-line traders, flashing wads of green and packing heavy artillery in case the money wasn't enough to catch someone's interest. Julio signed on from the get-go and fed the higher-ups enough street news to keep the cash rolling in, but not enough to chart his name on anyone's radar panel. The hours were light and sea-breeze easy, giving Julio more than enough time to devote to the one true passion in his life: running.

Julio never missed a day's run, regardless of weather or time of year. He kept to a steady routine, hitting the streets in the slow-tick minutes just before dawn to scale the hills of the Heights, logging a steady eight to twelve miles each day. He always aimed to up his speed or add a few more blocks to the day's tally. He kept his sneakers clean and looking as new as the day he bought them, and he changed his PF Flyers every three months, always going for the black low-cuts with red laces. He ran without a headset or a radio tuned to any particular station. The only sounds he wanted around him were those of the neighborhood shaking itself awake after yet one more night of gunplay and mayhem.

Julio Aguilera lived for his daily run.

Now he was running at his fastest clip, gliding over a large crack in the pavement, when the door of a parked car swung open and caught him flush in the center of his belly and legs. The force of the hit sent him spinning, arms out like wings, legs lurching toward the sky, his body free of breath and bristling with pain and confusion. He took a hard landing to the sidewalk, the back of his head knocking the concrete.

Through a set of glazed and glassy eyes, Julio made out the figure of a man stepping from the passenger door and walking closer to where he lay. The man had on what looked to be a black leather jacket, and there was a slight limp to his gait. He stood over Julio and stared down at him, his head doing a slow shake.

"I always heard running really wasn't that good of an exercise," the man said. "That across the long haul it did a fella more harm than good. I guess maybe there's some truth to that after all."

"I was just hitting my stride until you door-jacked me, shithead." Julio hissed out the words, the pain in his lungs causing his throat to clench.

"You must of taken a harder blow than I figured," the man said, holding a container of coffee in his right hand. "Scramble-egged your brains. That happens, you start to see things that you only *think* happened."

"Think, my ass," Julio said, his voice fast regaining its strength. "You could have killed me for real. Get my hands on a solid lawyer, sue your ass for any cash you got."

A second man walked over from the driver's side of the car and stood staring down at Julio. He had one foot on the curb and the other on the sidewalk, a half-eaten buttered roll in his left hand. "Shame he didn't run into the door with his mouth," he said with a shrug.

"Little early in the day for a Five-O shakedown, you ask me," Julio said, lifting himself on his elbows. "And I carry no cash when I walk, forget about it when I run."

"This little fucker's like 1010 news," Dead-Eye said as he slipped the last of the buttered roll into a corner of his mouth. "You give him twenty-two minutes and he'll give you his world."

"You good enough to stand?" the first man, Boomer, asked. "Maybe even walk it a few feet?"

"Do I got me a choice in it?" Julio asked.

"I could say yes," Boomer said, looking past Julio and down the silent street. "But it would be a lie."

"And I could step up and cap both your asses," Julio said, getting to his feet and wiping the blood from his mouth on his left forearm.

"Cap us with what, running man?" Dead-Eye asked, moving up to the sidewalk, his voice calm and polite, his eyes hard enough to bend iron.

Julio did his best to match that stare, held it for several seconds, then backed down. "I still got my ears, and I know you two Kojaks got more than enough lip," he said with a slight shrug of the shoulders. "So give me what you came to spread. What do you want to jab to me about?"

"A priest," Boomer said.

6

Bobby "Rev. Jim" Scarponi sat on the park bench and snapped open the lid to a can of Coke. He took two long gulps and rested the can between the soles of a pair of tan low-cut desert boots. He was on the west side of Central Park, just a long throw from a Broadway Show League softball game going on to his left. A small throng of people, some sitting in garden chairs with coolers by their side, cheered their team on while taking in what was left of the late-afternoon sun.

Rev. Jim leaned back against the bench's wooden slats, stretched his arms out, and checked the time on his watch. He was wearing a jean jacket over a dark blue long-sleeved T-shirt and an old pair of Macy's slacks. His body was still workout lean, kept that way by a vegetarian diet and three-times-a-week yoga classes that he attended with a fervor bordering on the religious. He was closing in on his fortieth birthday and, for the first time in memory, had finally landed in a good place both mentally and physically. Of course, the burn scars remained etched across his chest and neck, constant reminders of his years working the decoy beat for the New York Police Department, a short span in his life when his work was considered the best in the cop trade. But he had resigned himself to the handful of concessions he needed to continue his day-to-day without being haunted by the fire that had brought his career as a cop to a hard-brake end. The steady flow of nightmares had now been reduced to a few stress-induced occurrences a month, and the once strong-enough-to-touch urges to take his own life had all but dissipated. The salve to his wounds had been helped along by twice-a-week counseling sessions with a Lower East Side therapist and weekly visits with his father, Albert, a Korean War veteran who long ago had learned the harsh lessons of wrapping his world of pain inside a cocoon of silence.

But the scars were always there to serve as a reminder. It didn't matter that he hid them from public view by wearing long-sleeved shirts with high-rimmed collars, regardless of the time of year. Or that he never bared his chest to a woman, determined to avoid the look of pity he knew would be in her eyes—or, worse, the look of horror. But Rev. Jim had made his peace with the demons that raged within. He realized that his was, at best, a shaky truce, one that required a determined focus, but so far he was making it work.

Rev. Jim was, for payroll purposes, a drug counselor for a West Side not-for-profit clinic. He had been with the small storefront outfit in the Eighties off Broadway for close to three years, starting as a volunteer and offering advice to any teenager who walked through the glass-paneled door with the look of the lost in his eyes. Soon enough, even the well-meaning couple who ran the clinic, Jeffrey and Annie Parsons, realized Rev. Jim could be a much more useful tool in their losing battles against the onslaught of the drug trade. He had made some impact with a few of the kids, but not enough of them to alter the balance scales. He wasn't at his best or most comfortable in such situations, and they sensed his frustration at not being able to stem the problem. "Maybe we have you reaching out to the wrong group," Jeffrey said to him late one morning as the two of them sat in a small back room with an overhead fan and a window facing an alley. "You're good with the kids, don't get me wrong. I just think you might be better talking to the ones we can never talk to—and, even if we did, wouldn't care to listen."

"Who you got in mind?" Rev. Jim asked, already sensing the answer to his own question.

"The dealers," Jeffrey Parsons said.

Rev. Jim stood and nodded down at Parsons, the street juice of the adrenaline-junkie cop starting its mad dash through his veins. "I'll start in the morning," he told him. "On one condition."

"Name it," Parsons said.

"You feed me the names of the kids in trouble," Rev. Jim said. "I put a hand out to their street connection and take that to wherever it leads. The results will be there—trust me on that end. Just never ask me how I get those results."

———————

Rev. Jim saw the overweight white man in the Lawrence Taylor football jersey lean up against a side of the batting cage. He had on a sweat-stained Raiders cap, baggy shorts, and high-top black sneakers with no socks. The back of his flabby neck was a runway of thick, red, connect-the-dot pimples that snaked down his back and hid beneath the stains and shine of the tattered jersey. Rev. Jim left the park bench and walked up to the batting cage, stopping just a few feet short of the man, who looked to be in his mid-thirties and smelled like a rain dog.

"Got a minute for me?" Rev. Jim asked in his most polite tone.

The overweight man kept his eyes on the batter in the box, bat held high above his shoulders, neck muscles tight, arms ready to swing the wood against the fast-pitch softball coming down his way. "You a cop, flash me some tin," the overweight man said. "If not, take it back where you came from while you still got the legs."

Rev. Jim smiled and rested his shoulders against the cage, arms folded across his chest. "You guys take classes to learn tough talk like that?" he asked. "I mean, is there a drug-dealer training school where you all go to listen to some bent-over, smack-addled scumbag run you through the paces?"

"You been warned," the overweight man said. "There won't be a rerun."

Rev. Jim pulled a small photo from his jean jacket and held it up for the overweight man to see. He gave it a side-glance and then turned back to the game. "Her name's Rachel," Rev. Jim said. "Been on the street about two, maybe three weeks, a month tops. You know the drill. No place to go, nobody to see, and before you can say needle and spike some lard-ass loser who looks a lot like you has her living off the pipe."

"Don't mean shit to me," the overweight man said. "Not you and for sure not that skank."

"Rodney Phillips," Rev. Jim said. "Boys High honor student back when those zits on your neck first took root. Altar boy, decent family, father maybe put his lips to a bottle more than he should, but nothing more to it than that. You were excellent in both history and science, had your shit down cold as a keg. Could have gone to a decent middle-tier school, but somewhere along the way you lost the directions. Ended up where you are now, dealing and dialing little girls to morning highs and late-night scores."

Rodney turned and glared over at Rev. Jim, his cheeks puffed out and red as tree apples. "I find out who it is been feeding you that shit about me, I'll slap his tongue on a bun and have it for my lunch," he said. "And then I'll get to wastin' your sorry ass."

"Any play you want where I'm concerned is fine by me," Rev. Jim said. "But your days with Rachel ended the second I showed up. You need to think of me like AA, only instead of twelve steps my plan only comes with two. The warning you just heard was step one."

"And step two takes me where, tough boy?" Rodney asked, stepping closer to Rev. Jim, his stance open-legged, hands balled into ham fists resting against his hips, his manner making a move toward menace.

Rev. Jim lost the smile and leaned in close enough to smell foul breath and sweat. "Step two is the one I look forward to the most," he said. "Because that's when I fucking end you."

Rev. Jim heard the snap of the switchblade before he saw the knife. He stepped back and dodged a quick slash aimed at his chest. He leaned down and from a crouch position landed two hard body blows against soft flesh. He heard Rodney grunt and gasp for the breath rushing out of his lungs. Rev. Jim stepped back, the attention of the small crowd turned away from the game and squarely on the two men on the outside of the batting cage. He snapped a left jab against the side of Rodney's face and followed it up with a hard hook to his stomach. The second blow brought the overweight man to his knees, his eyes bloodshot and opened wide enough to pop. The blade in the fat man's hand fell to the dirt, and his sweaty back rested heavily against the lower end of the cage. Rev. Jim rammed his right elbow just above Rodney's eyes, causing two streams of blood to rush out his nostrils and cascade down his neck and onto the stained blue of his L.T. jersey. He then leaned down and put his lips close to the stunned man's right ear.

"Hear me good, dealer man," Rev. Jim said. "Find a place that's anywhere but here, and do it fast as you can. Want to duck and dodge me for a while, that's your right. But one day, sooner not later, I'll put eyes on you again. And that's the day I make your heart stop taking beats."

Rev. Jim stood up, kicked the blade toward an empty garbage bin, took one final look at Rodney Phillips, and turned away, walking at a slow pace, ready to enjoy what was left of the afternoon.

Boomer sat in a back pew of the small empty church, gazing up at the main altar. The flicker and glow of the votive candles that lit the faces of the saints lining the walls cast an eerie quality over St. Mary's Church. Boomer had, for as long as he could remember, sought comfort in the quiet shelter of the church he had first entered on the day he was baptized. He had spent many hours there since, including three years as an altar boy, helping an array of priests preside over Mass, weddings, and funerals. He preferred having the place to himself—a safe haven where he could be alone with his thoughts, where he was allowed to navigate his way through his many ups and downs.

Earlier that morning, Boomer had sat in stone silence, listening to a middle-aged priest drone on about the gift of death—one that allowed the body of his niece, her warmth, her smile, and her beauty shuttered forever inside a vacuum-sealed coffin resting in the middle of the aisle, to be brought inside a kingdom that knew only happiness. Boomer kept his eyes on the thick and shiny mahogany coffin, doing his best to ignore the words. His anger was running at a slow sizzle, but he held his temper, keeping his mind locked to the fact that a young woman yet to get a taste of the good that life could offer had been killed for nothing more than the whim and deadly needs of a heartless shooter. Four other innocents had also lost their lives that day, which now seemed so long ago. The story had earned page-one coverage from the tabloids and the local and cable channels, with most of the articles focusing on the escalating cocaine wars between the established Gonzalez Brothers crew, known industrywide as the G-Men, and the rogue priest, Father Angel, who was hell-bent on taking over their trade, one line at a time. Each story reinforced a belief of Boomer's: the drug trade was doing a shake 'n' bake on the world of crime, turning it from a universe with a unified, if violent, structure into one in which order of any kind was neither required nor desired. There had been a time, not too long ago, when top-tiered members of organized crime proudly followed the rule that was so flagrantly epitomized by Benjamin "Bugsy" Siegel, the New York shooter and Las Vegas dreamer who once boasted that gangsters "only kill each other." Today's new breed of criminal had a much more expansive thirst for blood, choosing to spread their deadly venom to the safest of places, the most civil of spaces, and never giving any thought to where a stray bullet might land.

The murder-fueled world of organized crime was rapidly being replaced by the drug-injected madness of disorganized crime. And as long as that siege lasted, no civilian would ever be truly safe.

It was a battle Boomer knew he would soon join.

He would not hesitate this time, not give it a great deal of thought, not as he had done before he last journeyed into the war zone, engaged in a long-odds fight against a ruthless cocaine queen that cost the lives of three good friends and brought further ruin to his already damaged body. He would gladly go it alone now if it fell that way, but he knew that once he was inside the heat of the fight, he would turn to find Dead-Eye by his side. And there would be others to join in their potentially fruitless cause, much as there had been three years earlier. Small squadrons of wounded warriors eager to return to a street fight they had been pulled away from long before its completion. Back in 1982, Boomer and the others had dubbed themselves the Apaches, because they were cops who had been forced into retirement by their scars and ailments, left to fend only for themselves.

He saw no reason now to change the name.

Boomer stared at the coffin of his niece and thought of the moments so brutally taken from her reach. There would be no man to steal her heart, no children to love and nurture, no job to perform with passion and commitment. She would not grow old and be burdened with the good and bad weight that the passage of years brings. She wouldn't laugh at silly jokes or cry at sad movies. She was now a statistic in a drug war, as much an innocent victim in this battle against the dealers as the hopped-up single mother selling her soul and her child for the next warm rush of the needle. Or the wasted skells he had seen huddled inside doorways and hallways, seeking the next score. All had been brought to their dark place by the greed of the men and women who turned white powder into power and money, leaving in their wake ruined lives, decimated families, and crumbled cities. Boomer knew he could not clean it all away, regardless of how many ex-cops he could muster into a force. But what he did pray for, on that sad and soul-crunching morning, sitting close enough to his niece's coffin to touch it, was that his ravaged body had the inner strength needed to take down the gangs that had brought about this death, which had reached deep into his heart.

He was free now, no path ahead of him except the one that would lead him straight into the enemy's scope. He would go into this last battle unburdened by the rules that bound a cop to society. A bullet in the night would serve as his Miranda warning. A hard kick against a wood door would make up his search-and-seizure warrant. A gun jabbed into a dealer's mouth would stand in for the right to legal counsel. The non-rules of the drug lords were now the only ones Boomer would follow, the justice to be dispensed as he saw fit. And he would allow them only one right: the right to die by his hand.

He heard heels clicking in his direction, and when he looked up he saw his sister standing next to the pew, her face smeared with the tears she had shed since he had sat at her kitchen table and told her the words it tore at him to utter—that her only child was now dead. Maria was the younger of his two sisters and had always, in his eyes, been the toughest member of the family.

It was Maria who had held them all together in the years after their father's senseless murder in a New York subway car. Despite her youth, Maria had kept their mother, Theresa, from crumbling from the sheer weight of the sadness she bore, and made sure that he and his older brother and sister stayed on a path that their father would have approved. Now here she was, years removed from that self-imposed obligation, standing before him, a young widow and a mother stripped of her own child.

"I figured this was where I'd find you," Maria said, sliding in beside him, a trembling hand reaching out to grip his arm. "Everybody else is up at the house having coffee, not really knowing what to say."

"That's because there's nothing left to say," Boomer said. "I couldn't sit through that. Watching her get lowered into the ground was about all I could take."

"I know you well, Boomer," Maria said. She turned toward him, her face thin, her dark eyes shadowed by tears, her black hair hanging loose across her cheeks. "Better than anyone except maybe for Dead-Eye, and even he hasn't seen you on your darkest day. And I know what you're sitting here thinking of doing."

"And you left a house filled with your friends and family to find me and talk me out of it," Boomer said.

"If I could, I would—believe me when I tell you that," Maria said. "As much hate as I have for the people who killed our Angela, I would never ask you to put yourself at risk in order to get back at them."

Boomer leaned closer to his sister and rested a strong arm across her small shoulders.

"You don't need to say any more," he whispered into her ear.

"I've been to too many funerals," she said, lowering her head, the words mixing with sobs. "Buried too many people I loved. I don't want to lose you, too."

"It'll be different with me," Boomer said, his voice calm, assured, and confident. "The way I've lived, it's bound to happen sooner than later."

"She was a lot like you in so many ways," Maria said. "My husband used to tease her when she was a teenager, tell her he fathered Uncle Boomer's kid minus the gun and the shield. Angela had your spirit, your courage, kept her fears to herself. She put a hundred percent into anything she tried, and even when it didn't go her way she never let it get her down. And she had heart."

"She saw the good side of people," Boomer said, his strong voice easing into breaks, tears sliding down his face. "No matter who they might be or where it was they hailed from. I figure that's how it's supposed to be when you're her age and looking at life through her eyes. She never got a close-up glimpse of the evil that's out there.

Not until that last day. And by then it was too late. And I wasn't there to keep it away. I had sworn to her that I would always be around to keep her safe, keep her world clean. I couldn't and I didn't. Those were nothing more than wasted words said to make a little girl feel safe."

"There was nothing you could have done to prevent what happened, Boomer," Maria said. "You should know that better than anybody."

"I could have told her the truth instead of hiding it in a corner," Boomer said. "Show her the world through my eyes. Give her a better feel of what really stands outside our walls. Have her be ready for anything, anyone, at any time."

"And it *still* wouldn't have been enough to save her," Maria said. "She would have been a girl going through her day-to-day afraid to live her life. Our Angela would have hated to live that way."

The two sat in silence for several moments, lost in their private thoughts. "I need to get back," Maria said, starting a slow slide out of the pew. "Would you walk with me?" Boomer nodded, genuflected, and then stood and followed his sister. They walked down the main aisle, their backs to the altar, his right hand gently holding on to her left elbow. "Would you do me one favor, Boom?" Maria asked, her head bowed and her voice low.

"Name it," Boomer said.

"Don't keep me in the dark on this," Maria said, slowing her step. "These people killed my daughter. If I can't stop you from going after them, then I think I deserve to know who they are."

"You'll know," Boomer assured her. "And you won't need me to tell you."

Maria stopped and stared at Boomer, chilled momentarily by the dark weight of her brother's words. He looked back, his hard eyes telling her all she needed to know about his vengeful intent. "This is a side of you I had once hoped would be buried away," she said. "I hate to see it keep coming back. And I just don't know how many more of these wars you can go out and fight and how many more you can walk away from."

"With luck and a few prayers, this one," Boomer said, leading his sister by the hand out of the darkness of the empty church. "This last one."

3

------ CHAPTER ------

Buttercup crouched against the cold side of a cement wall, head tilted to her left, her thick paws curled under her muscular brown hide. Her tongue hung low and lapped against the sharp teeth on her lower jaw, and her droopy cocoa-colored eyes gazed down the tenement hall with a look of casual indifference. Two detectives were braced on either side of her, guns drawn, Kevlar vests strapped on over their dark blue NYPD T-shirts. The corridor, cracked and graffiti-riddled, was empty and smelled of dry urine and burnt coke. Loud rap music, mixed with the sound of televisions on high volume, filled the hall. One of the detectives, a young man in his mid-twenties with thinning hair and an Old West mustache, rested a hand on Buttercup's neck, his eyes focused on the door leading to apartment 4F. "Get ready, sweetie," the detective whispered. "It's just about showtime."

"That snitch better be on the money about this shit," the second detective said. He was older, mid-thirties, the routine of daily work-outs replaced across the years by a running tab at a local cop bar. "If he's off by one nickel bag, I'll have his ass dry-iced to Rikers before rush hour."

"Take a breath, Frank," the first detective said. "The guy's always been on the square with us. No reason to sense any doubts about him now."

"He's a fuckin' junkie, Stevie. There's reason number one with a bullet right there," Frank said, barely able to contain his voice to the required whisper. "And one of the crew dealers he's throwin' our way happens to be his brother-in-law, which, right off the bat, smells to me like a fart in a spacesuit."

"There's three of us and, if the intel is even close to home plate, four of them," Stevie said, shrugging his shoulders, anxious to bring an end to the talk and a start to the action. "Not like we got ourselves a Butch and Sundance situation here."

"I'm gonna try and break this to you gentle," Frank said, frustration masking his fear. "I only count the ones with two legs as cops. I give a toss to the one that lifts a leg to take a piss and, if the opportunity is there, will jump at the first chance she gets to chew on a hunk of dry shit in the street."

Buttercup lifted her massive head and gave a blank look in Frank's direction, her breath and manner as calm as if she were in the middle of Central Park halfway through a late-afternoon walk. Buttercup was a full-grown Neapolitan bullmastiff topping out at 125 pounds. She was a narcotics dog, trained to sniff out cocaine, heroin, and, if the occasion warranted, large packets of marijuana. She had been assigned to the K-9 unit for three years and was considered the best field dog in any of the five boroughs. "That fucker could find a line of cocaine in the middle of a twenty-inch blizzard," undercover supercop Jimmy "Eye Patch" Mendoza raved the day he passed Buttercup on to Steve. "I made twenty primetime busts in my eighteen months working with her. And she wasn't just a sniff-and-stop hound. The bitch jumps into the line and fights, watching your back better than any partner you ever could wish for. No way she's a dog. Buttercup is all-star, all-cop, all-the-time."

Buttercup was always assigned the high-end takedowns, and possessed an eerie and innate ability to read a situation and react seconds before the trigger click kicked in. Off the job, in the company of other cops or her handlers or, most especially, around children, Buttercup was playful and relaxed, her sweet, puppylike disposition more than negating what, on the surface at least, gave the appearance of a fierce presence. But out in the field, in the heat of the moment, she thrived on the nuances of police work, always on the alert, quick to sense danger, and even quicker to pounce.

In her three years as a narcotics dog, Buttercup had sniffed out more than $200 million in cocaine hauls, covering a span of two dozen arrests, and was in front of the firing line during a $150 million middle-of-the-night heroin score in a Brooklyn warehouse. Her success rate came with a price tag, though. Buttercup had sniffed out so much cocaine and heroin that cops from other units were leery of working with her, afraid she might go off on a drug-fueled frenzy. "She's seen way too much shit for any K-9," Mendoza reminded Steve. "She could snap, crackle, and pop any second for any reason. She can be sweet as a nursed baby at five to the hour. And then, before you can unzip your pants for a late-night piss, she can take a dealer's head off with one chomp and roll it down center lane. She's no different and no worse than any other undercover narc. But I tell you, when the nasty turns ugly and you can smell the gunpowder coming your way, Buttercup is who you want standing next to your ass."

Detective Steve Ramoni had learned to take those words and tuck them close to his heart. In their months together, he had grown not only to love Buttercup as a dog but to admire her as a partner. Despite her size, she was a gentle dog and would easily adapt her moods and manner to the moment. In the squad room, she sauntered through the cramped floor space, littered with old arrest warrants, wanted posters, and crumpled-up papers, as if she belonged, pausing to accept a gentle rub of the head from a cop working the phones or grab a nibble on the cold remains of a hot hero left behind by an undercover off on a buy-and-bust. On the streets, free to strut alongside Ramoni without the burden of a leash, a replica of his detective tin hanging on a thin chain around her neck, she walked with the confident strides of a cop on the job, primed and ready for whatever action might head her way. She always let the local kids pet her and rub the bottom of a jaw thick as a barbell, her head lifted, her eyes closed, and her tongue lapping up against the fingers and palms of the tiny hands pressed to her flesh. But, as Ramoni learned in the time it takes for a traffic light to go from red to green, Buttercup was at her cop best when she stood paw to toe up against the hard drug dealers working the streets of what she had grown to consider her turf.

"I remember this one time," Ramoni once told a cluster of fresh undercovers, standing around the edges of a dimly lit cop bar, empty bottles of beer lined up like bowling pins on top of the wood, Buttercup sleeping it off at his feet. "Me and Buttercup were working an operation against a dealer named Fernando Chin. Hand to God, that was the fucker's real name. Half Chinese, half who the hell knows what else. Guy had himself a small crew of about a dozen or so wack-outs, moving that double-cut shit they sprayed with Raid to give the junkies a fake kick, hide the fact that it was about as primo as sauce out of a jar."

"This was in our sector or somewhere else?" asked a young cop with a face out of a high school yearbook.

"No, up in the East Bronx," Ramoni said, his shoulders tossing a who-gives-a-shit shrug. "Dominican turf and, as you will soon learn, those bastards like to play fair and share about as much as two homeless mutts do over an empty can of Seven Up. Anyways, we had set up shop, with me posing as a buyer for a heavy pocket user living in some ass-pimple town upstate, working this half-breed and his crew one dead worm at a time. Made like the dog was part and package of the price of me doing business, sweating down a heavy-vig gambling loan. We started our run with small buys, couple of bags a week—nothing that would make Chin raise an eyebrow. It was moving at a nice, downstream pace, each day me getting closer to the Chin man, connecting the dots on where he got his dope and who it was asking him to wax the lower floors. We were about a week, maybe two, from a middle-of-the-paper bust."

"He got wise he was being played by a hidden badge?" one of the cops asked.

"Or some stool toss a finger at you?" a voice from the middle of the bar shouted. "You know, caught your act from some other job?"

Ramoni sipped from a fresh bottle of beer and shook his head. "You guys need to get your ass out of the movies and into the real deal," he said. "That shit you're talking works for Hollywood, not the Heights. No, it was Buttercup that moved our closing date up. She smelled out that the Chin hated middlemen and dogs and was always on the look-see to rid his eyesight of both."

"How'd she manage that?" the cop closest to Ramoni asked. He was a beefy Irish kid with an easy smile and a wrestler's upper body.

"She pulled off the first rule of undercover work and made it happen on her end of the court," Ramoni said. "She was a smart enough cop to make sure the guy we were looking to tag felt comfortable in her company. In no time flat, that fuckin' Chin was so taken with Buttercup you'd think he had nursed her off his own tits. And that's no mean task, given the Chinese history with dogs."

"What history's that?"

"The history that tells you they fuckin' eat them," Ramoni said. "Think of that next time you lay down a five-spot for the Hunan special. At any rate, Buttercup winds up so tight with Chin it's like they're going steady. She's with him more than she's with me, taking meetings, running errands, and planning out jobs, including the one where it's mapped for us to take the slugs that send us both to the end of the conga line."

"When did you get a whiff of what was going down?" the beefy Irish cop asked.

"Not till the day of," Ramoni said. "We're in the back of some wok-and-rolls grease spill, trading laundered cash for cut cocaine—me, Chin, Buttercup here, and two other guys I never seen before. But she had. There she is walking around the room, tail wagging, breath coming out heavier than cloud cover, acting for all the tea in China like she's the night manager or some shit. But whenever she crosses over in front of the two new guys, both standing up against a stained wall—you couldn't wash the dried fat off with acid—she turns her head to me and barks. And you gotta understand one thing. The only time an undercover dog barks in a situation such as the one I just laid out is if there's about to be a show of guns. Based on her level of agitation, I took a hunch that I had less than two minutes to work out a solution. I figured Chin I could take down and out, no problem. You didn't exactly think of Bruce Lee when the fucker made a move your way—more like Stagger Lee, if you get my drift. But the two up against that wall, well, they for certain posed a problem. They no doubt came in the room heavy, that was for one. They were also to my left, which meant that I had to move like *Lethal Weapon* Mel Gibson to maybe even have a better than fair chance at bringing them both down to knee level. And that was without knowing if or if not Chin had extra artillery stashed behind one of the curtains or under the slop sink. I thought, Here is where I die, in some sinkhole of a Chinese restaurant, my last breath a lungful of oil thick enough to stain shoes."

"Could you have made a reach for backup?" one cop asked, shoving aside three empty bottles and leaning in closer, both elbows on the wood.

"How, exactly?" Ramoni asked. "Tossing a veggie roll out through the cracked window? I had nothing on me but my crotch gun and my ankle gun—neither one easy to get to, mind you that. No, if it wasn't for my lady friend sleeping by my feet here, this is one story would have been told you back in the Police Academy—as a way of *not* going into an undercover op."

"So, what'd she do?" the beefy Irish cop asked. "Christ, this is better than the movie I took my girl to see the other night. From now on, fuck going to the shows. I'll take her here—she'll get a better story and I'll save some dough."

"And you still won't get laid end of the night," another cop said. "That's the part never changes."

"Let me tell you what Buttercup did," Ramoni said, the cold flow of the beer and the cliff-hanger tale helping to hold the attention of the cops leaning on the wood. "She waited. And she waited. And she waited, like she was ticking off the seconds in her head, timing it down to match me move for move. She stayed breath-mint close to the two shooters, even let the fuckers pet her, they felt like it. They started to follow her around the room, leaving their assigned slots, their eyes more on her than on me, where they should have been every inch of the trip. Meantime, Chin, thinking his back's covered, is as relaxed as if he were sipping a Jack straight up at a Club Med pool. He's looking down, elbows on a small poker table filled with cash and bags of dope, thinking for sure he was going to clean up on both ends. Gave me the time I needed to cut to the quick."

"How did you signal the dog?" the bartender, an overweight fellow in a starched white shirt, asked.

"This dog you don't signal," Ramoni said. "She signals you. Lets me know when it's time to pull my piece and start the fireworks."

"You pulling at it, or you telling me straight?" the bartender said, sliding two more cold ones across the bar.

"Learned long ago never to bullshit the man pouring my drinks," Ramoni said. "There's no upside to the exchange."

"So, how then?"

"Simple as a front-seat stop-and-blow," Ramoni said. "Buttercup eyeballs me one last time, turns, and locks her jaw around the shooter standing furthest away from me. Doofus-looking badass sporting a blind man's haircut. She takes a chunk out of his thigh big as a Christmas ham and rips at it like she hadn't been fed for three months. Guy lets out a scream loud enough to crack paint. I reach down, pull the .38 from my ankle holster, and peg two at the second guy, one close to me, gun already in his shooting hand. Plant both in his chest plate, and he drops like a tree branch in a storm. First guy is doing some fucking dance around the room, Buttercup chewing on his skin and clothes, going at him as if the dealer had a Ben Benson steak bone jammed in his pants. That now brings it down to me and my pal Chin, and he's sitting there as stunned as if he just took one between the eyes with a baseball bat—woulda shit his pants if I just pointed the gun his way. Within seconds, I got total control of the room—from the two shooters to Chin and the dope and all the cash. The only noise in the place at this time was the shot guy on the floor moaning, clutching his chest, eyes bugged out wide, and the other nimrod on his hands and knees begging me not to let Buttercup eat any more of his ass. And that, my drunken friends, is what's called a prime-time takedown. And all because I have me a partner who knew how to read a situation and react like a top-tier pro."

"You got the collar and a letter from borough command, no doubt, for a bust that size," the beefy young cop said. "What'd the dog get from all that action?"

"Grilled skirt steak and a chew toy," Ramoni said, leaning down and giving Buttercup a soft pat on the head. "And she was as happy as a pig in slop to get it, especially since skirt steak is her favorite meal on the whole planet."

"Other than maybe a drug dealer's thigh," the bartender said with a full nicotine laugh.

———

The tall man's heavy steps brought Buttercup to full attention, her head still resting against the tenement wall, her eyes staring down at the dark green cement floor, following the shadow as it made its way toward the door of apartment 4F. Steve Ramoni lowered himself to the floor, eye level with Buttercup. He gave a quick glance down the hall, spotted the dealer, decked out in tight jeans and a red shirt loud enough to belt out a tune. He had a .9 millimeter handgun in each hand and a gold shield hanging on a chain around his neck. He glanced across at Buttercup, gave her a soft nudge with his shoulder, and threw her a wide smile. The dog tilted her head, leaned it over, and licked the right side of his face.

"Just a few seconds more," Ramoni whispered to Buttercup. "Soon as that door swings open, you move and go. Me and Frankie will be right behind. And remember, no bark—just bite."

Ramoni looked away and heard the lock snaps and the chains being unleashed from the inside of apartment 4F. He saw the tall man tense, resting his hand against his lower spine, feeling for the handle grip on a .357 revolver. He heard the cheap wood door creak and saw a thin shaft of light slip out of the opening, the stale odor of low-end grass seeping through. He looked at Buttercup and nodded. The bullmastiff rose to her feet, turned the tight corner, and charged down the narrow hallway.

A cop primed to nail another bust.

9

CHAPTER

Boomer was on his third lap around the Central Park running track, enjoying the heat of the morning sun warm on his back and neck. He gazed out at the city's landscape through a chain-link fence, ignoring the sharp pain shooting up and down his right leg like a pinball in a machine. It was part of a physical fitness ritual he had adhered to since the afternoon of his first day at the Police Academy. That morning, the young cadets were given a speech by a silver-haired retired cop with tree-trunk biceps and a chest that looked as if it were chiseled from stone. His name was Vince Dowd, and even Boomer, with his inexperienced ears, was quick to understand that he was in the presence of a department legend, a gold-shield homicide detective with more than twenty years of active service and enough medals and commendations to fill a U-Haul. Dowd spoke in a clear voice, his body language matching the power of his words. He gave a talk that filled Boomer simulta-neously with passion and dread, as he took in a speech that was cupboard-crammed with the dangers faced by an unprepared cop on the streets. One of the pure essentials preached by Detective Dowd was always to be prepared for any given situation at any given time. That meant physically as well as mentally. "An out-of-shape cop might as well stay home and pop a cold beer," Boomer recalled Dowd telling them. "Save the medical examiner and the body-bag boys time and trouble, because if he hits the streets like that he'll be found dead on those streets. You go out there looking like you're not ready for a tussle, then count on being taken out. That's the clear and simple of it. You don't care, they will take the dare."

Boomer dedicated himself to cop work.

He maintained a physical workout routine that rivaled that of a professional athlete. In addition to the daily five-mile rain-snow-or-shine runs, he lifted weights four days a week; took boxing and martial-arts classes; meditated and practiced yoga; and ate only one meal a day (chicken, fish, or pasta in a plain red sauce, with a vegetable side dish). When it came to the mental part of the job, Boomer's stance was even more aggressive. He read all the books dealing with the history and intricacies of organized crime, from as-told-to clip-and-paste bios to sociological studies and page-turner novels. He studied weapons and tactics, spending hours in three-credit night classes at the John Jay College of Criminal Justice or at mind-numbing Police Department–sponsored weekend seminars. He watched documentaries that dealt with police work and even took lessons from the shoot-'em-ups he paid to see in movie theaters, figuring he could learn much about what not to do and maybe even pick up a few usable tips on the edgy attitude that was sure to come his way from the street skells he would be going against face-to-face.

"Keep it in the back of your mind and never lose it," Detective Dowd told Boomer late one night as the two sat in a back booth of an empty downtown diner, each drinking more than his fair share of bad coffee. "Nine out of ten, hands to the ground, a wanna-be gangster picks up his street tics from what he's seen either on TV or in the movies. The lingo, the body bops, the tough hood-in-the-hood stance all come out of some movie you need to have seen. Give you an example. *The Godfather* hit theaters sometime in the early 1970s. Monster hit. Everybody from me and you to the corner pimp paid or swayed their way in to see it. Within a month of the movie earning money, there was a gang in Detroit and a second one in Brooklyn calling themselves 'The Godfathers.' Another gang, Hispanic crew up in the Bronx, tagged their group 'Sonny's Boys.' They're not rocket launchers, is all I'm trying to get across to you. They're crooks. Beat them at their own game and you'll always come out at the long end of the stick."

Boomer made it his business to know his business.

He learned to separate the neighborhood players both by routine and skill sets. The drug business didn't begin its day until late afternoon, when the runners and dealers took to the streets, which left the morning free to the numbers action, car boosters looking for a quick sale, and payback send-offs. Most of the organized mob crews kept to a standard schedule. The Italians did their daily business inside social clubs, with the windows either heavily shaded or painted black. On cool spring or fall days, they preferred to sit outside, gathered around small tables large enough to hold espresso cups and sambuca bottles. The Hispanic gangs mingled at the local bodegas, while black outfits spread their action inside the neon lights of after-hours night spots, booming background music blasting out any attempt at a wiretap. In those early years, as Boomer rose up the PD ranks—from beat patrol in Harlem to plainclothes work in Brooklyn and undercover stings in

Queens, until he hit the main event and was pinned with a detective's tin, rotating between homicide and narcotics—it seemed a simple task to decipher good from bad. The arrival of crack cocaine, coupled with the emergence of street gangs and the influx of ruthless gangsters from Colombia and Russia, forced the criminal leagues to toss out the rule books and ply their trade free of any of the time-honored traditions. What had once been so clear and organized that an aggressive cop could follow ongoing criminal activity with a flow chart was now a chaotic crime scene, and that left the terrain wide open for new crews to enter the fray and dominate the street action, amassing fortunes in less time than it took to buy a Manhattan co-op. As the dollars mounted, so did the dead bodies, leaving behind ravaged and ruined families and a city that would never again be the same. The Wild West had arrived in New York, and it gave no indication of leaving anytime soon.

Boomer slowed his run to a fast walk, body washed down in sweat, aches and pains slapping at his legs and lungs, his body rebelling somewhat against a daily habit it was no longer fully equipped to handle. He leaned against a rusty fence, breathing heavy and gazing up at a cloudless sky.

"I keep telling you the treadmill would be a better idea." Dead-Eye was standing next to him, two cold protein shakes in his hands, his sweatshirt drenched through with sweat. "You go at your own pace and stop when you feel the need. Keep going at it this way, one day or the next you're bound to fall flat."

"Remember Augie Petrocelli? That undercover working out of the two-eight?" Boomer asked, taking one of the shakes from Dead-Eye. "Took to a street chase like he was in the middle of a gold-medal run?"

Dead-Eye sipped his drink and nodded. "Worked with him on a

few jobs back when I was on the Black Liberation Task Force. Good cop, even better when there was some heat coming his way. What about him?"

"He retired about five, maybe six years ago," Boomer said. "Took a large chunk of his savings and borrowed against his pension and invested in a gym upstate, less than a mile from his house."

"I can just tell this is not going to be a happily-ever-after tale," Dead-Eye said.

"Bet your ass it's not," Boomer said, finishing off the protein shake with one long swallow. "In less than a year's time, he was flat broke—on the balls of his ass, fighting three court cases, and there was a lien on his pension. All because of that damn gym he threw his money at."

"And this has what to do with you going into one and using a treadmill?" Dead-Eye asked.

"The reason Augie found himself in such a hole is that one of the regulars in the gym sued his ass," Boomer said. "Did a scream-and-shout that his right leg was all fucked-up because the treadmills in the place weren't up to standards. Got himself one of those let-my-heart-bleed-for-you outfits to argue his case and a bent-eared judge to believe it, and there you have the sad tale."

"That the case, feel free to scratch it off your to-do list," Dead-Eye said. "It was only a throw-out idea on my part, nothing more."

Boomer and Dead-Eye moved off the running track and slow-walked up a steep hill, the shade from the surrounding trees cooling the sweat on their backs and necks. They were both still on the safe side of forty, but they moved with the gait and groans of older men. Two ex-cops who had suffered too many wounds in too short a period of time. Boomer cleared the hill and sat on a park bench facing the touch-the-cloud co-ops that lined Central

Park West, his hands resting flat on his legs. Dead-Eye stood, stretching out the kinks in his lower back, and looked down at his friend. "Don't grow shy on me now, Boom," he said with a hint of a smile.

Boomer returned the smile and leaned against the wooden slats of the bench. "I'm going to make a play against the restaurant gunners, soon as I pin down who they are and who pays them," he said, the words, as always, spoken with a calm and resolute confidence. "And the rest of their crews and the bosses who put in their orders. Every single one of them. They go down until I go down."

"Ballpark me a number," Dead-Eye said. "How many we talking about here? Total?"

"I haven't put the final layout together yet," Boomer said. "But from what I've been able to pick up so far, if we look the South Americans' way, then we're staring at three full crews, about one to one hundred and fifty members in each, every one with tons of washed cash and warehouses stashed with ammo. If it's the Russians, then double the numbers all around."

"How many on your side of the table?" Dead-Eye asked, already knowing the answer—and knowing that it would have little impact on Boomer's decision. Boomer had turned his back on reason and was about to run full steam now into a battle that seemed less a full-scale war than a final stand. "And let's not count your ass for the moment."

"I'm not asking you in on this, Dead-Eye," Boomer said with a slow shake of his head. "I can't. Not again, and not this time. You got a wife who loves it when you walk through your front door, and a kid that wants you at all his graduations. If I had either one of those, I might even take a step back from all this myself."

"Let's save that you-got-too-much-to-live-for bullshit for when we're both so fuckin' old we can't remember our names," Dead-Eye said, stepping in closer to Boomer. "And if dying is the endgame of this plan you can do it a lot faster and a lot less painfully than by going up against an army of cocaine cowboys. And you have to know, sure as I'm standing here, that there is zero chance of me watching this war from behind a glass door."

"We got lucky the last time, there's no doubt," Boomer said. "And we've been lucky our entire run, both on the job and off, wounds and all. But luck can turn on you with a vengeance, leave you standing with an empty gun and your back flat against a wall. And even if it doesn't break, we still don't stand much of a chance against any one of these crews. I don't know how this will all play out or how much of a dent we'll be able to put into this band of fuckers before it's our turn to fall, but I don't see us riding off into the sunset. Not on this one. You need to give that some serious thought before you jump in with me, that's all I ask."

"Then why do it at all?" Dead-Eye asked, a sad weight to his words. "On the one hand, it won't ease the pain of losing somebody who owned your heart. On the other, we're looking across at drug dealers, living inside a two-bullet-deductible world. They're on short time. These crews will all taste the drop, Boom, and soon. It just won't be our bullets that take them down."

"It's what we do, Dead-Eye," Boomer said. He stood up, and the two men started a slow walk up a path that would lead them out of the park. "And it's who we are. And deep down, whether we cop to it or not, it's all we've ever lived for. It's what keeps us alive. At least it does me."

They walked in a comfortable silence for several minutes, the grinding noise of a big city coming to life in the distance. They watched a young couple holding hands and walking a puppy in the tall grass and a middle-aged rummy stretching out near a bench, gearing up to begin yet another day. A man in jogging tights and a heavy sweatshirt brushed past them, making a beeline for the track and a long morning run.

"You have any sort of plan in mind?" Dead-Eye asked as they stepped out of the shade of the park and into the pedestrian traffic of Central Park West. "Or you just counting on pulling a Helen Keller and walking into this blind?"

Boomer looked at Dead-Eye and smiled. "I *always* have a plan," he said. "And this is one you're going to love. It's a real killer."

10

CHAPTER

He sat with his back to the wall, thick long hair brushing up against the gray cinder blocks that surrounded the four sides of the dark basement. The man was young, no older than twenty-five, and was dressed in a style well-schooled Brits call smart casual. He glanced down at a yellow legal pad resting in the center of a dark-oak table and shook his head in mock disappointment. He looked up and glared at the trembling man sitting across from him, stripped down to his shorts and a sweat-soaked T-shirt, blond hair, scraggly beard, and double chin coated with the gleam of fear.

"You know me?" the young man asked, his voice strong and calm. "Who I am and who I work for is what I mean?"

"Yes," the trembling man muttered, his lower lip quivering at a NASCAR pace.

"And yet you still went ahead and did what you did," the young man said, flashing eyes as cold as winter rain. "Which can only lead me to conclude that you don't give a bear's shit about who I am or who it is I work for. You're a player, and a player picks any field he wants. That's the photo snap I get."

"No, no, that's not it at all, Carlos," the trembling man said, sweat flowing off his head and neck like a small waterfall. "I needed to move the six kilos fast, didn't want to give a tip-off to the narcs that always seem to be on my ass."

"They're on your ass for sound reason, Walter," Carlos said with disdain. "They know that if they catch you they break you. Simple as the alphabet. And when they break you they know you'll toss out names at them faster than if you were reading them from a fuckin' phone book. It's prison you're afraid of, little man. But ratting out those who play on the same streets you do? It don't carry the weight. And selling shit that ain't yours to sell, you give a fuck about even less."

"I'm trying to explain it all to you—please, just hear me out on this," Walter pleaded. "First off, I didn't know the shit came from your crew. I bought it fair and on the square from Johnny the Clerk, hard runner with El Lupe and the Purple Gang in the East Bronx. Worked a good deal and made back six bangs more than what I paid, and I did it in less time than it takes to watch an extra-inning ball game. Then, once I knew I was in cloud clear, I was gonna come find you and hand over fifty percent of the haul. Plus any adds on top. My hand to my mother's grave, I'm talkin' truth here."

"I'd bet better than even money you never even laid eyes on your mother or any woman claiming such," Carlos said. He pushed his chair aside, walked around the table, and stood behind Walter, who was trembling so hard now that his bare feet shook on the cement floor. "And I don't give a fuck about the where and the how my drugs ended up in your greasy little hands. But I care, and I care a great deal, that you moved my brand out on my streets. I let shit like that stand without a Western Union going back the other direction, soon enough my name is ground down to what yours is now. A flat nothing with a target large enough for the blind to see splattered on my back. Even someone as shit-sure stupid as you can see the bind that puts me in."

Carlos McEntire was a seven-figure drug dealer, running hundreds of kilos a month from the hills of Bogotá to the streets of New York each and every month. He had set up shop in a candy store on East 233rd Street and White Plains Road in the Bronx while he was still in his freshman year at a local Catholic high school. He worked four-hour shifts behind the counter and used his time there as a base to sell marijuana packets to the older students who flocked in after class to buy cold sodas, small bags of chips, and enough weed to get them through the week. Every Saturday, he split the cash profits with an elderly Irish couple who didn't care how the money supplementing their monthly income came through the door. Within six months, Carlos had taken over the candy store and partnered with a narcotics detective with a habit of his own who was working out of the local precinct. The cop offered both protection and connections and, in return, had asked for a 15 percent cut and all the free coke he could jam up his nostrils.

Carlos had diversified his inventory to include pills and small vials of weak coke cut and danced on so many times it ranked just above Johnson's baby powder for a full-tilt buzz. He would spray a few hits of Raid ant and roach killer over the dope to give it an extra boost. "Raid is, like, the fuckin' Gatorade of dope," he once told a rival dealer. "It gives it that energy kick to get you over the top of the hill. Until you hit the big time and land your ass in prime-time heaven, you got no choice but to swear by that shit. Anything that's strong enough to kill bugs has got to be more than good enough to milk the flakes we're moving on these losers."

The increase in Carlos's street activity brought him to the attention of two equally young and hungry drug runners, Hector and Freddie Gonzalez. For a few brief months, the trio circled around one another like circus cats in a cage, watching and waiting, deciding when and where to make the first move. But in a unique show of restraint that is seldom witnessed in the drug world the three on-the-rise dealers decided to unite their small forces and move as one against the stronger and better equipped coke lords of the city. Across a two-year period, starting in the summer of 1982, the three hoods and their ruthless G-Men, numbering no more than twenty-four strong at the outset, lashed out against rival gangs with a viciousness not seen on New York streets since the Gallo-Profaci wars of the early 1960s.

"Every day on the job, I knew I could count on finding another body tossed in a garbage dump or left burnt as a slab of bacon on a rooftop," Sonny Rottillo, a detective working the narcotics beat during those twenty-four brutal months, recalled. "And they never hid the fact it was them that did the killing. They *wanted* us all to know, especially the other gangs. We just could never get enough on them to tag them with the hits. Sooner turned to soon, and the other gangs got tired of having their wives start their cars or looking both ways when they walked out of one of their social clubs. They didn't have the same stomach for the fight that the brothers and McEntire did. And in that crowd the one with the biggest hunger for blood always walks away with the title."

The Gonzalez brothers did the five-borough walk and talked with the other gangs in town, brokering deals that would eventually stem some of the bloodshed, cutting partnerships with the five Italian crime families and the smaller South American crews that were in play. Carlos worked at building up the sale and distribution end of the multi-tiered business, ensuring that a cut of any cocaine or heroin that moved into New York City ended up in the offshore bank accounts of the G-Men. In return, the upstarts offered blanket coverage to all participating members of the organization, turning loose their murder machine on any late arrivals that failed to grasp the rules of the agreement. If a new crew or dealer emerged on the scene, the offer was put out to send a share of the profits down toward the G-Men or risk a penalty fee. The initial cost was the life of a player who was close to the dealer. If that move was either ignored or not acted upon with the required speed, the G-Men took it to the next level. "They were the first New York City gang to reach out and touch someone's family," Timmy "Goat" Reynolds, one of the NYPD's legendary narcotics undercover cops, later said. "Before them, dealers only looked to take out one another. Their families could sleep safe and sound at night. These guys came in and changed all the rules. They did a top-to-bottom wipeout—wife, mother, father, kids, pets. You fucked with them and they left behind a trail of blood Mississippi River thick. That left dealers and their crews with two clear-as-a-sunny-day choices: you either do business the G-Men way or you get the fuck out of Dodge. You could be a hundred a day and on-the-nod deep into drugs, that's the kind of message that blasts its way through any smoke and haze you toss in its path."

"I'll give you all my money from any deal I make here on," Walter said, trembling as if he were in the middle of an ice storm. "From this second, I work only for you, fuck anybody else. I'll bring it in heavy, too—you know you can count on that plain as shit on the street. I'll be your number-one mover, work my ass off night and day. You'll see, Carlos, believe it when you hear it. You'll see."

"How can I believe you on that?" Carlos asked, taking several steps away from Walter and putting a light to a thin brown cigar. "An air-sucker like you would lie in front of the fuckin' Pope if you figured it would help out your angle. So words out of your mouth are like tits on a bull to my ears. Don't mean shit."

"I put it on my honor to you as a man," Walter said. "No way for me to make it any cleaner than that."

"There's a way," Carlos said, giving a slow nod, his thin lips pursed in a tight smile. "One that would show me you had the courage and the balls to back up all your words, make me toe-tap my way out of here knowing I had just traded for a stand-up and true team member."

"Tell me what it is and I'll do it without wasting a blink," Walter said, finally starting to see the emergence of a sliver of light at the end of his barren tunnel.

"You sure now?" Carlos asked. "You can still back away from your Custer stand, take the fast ride upstate with the ice pick in your neck. Not too late for that. All nice, clean, and easy. This other road that's open to you—not as quick, not as painless, not as final. You have to live with what happens, you make it your choice to travel down there. Am I coming across clear?"

"Whatever it is," Walter said with nervous conviction. "I won't take a step back. I'm from the barrio, my brother. We born with the hard brand burnt into us."

Carlos nodded and tossed his half-smoked cigar against a corner wall, a hard set of eyes glaring down at the sweat-stained dealer, who was breathing loud enough for it to echo in the empty room. "All right, then," he said, his voice, tone, and manner as relaxed as if he were in the middle of a Sunday-afternoon golf outing. "You leave me something behind, something that means the whole planet to you but would show how serious you are about working for me alive as opposed to not working for me dead. You willing to do that, to take it that far down the road, then we might have ourselves a solid deal."

"Anything, Carlos, I swear it," Walter said. "You just name it and whatever it is, if I got it, it belongs to you. All you need do is tell me what it is you want."

Carlos stared at Walter for a long and silent stretch of time. He then took a deep breath, smiled, and rested his hands against the cool cement of the wall at his back. "Your legs, Walter," Carlos finally said in a low voice. "You leave behind both your legs. You work for me, you'll do it from a wheelchair. Don't worry, though, I'm not going to keep them. I'll have them left for you in your apartment. You'll see them again once you're out of the hospital."

Tears streamed down Walter's scarred face and he choked back a mouthful of vomit. His heart was beating so loud that it made him dizzy, his mind filled with a vision of pain and bloodshed. He didn't turn to watch Carlos leave, unable to either speak or move his head, trembling hard enough to rattle the wooden slats of his chair.

"Welcome to my crew," he heard Carlos say.

11

Boomer waited as the woman walked toward him, the lights from the Whitestone Bridge overhead helping to guide her way. The ground was wet, the middle-of-the-night dew settling in and turning the brown dirt at his feet into soft mud. "I was starting to think you might not show," he said as she stood across from him, hands shoved inside the pockets of an expensive black coat, the shine on her boots strong enough to reflect the glare of the passing headlights from above.

"I'm always late," she said, her voice coated with a rich Eastern European accent. "A family habit, I'm afraid."

"Late or not, I'm glad you're here," Boomer said. He handed her a container of deli coffee, the lid jammed down tight. "I took a guess as to how you like it."

"Which is how?" she asked.

"I had a nun when I was in grammar school used to say she took her coffee black and bitter, just like her life," Boomer said. "That's how I take it, figured you for the same."

"Good call," she said. She lifted the lid of the container and took a long sip of the hot coffee. She was in her mid-twenties, dark hair flowing long and straight down the sides of her face and shoulders.

"Do you know why I wanted to meet with you?" Boomer said.

"Our friend said you had something important to ask," she said. "He thought it would be best if it was done face-to-face. And I agree with that thinking. It's always best to be able to look in the eye of either a friend or an enemy."

"He tell you anything about me?" Boomer asked.

"He didn't need to," she said. "I've always done my own homework. So I know you're a cop, or were. And who I am should be no secret to you."

Natalie Robinov was Russian organized-crime royalty.

She was the only daughter of the feared and respected Viktor Robinov, known to both cops and criminals as the Red Wolf, a thug and killer who ruled the Russian underworld from the Cold War through the odd dance of détente by murdering upwards of fifteen hundred men and women who sought to block the growth of his empire. Viktor was the Charles "Lucky" Luciano of the Russian mob, moving it out of its simple nineteenth-century mind-set, in which tribal gangs were happy and content to rule over the small villages within their domain and share the profits only among themselves, and into a national crime syndicate where the nation was sliced up like a thick oven-fresh pie and all factions gathered to share in the wages of fear.

Such a bold move did not come free of bloodshed, and it took several decades and many mutilated bodies before Russia was finally able to waltz into the twentieth century armed and organized, its reach now of global proportions, its power vast, the numbers beyond the scope and abilities of any other criminal enterprise or law-enforcement entity. "In time—and we're not talking a long time here, either—the Russian mob will dominate and rule the world of crime," FBI field director Ralph Vecchio once said to a gathering of federal agents at a Washington, D.C., government-sponsored conference. "At the height of their power, there were no more than five thousand members of Italian organized crime in the United States and as many as eight thousand in Italy. The same numbers, more or less, hold true today for the South Americans and rank a few thousand or so higher for the Chinese Triads. The Russians? They are a criminal nation all their own. At last count, there were three and a half million sworn members of the Russian mob, with anywhere between thirty and forty percent of them holding degrees in chemistry and physics. That makes them both deadly and dangerous. And, in the minds of many at our end of the line, be they federal or local, damn near unbeatable."

Viktor Robinov chose his daughter, Natalie, to lead the Russians in their quest to conquer and rule the criminal world. She had trained by his side since her youngest years, and had been educated in both the best schools mob money can afford and the day-to-day lessons of running a vast and expanding criminal enterprise. She was fluent in four languages and had martial-arts and weapons expertise, as well as a business degree from Oxford. She was tall, angular, and beautiful, and she understood that in her work such beauty could be as vicious a weapon as a loaded gun or a jagged knife. Viktor was sixty-seven and succumbing to lung cancer when he last spoke to his daughter, anointing her the most powerful member of the Russian underworld.

"You're ready now," he said to her, his once full-bodied voice reduced to a mere rasp. "It is my time to die and your time to rule."

"I don't want to be without you, Papa," Natalie said, not allowing herself the luxury of tears. She knew how little her father approved of any sign of weakness.

"And you won't ever be," Viktor said, reaching for her hand. "As I ruled with you by my side, so, too, shall you rule with me by yours. I will never leave you. My presence will be felt in every action, every decision, in your every thought. Know this, my sweet girl, and never forget it."

"I won't," Natalie said with a slow shake of her head. "I swear it to you."

"You will be tested, very early on," Viktor said to her. "Not everyone is pleased that my only child, and a woman at that, has been chosen to run the operation. They will look to kill, rid you from the scene before you even have a chance to enjoy a taste of the vast power you will have at your disposal."

"Who do you think it will be?" Natalie asked.

"The who, in this case, doesn't matter," Viktor said, his eyes the color of a wolf's winter coat. "They are *all* thinking you are too weak, ill suited to command them. So you must act within the first hours of taking the reins, even before my body is buried. Send a signal to all that you are even more vicious than the Red Wolf they so feared. It is the only way you can assume control and keep it. You must do it fast, make sure it's bloody, and, most of all, make sure it's visible for all to know and see."

"How many?" she asked.

"As many as it takes to get the message delivered," Viktor said. "No soldiers, only those with high ranks and powerful posts. Include in this initial group the one who is your most trusted adviser and who all suspect has your heart."

Natalie stiffened a bit, just enough for Viktor to notice. "Do you suspect it as well?" she asked. "That Vlad has my heart?"

"I have learned never to suspect," Viktor said. "Only to believe. And, yes, I believe your heart belongs to that young gangster."

"And yet you would have me kill a man you believe I'm in

love with," she said. "A man I may wish to wed and have by my side."

"You can never love, Natalie," Viktor said, wiping at his mouth with a cloth napkin. "In your position you can only taste love, be near it perhaps, embrace it on occasion, but never give yourself to it. Love is as big an enemy to you as trust. They can only bring you to ruin. You must never surrender to either one."

"But you have loved me," Natalie said. "And, before me, you loved Mama. Or am I wrong?"

"You speak the truth, I loved you both," Viktor said, his words hard and as cold as the Russian air. "But even with that I made sure to have ears to your words and eyes to your movements. And, despite such caution, I was caught off guard by your mother's betrayal, so much so that initially I doubted the evidence I knew to be valid. I questioned the truth that stood before me."

Natalie leaned in closer to her father. "What are you telling me?" she asked.

"That if you are indeed to follow in my footsteps you must be prepared to have an even harder heart than I could ever have," Viktor said. "Anyone can order a kill or do it himself, be it the death of a stranger, an enemy, or a friend. But not anyone can put to death a person to whom he has professed an unending love, someone with whom he has exposed his true self. Someone for whom he would risk all that he has worked to gain."

"It was you that had Mama murdered?" Natalie said, barely able to get the words past her lips.

"Even worse than that, my Natalie," Viktor said, taking in a series of deep and painful breaths. "Your mother met her death by my own hands. It was done in this very room and on this very bed. And I shed not one tear. Not back then and not now, even with my own death so close at hand."

"Why are you telling me all this?" she asked, glancing for a brief moment at a framed photo of her mother on a night table, dressed in a black dress, a white string of pearls hanging loose around her neck. "And why now?"

"So that you are fully aware of the type of man I had to be in order to retain my position of power," Viktor said. "And the kind of woman you need to be in order to maintain yours. And now is not just the only time I have left to alert you to this painful fact but the best time as well."

"I don't understand you, Papa," Natalie said. "What are you trying to do to me?"

"My lesson is a simple one, my little Natalie," Viktor said, gripping both her hands in his, thick purple veins coursing up his arms. "I need to know before I breathe my last that I have prepared you to run this organization in the manner required. I need to see the proof that I have indeed chosen the right person to succeed me."

"And how am I to prove it?" Natalie said, wondering now if her father was merely lost inside the fuzzy haze of the various drugs his doctors were giving him to help him cope with the pain.

"End my life," he said, his voice at full strength for this brief moment. "Do not allow your mother's killer to breathe for one more pain-free second. Make me pay for what I did to her and for what I took from you."

"Isn't living with it pain enough for you?" Natalie asked.

"If you do indeed believe that, then my choice is already doomed," Viktor said. "There is no pain in taking a life, only relief that you were the one spared. No matter whose life it was that was brought to an end."

Natalie stared at her father and gazed into the harshness of his eyes. She leaned down and kissed him gently on both cheeks. She then reached across the bed, grabbed a pillow, and held it above her father's face. She watched as he smiled up at her and gave her a silent nod. She eased the pillow down on his face and held it there, holding it tighter and with strength the moment she felt her father jostle and squirm. She kept it there until the life was drained from the wilted body of the most feared man in the Russian underworld.

"Your father never made mention of having a kid," Boomer said to Natalie. "Then again, our meetings were never weighed much on the social end."

"You knew my father?" Natalie asked, not bothering to hide her surprise.

"We butted heads once or twice," Boomer said. "Other times, when it served both our interests, we buttered each other's bread. He was a tough bastard, but old school all the way. He knew the rules and, while he may have bent them here and there, he usually stayed within the foul lines."

"And you're wondering if the same is true of me as well?" Natalie said.

"Only when it comes to a restaurant takeout," Boomer said. "I want to make sure I aim my guns at the right targets."

"You lost someone in that shooting," Natalie said, both hands gripped around the now empty coffee container.

"My niece," Boomer said, his eyes suddenly sliding from hers.

"I'm sorry for that," she said, drawing in on Boomer's sense of loss and despair. "But none of my guns were involved. It's your choice whether you believe that or not."

Boomer stared at Natalie, looking into a pair of eyes the color of night, and nodded, surprised at the warmth she conveyed. "Viktor never lied to me," he said. "I'm going to take the points and spread that trait to his daughter."

"Do you need anything else from me?" she asked, her unlined face shimmering under the lights of the bridge.

"If I do, I'll reach out," Boomer said.

"And if you do I'm sure we'll meet in a spot equally as romantic," she said, gazing out at the river water lapping against a shoreline littered with old tires, blocks of cement, and rusty old train rails.

"I'll make a point of it," Boomer said.

Natalie turned back to him and smiled.

"I was sorry to hear about your father," he said. "I lost my dad when I was young, too. It's not something you shake off easy, doesn't matter what end of the fence you play on."

Natalie stayed silent, caught slightly off guard by Boomer's words, watching as he turned and disappeared into the darkness and the low-hanging mist of the muddy path.

12

Andy Victorino ran a rubber-gloved hand slowly across the dead man's bare chest, his long fingers resting on the two large bullet wounds just below the breastbone. They were in a dark tunnel, the rumblings of cars and trucks racing across the Cross Island Expressway sending loose dust particles and paint chips to the damp ground around them. The body belonged to a middle-aged white male with a swollen stomach and a Klondike Bill black beard. He was in full rigor, and his low liver temperature meant that he had been dead a full day shy of a week. Rats had feasted on the body, gnawing gaping holes in the areas around his neck and thighs. He was naked except for one soiled brown construction boot, minus laces and leather lip. "Has the look of another pump-and-dump," a voice to Victorino's left said. "It's that time of year. This and half a dozen or so floaters are what come in like clockwork every spring. Sure as bees work flower beds."

"Maybe," Victorino said. "I'll know more once I break down the crime scene, or what's left of it, and then have him autopsied downtown."

"You're not going to find yourself much in either place, you ask me my thoughts on the matter," the voice said, stepping closer to Victorino, the soles of his shoes leaving thick marks on the dark soot piled up next to the right side of the dead man's head. "Both the scene and the vic have been stepped on like they were a fuckin' dance floor."

"You've been working homicide, what is it now, six, seven years?" Victorino asked, still not looking up at the man hovering over his crime scene. "And you still know as much now as you did six months in. It's what's *not* here means more to the solve than what you can see. You're a good cop, Bennett, solid. But what keeps you from the next level is you always come in looking for the easy, and there's never anything easy about death."

"All right, Quincy," Detective Sam Bennett said, calling Victorino by the nickname the department had pinned on him within weeks of his joining the Crime Scene Unit, Forensic Division. "Educate me. What am I not looking for that for sure you can plainly see?"

"The ones who killed him weren't the ones who stripped him down and took away all his biologicals," Victorino said, his words calm, measured, and confident. "That was done later—a day, maybe two on the outside, after the murder. The killers left him clean, didn't take anything that belonged to him. Other than his life."

"How do you know that?" Bennett asked, the sarcasm replaced now by a raised police antenna.

"First, the vic took two close-contact hits—first bullet stopped his heart, second was pumped in just to make sure there wouldn't be a curtain call," Victorino said, standing now, hands folded across his thin chest, eyes still on the dead man. "The doer was a pro, knew why he was sent here and wasted little time in getting it done. He came in clean and calm, pocketed the shell casings. Even if we had the gun in hand, the prints would lead us nowhere but some upstate cemetery."

"How does all of that take you to where the shooter leaves here without doing a Salvation Army on the clothes?" Bennett asked.

"Logic, for one," Victorino said with a slight shrug. "I mean, give it a second of thought and then tell me why a pro, paid in cash left in a safe-deposit box in a city that's not this one, would strip a guy he just killed down to next to nothing. There's no link between the two—none that we'll ever find, at any rate. Two, you're telling me he walks away from a murder site with his arms filled with a dead man's clothes or, even worse, lugging a large black Hefty bag? Just so some pain-in-the-ass innocent bystander out taking his dog for a quick piss could spot him doing so? Never happens."

"That's your gut talking to you," Bennett said, his gray jacket and crisp white shirt tight against the expanse of a set of broad gym-worked shoulders. "And, while all of what you say may be on the mark, you can't really prove it; you can only argue in favor of it. You still don't know with one-hundred-percent certainty that the shooter didn't also lift the clothes."

"Riddle me this then, Bennett," Victorino said, leaning across the much taller detective and pointing toward the dead man's feet. "Why would he go to all the hassle of a clothes raid and then leave behind one lonely little construction boot? And, before you answer, toss this little factoid into your head. The boot in question doesn't belong to the vic."

"To who, then?"

"If I had the answer to that, I would know who it was that took the clothes," Victorino said. "And then you and me would maybe both be one step closer to tagging the hitter."

"So who is it I'm supposed to go hunt down, exactly?" Bennett asked. "Other than maybe a construction worker minus a boot."

"Soon as I get an ID on the departed I can maybe start to give you an idea," Victorino said, turning to look down the length of the dark passageway. "Meantime, while I finish up here would you do me a solid?"

"If it's doable," Bennett said.

"Ask the lab boys to bag that large dead rat up against the wall behind us," Victorino said. "And have them do a perimeter search around his body—five feet on either side ought to do the trick. They can bring everything they find to me down at the lab."

"And what the fuck would I ask them to do all that for?" Bennett asked, disgust mixed with displeasure.

"The rat's got a bullet in him," Victorino said. "Could be just a strange coincidence—that happens every day, as you are well aware. Or it could be our shooter didn't leave with all his shell casings. Either way, it's worth us taking a look."

"You are indeed one odd duck, Quincy," Bennett said, walking away, careful not to step with too heavy a foot on the dirt patches in his path as he made his way toward the dead rat and the two technicians in blue windbreakers.

Victorino watched him leave, one gloved hand resting on the dead man's chest, and nodded. "You have no idea," he whispered.

Andy Victorino was raised among the dead.

His father, Francesco, arrived in New York City from his birthplace of Naples, Italy, fresh off a four-year sentence as an Italian POW in a camp run by a force of British and Australian troops.

He was one of 272 prisoners, all of whom were treated as nothing more than mild annoyances who needed to be tolerated and, on rare occasions, admonished. Francesco moved into a back one-bedroom in a cold-water walk-up near the Manhattan West Side piers and, in less than a week's time, found work at a local funeral parlor. There, working under the steady gaze of Gerald Miller, a thirty-year veteran of the death business, Francesco loaded and unloaded coffins into the back of idling hearses; picked up bodies from cramped apartments, stifling workplaces, and overrun hospital wards. He found comfort in the silent and difficult work, and solace in bringing a final peace to the suffering bodies he saw on a daily basis. He had grown accustomed to the face of death after the onslaught of a major world war in his native land had stripped him of his only home and the few relatives he had left. In his spare time, he mastered a new language by reading the daily tabloids tossed aside by the other workers at the funeral parlor, always with an English dictionary close at hand. And through those early months of hard work and peace, Francesco began to set his sights on two major goals, both key ingredients in any immigrant's dream: he wanted to open his own business and start a family.

He met his future wife, Lucia Selvaggi, at a funeral Mass for a middle-aged butcher who suffered a fatal heart attack as he sliced his way through a thick double-cut rib eye. She was twenty-five and had been married to a handsome young man who lost his life in a gambling dispute in a Tenth Avenue bar. The few friends Francesco had made during his short time in the States all advised him to wait and perhaps find a more suitable bride, one who wasn't "tainted" by the widow's stain. But living through the end trails of a war had drummed into Francesco the simple but uncomfortable fact that death reaches a hand to touch everyone, some sooner than others, and leaves in its silent wake a vast ocean filled with altered lives. He felt safe in Lucia's presence, finding a comfort zone he had never known before, and allowed her entry into the gates that he kept locked and lowered to ward off any intrusion. There existed a mutual understanding between the two, shared sentiments that life was indeed a fragile gift—one that could be quick to evaporate. So he ignored the dire warnings pressed on him by concerned friends and settled down with the only woman he would ever profess to love, and they began their life together.

Within five years of his wedding day, Francesco opened the doors to a small funeral parlor that bore his name. He worked the long hours required to get a competitive business off the ground, catering to the needs and requests, religious or otherwise, of the working-class Italians who made up the bulk of his clientele. While he serviced the dead on the first two floors of the four-story brownstone that housed the parlor, Lucia worked out of their third-floor apartment, designing and stitching white dresses and dark suits. These would then be offered up for sale at reduced prices to bereaved family members eager to make the dearly departed look their best in their final resting place.

The couple had enough money to cover the mortgage and their monthly expenses, with enough to put aside for the occasional dinner at a restaurant outside their neighborhood. They enjoyed each other's company, treated each other with a mutual respect not common in most of the marriages in their circle, and were not afraid to display their affection in public. All was perfect, except for the fact that they had yet to have children. "It will happen when it's meant to happen," Francesco told his wife after yet another futile visit to a doctor long on sympathy but short on answers. "And when it does, it will be more than worth the wait. A special kid just takes a little longer to arrive."

Andrew Victorino made his appearance one week shy of his parents' tenth wedding anniversary, on a sultry August night in 1956. The couple, as expected, doted on their only child, happily catering to his every wish, and allowed to do so by the substantial income Francesco enjoyed from his now thriving business. There were camps for gifted children and trips to Europe in the summer, and private school the rest of the year. And if these outlets could not provide or fulfill a need, Francesco and Lucia brought in a tutor who could and did. For Andrew, it was, both above and beneath the surface, an ideal childhood. "My mom used to read me these bedtime stories—some in English, others in Italian, most of them sad—about kids my age going through all sorts of hardships I could never imagine existed," he once told a college roommate. "I would sit in my bed at night, long after she had turned out the light and closed the door to my room, and wonder what it would be like to have to live like one of those kids. By the time I hit my twelfth birthday, I didn't have to wonder about it anymore. I was one of them."

———————

Francesco Victorino was putting the final touches on the corpse of a young man who had fallen victim to an unforgiving lung disease. It was late, closing in on midnight, the large basement room shrouded in darkness and enveloped in silence. Francesco stared down at the young man with the sunken cheeks and the thinning hair and slowly shook his head. It was indeed a thin line that separated those who lived from those who died, those who were spared illness from those who were haunted by its hard clutch. The longer he lived, and the more days he spent working in the company of those who were touched by death's hand, the more Francesco had come to appreciate life's short attention span. He had long ago come to the realization that he ranked among the lucky few, the ones for whom death had yet to reach out its iron grip: He had skirted its grasp during the madness and suffering of the World War II years and had emerged from that period a determined man, made much older than his age by the horrors he had lived to witness. This, he had later realized, was why he had chosen a profession that kept him in death's company on a daily basis. And it was also why he took such pride in ensuring that the deceased were afforded as comfortable and as warm a final parting as he could conjure. If you walk among the shadows of death, it might make you a less appealing target, he reasoned. Or maybe it was all just a matter of luck: the unseen flip of a celestial coin that ultimately decided who would live and who would die.

Francesco Victorino's coin flip was about to turn on the losing side.

The man stared in silence at the undertaker, drugs and drink soaring through his frail body in lethal doses, his mind racing with images that bore no connection to reality. He kept the thin fingers of his right hand wrapped around the hard black handle of a thick, sharp knife, the knuckles red and the skin peeled back raw. His legs trembled as he stood with his back to the wall, his body partially hidden by a dark curtain. He had not tasted food in three days, and his only nourishment came courtesy of a warm six-pack of Colt 45 malt liquor. He was wearing jeans that were both frayed and stained, and a Deep Purple T-shirt that had once been white as a morning cloud. The veins in his arms were swollen, jabbed full with Blackbeard, the newest and the best low-grade, crumpled-singles heroin for the habitual on-the-nod user. He kept his eyes on the undertaker, gazing out at him through a glazed-doughnut stare, watching as he worked with quiet precision on the body of a young man less than seventy-two hours dead. He tried to keep his breaths short, taking in the cool, moist air of the room through clogged and caked nostrils. Every two minutes or so, he let out a sudden shudder, sending his entire body, from felony-flyer feet to greasy hair hanging loose across his forehead and eyes, into a long, rhythmic series of low-wattage spasms.

The man gripped the knife handle as tight as he could muster and took several silent steps forward, inching closer to the undertaker as he quietly and carefully neared the end of his death ritual. The man's every movement was fueled by the insane drive of the desperate addict to seek out the easy mark, to find the quickest route to fast cash that would pay for the next high that lay in wait. The warm needle that just ached to course its way down the glory roads of his arms and legs there, just waiting for the cash transfer and the grab. The man, James Pelfrey, was a twenty-two-year-old twice-convicted petty thief and doper, hectored and hounded by the police since he first cracked the puberty mark, who lived hand to nickel bag by pulling down small-time scores and late-night widow push-in-and-snatch jobs. He got the idea to reach for a hit against Victorino's Funeral Home while nursing a series of cold taps at a local alehouse, his head resting against the old stone of the bar that his family had once owned and gambled away. He was doing a bent ear to the two men in cheap suits off to his left, discussing matters of money—mostly, who had it and who didn't. That's when he first heard mention of the small parlor nestled between a Met supermarket and Eliot's Dry Cleaners just under the IRT number 2 elevated subway line along White Plains Road in the East Bronx. "The place is a fuckin' gold mine," the cheaper of the two cheap suits said. "Wives, mothers, sons, and daughters all paying out cold cash to bury a young husband or an old father. And the dead doin' nothin' but layin' there, not able to breathe one fuckin' word about their hard-earned dollars taking a fly out of their relatives' pockets and into the clean and crisp pockets of the dago gravedigger."

"Owning one of them funeral places is like owning a piece of a fuckin' casino, is what I heard tell," the other cheap suit said, his words coated with anger. "Every day, every night, some poor bastard bites the bit and his ass ends up on that fucker's cold slab while his cash does a fast fade."

"Somebody with a head on his shoulders and a pair as big as this room could make a move on a place like that," the first cheap suit said, slugging down another in a steady line of shooters. "Walk himself away with a nice and sweet payday. Fuck, if I had the time and was the type who leaned in that direction, for sure as shit I'd take a jab at a hit myself. But, if truth be told, a cold room packed top to bottom with the fresh dead is more than enough to make me want to take a step back."

"The dead can't fuck with you," James Pelfrey said, the words meant to be more a murmur than spoken aloud as he interjected himself into the conversation that would alter the course of his one-way life. "Seems to me the best place to go for a prime-time score would be a place where the dead outnumber the living."

"Listen now to the doper's words," the second cheap suit said, raising an empty glass in Pelfrey's direction. "As fucked-up as he is, even he knows a good plan when he hears it."

"Well, go ahead then, you think it's so fuckin' easy," the first cheap suit said. "Take down that undertaker and make your score. But don't you forget to come back here and square us a few rounds on the arm once you do."

Andy Victorino was in the spacious and elegantly furnished third-floor dining room, helping his mother arrange cups and plates on the thick, hand-carved table. It had, down the years, evolved into a family tradition shared by the three of them each evening: a hot cup of espresso and two chocolate biscotti when Francesco closed up shop for the night and made his way up the hall steps. It gave them a chance to reflect quietly on the day or discuss a variety of matters big or small that pertained to all three, but mostly school or recreational activities built around Andy's often overloaded schedule. On a few of the nights, they would just sit through dessert in silence, each lost in his own world of thought.

"Papa is running late," Andy said, glancing at the wooden clock positioned in the center of the wall just above an antique hutch filled with silverware and dishes. "As usual."

"He loses track of time," Lucia said with an understanding shrug. "He concentrates on his work, not on the hour."

"Should I go down and get him?" Andy said, this time looking at his mother and giving her a wide smile in anticipation of the answer he knew he would get.

"Go," Lucia said with a wave of her right hand. "And don't you keep him too long. Help him clean up, and then you both get back here before my coffee tastes like old rubber."

Andy had already made a hard dash out the door and was halfway down the hall stairs by the time she had finished her admonitions. Lucia slid a chair from the table and sat down, her slippered feet folded one over the other. She shook her head, the rich dark strands of her black hair coating the sides of her face, and smiled. This time of the night, long after the mourners had left the parlor and the house was as quiet as a country morning, belonged to her son and her husband. The special few minutes the two shared in the basement, their evening talks covering a wide variety of topics, further cemented the cast-iron bond that existed between them. "They are so very much alike," Lucia once told her best friend in the city, Angelina Cortese, a widow who owned the florist shop across from their parlor. "It's as if they were one person. Andrew is so driven—sometimes I think too much so—but then so is Francesco. And both treat work as if it were its own reward. Andrew asks his father hundreds of questions, and each one is patiently answered. And if Francesco doesn't know or isn't totally sure, they both make their way to the library and don't come back until they have the answer they need."

"Does Andrew want to be an undertaker like his father?" Angelina asked.

"He wants to be a doctor," Lucia said with a glint of pride. "He respects the work his father does, but he would much rather save a life than prepare it for its departure. Still, the time spent down in the mortuary with his father will serve him well once he's in medical school. He has already seen the dead, and learned that from them he has nothing to fear. It's the living who give us all our grief."

Francesco Victorino turned when he felt the shadow descend. He looked at James Pelfrey, saw the shaky smile on the thin man's face and the large blade of a knife hanging from his right hand. He saw the violent tremors in the legs and upper body, and the lost look embedded in a set of eyes the color of old chalk. Francesco Victorino had seen more than enough bodies in his life, both living and dead, to know what the one now standing before him had come to do.

Bring his dream to an end.

"Give me the money," Pelfrey stammered, his voice sounding as if it were delivered through a clogged drain. "Every single fuckin' dime you got, and maybe I let you live. Maybe I don't leave you dead on one of your own slabs. How fucked-up would that be, undertaker? Your ass found on one of your own slabs?"

"I keep no money down here," Francesco said in a manner as calm and relaxed as he could muster. "Look around for yourself and see. But, believe me when I tell you, there is no money in this room."

"You lyin' bastard," Pelfrey said, the low gurgle of his words reaching for a harsher tone. "Who you tryin' to bullshit? You got funerals coming in and out of here all day long, like it was some fuckin' parade of the dead. I seen it myself, with my own eyes. Even came to one of your fuckin' funerals a while back, for some cousin of mine got shot up near the Wakefield movie theater. And knowing all that, you got the balls to tell me you got no money?"

"I said I keep no money down here," Francesco said.

Pelfrey ran a white-coated tongue across a set of parched and chapped lips. The fingers gripping the knife handle were drenched with cold sweat and the veins in the back of his neck were doing a drum solo, the pounding reaching all the way up to his temples. He lifted the knife closer to the undertaker, the sharp blade now mere inches from the man's chest, and glared at him through drug-infested eyes. "Then give me what you have on you," Pelfrey said.

Francesco stared back at the young man for several seconds and then slowly shook his head. "I have no money," he said in a low voice. "Not in the room and not in my pockets. I have nothing to give you."

Pelfrey's eyes widened as if they were shocked awake by a cold blast of air. He reached out his left hand and grabbed the back of Francesco's head, his fingers clutching a thick mound of brown hair. He pushed Francesco closer and managed to curl his lips in what passed for a snarl. "Then I have something to give you," he said.

The blade of the knife wedged in Francesco's stomach, the blood flow running in a tight pattern down the front of his starched white shirt and onto the creases of his blue slacks. It formed a puddle over the top of his black loafers and coated the gray concrete floor, looking as still as a lake under the sharp glare of the mortician's light. A thin line of blood rolled down the right side of Francesco's mouth, his eyes did a flutter dance, and the color began to drain from his face. His knees buckled and he was held in check by the shaky grip of the addict, who jammed the blade of the knife deeper into his stomach with every fresh wheeze he took. "You spend all your time taking care of the dead," Pelfrey whispered. "But now, who the fuck will take care of you?"

Pelfrey let go of the knife and took two steps back, watching the undertaker fall to his knees, both hands gripped around the blade jutting from his stomach. The junkie stared with openmouthed amazement as the life slowly seeped out of a good man, the adrenaline rush now doing a mix-and-blend with the heroin, giving Pelfrey the most sustained rush of his wasted days. He winced when Francesco fell facedown to the hard surface, the knife now buried handle-deep inside his body, the thick pool of blood around him taking the shape of a full moon. "Sweet dreams, undertaker," Pelfrey said, and turned to leave the room.

He stopped when he saw the boy standing in the shadows off to his left, a cocked .38 revolver held in two thin hands. The boy kept his eyes on Pelfrey, his breath coming out in a rush, his calm manner betrayed by eyes that welled with tears. Pelfrey took a quick glance around the room and then looked back at the boy and gave him a slow smile. "You lookin' to rob the place, too, little man?" he asked in hushed tones. "If so, it'd be nothing more than a time killer. Ain't nothin' here but the dead."

"The man you just killed is my father," Andy Victorino said, the barrel of the gun that was kept hidden in the bottom drawer of Francesco's desk aimed squarely at the junkie's rail-bone chest.

"He's dead because he lied," Pelfrey said without a hint of remorse. "Tried to sell me some wolf tickets about him having no money."

"He never lied," Andy said. "He had no money to give. But even if he did have money and gave it all to you, it wouldn't have mattered. You would have killed him anyway. It's what people like you do."

"And now what are you going to do about it, little man?" Pelfrey said. "You gonna kill me? Shoot me dead with your papa's gun? Why, I'd bet a cold turd like you ain't even shot off a round before. And even if you did, you've never pulled on somebody alive—somebody that can walk and talk and breathe. I ain't no fuckin' tree, kid. You pull that trigger and you're gonna have a murder pinned on your ass. And you ain't ready for any kind of shit like that. Because that's *not* what people like *you* do. Or am I wrong on that, little man?"

Andy Victorino did his all not to gaze at his father's body, the dark puddle spreading far enough to reach down to his legs and feet, the life gone, replaced now by the cold stillness of the dead. He had heard his father's and the stranger's initial verbal exchange as he moved down the stairwell into the dark void of the morgue and had frozen in place. He couldn't figure out who it could be or what he could want, especially as it was three hours past the parlor's closing time. He took a long, deep breath and eased down the final three wooden steps leading into his father's work area. He had his back to the old wood desk that his father used to file his large amounts of paperwork and, when time allowed, to write letters of comfort and hope to those who had left their recently departed in his care. The voices in front of him were gaining in strength and threat. With ghostlike moves, Andy slowly slid open the bottom drawer of the desk and reached for the loaded .38 Special his father kept there. It had been a gift left to him by a longshoreman's widow, her husband lost to her in a barroom brawl that had escalated from closed fists to bullets in less time than it took to pour a full pint. His father was initially reluctant to accept such a gift, not being a man who found comfort or need to back up his words with a weapon, but the widow insisted. "Trust me, it won't do anybody a goddamn bit of harm at rest in your desk drawer," she said through her veil of tears. "And in this world you have no idea when it might come in handy."

Andy gripped the gun, cocked the trigger, arms held out in a shooter's pose, and turned toward the voices. In the flash of an instant, he saw the knife plunge into his father's stomach and stood helpless as Francesco fell first to his knees and then on his face. He had trouble keeping his footing, the room spinning, a mass of bile forming in his throat, heart pumping loud enough to echo. In less than a second's time, the safe world that his father had so carefully woven for Andy and his mother was torn aside and stepped on. All by a junkie in need of fast cash and a quick fix.

"You hearing me, little man?" Pelfrey asked, not comforted by the moments of silence that had passed between him and the boy. "How about I walk away from all this mess, clean and quiet, like I was never here, and you run your tiny ass over and be with your daddy? Might be the best way for the two of us to clear away from something that maybe should never have happened."

Andy held the hard gun barrel and the tough look, his body taut, his index finger curled around the trigger. All he needed to do was give the trigger a light touch, a gentle reflex push, and a bullet would warp-speed its way toward the man who had just murdered his father and send him blood-splattered against the wall. Andy wanted so much for the man standing across from him to suffer—to feel the same intense pain that his father had felt, to grasp, during those final, lost seconds, what it meant to die for nothing more than the whim of a stranger. And he would be the only one to bear witness, standing over the dying man, watching as he fought for his final breaths, knowing that his father's death had been vindicated. This was not the time to consider legal implications. Andy was old enough to have learned that the wheels of justice often spun in favor of the career criminal, and always at the expense of the innocent victim. A savvy street hood like the one who stood less than five feet from him, the soles of his shoes stained with the spilled blood of his father, would know how to manipulate the system as expertly as any seasoned lawyer. His was a sermon that was at its most effective in the presence of a soft judge and a jury whose collective hearts would bleed for yet another damaged soul held hostage by the life-sapping demands of a drug plague now in its third destructive decade.

Nor did it matter that the loss of James Pelfrey would not be felt by any sector of humanity. He would leave no family behind, no mourning widow or grieving son. James Pelfrey would simply be yet another abandoned craft in a long urban chain of predatory vessels, destined to be moored across a cold slab, a thick white sheet hiding what remained of him. And all it would take for that cycle to be set in motion was for Andy Victorino to squeeze down on the curved trigger and let his anger and pain and sorrow guide his motions.

Andy took a deep breath and flashed on an image of his father smiling. He knew that he wouldn't be the one to end James Pelfrey's life. He and his father had shared many ideas during their many hours alone together, discussions that touched on all the matters that Francesco deemed important to pass on to his only child. Killing a man in cold blood, regardless of the reasons, never entered into any of those long conversations. For Andy Victorino, it was more important to keep the memory of his father intact than it was to exact cold-steel revenge on the man who had just ended his life.

James Pelfrey caught the look in the boy's eyes and knew that this was not the day he was meant to die. "I don't want to ever come back here," he said to Andy. "So don't do or say anything to anybody that would give me cause. You tell the cops the same story you're going to tell your mother. That you walked down them steps behind you and found your daddy the way you did. If you can keep your shit together long enough to do that, then me and you won't be nothin' to each other but a bad fuckin' memory."

Andy Victorino lowered the handgun and nodded. "We'll see each other again," he said, his voice small and hollow but steady.

James Pelfrey managed a smile and wiped his runny nose with the front of his right hand. He lowered his head, turned, and did a quick fade into the darkness of the room, heading for the back door that would lead to a dark alley and freedom. Andy waited a few long, lonely seconds and then walked to his father's desk and rested the gun in a bottom drawer. He sat on his father's old, creaky wooden chair, the wheels squeaking from his slender weight, and stared across the room at the still body. It was then that the tears began to rain down his face, his chest and stomach heaving from the heavy and painful spasms. It was there, less than an hour later, that his mother found him, her screams only adding to his pain. And it was there that he stayed, through that long night, as the room filled with police and crime-scene investigators, an unfolded black body bag spread out in the corner, two burly men standing off to the side, waiting for the signal that the corpse could at last be removed.

"You ready to do this, Quincy, or what?" Bennett said in his thick baritone, snapping Andy Victorino back into the present. "Not like this poor bastard's gonna up and fill us in on who it was did him in."

"You go on ahead," Andy said. "I want to go over the body once more, make sure I didn't overlook something easy to miss. Check in with me in a few hours. I'll have a bone for you to chew on by then."

"That's a call for you to make," Bennett said with a slight shrug of a pair of massive shoulders. "And it's not in my nature to tell people how to go about their business. If you find anything sooner than you figure, give me a blow and I'll head down your way. In the meantime, I'll deal with his bios and kick-start the paperwork."

Andy Victorino waited until he was alone with the victim. He knelt down over the man, slapped on a pair of latex gloves, and probed the fatal wounds once again, looking for the one mistake that would eventually lead to the track and takedown of a killer.

He was where he knew that he truly belonged.

Alone, in the company of the dead.

The Boiler Man listened and nodded. Nothing the tall man standing across from him in the empty men's room at the rear of the midtown steak house was saying was new to his ears. In the end, after you broke it all down, his business was a very simple one. There was a price, a target, a preferred date of execution, and the clean walkaway. It had been his experience that anything beyond those basics that was added to the mix was done either because the client was looking to impress or because what was being tossed on the table wasn't as clean a deal as he was expected to believe. The Boiler Man had been around the murder track enough times to have learned that if either of those two factors entered into play, it was a clear signal for him to turn his back on the deal, regardless of the sum of money being dangled.

"Three hundred thousand in cash just to put to waste a fuckin' accountant with millionaire taste and a turncoat's instincts," the tall man said, his voice thick with disdain, the attempt at the tough talk more wholesale than retail. "And they say I'm in the money end of the pool. I did your kind of work, I'd be wiping my ass with a handful of hundred-dollar bills. Hear what I'm saying?"

"There's no one here but you saying you can't do my kind of work," the Boiler Man said, his tone laid-back and matter-of-fact as he gave himself a quick glance in the large bathroom mirror. "It would save you all that cash you jammed into that little satchel over there, not to mention give you the total satisfaction of taking out your own garbage. Of course, if you in any way fuck up and either botch the job or get pinched hard by a young badge eager to make homicide first grade before his hair starts to thin, then, first offense or predicate, you would no doubt be staring down hard at natural life. And you don't have the balls, the money, or the head to handle that kind of weight. Which is why here I stand, in a fucking men's room, talking to you instead of hanging my dick over a urinal."

"I didn't mean to set off your alarm," the tall man said, the bravado behind his words taking a long step down. "I was just making conversation before we got down to it, is all. Didn't mean to offend."

"If I'm lonely for conversation I'll dial one of those all-night radio stations," the Boiler Man said. "Or maybe see a shrink and figure out why it is I visit my father's grave once a year and piss all over the headstone. Or, better still, I'll find an Irish bartender. What I would never fuckin' do, no matter how desperate I might be, is seek you out and start to shoot the shit. Now, are we ready to get on with the business at hand?"

The tall man nodded and kicked the satchel closer to the Boiler Man. "It's all in there," he said. "I took the cash out of the office safe late last night, long after the place had cleared. I didn't go home, as I was told not to do, but got a room at a motel in Queens over by LaGuardia."

"You check in under your own name?" the Boiler Man asked.

"Look, I know I don't play in your league. But a moron I'm not. I have this alias I've used as far back as when I first started stepping out on the wife. It's a character from a favorite book of mine."

The Boiler Man held up his right hand. "Save the details for your obit," he said. "All I need to be sure of is no one saw you take the money or leave with the money, and no one knows where you've been for these last twenty-four hours. And if the answer to all of the above is a yes, I can die happy."

"Hand to God, nobody's seen me since I took that dough out of the safe, not unless you count the dim-bulb clerk working the front counter at the motel," the tall man said. "And I wouldn't, not since the guy was so fuckin' stoned he couldn't pick Ronald Reagan out of a police lineup."

"We can move on then," the Boiler Man said. "What else do you have for me other than the money?"

"What else do you need?" the tall man asked with a hint of surprise. "All I was told was to get the cash, bring it here, and hand it over to you."

"I'm sure that's exactly what you were told," the Boiler Man said. "That may be due to the fact that those in the know weighed you in as smarter than you turned out. In all of these situations, the less said is always the cleanest path to go, which, by nature, leaves a lot of unresolved issues. It's then left out there for the buyer to figure out what else there is to be done. You then, using the old pasta bowl, provide us the answers without being told to do so."

"I didn't know," the tall man said, the concern on his face real enough to touch.

"That's as clear as that fucking mirror staring back at us," the Boiler Man said. "What isn't clear is what I need to know in order to bring the job full circle."

"Can I get a for instance?"

"You want someone dead," the Boiler Man said, keeping his temper in check, confident that this part of his evening would soon draw to an end. "You set up a meet with certain people, settle on a price and all that followed which put us both here in this shit-house. You still on the same channel as me?"

"Right next to you."

"You delivered the dough, covered your tracks better than an old Indian scout, and got as hot as an Indy 500 engine over it all going down as planned," the Boiler Man said. "You were in the fucking end zone, money man, getting ready to slam down that ball and do yourself a TV time dance."

"So what's the fucking problem, then?" the tall man asked, sur-rendering to his feelings of frustration.

"Here it is, slow and simple," the Boiler Man said. "You need to tell me who the fuck is it that's supposed to get iced. I got every-thing I need but the fucking name. And if I have to guess, it's going to cost you a lot more pesos."

The tall man gave a nervous laugh. "Jesus Christ, what the fuck was I thinking? I suppose I never mentioned it since no one ever bothered to ask."

"In my line, that's not the sort of information you seek," the Boiler Man said. "You just expect it to be given, after all the details have been worked out."

"Okay if I give it to you now?"

"Be better if you wrote it down on a slip of paper," the Boiler Man said. "Otherwise, there's a good chance I'd forget, and then we'd be back on first base."

The tall man pulled a thin silver pen from his shirt pocket and reached behind him and grabbed a thick paper towel from the dis-penser. He leaned over the sink and, with the paper against the wall, scribbled two words across it. He then turned and handed the paper to the Boiler Man.

The Boiler Man glanced down at the name and smiled, shoving the paper into the pocket of his thin leather jacket. "I know this man," he said. "I met him two nights ago. In this very same shithole, truth be known."

"You met him?" the tall man said. "Why the hell would you meet with him?"

"He offered me a job and the money was good, a hundred larger than what you put on the table," the Boiler Man said. He walked two steps closer, his eyes in full focus, his body relaxed but poised.

"Who was the job?" the tall man asked.

"You are," the Boiler Man said.

The first shot put the tall man down. The second, landing right above his nose and crashing through the bone and tissue of his forehead and lodging in the center of his skull, killed him. The Boiler Man bent over, picked up his two shell casings, and shoved them into his pants pocket. He opened the satchel, checked to see if the money was all there and tossed the gun in, then locked it shut.

He opened the bathroom door, turned left, and walked out of the quiet restaurant. The Boiler Man's long day had finally reached its end.

"The both of you should mourn your dead and count your blessings," Tony Rigs said, sitting back against the strained sides of a lounge chair, late-morning spring sun warming a tanned face topped by razor-cut silver hair. "You dug down and hit the mother lode, fuckin' policeman's lotto, for Christ's sake. You land a tax-free three-quarter pension plus health coverage till the day you drop like you two did, you go to church and light a fuckin' candle and tip the first priest you see. You think I got anything close to that kind of shit in my line of work? Even our fuckin' life insurance comes with a two-bullet deductible."

"I thought when you guys retired you headed off to Florida," Boomer said. "Buy a boat, fish for marlin, and hope you don't reel in a floater by accident. Yet here you still are, soaking up the Ozone Park rays, sitting in front of your little candy store, just waiting for the results of the first race to come in and your action to start."

"Sun up here is just as hot as the one down there," Tony Rigs said. "The restaurants are better, and I don't have to wait in line behind a bunch of oldies who'd put a pin in me just to jump-start the early-bird special. But you two busted tins didn't drag your asses all the way here just to check on my day-to-day. You came with empty ears, looking for me to fill them. So, knowing that, how about I have Gracie make us a fresh pot of her heart-stopping coffee and you tell me what's up?"

Tony Rigs was an old-school gangster, the kind of hood who ran his businesses and his neighborhood with wide eyes and closed lips. He had been a hard-earning capo in the Banelli crime family back since both Boomer and Dead-Eye were fresh out of the Police Academy. And despite all the wiretaps, surveillance photos, witness-relocation deals, and stool bustouts, neither the Feds nor the locals had yet to come even close to typing in his name on an indictment. Tony put as little as possible on paper, treated any phone as if it were a radioactive device, and kept his own counsel, having seen more than his share of crime bosses head off to triple-digit slamdowns on the courtroom testimony of a trusted adviser.

"Know what a right-hand man is?" he asked Boomer and Dead-Eye the last time the two came looking his way. "That's a guy who's biding his time, walking next to you, acting like he lives only to make you happy. Sooner than later, your right-hand man will make a move to being a two-hand man. In order for that to happen, he needs for the boss, the guy he no doubt named his fuckin' son after, to go down. And that's when he makes the call and does his flip. As quick as that judge hits his hammer to the wood, his ass is in the boss's seat, talking to his own right-hand man. Meantime, the former hombre sits in a top-tier bunk over at Allenwood just off a fake egg, Wonder bread, and some cherry Jell-O, waiting for his one-hour stretch in the yard. And that holds true for whatever line of work you fall into, criminal or not so. You think the vice president of the United States doesn't hit the pillow at night dreaming up ways for the top guy to fall flat on his ass?"

Tony Rigs knew the rules and followed them. If he could lend a hand to a tough street duo like Boomer and Dead-Eye, he knew it would come back his way. He steered clear of the drug trade and earned his take-home with the daily numbers action and a clear and steady stream of betters who always laid their money down, convinced it would be worth twice that by end of day. Neither of those crimes ever surfaced on the radar of any action cop working the streets. "You should nail a bookie, but you have to turn your back if it's an OTB parlor," Boomer once said to Dead-Eye. "Explain the logic on that to me. One haul goes into the pocket of some wiseguy trying to make a go of it on the street. In return, he helps keep trouble off his turf. Not because he's the Mother Teresa type but because he knows anything that hurts the people hurts him and his business. OTB, on the other hand, sends their haul up to Albany and there it lands in the hungry pockets of a pack of assemblymen whose names we don't even know. And they don't look to keep trouble off their elected turf, since they don't give a shit about it and wouldn't know the how and when even if they did. So if I'm put to the wall and need slapping the cuffs on one or the other, I'll make for the assemblyman. That's a bust that'll stick and hold."

Tony Rigs poured three sugars and a half shot of sambuca black into his espresso cup and let it sit to cool. He sat back and listened as Boomer and Dead-Eye began to walk him through their initial plan, step by step, working within the comfort zone of trust, no matter which end of the table Tony Rigs chose to rest his ample arms.

"I'm not saying it's a shoo-in," Boomer said, wrapping up his proposal. "But with a handful of angel dust on our side and playing off a warehouse full of greed from theirs, we might be able to hold our corner of the court."

"Who you figure is your endgame target?" Tony Rigs asked, clearly intrigued by the sheer audacity of the venture.

"Angel," Dead-Eye said without any hesitation. "He's making the hard moves and the overtime plays, which means all the green lights point to him being the one that gave the thumbs-up to the blastout at the restaurant."

"And these other two crews?" Tony Rigs asked. "If they don't mean anything to you, why bring them into a fight that's one-sided off the first whistle as is?"

"A lot of innocent bodies have taken a drop since these crews began to blast their way into town," Boomer said. "My niece wasn't the only casualty. These hard jaws took a night drop into our city and they're treating it as if it were just another open sewer for them to toss their shit in. They're packing the streets with heavy doses of Colombian snow and leaving behind a dust trail of ruined lives. They get to pocket their millions, and we get to bury our dead. I figure somebody's got to put the pain back into the slap—why not us?"

"You can't win, if that's what you're thinking," Tony Rigs said, downing the last of his coffee and nodding toward a curtained window for a second cup. "Shit, the shape you two are in, you plant half a dozen of these cocksuckers in rich soil the Pope would declare it a miracle."

"What if we don't go it alone?" Boomer said, catching the surprised glance thrown his way by Dead-Eye. "I'm not talking a full crew here, just something along the lines of what we put together a few years back."

"When you butted heads with that prime-time coke queen is what you mean," Tony Rigs said. "You went in with six and came out with three, as I recall. And the three of you that were left had more holes than a half pound of Swiss."

"But Carney and her gang went belly-up," Dead-Eye said. "We finished what we went in to do, from our way of breaking it down."

"That may well be so," Tony Rigs said. "But it bears no weight with the door you're about to open this time. Next to any one of these three outfits, Carney and her bunch wouldn't have made it to the six o'clock news."

"Say we catch ourselves a little luck," Boomer said. He leaned in closer to Tony Rigs, calm and in command of the situation as it began to take its first steps toward a business offer. "We add to our group one of the guys from the last go-around, plus a few fresh faces to round out the team."

"If one of them wears a cape and can fly, then just maybe your chances might go up a few notches," Tony Rigs said. "But not by all that much."

"How big a bite are the SAs taking out of OC pockets?" Boomer asked. "And I'm not looking for an on-the-money quote. Ballpark's good enough."

"Depends on the family and the crew," Tony Rigs said. "Most of the south-of-the-border crowd like to deal dope and guns. Maybe some track action, but not much of that. They leave us the horses out of the starting gate, and we leave them their cockfights in a Bronx barn. But overall, I'd say business was off about twenty to thirty percent since they rolled. They're not exactly the group-hug types. They see a piece of action that's of interest, they make their move. Could give a fuck whose turf it is or who's spent years working it to get it to a profit point."

"That hold true for all of OC, or just the Italian end?" Dead-Eye asked.

"The Crips' and Bloods' idea of doing a deal with the SA crowd is handing cash over the counter at Taco Bell," Tony Rigs said. "The Chinese Triads don't work with anyone other than their own kind. The Russians are biding their time and building up their trade, looking to eventually run the whole room. They never deal with who they don't trust, and they don't trust the SAs. And the Irish, what's left of them, can barely stomach being in the same room with the Italians, let alone a bar crammed with guys with thick accents."

"Not like any one of those crews just to fold their hands and watch their action get sucked up by strangers with guns," Boomer said. "Been my experience they turn to bite soon as they hear a bark."

"When the time's good, maybe that's what they'll do," Tony Rigs said. "But for now the smart play might be to buy a sideline pass and watch the game play out for one or two quarters. Learn how the other team plays before you call in your offense. At least that's what I would do, providing that was the line of work I was in, which as you both know, it isn't."

"These fuckers are here to stay," Dead-Eye said, his eyes doing a quick scan of the quiet street. "They're buyers, not renters. They want what you got and then some. You've been around long enough to smell it yourself, don't need me to spoon-feed you. And I don't give a shit what line of work you like to pretend you're in, they're going to come at you like wolves on a deer and swallow you."

"But that's not going to happen, because if I heard it right you and Boomer here are going to hook up with a few more crippled cops and tangle with the SAs and Batman them out of town," Tony Rigs said with a wide smile. "Which means to my ears that I don't have need for any worries. At least not when it comes to my new friends with the thick accents."

"Shave off the cute," Boomer said, staring hard at Tony Rigs.

"You know what I'm asking here. I don't need to go through it letter by letter. But I want to walk away from this meeting with something other than heartburn. I want an answer. Whichever way you go with it, you and me will still be good. This is a big decision, I realize, and we're only coming to you. Where you bring it from here is your business."

"Can you give me some think time at least?" Tony Rigs said. "Not like you come in here asking for a lower hit on a weekly vig. This is major-league play here, and I need to make sure it's right for all involved."

"We need our answer now," Dead-Eye said. "You've been thinking about moving on the SAs since long before we sat here and spun our tale. We're just helping to speed up the process, like putting a little STP in your gas tank. But before we make our first move we have to know no other crews will get in our way. If we're going to slam into roadblocks, be best if we knew about them before we got on the road."

Tony Rigs shook his head and rested a hand on Boomer's right shoulder. "Put a gun to my head and I wouldn't be able to finger which one is the craziest of the bunch," he said. "The two of you or the SAs and their posse? But you know, that's just what it might take, a band of busted badges with nothing to lose but bullets. You might not win the all-out, but you could dent them enough to give the other crews in town the idea to do the same. And then, if that happens, we got ourselves a nice little war."

"I'll get word to you when we're ready to move," Boomer said. "I won't weigh you down with details, just the bare bones. And if you pick up any intel from your way, you can spread it to me on the quiet. The rest of it, you'll either read about in the papers or hear about on the street."

"You need anything from this end?" Tony Rigs asked. "Those

police-issued water pistols you two still carry not going to be much help pointed at the artillery these guys jam inside their pants. Might be nice to have something with a bit more kick to it."

"How would you go about getting equipment like that for us?" Dead-Eye asked. "Especially since, as you've said on more than one occasion, you're not involved in any illegal activities."

"That's simple," Tony Rigs said, smile back in place. "I spend a lot of time in prayer. And the Lord above must care an awful lot about me, because he sees to it that my prayers are always answered."

15

Stephanie Torres held a mound of black dust in her gloved right hand and sifted through it with the fingers of her left. The room was crammed with the acrid smell of spilled gasoline and smoldering pieces of old furniture. The wall's paint had been burnt away, leaving in its wake thin, dark slabs of wood that would break to the touch. The charred floorboards creaked under the weight of Stephanie's light step. The faulty wiring in the room was seared and hanging off the sides of each wall, the skeletal remains of a fiery wreck. Stephanie walked over to a cracked window and gazed out at the rooftop of the next building, close enough for her to reach out a hand and touch, its brown-brick façade turned black, the tar that overlapped the sides bearing melt dents from the heat of the recent blaze.

The fire in the building had been set. Stephanie Torres knew it, felt it, believed it, and now needed to find the evidence to prove it. She had a gut feel for the cause of fires and would spend hours, days, weeks sifting through mounds of dust large and small until she found the one clue that would back up her initial theories. The other cops in her unit had long ago learned not to dissuade her from her quest, that the arson investigator they had nicknamed Ash was always spot on the money when it came down to the cause of a burnout. "I've worked with the best, but I've never crossed paths with anyone like her and I been on this job closing in on twenty-five years," Captain Peter Perelli once told two detectives fresh off hauling in a suspect wanted in the arson deaths of three children, based solely on evidence dug up by Stephanie "Ash" Torres. "She sees not only what's there but what isn't. When she's at a fresh crime scene, it's almost as if she can visualize what happened and how. Play it out in real time, like she's standing there, with the smoke and the stench, watching a fucking video reel off in her head."

"She just might be really good at what she does," one of the detectives, Richie Monroe, said. "Credit her that and forget about the watching-the-dead-burn bullshit."

"She's not good, she's Hall of Fame great," Perelli said, jabbing his finger in the air. "But what I'm digging at is what it is that makes her great. How in the hell can she walk into a burnt shell and see something that an investigator with ten years more experience than her just up and misses? She can enter those dark places most of us fear and find her comfort there. I don't know much about her doings off the job—few of us do—but my sense is that she's most at home when she's surrounded by the rubble and ruin of a fire. It's the one place she knows she belongs."

"She's a pretty hot-looking plate," the other detective, Tommy Rolo, said. "Even if you just went and made her sound like that fucking chick from *Sybil*. She into men, do you know, or she a muncher?"

"That's on a need to know, and none of us need to know,"

Captain Perelli said. "I'm talking here about pure police work and on-the-scene gut instincts, which, it's now clear to me, travels down a lonely road with the two of you. So I'll just end by telling you that hands down, for my money at any rate, Stephanie is the best arson investigator to ever pin on the NY tin."

"If I ever get close enough, Cap, that would be one of my top-five whispers in her ear," Rolo said with a fast and easy grin. "Swear it on my mother's grave."

"And now let me whisper a few words of sweet in your ear," the captain said, his anger directed at both detectives. "Make your case and make it stick. Torres practically hand-walked you through the evidence and threw in motive and method as a side dish. So if either of you two Wonder bread wonders fucks it up, I hope you can make your way to the front entrance of the Holland Tunnel at rush hour, because that's where your asses will be standing, come snow or sun, until you put in your full twenty."

———————

Stephanie stood on the fire escape, the railing and the steps covered in soot, and honed in on the burnt butane lighter. She held it as gently as a newborn in her right hand, running her fingers across its scarred surface. The apartment, a two-bedroom railroad with a tub off the kitchen and a shared bathroom down the hall, was a known drug drop used by the local dealers to make buys to their regulars and bag fresh quantities of the cheap crack and coke shipments that arrived on a weekly basis. It had little in the way of furniture except for a leather couch, a wide-screen television, and a foldout cot. But it did have three full-size, double-door self-defrosting fridges—no doubt, she surmised, used to keep the drugs cool and the vodka and beer cold. There was no food in the cupboards and no clothes folded in a bureau or hanging in the closets.

This was not a residence. This was pure and simple a place of business—what passed in the drug world for an office, complete with two-way radios and spotters positioned on the four corners of the street below. Which meant that this fire, the one hundred and tenth she had been assigned in her three years of working the burn beat, was tied into the drug trade. She placed the butane lighter inside a clear plastic bag and dropped it into her evidence kit, the first solid piece of a puzzle that, once complete, would lead her in the direct path of the primary. She took a deep breath and stared up at a cloudless blue sky, the rooftops around her littered with empty beer cans, discarded condoms, and scrunched-up cigarette filters. She could follow the illegal cable hookups flowing from one Tar Beach antenna to the next as they snaked down the sides of the building and into a series of open windows.

Stephanie Torres was thirty-one years old and already a ten-year veteran of the NYPD. She had a college degree from Fordham University, having worked her way through the four-year program in six and leaving with dual degrees in English and science. She ran five miles every morning on the small treadmill she kept in the foyer of her one-bedroom Corona, Queens, condo. She was a vegetarian, meditated three times a week, and spent her free time renting 1930s and '40s gangster movies and watching them deep into the night with her best friend and next-door neighbor, Vivian Marsalla, a thirty-three-year-old curvy widow who worked at the downtown post-office depot. Her antique night table was always packed with thick stacks of crime thrillers, true-crime tales, crossword-puzzle magazines, and forensic and arson-related textbooks—all resting alongside a tall, chipped statue of Saint Jude, the patron saint of lost causes and cops. She had no steady boyfriend, no desire for a pet, and hadn't taken a vacation in three years. She drank two glasses of red wine most nights of her life, stayed away from hard booze, and suffered from chronic bouts of insomnia, sustaining herself on three half-a-doze hours of sleep each night. On those rare occasions when she did manage to close her eyes long enough to earn a rest, Stephanie Torres would wrap herself in the warm dreams of the happy childhood she had enjoyed before tragedy redefined her reality. But when the nightmare of the horrible deaths of her grandfather and her mother crept into her float-away moment, Stephanie would jolt herself awake and step away from either the couch or the bed and spend the rest of the hours until dawn sitting upright in front of her television set. There, in the blue glow of her favorite movie hoods, James Cagney and Humphrey Bogart, she would be able to regain the lost strands of her composure.

And she would once again find peace.

Stephanie smelled the gasoline before she felt it fall across her back and shoulders. She reached behind her thin leather jacket and grabbed for her .38 Special, spinning in a semicircle as she did, her eyes following the shadow that hovered over her from the rooftop. The gas flowing from the full canister coated her jacket and splattered her slacks and soft black loafers. The rest fell through the open slats of the fire escape, landing in the cement garden five stories below. She jumped back into the burnt-out apartment, landing chest hard against a mound of dust and splintered wood. She lay there, cocked gun in her right hand, in silence for several moments, her breath coming out in slow spurts, her mind racing in an attempt to put all the pieces on the board and map out what would happen next. Her thick dark hair was matted against the sides of her face, filled with gasoline as it dripped off her fingers and onto the burnt rubble of the floor. She closed her eyes, took a deep breath, her throat and nostrils burning with the aftertaste of fumes, and knew that in a few moments she would need to kill a man.

"I'm glad it was you," the male voice coming up from behind her said. The words were spoken in a soft and polite manner, like a young student chatting with a favorite teacher. "You're the one I most wanted."

Stephanie didn't move, her mind doing laps as she tried to place the voice and put a face and a connection to it. She held the grip on her handgun, not knowing if the man behind her was armed with anything more deadly than a match. "Do we know each other?" she asked, making a strong attempt at staying calm.

"Let's just say you're aware of me," the man said, shifting his feet slightly across the ruined floor. "At the very least, you should be more than familiar with my work. After all, you've seen so much of it down the years."

"You're a torcher," Stephanie said, her cop confidence back, her radar at full power. "Gas and electric are your way to go, based on the work in here."

"If one doesn't get you, the other will," the voice said, adding a low chuckle. "The method has been around forever, and is practically foolproof. I'm afraid in that regard I get no points for creativity. It is most effective in firetraps such as this building, but not exactly a true test of my skills."

"What would be?" Stephanie asked.

"There was a fire about a year back," the voice said, the man stepping closer toward Stephanie. "It was in one of those odious new downtown high-rise buildings. You know the ones, don't you? All glass and steel, with a security system out of a James Bond movie. But if you and I share any common ground it's in knowing the very basic and simple fact that everything can and will burn. It's all in the execution. At any rate, I know you weren't the one assigned to that masterwork, but I'm more than certain you read as much about it as you could, practically marking to memory the full details of the case file."

"Eighteenth-floor corner office," Stephanie said, doing a full-speed recall on the still unsolved arson investigation that took the lives of an on-the-come stockbroker and his even younger intern. "It was a flash fire contained in the one room, probably started off a timing mechanism, hard-tick explosion working off a gas-soaked detonator. Very professional work, and a long way removed from a tenement torch like this one."

"You'll get no argument from me on that," the voice said with a hint of resignation. "But you can only take the jobs that come your way, and it's a seller's market out there, as I'm sure you're well aware. After all, anyone can set a fire. It's just not anyone who can do it with a certain sense of style."

"How did you know I would be here?" Stephanie asked. "The scene was sealed a few days back, and I didn't tell anyone where I would be today."

"Why would you?" the voice asked. "Technically it's one of your off days, but like me you never tire of your work. I've not had anyone of your skill level assigned to one of my jobs, and I enjoy the cat-and-mouse game as much as the next fire starter."

"I'm the one who should be on your tail, not the other way around," Stephanie said. The realization that a top-tiered torcher was tracking her daily movements had sunk in fast, her heart rate pounding into overdrive.

"That would be true, in theory at any rate," the voice said. "But just as you would learn all you could about me, I found I needed to do the same with you. Just to keep our hide-and-chase on level ground."

"Which leaves us where, exactly?" Stephanie asked.

"We've just reached the finish line," the voice said.

Stephanie heard the click of the butane lighter, wheeled, turned, and fired off three fast rounds at the well-dressed man standing above her, his pale blue eyes glaring down at her as he clutched his chest and fell to both knees, blood gushing past his fingers and running down the front of his starched blue shirt and blazer.

The open lighter landed with a soft thud against her right shoulder, and she felt the rush of the heat from the flames set off by the gasoline that had been poured on her clothes and body. Within seconds, she felt the searing burn of the fire that was shredding through her clothes and scalding deep into flesh and bone. She rolled around in the soot and the splintered wood, attempting to douse the flames and bring smoke to the heat, the rush of intense pain she felt around her head and neck bringing her close to blackout, her mouth charred, her lungs clawing for air. Through the smoky haze, she caught sight of the man, still on his knees, his back against a wall, a thin smile on his face.

"Looks like I win," he said, his eyelids doing a slow flutter. "I'll die here, but I will always be a part of you. We are now as one, linked to the end."

The man slid from the wall to the floor, his body still, his eyes open, soot covering half his face, a pool of blood forming around his waist.

Stephanie Torres was ten feet from the dead man. Her upper body was smoldering, the flames burning down to their last embers. She was numb to the pain and lay coiled with her legs up against her chest. Her breath came through her open mouth in small doses, puffs of smoke following gently in its wake. Her eyes were shut and tears formed at both ends and rolled down her cheeks, disappearing into the thick mask of burnt skin and soot that had been her face. Outside the charred window, a black-and-gray pigeon perched on a shaky sill and stared silently at the two bodies. Below them, police sirens swirled and twirled down barren streets and a small cluster of the curious had started to gather around the front of the burnt-out tenement. But Stephanie Torres was long past seeing or hearing any of the commotion that her shooting would cause. She was no longer an on-site investigator working the dead leads of a live case; she was a burn victim with a bled-out doer at a crime scene that was once again fresh.

But, in that burnt-out shell of what had once been a prosperous drug dealer's den, within easy reach of a dead arsonist, Stephanie Torres had found the peaceful rest she had sought for so long. As the pace of her breathing pattern slowed and her blood pressure continued its downward spiral, Stephanie Torres was lost to the world that had consumed her since childhood and the horrible moments that led to the tragic deaths of her mother and her grandfather. On this day, Stephanie Torres finally rested.

16

Buttercup landed with the full weight of her chest and paws against the muscular man's back, sending them crashing into the half-open door that led them inside apartment 4F. The two lead detectives were right behind them, guns cocked and drawn, aimed at the four men crouched and geared up for action in a crowded living room that was now a bevy of strewn furniture, tossed lights, and a television blasting out a recap of an early-season Mets-Phillies game. Buttercup held her position, eyes on her target, massive jaws locked around the fat of the man's thick neck, two sharp teeth teasing his pulsing veins.

Steve Ramoni was crouched down, hovering just above Buttercup and the muscular man, whose face was scrunched against the patch of thin blue carpet that lined the foyer. Ramoni kept his eyes out for the other three men he knew were hanging bodies low and guns high deeper inside the apartment. "Nobody needs to die here today," he said to the tall man. "Not least of all you, and if not me then the dog will see to it, buckets to bullets, that you sure as shit will be the first."

"I give a fuck about you and your dog," the muscular man said, drool forming against the edge of a lower lip. "So pull down and shoot it out if that's what you came in here to do, but you picked the wrong room if you figure me to roll over on the words of two tea-bag narcos."

"Not you I want," Ramoni said. "You live, you die—don't mean a dime's worth to me. We're here for Santos. If he's in the room, we take him and him only. Neither me nor my two partners got a beef going with anybody else in here. The only one who can change that is you."

"If it's Big Moe Santos you huffin' about, then you can pack your mutt and your partner and find yourself a cheap bar," the muscular man said, finding it a struggle to both breathe and talk with Buttercup's mass resting square on his back. "Leave his bald ass to me. I'll jack him for you and earn myself some after-school credits."

"You're looking to tag him," Ramoni said, "we're looking to bag him. He's got a full natural hanging over his head, and we got an eager ADA ready to offer him a nickel ride in return for some hard-nail finger pointing. Once he talks, he walks. What happens from then on, we can leave to the two of you."

Bullets cascaded down on Ramoni, Frank, Buttercup, and the muscular man, nicking paint, floorboards, and ceiling, and the two detectives dived for wall cover and fired back with a heavy load of their own. Buttercup lay down flat across the body of the muscular man, her head tilted to one side, jaws still held tight around his neck. "I guess Big Moe can hear, no doubt over that," Frank said, shouting above the rapid exchange of gunfire. "I'm surprised you just didn't invite him over and ask him to pull up a chair."

"I wanted him to hear us," Ramoni said. "This way, he knows now he's got a choice. Walk out the front with us or be carried out the back by Wilson here and his crew of hitters."

"Looks to me like Big Moe went and decided on a Plan C," Frank said, slamming a fresh ammo clip into his gun and firing three rounds into the smoke-filled room.

"Which would be what, you think?" Ramoni asked.

"Kill us all, right here and now," Frank said. "And then run, balls to the floor, to the first out-of-town bus he can find. Disappear inside a no-name town where nobody but the local dealer will give two shits and a spit about when he comes and where he goes."

"You two motherfuckers gonna go in there and wipe some ass or you plan to Lucy and Ricky the bastards to death?" the muscular man, Monroe Wilson, shouted back at them. "If that's your direction, be wise to let me and this fuckin' mountain dog loose to take care of some business while the two of you just talk it out."

"You going to let me leave here with Big Moe?" Ramoni asked. "Take him where he needs to be before end of day?"

"I get him back when you set and done?" Monroe said. "And I don't want to hear any of that witness-relo bullshit. I'm too old and too fuckin' tired to go hunt his ass down in Phoenix, or whatever desert town you toss the flippers in."

Ramoni looked across the small foyer at Frank and waited for his nod. "Your call," Frank said. "But I don't know how the fuck you can get him back once we hand him over. The marshals will have a new name sewn in his clothes long before he even steps into a court-room."

"Then all you need to do is make sure I can spell that new name," Monroe said, lifting his head less than an inch, but enough to catch the blur of the shadows closing in on them from the other room.

Steve Ramoni took a deep breath and shrugged his shoulders. "I'll make sure you get a name, Monroe," he said.

"All right, then, blue bloods," Monroe said after a short pause.

"Now hows about you get Lassie here off my fuckin' back and let's see which of these homers screams when he catches a bullet."

———————

The firefight lasted four minutes, a fusillade of bullets bringing blood and ruin to a sun-drenched New York morning. Buttercup had rolled off of Monroe, on a head signal from Ramoni, and run into the darkness of the living room, the sparks from an array of weapons her only light and a series of harsh voices and loud moans her signal as to where she should bring into play her seek-and-stop police expertise.

One of the cornered shooters, a lanky Hispanic man in stained blue Fruit of the Looms and knee-high sweat socks with red-dye toes, stood with his back against a deep purple wall, a semiautomatic in each hand. The rapid-fire flow of his bullets pinned Ramoni in a corner of the small kitchen, a splintered white cabinet door and a Kevlar vest his only protective shields from the barrage. The bullmastiff moved like a ghost amid the firestorm, swinging her girth through the dark shadows, seeking out the best vantage point to take down her foe.

Buttercup was coiled across the room from the shooter, her hind legs ready to pounce, her mouth open and her large teeth exposed, eyes alive and alert. The shooter shot off the final salvo in his ammo load and let the two empty clips fall to the wood floor. He was quick to reach behind him for two fresh clips, taped to the small of his back in a row of six. Buttercup saw the move and was even quicker to make hers.

She hurtled across the room and caught the dealer at chest level, draining the air from his lungs and sending them both crashing to the floor, the guns scattered at opposite ends.

"Get your ass over here, Toilo," the dealer shouted, unable to fend off Buttercup's attack, her thick head hovering several inches above the man's face, her breath thick as fog and clouding his already blurred vision. "And get this mountain lion the fuck off me."

"Chill, Paco," a voice from the far end of the room shouted back. "It's only a fuckin' police dog. Stop playin' and toss him aside."

"He's as big as a fuckin' police *car*," Paco said, fighting to regain his breath, his lithe body hosed down in sweat. "I can't do it by my own."

"You're right on that, Paco," Ramoni said from the other end of the room, holding his fire. "Your best play is to give it up. You can do that by resting your hands flat on the floor, palms up. Once Buttercup sees that, she'll know not to rip out your main vein and use it as floss."

"Buttercup?" Toilo said, sneering out the word and not holding back on the chuckle that followed in its wake. "You can't be straight serious? You hear that, Paco? You about to hand your balls up to a fuckin' dog with a soft-toss name. You do that, you better learn how to sleep with your ass in the air."

"She will kill you," Ramoni said in a low but commanding voice. "Buttercup loves playing fetch and swimming in a cool stream. She likes to ride in my Mustang, the top down—rain, snow, or shine. She likes her steaks medium rare and wants her Italian bread dipped in homemade olive oil. But there's only one thing that she really loves. Want to guess?"

"I give a fuck," Paco said, trying to squirm his way out from under Buttercup, the bulk of the dog's weight now resting on his chest. "And if you don't say what you need to say to get her the fuck off me fast, she's gonna love the feel of my gun up her ass."

"If you're thinking that, then that ganja has really fried your brain," Ramoni said. "That dog will Dirty Harry you before you have a chance to lift one of your arms."

Paco looked up at Buttercup through his glassy eyes and got back a gaze that made him shiver. "Can you and me talk it out, then?" he asked.

"I'm all loaded, guns and ears," Ramoni said.

It was Buttercup who first saw the shadows of the two men in the hallway.

She lifted her head away from Paco and looked over Ramoni's shoulders. Ramoni caught the move and turned. Frank had his head down, blood oozing out of a flesh wound in his right arm, and Monroe was nowhere to be found. Ramoni snapped his fingers and Buttercup eased herself up off Paco, her front paws rubbing now against the wood floor, her body poised to make a run and leap past the drug dealer and the two detectives in the vestibule, aiming for the hallway and the men lying in wait.

The two men jumped into the open doorway, each with two .357 Magnums in his hands, and began to fire down at the two detectives. Ramoni whirled and let off several rounds of his own in their direction. Frank was slower to react, reaching for his gun with his good arm, fingers gripping the handle, his strength sapped by the flesh wound. Within seconds, bullets once again began to fly, this time both inside and outside the apartment, the two detectives caught in a vicious cross fire, the risk of taking a hit coming at them from front and rear. Monroe jumped out of his hiding hole in a back bedroom and let loose with his own hailstorm, not caring who his shots took down, cop or thug. The gunmen were separated in distance by no more than fifteen feet.

Frank took a series of slugs to the chest, neck, and leg and fell over in a heap, his head landing hard against the wood floor, thick specks of dust coating the bloody left side of his face.

Monroe blasted away, heard a death grunt from the back of the apartment, and knew that he had dropped one of the three dealers. He looked to his left, saw Paco on the floor, jamming two clips into his semis, and smiled. "I told you not to go and fuck with a player," he said. "Look around, motherfucker, and grab a deep breath. This is what the business smells like. This is what it brings."

Paco managed to get off a round, which caught Monroe just above his right knee. Monroe grunted and tilted to one side, then emptied his chamber into Paco's prone body, the kill shot blasting out the dealer's left eye and causing his legs to twitch and spasm, blood doing a slow run down his face.

The two gunmen closed in on Ramoni, who was low on ammo and running out of room to seek cover. He tossed aside an empty gun and rushed the shorter of the two gunmen, both of them landing hard in the narrow hallway just outside the apartment. The second gunman turned, followed the flow of action, and took dead aim at the back of the cop's head.

Buttercup caught him a second before he could push down on the trigger. Her jaw was locked on the gunman's shooting arm, her teeth cutting through clothes, skin, and bone, sending a thick flow of blood across her face. The gunman landed a series of hard, closed-fist blows on Buttercup's head, but the police dog held firm to her grip. The loss of blood and the weight of the dog brought the gunman down to one knee, his flurry of punches losing some of their force. Buttercup shook her head from side to side, ripping tendons and nerve endings in the gunman's arm, eager to bring his movements to a halt.

The bullets were strays, shots from the gun of the man waging battle with Ramoni in the hallway.

The first shot caught Buttercup on the right flank, just about center mass, and pierced one of her lungs. The blow stung and weakened her rear paws. The second landed higher, creasing through the skin folds on her chest and bursting through several blood vessels. Both Buttercup and the gunman were soaked through with blood, the blue cement floor now the color of melted cherry ice. But despite the wounds, Buttercup held on to the bite, her teeth clenched, jawbone locked in, the man's arm tattered and torn, muscle and bone visible beneath the sheared clothes. The gunman was fast losing his grip, his eyes doing a slow roll toward a blackout.

Ramoni heard the shots, and the two low yelps that followed, and glared down at the gunman who had fired the rounds. He unleashed a flood of hard blows against the prone man, his fury fueled by anger and the sense of dread and loss any cop feels when a partner takes a hit. He lifted both knees to where they pressed heavy on the gunman's shoulders and reached his right hand toward his ankle holster, his fingers gripping the handle of his loaded drop gun. In one swift move, Ramoni, ignoring the sharp pain of his own wounds, had the gun cocked and pressed against the gunman's forehead. Ramoni gazed down at him, drops of blood dripping from a cut on his face and a sliced lower lip, his right eye shut tight from a series of blows to the head and a bullet that caught him just below the neck. "Shitty fuckin' place we both picked to die," he said, then pulled the trigger.

Ramoni fell off the dead gunman and crawled over toward Buttercup. Her head was resting on the blood-soaked floor, her eyes half open, her breathing a series of pained wisps. Ramoni stroked her cocoa-colored coat and ran a finger softly against the sides of her two gaping wounds. "You did great," he said to her. "I'm the one went and messed it up. But I won't let you die, Buttercup, you hear me? Not on me, not here, not now."

Buttercup stared back and licked the right side of Ramoni's face, tasting blood and bone matter, her massive head giving his a gentle nudge. "Hang to it," Ramoni said to her, his vision starting to fade, the loss of blood from his multiple wounds turning the room into a drug-ravaged carousel. "Nobody good is gonna die here today."

"Except maybe the two of you, that is." Monroe Wilson's immense shadow hovered over the badly wounded partners. "You got as much chance of seeing a police pension as I do of drawing a legit payday."

Ramoni lifted his head and managed a weak smile. "I guess you won't need that name from me, either."

"Not unless that dead fucker Big Moe had vampire blood in those fat veins," Monroe said. "But I appreciate you making the deal. I wouldn't have trusted many badges to back up their word, even in the middle of a lost cause like that. But you were one of the few that wouldn't step back from his end."

"Save it for my eulogy," Ramoni said.

"I'm sorry, Ramoni," Monroe said, holstering his gun and gazing down at his blood-splattered clothes. "About you *and* your dog. She's a fighter."

"Take her, Monroe," Ramoni said, lifting his head and reaching an arm out for the big man. "She doesn't need to die. You can get her help, make her right again."

"She took two hard ones at close range," Monroe said, his hard voice touched with sympathy. "Best thing might be to just let her be."

"She's a cop," Ramoni said. "She's tougher than you and me glued together. Take her, Monroe, and save her life."

"What about you?" Monroe asked.

"I can wait for backup and EMS," Ramoni said. "I make it, I open a bar and you can drink your fill for free the rest of your days. But Buttercup can't wait. You're her best shot."

"And what do I tell the cops?" Monroe said. "Police dog and me waltzing into an ER, both streaked with blood and running leaks like two garden hoses. Don't need to be no fuckin' Columbo to put together the two-and-two."

"Tell them you were part of my undercover team, working Big Moe and his crew," Ramoni said. "I'm still breathing when they locate me, I'll back it. But even minus me there, they'll believe you. Shit, you're a shot-up man walking in with a wounded police dog. If Buttercup lives, the cops will be looking to pat your back instead of patting you down. You save a cop's life, that's a truth no one forgets."

Monroe looked down at Buttercup, her breathing shallow, her back paws doing a slow shake, her closed eyes twitching. The blood was just easing out of her two wounds now, but she had lost more than enough to put her life clear in the red zone. "I hope to Christ you're right about this shit," he said.

"Bet your life on it," Ramoni said, easing himself clear of the dog and giving Monroe the space he would need to get her in his arms.

"I am, dude," Monroe said.

Monroe got down on his knees, wincing from the pain of his own wounds, jammed his hands and arms under Buttercup's body, and lifted her to his chest, instantly feeling the rush of the warm blood flowing out of the dog's body. Buttercup lifted her head up and rested it on Monroe's chest, her eyes half open. Monroe looked back at her and shook his head. "You would have killed me in there," he said to her. "And now here I go looking to save your ass. Bet you think I must be the biggest black fool this side of the East River." Buttercup whipped out her thick tongue and quick-licked Monroe's neck, then rested her head back down and shut her eyes. "Just like any woman," he said to her. "You only turn nice when you want something."

Monroe moved with a careful and steady purpose. He walked past shuttered tenement doors, the smell of gunpowder still strong in the air. The two of them, the wounded cop and the street shooter, leaving behind a thick trail of blood.

Ramoni crawled to a wall, pushed himself up to a sitting position, and watched them as they walked toward the shot-up exit sign at the end of the long hallway. He leaned his sweat-soaked head against a greasy door, closed his eyes, and rested his bloody hands at his sides.

"Good luck, partner," were his last words.

Angel sat in a dark room, rolling the base of his wineglass between the fingers of his right hand as he listened to the man in the brown suit across from him, his slim frame lost in the center of a thick black leather chair. "I put the feelers out as per your request," the man said. "And, as expected, I was given the answers I knew would come back my way."

"Were there any surprises?" Angel asked.

"The band that likes to call themselves the G-Men were the most receptive," the man said. "The two brothers who run that crew were open to a deal—more so than any of the other gangs, South American or otherwise. But again, they're mercenaries. They hire out to whoever pays the most. If that ends up being you, then they will be loyal to you. At least until the next big offer comes their way."

"What was the surprise, then?" Angel asked.

"They were the only ones who were aware of you," the man said. "They didn't say it with words but, rather, with their lack of them. The other gangs, they all asked me many questions. Who you were. Where you were from. Why they had never heard of you, either here or back in the home country. But not the G-Men. They said they knew you were good for the money and would make sure that your cash was well spent and not wasted in their hands."

"Which gang will give us the biggest problem?" Angel asked, slow-sipping his chilled rosé.

"Take your pick," the man said. "These crews, big and small, have fought hard to grab whatever turf they control. And they will do anything and everything in their power to ensure that turf remains in their grip. They're not looking for partners, have no interest in bringing in new blood, and don't lack for money and weapons. We're walking into the middle of their gold rush, and up till now anyone who's even attempted to take them on has been left in the marshes off the Whitestone Bridge. And not just their ene-mies, mind you, but their entire families as well. They leave no one and nothing behind. No family, no property, no witnesses. It would be as if you had never existed."

"I don't plan on being caught," Angel said, resting his glass on an empty marble table to his right. "What can I expect from the other end?"

"The police here are very active," the man said. "They are young and have no fear of getting into the middle of the action. And bring-ing down someone like you would be a huge notch on any young detective's arrest sheet. Graft is at a minimum. They are, however, dealing with a city that has a high crime rate. Murder is rampant and drugs are in great demand, and there's just so much an over-worked police force, no matter how fierce and dedicated, can do. So from that end my advice would be to act with your usual care and keep a safe distance from the day-to-day activities. If you can sustain that, you should expect little police resistance."

"Have you found anyone of interest we can reach?" Angel asked, digesting the man's information. "Anyone who doesn't seem to enjoy the pleasures of being overworked and underpaid? Anyone we can trust—to the extent, of course, we trust anyone at all?"

"A black rock can be found on the whitest beach," the man said. He was short and well dressed, choosing for this first New York meeting a dark Brioni suit with matching loafers, crisp blue shirt, and a wine-red tie, looking a decade younger than his actual age of fifty-six. The man, whose name was Jonas Talbot and whose ethnic origins remained a mystery to all but his closest associates, was one of the most valuable criminal weapons a man newly launched in his venture could possess.

Jonas Talbot was a fixer.

He had connections spread across every major city and small town where the potential for corruption existed and the opportunity for criminal profit was evident. He had come to his profession by birthright, the only son of Lawrence "Bull Run" Talbot, the most renowned and respected fixer in the index of organized crime. Bull Run had worked for the legendary Arnold Rothstein and was rumored to have been instrumental in the setup of the notorious Black Sox scandal, involving the rigging of the 1919 World Series. From there, he went on to hone his craft and perfect it to the point where he could help a gangster establish any arrangement he sought, from opening a brothel to assassinating a dictator. He died at the age of eighty-seven, staring out at a two-hundred-acre horse farm complete with a freshwater pond and a running track, content that his life had been well spent. He had devoted a number of years to dispensing that knowledge, along with all of his worldwide contacts, to Jonas, who, from the time he was old enough to toddle into his father's elegant Upper West Side office, would sit, kneel, crawl, or stand as he listened in on his father's often into-the-night business meetings, devouring the lessons that were learned in that room. It was a given to the few allowed to enter the tight Talbot family circle that Jonas would one day carry his father's lucrative business to even more sophisticated heights, bringing the talents of a fixer into the new world order of organized crime. And this Jonas Talbot did with a master's flourish.

Jonas was a determined and driven young man who would allow nothing to get in the way of the goals he had so lavishly set for himself. By the time he stood across the room from his newest client, Jonas Talbot had elevated the role of fixer to such a rarefied status that no high-end criminal working on any continent would set up shop without such a person in his employ. And of the two dozen men and three women who were ranked at the peak of their profession, none were a match for his talents.

"And does our black rock have a name?" Angel asked. "And worthwhile information that would constitute money well spent?"

"The very existence of a black rock necessitates that he does," Talbot said. "As far as it being money well spent, that's between buyer and seller."

Angel refilled his wineglass from a crystal decanter and nodded. "Then let me hear what this police official can tell me for a price that I couldn't find out on my own for free."

"Sean Valentine is a former Brooklyn precinct captain now working out of One Police Plaza headquarters," Talbot said, shifting his weight slightly as he moved closer to the warm waves of sunlight coming at him from an open window next to the floor-to-ceiling bookcases. "Valentine works in the community-relations division, a valuable place for him to be, since it allows total access to all police activity covering the five boroughs. On top of which he's been with the department for slightly over two decades and is well liked by the upper tiers of that inbred culture. At the same time, he is respected by those who do the actual grunt work of arresting those who operate on the opposite side of the law."

"And how much does such a talent cost?" Angel asked.

"You're setting up a new business in a very complex and competitive city," Talbot said in a professional tone. "And add to that the fact that yours is an illegal enterprise, one that often ends in either death or a multi-decade prison term. Not the best inducement to place on a recruitment poster. But, as luck has a tendency to embrace the profit side of the ledger, there has always been an overabundance of people eager to run such a risk for the reward. And Captain Valentine is one such individual."

"You still haven't answered the question," Angel said. "How much am I into him?"

"Fifteen thousand a month," Talbot said. "Double that for the month of December, plus five thousand every two weeks in spread-around money. The cash is to be placed in a PO box in Middle Village, Queens. The box will be paid and signed for by someone not known to either of us, but we will be given a key in order to gain access and make the required drops."

"For that kind of money, this badge better come across like CNN with all news, all the time," Angel said, waving his right hand in disgust as if brushing aside a gnat. "Otherwise, the last envelope I have put in that PO box will be his fucking ashes."

"I agree," Talbot said, having learned many years ago never to argue with or engage a client in anything beyond the business at hand. "The price is a steep one. And chances are better than good they will only go up in time. But you are the new face in the city, an unknown commodity, and in order for me to entice him to part ways with his last employer I needed to put forth the most attractive package I felt you could afford."

"Who was his last employer?" Angel asked. "What lucky bastard got out from under his weight?"

"Rodrigo Duarte," Talbot said. "A low-end heroin distributor loosely connected to and, on occasion, financed by the Paolo Murino crime family. In return for his monthly payouts, Duarte was told about any Joint Task Forces that might be picking him up on their radar and whether they had managed to place undercover agents or video surveillance anywhere near where he conducted his business transactions. It wasn't what I would call fair market value for his money, but it helped Duarte feel that much the better for it and, in the end, that's what matters."

"To my ears, that's fifteen thousand a month for two phone calls," Angel said. "And if Duarte had himself stronger street antennas he could have a crew man make those two calls for him, keeping that money in his pockets."

"Possibly true, but not a decision for me to make," Talbot said. "And Duarte's monthly bill wasn't fifteen thousand. It was seven five. You're paying double because that's the only way I could get someone in Valentine's position to come to your side."

Angel stiffened in his chair and glared across the room at Talbot. He knew that he needed to have a man with such talents and connections in his employ, but he despised the very notion of such a need. Angel worked and thrived in a business where dirty hands were primary requirements and death a constant threat. He had little regard, then, for men like Jonas Talbot, who walked into their deals with clean hands and left the same way, with no track marks to even hint at their presence. Angel distrusted and disliked anyone who moved through life free of risk.

"And what has he told you about my side that I don't know?" Angel asked.

"Several items of note," Talbot said, ignoring Angel's sarcasm.

"The police investigation into the restaurant shooting has yet to gain traction, this despite mounting pressure from the mayor's office to get a suspect—any suspect—in front of the television cameras. They are desperate to soothe the anger over the innocent bystanders the shooters murdered. The press, of course, has been playing the story for all it's worth, citing it as one more example of a city where no one is safe with a clueless mayor at its helm."

"They're spot on when it comes to their mayor," Angel said with a smile. "That guy is a drug dealer's wet dream. Far as my money goes, he's hands down the best this city has ever tossed into Gracie Mansion."

"The police commissioner will add a dozen more detectives to the task force cobbled together to find the shooters, hoping the additional manpower will unlock a few doors."

"Only if those doors are in downtown Bogotá," Angel said. "Anywhere else, it would be nothing more than a waste of detectives, who could be out arresting muggers instead of hunting for ghosts."

"The point being, I suppose, that this case is not going away, and if the NYPD should somehow fall across your name and activities it could have them looking your way," Talbot said. "And that's something none of us want to see happen."

"Then you and Valentine make sure it doesn't," Angel said. "Because if it does, then it could have me come looking your way, and that's something neither of *you* want to see happen."

"There was one more item Valentine made mention of," Talbot said, allowing the direct threat from Angel to fall by the wayside. A drug dealer, especially one attempting to scale the heights, had a life expectancy of anywhere from three to five years. And that's only if he was both lucky and good at his work and had a crew that fit the same description. On both those ends, the jury was still out as far as Angel was concerned. A good fixer—or, in the case of

Jonas Talbot, a great fixer—on the other hand, could stay in business until he died a rich old man. So most threats, if not all, were just lines in the ledger.

"Let me hear it," Angel said. "Anything more, we can save for our next meeting."

Talbot nodded and leaned against a thick mahogany wall. "One of the victims in the shooting was a young waitress making her way through school," he said. "Wasn't on the job very long and died at the scene."

"So?" Angel said.

"So her uncle is a retired detective," Talbot said. "Not the security-guard type or one of those who turned to low-level private-eye work for extra rent money."

"What's he do, then?"

"It's not what he does that should be of any importance to you," Talbot said. "It's what he once did. About three years ago, he formed a unit made up of detectives like himself. Fresh off the job, wounded, collecting a decent disability pension, but all young enough to miss the street action."

"A unit that went and did what?" Angel asked, his interest piqued.

"They took down a drug queen named Lucia Carney," Talbot said. "Wreaked havoc on her and her entire crew. In the process, they lost three of their own. Three of the original members are still around."

"And Valentine thinks they're going to look into this?" Angel said. "Come after the ones who did the restaurant shooting?"

"They went after Lucia Carney because a friend's daughter was taken off the streets, tortured, and raped," Talbot said. "This time, one of them had to stand and watch a young niece buried. I'm not saying they will, but there is a chance."

"And it's not just the shooters he'll want," Angel said.

"No," Talbot said, shaking his head. "He'll come after the man who hired the shooters. He'll come after you."

"This unit have a name?" Angel asked.

"They called themselves the Apaches," Talbot said. "They claimed it was in honor of the wounded warriors left behind after a battle. True or not, they were an effective team—this despite the heavy manpower odds they found themselves up against. As of this moment, there's no reason to believe they will reunite and come after anyone, let alone you. But the possibility does exist, and it is always best to be aware of the situation."

"What do you suggest we do about these Apaches?" Angel asked, not so much concerned as curious.

"For the moment, nothing," Talbot said. "There's been no indication that a fresh unit has been formed or that new members are actively being recruited. They may well decide to sit this one out, nurse their wounds, and cash their pensions. But if they do choose to come at you hard and fresh, that's where having Valentine in our back pocket comes in handy. He will, presumably, give us ample warning as to any potential red flags."

"Which ex-badge calls the shots?" Angel asked.

"John Frontieri," Talbot said. "Answers to the name Boomer. He was something in his day, but time and numerous bullet wounds have more than done their part to slow his engine down a few notches."

"Slow engine or no, he still had enough left in his tank to take out Carney and her mad bunch," Angel said with a tinge of respect. "Badges like these are rare as virgin brides. They don't live for the check, and give a rat's tit about the pension comes with it. They get into the game for the action, feed off it the way a junkie feeds off the pipe. They come into it heavy and are never eager to leave. Just based on the few bits you gave me, if this guy saddles up and puts together a new crew it could be a problem."

"They have no jurisdiction in any area—local, state, or federal," Talbot said, as aware as Angel of the potential risks a rogue team of skilled and desperate cops would pose for their overall operation. "They would get little, if any, backup support from within their own department. And, above all else, even fully armed and financed to the hilt they would be no match for your team. It's not among my habits to patronize, so take what I have to say to you in the spirit it is meant. Lucia Carney, were she still around today, would have risen no higher than midlevel in your organization."

"His niece is dead and he'll come looking for me, team or no," Angel said, not able to hide the hint of glee in his voice. "He's out for revenge, with nothing to live for but watching me. Count on it, Talbot, he is one cop we are destined to meet. Let's make sure we're ready when we do."

"We could have him handled before he makes any move your way," Talbot said. "If he is indeed the kind of man you say, then we can simply settle the matter before he gets to fire off a round. Why allow the shadow to be cast when we can just make it vanish with a phone call?"

"Because I want to meet him," Angel said, pushing his chair back. "And I want to be the one that stands across from him and puts him down. If this Apache is looking to target me, then it should be by my hand that he goes down."

18

Andy Victorino leaned against a cold green wall, clutching his stomach with both hands. The sharp pain caused his knees to buckle and his eyes to water; his back, chest, and forehead were all drenched through with cold sweat. He was standing in a dark corridor, empty gurneys lining both sides. Old and scarred medical clipboards hung from the wall he was using to support his weakened body. He looked down at his lab jacket and dark slacks and saw that both were streaked with blood. He took a deep, painful breath and slowly moved his feet deeper into the corridor, standing now less than twenty feet from the office he shared with two other detectives who worked out of the science lab. He felt as if he were drowning in a sea of his own blood, the betrayal of his body so fierce and so sudden that it was all he could manage not to shout out and curse the strange and deadly disease coursing through him like a snake down a canyon road.

Andy Victorino, a young man who had devoted his life to the study of the dead and the information they could pass on to the living, was now staring down at a cold slab, and his eyes could see only his own face gazing back. He didn't need myriad expert medical opinions or a battery of blood results to tell him what his body had been actively devoting the past three months to telling.

He was dying.

It started as a red blotch on the upper end of his right arm. Andy was working a multiple murder during that cold week in mid-January when the rash first appeared, and he wrote it off as nothing more than a stress-related side effect. He was putting in double-overtime hours, and his social activity had been relegated to late-night phone sessions with a new lover he had met at a Christmas party in a friend's downtown loft. This newest and latest in a series of quick-burning flames matched both his temperament and his devotion to work, racking up seventy-hour weeks as a new associate in a white-shoe East Side law firm. For both of them, then, those middle-of-the-night chat sessions were a welcome anti-dote to a grind whose grip never eased. It was their time to sit back, sip a glass of wine, and share a conversation that lacked a rush to deadline or needed to be charted in any particular course. And it was only then, under the guise of night, that they could toss aside the masks and bask in being their true selves.

But as the rash spread and the flulike symptoms he had been feeling for more than a week persisted, Andy knew there was more at play than the work-related stress he normally embraced rather than shunned. Still, it wasn't until that moment that seemed to last for hours, standing in the lobby of the ME's office, gripping the thin sheet of paper with the results of a blood test administered by a friend at a Greenwich Village clinic, that the first cold wave of reality soaked his rapidly thinning frame.

"Let me help you to your office." Andy recognized the woman's voice and felt her warm hands on the small of his back. "I know you wouldn't want anyone around here to see you like this."

Andy glanced over at her, nodded his head, and managed a weak smile. Not even the dead, he thought.

She guided Andy down the corridor and into his office. She eased him into his brown swivel chair and watched him stretch out his legs and ease the back of his sweat-soaked hair onto the thick foam of the headrest. "Thanks a lot, Jackie," he said, his eyes closed, his breath returning to normal. "I was about one step away from falling flat on my face. It serves me right for not getting that free flu shot."

"It's none of my business, I know," Jackie Pavano said. She was tall and shapely, with rich dark hair and eyes to match. She was in her early thirties, coming off a failed marriage to a uniform with wanderlust, and was a first-rate second-grade homicide detective, with the most solved cases in the unit for the past two years. "But I'm going to ask anyway. You seeing anybody for this flu you have? Somebody to help you until you get over it?"

Andy opened his eyes and lifted his head, staring across his desk at the young detective with the raised antennas. "There really isn't anyone to see," he said in a soft, low voice. "Because there really isn't anything that can be done."

"How long have you known?" Jackie asked in a voice as warm as an old quilt.

"It will be four months come this Tuesday," Andy said. "I'm still in the very early stages and, except for the occasional horrendous day like this one, can hide it pretty well. Most days, in fact, I don't feel ill at all, and there are even a few moments here and there where I can put it out of my mind altogether."

"Is there a clock on something like this?" Jackie asked.

"It's uncharted waters, as much for doctors as it is for patients,"

Andy said, dabbing at his forehead with a folded tissue. "Based on what they do know, which isn't much, they came out with an any-where between six months and five years scenario, depending on any number of factors out of their control."

Jackie Pavano walked over to a counter and reached for a pot of coffee that looked as if it had been sitting there since the Nixon administration. "I'm going to risk a cup of this," she said, holding up the pot. "You care to join me, or are you just going to sit back and let me take a dive in by myself?"

"There should be some rancid cream in the mini-fridge," Andy said, tossing her a smile. "If you add that and three sugars, you found yourself a partner."

They were both silent as Jackie fixed the two cups of coffee and Andy sat up in his chair, the pain in his stomach subsiding, the sweat no longer pouring off him like running water. Jackie handed him a Styrofoam cup and sat back down across from him, taking a long sip of her coffee. "This isn't as bad as I thought it would be," she said with a grimace. "It's a lot worse."

"When I was first on the job, I couldn't help but notice the foul mood most of the on-the-scene homicide cops always seemed to be in," Andy said, the strength back in his voice, the coffee cupped in both his hands. "Initially, I wrote it off to them spending the bulk of their time at a murder site, torn over the loss of one more often innocent life. But after I had been here awhile and got to know most of the crew, that theory was tossed for a loss. Then, early one predawn, I happened to look up from a multiple and spotted all the tins hovering around me drinking coffee. And not fresh-roasted South American joe. I'm talking pre-dug, foot-brewed Manhattan mud."

"They should warn us about it at the Police Academy," Jackie said. "Give us a chance to get used to green tea. The lou back in my old precinct told me early in my run there that cop coffee was like a cop paycheck: it came in steady and it came out steady, and you can count on it straight through to that first pension package. It just happens to be a lot worse down in the science lab for some reason."

"There are fewer people around to piss and moan about it," Andy said. "So I'm afraid we're stuck with it, at least until the spring floaters lodge a complaint."

Jackie laughed and rested her cup on the edge of Andy's desk. "Who else knows?" she asked.

"About the coffee? Pretty much everyone," he said. "About me? You'd be the first."

"You can hide it for a while longer, I'm guessing," Jackie said. "But sooner than later the word will leak, and it'll run through here faster than you can run out."

"I've lived with secrets most of my life," Andy Victorino said in a tone that was free of regret. "I was hoping to treat this as just one more in a long line."

"I don't know what those other secrets are," Jackie said, "and I don't have to know. But any of those you could pretty much bury and hide without anyone giving two shits. This one is in a league of its own. This is about a disease they'll think can be spread from you to them with just a nod of the head. And when it comes to shit like that, nobody—and I swear to you nobody—goes over-the-top paranoid more than a cop. They'll treat you worse than a basement on-the-nod skell."

"And you think I should do what about it?" Andy asked, not liking what he was hearing but knowing that it came to him out of truth and friendship. "Other than live with it the way I have been for as long as I have been."

"I don't have an answer for that, Andy," Jackie said, reaching out a free hand to rest on one of his folded ones. "I wish I did, swear to

God. I just know as bad as it is for you now, keeping it under lock and key, it's going to come down on you like a fucking hurricane soon as it's out in the open. And you won't just feel pain then. You'll feel shame, too. They'll do all they can to make damn sure of that."

"This has been my world for so long," he said, "and I've known for a while that I'll need to leave it behind. I've just been trying to hold on to it for as long as I could."

"And what happens to you then?" Jackie asked. "You have somewhere to go? Or someone to be with?"

"I haven't planned it that far ahead," Andy said in a slightly sheepish manner. "Which is par for the course for me, I guess. After all these years working a job with no reruns, it's hard enough to map out the next day, let alone a month or two down the road."

"It might be time to start giving that some thought, then," Jackie said. "There are places that can lend a hand with that sort of situation, or maybe just a friend if you want to keep a lid on it."

"Does it really matter?" Andy asked. "I'm going to die—that's the plain and the simple of it. I doubt that whether I'm alone or I'm surrounded by friends will have much effect on the final outcome."

"It's better not to be alone," Jackie said, finishing the last of her bitter coffee.

They sat in silence for a few minutes, both absorbed in their own thoughts. Andy tossed a folded tissue into a wastebasket by his right leg and looked up at Jackie, her face marred by sadness. "Go ahead and ask me the question," he said to her. "You're too good a cop not to want to, and too good a friend to get a lie tossed back your way."

"You want me to know, I won't stop you from telling me," she said. "Otherwise, both the question and the answer stay where they belong."

"I'm not a drug addict, and I didn't get it from a blood transfusion," Andy said. "That leaves us looking at only door number one. But I guess you knew that even before you sat down to drink the coffee from hell."

"You're wrong about that, Quincy," Jackie said with a sad smile. "If I did, it would have saved me a lot of worry time, leaving here at night wondering what the hell I had to do to get you to notice me."

"And that's where you're wrong," Andy said, returning the smile with a wider one of his own. "I noticed you on your first day here. I may not want to sleep with a woman but, like anyone else, I can appreciate her beauty."

———————

Seven years after AIDS first began to cut its deadly swath, it left in its horrendous wake thousands of dead homosexual men. By the time Jackie and Andy were sitting across a desk from each other, more than 35,000 cases of AIDS had been diagnosed nationwide, with 60 percent of them ending in a long and painful death. In March of 1987, the Food and Drug Administration approved AZT, a drug manufactured by Burroughs Wellcome that would relieve some of the symptoms of the disease and extend the lives of those suffering from it. The total cost of $10,000 a year per patient was covered under most medical plans but was ignored by many patients out of fear that news of their illness would cause them to lose their income and be shunned by those closest to them.

Andy Victorino took his disease and the suffering that went with it even closer to the edge of an abyss from which there was no return. He was a homosexual man working in a heterosexual world. He was a cop who logged long hours within the confines and the strictures of a paramilitary organization with little room in its ranks for gay men, closeted or not. He had kept his private life a secret in the same manner that many who were bound by a similar situation chose to do, partaking in many of the social activities that went along with being a cop and ducking and dodging matters of dating, marriage, and family. It also helped his cause that a number of cops held off on marriage until they were close to retirement due to the high-voltage dangers of the work, allowing him to apply the same reasoning to his status without red flags being raised.

The incessant demands of his job, more than any other circumstance of his life, was what curtailed Andy's potential for meeting anyone with whom he could establish a lasting relationship. As a rule, cops have always had difficulty dating outside the parameters of their blue world. "Think about it, Andy," Jimmy McReynolds, a twenty-five-year battle-scarred homicide detective had told him a few years back during a long night of marathon beer gulping. "Why would anybody who didn't have to even think of dating a cop? We got the hours from hell, our take-home sucks, and most of us don't have any hobbies outside of busting down doors and hunting up leads. Plus—and this is the dark truth about all of us, man, woman, dog—we would rather hang with each other than be with somebody that's not a part of our fucked-up world."

"Maybe so, but we're not the only ones who are like that and who put in the hours we do," Andy said. "These investment bankers never seem to go home, either. Might as well put a pullout in their office and grab a few that way. Same as us. So what makes them a better grab for someone on the prowl? And don't say the money, because it's never just that alone."

"You better start drinking something a lot stronger than beer if you don't think money comes into play," Jimmy Mac said. "Sure, they put a pullout in their office—except theirs is a leather number imported from some factory in Northern Italy and costs more than we make in two months. Ours we buy from a brother-in-law who can make a grab at a Macy's. And the only reason they won't make it back home alive at the end of a long shift is because they pulled a suicide squeeze off an eight-digit merger deal gone sour. And not because they took two to the head and chest in a hallway stare-down with a cracked-out predicate felon. We talk and live in two different worlds, young Andy. They live in one and we live in the other, and there's no point in sneaking across their border even if we could swing it. They could pick us out of any six-pack with their eyes sealed."

————————

Jackie pushed her chair back and tossed her empty cup into a wastebasket to her left. "I need to get back to my case," she said, standing and looking down at Andy. "And you need to get back to yours."

"Thanks for taking the time," Andy said. "Not just out in the hall there, but in here as well. It felt good to talk about it, even if it was just for a few minutes."

"It's what a friend does, Andy," Jackie said. "You shouldn't have to go through this all alone. You might think you can, and you may even be strong enough to get past the dark days by yourself. But it's not just about that. It's about having a hand you can reach for when you feel the need. Nothing is going to help make this fight you're in go down any easier, but it just might make the day-to-day of it not as hard."

"You have your own life," Andy said. "You don't need this. This is an ugly disease that's only going to get uglier. Some of the people we work with think you can catch it just by standing close to me. And I don't know enough about it to tell them they're wrong. I'll be shunned, as will any friends I have left. And I care too much to put you in that place."

Jackie stared at Andy for several seconds and then walked past the desk and over to his chair. She rested her right hand on his and leaned down and kissed him gently on the cheek. "You're a good man, Andy," she whispered. "And a good man should never die alone."

She moved her hand away, turned, and walked quietly out of his office. Andy Victorino sat and watched her go, listening to the slow hiss of the door as it closed behind her. He then pushed his chair back, picked up a thick case folder, and took a slow walk to the morgue room.

19

——— CHAPTER ———

Boomer sat at a corner table in the back of Nunzio's Restaurant, across from Dead-Eye, two open folders spread across the starched white cloth. Both men were sharing a large bottle of flat mineral water and gazing down at the information laid out before them. The owner of the restaurant, Nunzio Goldman, walked their way, a bottle of red wine in one hand, three glasses in the other. "You should always have a glass of good wine when you're planning a job," he said. "No matter what kind of work it is we're talking about. Even a suicide mission."

"The last job we just got a glass," Dead-Eye said, moving aside a handful of papers in order to make room for Nunzio and the wine. "This time, we're getting the whole bottle. That can't be a good sign."

"So long as it's a good wine," Boomer said, nodding at Nunzio and watching as his old friend sat and poured out three glasses and passed two across the table.

"I would drink to your health," Nunzio said, raising his glass, "but I learned long ago what a waste of time that is when it comes to you two. So how about we just drink to mine?"

"How about we just drink?" Dead-Eye said, clinking glasses with Nunzio and smiling at the older man. "I hate to get into any situation where there are conditions put to it." Nunzio sipped his wine and glanced down at the pages that were nestled on the table. He looked at Boomer and Dead-Eye and shook his head. "I never took you two for the going-on-a-vacation type," he said. "And even if I was wrong on that score, I would figure it to be someplace in Europe and not down South America way."

"You'd have a hard time finding a more beautiful spot in this world than the triborder region," Boomer said, pointing to a black dot on a small folded map by his elbow. "It's where Paraguay, Brazil, and Argentina meet and greet. Rain-forest country."

"At a sweet little wet spot called Ciudad del Este," Dead-Eye said, setting his glass off to the side. "And for my money it's the most dangerous city in the world sitting in the very middle of the most corrupt region known to cop or crook. The rain is just added in for a little dash of color."

"And this is where you both pick to grab some sun and fun?" Nunzio asked. "What? All the gulags were booked?"

"Every new drug crew to dance into this city has either had its start there or does a large chunk of business out of its port," Boomer said. "It's what Marseilles used to be in the 1970s, and Palermo in the years before that. If the cocaine business had a heart, it would beat in Ciudad del Este."

"It's where crime begins and where it goes on holiday," Dead-Eye said. "You name it, this city has it. From a tax dodge to a terrorist hookup, you'll find it on their shore. You can't buy anything or anyone that's not contraband, elected, or appointed. Shit, me and Boomer were out looking to be pirates, this is where we'd dock our boat."

"These new guys seem cut from different cloth than the ones that did business out of France and Italy," Nunzio said. "At least that's what I get from reading the papers."

"Hoods are all cut the same, Nunzio," Dead-Eye said, his hands resting flat on the tabletop. "Africa to Amsterdam, they're all one. They earn their money off somebody else's hard sweat and they snap out a life easy as blowing out a candle—some for pleasure, some for profit, most for both."

"Are you passing these nuggets along just to educate?" Nunzio asked with a hard look. "Or has your madness latched itself on to a new method?"

"You know what else they all have in common?" Boomer asked, leaning forward in his chair. "The mob guy, the Crip and the Blood, the Russian, the SA dealer, the shooter sets up shop in a French art gallery? The one thread they all share?"

"You got my attention," Nunzio said.

"They believe there's nobody going up against them with a badge that's as crazy and as desperate and as deadly as they are," Boomer said. "That's why they all think that if they're going to go down it will be at the hands and guns of another crew set up just like them. They never think they'll take the fall because of a cop or even a team of same. In their minds, there are no cops out there to be feared."

"But you guys are different?" Nunzio asked, looking from Boomer to Dead-Eye. "Is that your bullet point?"

"Yes," Boomer said. "We *are* different, and we've always been. That and a handful of luck are the only reasons guys like me and Dead-Eye are still on our feet."

"Be a good idea to toss the word *barely* to that thinking," Nunzio said. "Look, I'll give you that you were balls-to-the-wall cops, and if I was a hood on the run you'd be the last sons of bitches I'd want after my ass. But that was about a dozen bullet holes ago. You made all the right moves the last time out and you just managed to eke it to the finish line. How much closer do you want to cut it?"

Dead-Eye drained the wine out of his glass and rested it back on the table. He looked at Nunzio and smiled. "My son always wonders why it is I miss being a cop but would cringe at the idea of him strapping on a gun and shield. He thinks it's because I'm afraid he might get hurt, or even worse. Or that maybe I don't believe he would be up to it, be able to go near the same levels I once touched. I let him think either one is on the money, because he's still a little too young to know the real truth."

"Which is what?" Nunzio asked, leaning with his back against his chair, eyes focused only on Dead-Eye.

"That he's too much of a good kid to be a great cop," Dead-Eye said. "He looks for the goodness when all I see is pure evil waiting to pounce and make its play against a boy like my son. There's always going to be more criminals out on those streets than we deserve to have for the simple reason that there aren't as many guys like me and Boomer waiting for them on the other side. Taking them out is what we're about. No matter how many bullet holes we got in us or how much it hurts to walk up a flight of stairs, guys like me and Boomer have no say in how we play. We have made it our business to mess with theirs, till death."

"Well, if it's death you want, you're about to mix it up with the ones most eager to give it to you," Nunzio said. "Other than maybe the Russians, there's no one crew nastier right now than the SAs. And they won't care if you're in a wheelchair or breathing from an oxygen tube. You make a move on them and they will bury you. They don't think of it as just business. To them, it's a way of life."

"Does that mean you're going to help us?" Boomer asked. "Or

are you just going to sit by and watch two of your best customers go down the drain?"

"Customers I got more than my share," Nunzio said, pushing back his chair and standing, looking from Boomer to Dead-Eye. "But friends I don't have too many of, and I like to keep the ones I have. Whatever you need, if I can get it done it will get done. Once you get all the pieces to your plan in place, I'll try and fill in as many holes as I can."

"We're about a week away, even less," Boomer said. "The plan's there—we just need to put together the team to make it work."

"How hard you figure that's going to be?" Nunzio asked. "Finding a few more demented bastards like yourselves just itching to fight till they drop?"

"Desperate's always easy to find," Boomer said. "But they have to be good, too. And that part's never a walk."

"We'll get them," Dead-Eye said. "I have no doubt."

"In that case, I'll go in and check on the specials," Nunzio said. "A good meal is in order. Nobody should stare down death on an empty stomach."

Boomer and Dead-Eye watched as Nunzio made his way past the bar and through the double doors leading into the kitchen. "You think he's right?" Dead-Eye asked.

"About what?" Boomer said.

"The part about this being a suicide mission," Dead-Eye said. "That's the one that caught my ear."

"Have we ever been out on one that wasn't?" Boomer asked.

"We always did make it a habit to kick down the do-not-enter doors," Dead-Eye said with a smile. "Never wanted any part of nice and easy."

"And we're too old to ask for a fresh deck of cards now," Boomer said. "Besides, it's not death we're afraid of; it's living at half speed that gives us the night sweats. Truth is, I don't know if we can do this, Dead-Eye. These crews are primed and running on full tanks. They're more than not the best we've ever gone up against. It could be over for us in one round. Shit, it can end before we even get a chance to climb through the ring ropes."

"But?" Dead-Eye said.

"I just know this is something we have to do," Boomer said. "Because not doing it will kill us faster than any one of their bullets."

2
—— BOOK ——

"What do you want, Steve?"
"To enter my house justified."

— FROM SAM PECKINPAH'S
RIDE THE HIGH COUNTRY

1

Rev. Jim bounced the ball with his right hand, body coiled, eyes focused on those of the young man with the bulky arms by his side, both soaked with an early-morning sweat. He pushed the ball to his left and burst past the young man, head down, dashing toward the basket less than twenty feet away. Rev. Jim stopped short, knees bent, and got a good arc on the ball. The chain rattled and the rock fell to the concrete.

"That's game, Ty," Rev. Jim said, turning to the young man behind him sitting on the ground, arms folded around bended knees. "Unless you have a few points I forgot to add to your score."

"No, you took it, you keep it," Ty said with a slow shake. "And I'll live with it. But you know next time we play I will own your ass."

"How did you come up with a two-and-two that led you to that?" Rev. Jim asked, reaching down for the ball. "Given that you have *never* beaten me and we've been going at it for three years now."

"I got all your moves down now," Ty said. "And you're way too old to dig up any fresh ones, that's for one. And I'm due for a win—it's all just a matter of me catching some of the luck that's been floating your way."

"Sounds like you got it all worked out," Rev. Jim said, tossing Ty the ball and walking toward him, his eyes now on the two men standing under the shadows of the net. "So much so that it might all work for the best if I don't even bother to show for next week's game."

"Forfeit falls under a win for me," Ty said, smiling as he stood up. "But I'll make that your call. Don't want a guilt ticket floating my way down the road if that happens."

"I got a week to decide," Rev. Jim said, turning away from Ty and walking toward the two men. "But toss this in. If you nail that chemistry test coming up, I might lean toward spotting you a few points."

"How much of a spot we talking?" Ty asked.

"That depends," Rev. Jim said, "on how high of a grade you can take down."

"You shittin' me?" Ty asked. "I'll dunk down a straight and solid A if I can get some free points tossed that way."

"That's the plan," Rev. Jim said.

Rev. Jim waited until Ty walked out of the basketball court, taking a quick glance at the bumper-to-bumper traffic locking both sides of the FDR Drive. He then turned and faced the two men, both leaning against the steel basketball pole. "I never figured either one of you to turn into park lurkers," he said, giving each a warm smile. "At least not for a few more years, anyway."

"Beats hustling lowballers out of pocket change," Dead-Eye said. "That's scraping hard ground, little friend."

"You move pretty well out there," Boomer said. "If I had known, I'd have set up an Apaches basketball team years ago. Try to cash in on that corner jump shot."

"And what special skill would you and Dead-Eye bring to the table for our team?" Rev. Jim said with a wink.

"You know me, Rev.," Dead-Eye said. "I'm a shooter. I'll have that end covered like a bearskin blanket."

"I can whistle," Boomer said. "I guess that should be more than enough to make me the coach."

"We'll never pull it off," Rev. Jim said after a moment of thought. "We'd be picked off as ringers in no time flat. I hope you came with a Plan B along with your dollar and a dream."

"We did," Boomer said. "Only this one has more bullets than baskets. And it's not even close to being a five-on-five."

"And the chances of us coming out of it with a win are less than zero," Dead-Eye said. "But in the event you die the city of New York will spring for the funeral and the flag."

"I knew there would be a perk hidden in there somewhere," Rev. Jim said. "Your plans always come with the best perks."

"The temperature on this one, Jim, is a few clicks higher than our last job," Boomer said. "I'm not going to pour sugar on it. You come in with us, I don't know if you'll come out. I don't know if any of us will."

"You really suck at recruiting," Rev. Jim said. "You need to work on that win-one-for-the-Boomer talk. Ease up on the negative vibes, my friend."

"We could use your help," Boomer said, his voice gone suddenly soft. "But if I were standing in your place I'd take my ball and head as far away from the two of us as your legs can take you. Because coming in with us won't lead anywhere good."

"Me and Boomer figured we'd lay it out for you and then give you some think time," Dead-Eye said. "But there's no other way to spell it. This one has a one-way feel."

"There's no need to either lay it out or give me time to decide," Rev. Jim said, looking from one ex-cop to the other. "I'll get up to speed soon enough—that end has never been much of a problem for me. And as far as me giving a thumbs-up or -down to joining your team, I decided on that about the time I first spotted you standing under the basket."

"From what I hear, you carved a decent slice for yourself out here," Boomer said. "Make some decent money, do work that matters, and help kids in your free time. That plus your pension should keep you ahead of your mortgage and grocery money."

"To be truthful, we gave a lot more thought whether we should reach out to you than you did on signing on," Dead-Eye said. "Okay with you if I ask why?"

"Boomer's right," Rev. Jim said. "I landed a decent job and have more than a fair share of pocket money. And every now and then I make a reach-out and turn a kid around and get him off the side roads and back onto the main highway."

"Don't sound all that bad to these ears," Dead-Eye said. "It's not a buy-and-bust and a flurry of bullets blowing both ways, but it's better than doing a nine-to-five in a branch bank wearing a blue uniform and a fake badge and praying that some loser with a mask and a shotgun slams his way through the front door and brings a little juice to your day."

"What are you looking for?" Boomer asked.

"Same thing you two are," Rev. Jim said. "I want a chance to matter again. I want to make a difference, and not just to one kid or a small handful. Don't read me wrong. That's all well and good, but there's too much shit out there and it's too easy to get, and that Father Flanagan routine can only take you so far. I'm drifting. We all are. And maybe what it is you got planned will scare ten years of shit out of me, minute I get wind of what it is. But, even if it does, it might help bring the drift to an end and give me a chance to feel alive. None of us like to say it, but God knows we all think about it. It would have been easier to be dead than to have survived the wounds we did. Once you're dead, it's over with, gone and buried. Walking out of the hospital, that's the day the real shit begins."

The three stood under the warm morning sun, heads bowed in silence, the noise of the traffic swelling behind them. "Remind me again, Boom," Dead-Eye said. "Why did we think of asking Rev. Jim back on our team?"

"We were looking for somebody to cheer us up," Boomer said, looking up at Jim and giving him a slow nod.

"There had to be more to it than that," Dead-Eye said, squeezing out a smile. "As I recall, this sucker's as funny as a funeral party."

"We were looking for a great cop, too," Boomer said, turning and doing a slow walk out of the playground. "Remember?"

The small church was empty. The old woman in the black dress knelt in front of the main altar, blessed herself, and released a string of dark rosary beads from between a set of vein-riddled fingers. She bowed her head and closed her eyes, her thin, frail lips shaping the words of a whispered prayer. Around her, the slow and easy glow of the votive candles slid across the silent glares of saints and angels. She leaned her arms against the creaky wood railing separating the altar from the nave and began her slow journey down the beads of the rosary. Outside, the sun was in the early stages of its descent, bringing to an end an otherwise warm and peaceful spring day.

Angel slid in silently beside the old woman, bowed his head, and then lifted his gaze up toward the main altar. "Do you hold all your meetings in a church?" he asked. "Or am I simply a special case?"

"It's where I feel most at home," the old woman said. "I would think that would be true for you as well."

"There was a time, yes," Angel said with a slow, appreciative nod. "But that was many years ago. I'm not the same man I was then."

"The man hasn't changed," the old woman said. "Only the choice of profession."

"Perhaps, Theresa," Angel said. "It would be best for us to have such a discussion in a place with much better lighting. But for now it might be a sound idea to work toward the business at hand, which boils down to a simple transfer: my drugs, your money. Are you prepared to move forward?"

"You would be pleasantly surprised to know what a cure our proposed transaction can be for my tired old body," Theresa said in a firm voice, her eyes on the rosary beads resting on her fingers. "And, at the very least, I anticipate feeling two decades younger the closer we get to finalizing all the details."

"There isn't much left to do," Angel said. "You will transfer the money to the accounts stipulated in the last meeting between our attorneys—five million total, American dollars, low denominations, no bills newer than four years. And I, in turn, will transfer over to you one hundred kilos of cocaine and have them distributed as per your agreed-upon specifications."

"And I have your guarantee that the street value of the cocaine will be in the neighborhood of fifteen to twenty million," Theresa said, slowly turning her gaze from her hands and up to Angel. "And, I assure you, you will be held to that guarantee. Not one dollar less."

"Ease up on the threats, old woman," Angel said, standing and gazing down at Theresa. "I'm not in the mood. How much you earn from the drugs you buy from me is totally dependent on the skill levels of the crews you have in place. If they can slice it and dance on it enough times and sell large quantities in silk markets at high tide, then you will hit your target goal. If they can't, you won't.

Either way, it's not something that will ever pop up on my radar. I will be long gone from your rearview once the total numbers are in."

"There was a time I would have had you beheaded for speaking to me in such a tone," Theresa said.

"And there was a time I would have heard your confession and sent you home with a blessing," Angel said. "But both our universe and our places in it have changed. So my offer stands firm. Five million in cash in return for one hundred kilos of my finest. Take it or toss it—your choice, so long as you make it this very second with the knowledge that once rejected it will never be brought back to your table. At least not at the same bargain price."

Theresa folded her dark rosary beads and dropped them into the pocket of her widow's dress. She slowly lifted herself off her knees and turned to face Angel. "The cash will be in place before end of business tomorrow," she said. "I'll alert my runners to be on guard for a large and valuable shipment. And if this all moves as smooth as it no doubt should, I look forward to seeing you in church on a fairly regular basis."

Angel nodded and smiled. "With pleasure," he said. "I would even hear your confession if you liked."

"I appreciate the offer," Theresa said, turning to walk down the aisle, her thick shoes echoing off the marble floor. "But, as you yourself so clearly stated, our two universes have shifted. I will come to you only for the purpose of conducting business. I will find a priest if I feel a need to confess any sins I might have committed."

"Do you confess them all?" Angel asked. "Or simply the convenient ones?"

Theresa stopped and turned. "I confess the ones I feel most require the Lord's forgiveness," she said in a voice laced with anger. "As well as the ones for which I feel the greatest remorse."

"Does that include the recent death of your husband?" Angel asked. He took several steps closer to Theresa, hands by his sides, at ease inside this place.

"My Alberto died of a rare blood disorder," Theresa said, her right hand clutching the curled edge of a brown pew. "The only remorse I feel is in no longer having him at my side."

"If that is indeed the case and he died as you say, you have my sympathy," Angel said with a sarcastic smirk. "I should learn not to give much weight to the street gossip that has become so much a part of our business."

"That would be wise," Theresa said with a stern nod of her head. "It would prevent you from saying anything foolish and may even save your life."

"Or prevent me from taking one," Angel said.

Theresa stared at the ex-priest and nodded. "I have lived a long life in a trade not known to embrace experience," she said. "And that is neither idle gossip nor talk. Nor is it luck. It is simple fact."

"There's always a reason buried behind such a fact," Angel said. "What is yours?"

"I make sure the first bullet fired is always from the end of my gun," Theresa said.

CHAPTER

Boomer moved down the alley, lowered his body, and released the ball, watching it roll down the lane and crash against the pins with force, sending all ten sprawling. He walked back to the table and sat next to Natalie, watching as she penciled in his strike.

"One fifty-seven for you and thirty-three for me," she said, leaning back against the tattered leather bench. "But we have three frames to go, so there's still hope."

"A glimmer at least," Boomer said. "I'm guessing bowling doesn't rank high on the sports agenda back in Russia."

"If it's not violent or fast, we're not interested," Natalie said.

"Cops seem to love it," Boomer said. "When I was on the job, I played in the NYPD league. The only time I missed any of my team's games was when I was too banged up to get out of a hospital bed."

"Another reason, I suppose, for me not to enjoy the sport," Natalie said. "I try not to spend too much time in the company of cops."

"I'm glad you made an exception in my case," Boomer said.

"You're not a cop anymore, remember?" she said.

"Barely," Boomer said.

Natalie looked around at the long alley, all lights out and lanes shuttered except for theirs. "How did you manage to get in here in the middle of the night?" she asked. "Or is that something I would be better off not knowing?"

Boomer smiled. "It's all in who you know," he said. "My brother owns the place, lets me come in and play whenever I want. I usually like it better when I have it to myself."

"And how did I manage to earn an invitation to your party?" Natalie asked.

"I wanted to make sure I played against someone I knew I could beat," Boomer said with a half smile. "And I also needed to key you in on something."

"I assume it has nothing to do with bowling," she said.

Natalie stood and walked around the one lit lane before turning back to face Boomer. Her dark hair was hanging down loose around her shoulders, teasing the white collar of a designer shirt, its flaps pulled over a pair of tight-fitting jeans. Orange-colored bowling shoes wrapped up the outfit. It was hard for Boomer not to be distracted by her sheer beauty, and he knew that she was aware of her effect.

"I'm going to make a move against the SAs," he told her. "Go at them heavy as I can for as long as I can."

"I know," Natalie said.

"So much for a poker face," Boomer said.

"It's one of the traits cops share with criminals," Natalie said. "At least those who operate at our levels. You can always see the need for revenge in their eyes. They are incapable of masking it."

"We're not going to touch any of your operations," Boomer said.

"And if by chance we do, just know it was not intentional. Our beef is not with the Russians."

"At least not this time," Natalie said with a shrug. "In our business, there's always a down-the-road waiting for us both."

"I wouldn't worry," Boomer said. "I don't have that many more fights in me."

"I know how strong the crews you're going to face are," she said. "How will you match against them?"

"Not well," Boomer said. "But we'll bring down more than our share."

"You could do much more than that if you had help," Natalie said. "It's no secret that I'm not a fan of the SAs, and they feel the same about me. We would both be working toward the same goal, only for different reasons."

"Thanks for the offer," Boomer said. She was standing close to him, her hips brushing against the scoring table. "But I'm not ready to make that move just yet."

"Then there isn't much else I can do for you," Natalie said. "But the offer will stand, yours for the asking."

"There is *something* you can do," Boomer said, a smile on his face, his eyes locked in on hers.

"What?" she asked.

"Give me one more game," Boomer said. "I'll even spot you thirty pins."

"Only if we play for something," she said. "I'm always better if I know there's a chance to come away with a prize."

"Fair enough," Boomer said. "Winner's call, and anything goes."

"You have yourself a deal, Detective," Natalie said.

Boomer and Dead-Eye leaned against the mesh cage of the police K-9 compound unit. Rev. Jim stood across from them, sipping from a container of black coffee. "Neither one of you two ever struck me as the Lassie-come-home type," he said.

"We're not," Boomer said.

"And Lassie was no cop," Dead-Eye said. "Just a collie with a lot of free time. Rin Tin Tin, now that fucker was a cop."

"Still, both were dogs," Rev. Jim said. "And we're looking for partners, not pets. At least that's what I read on the last memo I got."

"You allergic to dogs?" Dead-Eye asked. "Or just afraid of them?"

"Both," Rev. Jim said.

The gate behind them was unlatched by a short, stocky bald man in a police sergeant's uniform. "I'm guessing you're the guys Fast Freddie was running off the mouth about," the man said, offering a stubby hand to Boomer and a nod and a smile to Dead-Eye and Rev. Jim. "I had heard some about what you did a few years back, and I have to give the tip of the cap to you for even trying a ballsy move like that. Now, I don't know what you're lining up to do next, but whatever it is and wherever it is Buttercup is the one you most want on your side of the door."

"What's a Buttercup?" Rev. Jim asked.

"She's a full-bred Neapolitan bullmastiff," the bald man said, flaunting his pride. "Weighs in at a solid hundred and twenty-five pounds—mostly muscle, fat only where it's needed. I've been working the K-9 teams going on eight years now. I've seen my share of good ones and a handful of near-greats. But no one comes near Buttercup. She's Hall of Fame great."

"Skully?" Boomer said, gazing at the name tag pinned across the front of the man's button-down. "You any relation to Ralph Skully from the two-eight?"

"He was my dad," the bald man said. "Died on the job nine years ago this month. Was taken down in a drug bust that hit a sour note in the East Bronx."

"I know," Boomer said. "Me and Dead-Eye were backups on the job. We rode in the unmarked with him, trying to get him over to Mercy Hospital. I'm sorry we didn't make it in time. If I had to bet, I'd say he was as good a father as he was a cop."

"If it matters to you," Dead-Eye said, "the dealer that shot him got his own funeral about a week later. Only his didn't come with a flag and an honor guard."

"It does matter," Skully said.

"What kind of dog are we getting?" Boomer asked. "What I'm asking is, she up to what we need her to do?"

"I won't lie to you," Skully said. "This last job, the one that retired her, cost her big time. She's got one lung, which slows her down quite a bit—especially given her weight and size. And her right rear leg acts up at times, locks when she's in full run. That happens, she turns still as a statue."

"Can she still smell out the dope?" Dead-Eye asked.

"She hasn't had to for a while," Skully said. "But that's an instinct she'll never lose, and there's a potential problem there, too."

"How so?" Boomer asked.

"In her time, no dog took on more drug work than Buttercup," Skully said. "That level of work goes hand in hand with a certain level of risk. She's sniffed more than her fair share of high-end powder and that can, in turn, make her behavior erratic. She could have an occasional flashback and maybe snap a bit. Me? I don't think it's that big a risk, but I can't let you leave here without knowing the full truth. I don't need to draw you a full-color map. You get the picture."

"Kodak clear," Rev. Jim said. "Old Buttercup's a walking, growling time bomb. One that needs to be fed more than a foreign weight lifter, walked whenever the need arises, and have her shit picked up twice a day."

"She also gets a nice paycheck and has all her vet bills covered by the city," Skully said with a back-at-you tone.

"That how it works with K-9s?" Dead-Eye asked.

"In some cases, not all," Skully said. "It's done at the discretion of the commish and the heavy medals down at One Police Plaza. If it's determined that a dog has gone above and beyond, then they use pull funds from the set-aside money and dole out a monthly stipend in accordance with the rank she's assigned. Given the number of cases and the high-wire danger Buttercup had a hand in, I'd say she did pretty well for herself."

"How well?" Boomer asked.

"They retired her as gold shield with her own tin and number,"

Skully said, chest slightly puffed out, as if he were talking about one of his own kids earning an Ivy League diploma. "She collects a three-quarter disability pension that comes out to about twelve thousand a year. Enough to feed her prime-cut organic dog food and bottled spring water."

"Who gets the money?" Dead-Eye asked.

"Whoever takes care of her," Skully said. "Right now, it's me. If you decide to bring her into your squad, I can sign her over to you or leave it as is and send you the checks as they come in. Your call on that end."

"Let's take a long, slow breath here," Rev. Jim said, taken slightly aback by the direction of the conversation. "And I mean no disrespect at all to Buttercup. I'm sure she's really a great dog and a penthouse narc. But a gold shield and a pension for a dog? And a three-quarter, tax-free one at that? Doesn't that seem a little off to you guys?"

"Cop's a cop," Dead-Eye said. "Whether she walks on two legs or four. This dog put in her time and dropped her share of blood on the way out, same as us. Far as I can see, she has more than earned her keep, at least to my way of thinking it out."

"How long she been off the job?" Boomer asked.

"Six months, give or take a day," Skully said. "She spent three of those at the animal hospital downtown until she was strong enough to get around on her own. Once she jumped that hurdle, I brought her down here with me. I take her to work every day. Figure if she can't be a K-9 out on the streets, being around them on a regular shift plays out to the next best way to go."

"I can't tell you what we have working," Boomer said. "Works better if you do a Mister Clean on that part. But I can tell you it's going to be a lot heavier weight than a bodega buy-and-bust. And you know enough about the action end of the business to figure the survival rate doesn't make us insurance candidates. Not everybody's going to make it back home, tucked and washed. You need to know at least that much before you trade her to our team."

"Right now, way I see it she'll finish whatever years she's got left hanging around an office, watching other police dogs head out to do the work she was born and bred to do, and too many days of that shit will kill her faster than a drug dealer's bullet. Now, I figure you'll head out for deep waters and cast your line for some big fish. No point in going out to do any of this shit if you were looking to hit some end-of-the-line crew."

"Now that I hear it said out loud, it doesn't sound at all bad," Dead-Eye said with a soft chuckle. "Disabled cops against disabled crooks. I could see us coming out of that head-to-head with a solid win."

"And if you did, you wouldn't have any need for a K-9 with Buttercup's skills," Skully said. "You guys are big-market players, searching out the heavy takedowns and the page-one busts. And those are the kind of jobs that don't fall easy and always total out to high body counts. The kind of jobs Buttercup was born to fight in. And if she's going to die in the process, then she'll go down the way she was meant to. Like a cop."

"We *are* still talking about a dog here, am I right?" Rev. Jim asked, not bothering to hide his smile. "Or did I miss a detour on the road coming down?"

"From here on, I don't want you to even think of Buttercup as a dog," Boomer said with a look at Rev. Jim and a nod to both Dead-Eye and Skully.

"Let me take a stab at a guess," Rev. Jim said. "She can go undercover, too, and make a conga line of coke addicts think she's really a cat?"

"Buttercup is now officially an Apache," Boomer said. "She is now one of us."

"All right, then, Skully," Dead-Eye said, slapping his hands together. "Let's put a shake to it. I think it's time we all went and met the bitch."

Rev. Jim laughed. "That's Detective Bitch to you!"

— CHAPTER —

The airport runway was pitch dark, the rustling of the weeds and high grass the only noise breaking across an otherwise silent night. In the distance, a long, thin line of blue, yellow, and green landing lights were shrouded in evening mist, and the muted moans and groans of small-craft engines were muffled by thick gray clouds passing overhead.

"I fucking love nights like these," Carlos McEntire said, cigarette smoke flowing out his mouth and nostrils. "You can do anything you want when the weather turns this way. Get your cock sucked, pump a dozen bullets into some loser's back, close on a big deal and nobody can see shit. It's like being invisible. I tell you true, you find me a city has weather like this day in, day out, twenty-four-seven, I'd set up shop there in a heart tick, no bullshit."

"You feel all that strong, you would have been better off hooking up with that fucker Dracula than with us," Freddie Gonzalez said, laughing as he elbow-nudged his brother, Hector, in the rib cage.

"The way I'm listening, you got a lot more in common with that coffin-hugger than you do with either one of us."

"Don't kid yourself," Carlos said, staring at the two leaders of the G-Men through thin drops of light rain. "He was for real, Dracula would be crowned a king in our trade. That's one dealer that can never die and never be killed. Sucker can be open for business any-place, anytime, forever."

"I wish he was for true," Hector said, his hands shoved deep inside the pockets of a tan leather coat. "Then it would be him instead of me standing out here talking shit and letting his balls freeze down to fuckin' raisins."

"Where is this rodeo clown?" Freddie asked, his eyes doing a quick dart dance around the barren field. "Should have been here ten minutes ago, and that's taking in him getting lost on the way."

"He'll show his ass, you can count on it," Carlos said. "If you're not from around here, this place isn't so easy to spot. And this weather we got don't toss out any helping hands, either. Shit, I *am* from around here and I still miss my mark most of the time."

"I wasn't late and I wasn't lost."

The man's voice came at them like a bullet in the night. They each turned in the direction of the voice.

"I was just taking a listen."

"You can listen all you want," Freddie said, the middle fingers of his right hand stroking the dark barrel of a handgun wedged in the center of his spine. "Take notes, if that brings a ring to your bell. Only do it over here where our eyes can meet."

The man appeared from their left, shrouded from the waist down in layers of swirling mist, thin clouds of cigar smoke obscuring his face. He was wearing dark blue slacks and a matching three-button jacket over a white shirt starched crisp enough to slice skin, the entire outfit designer-stitched. His body was workout lean, topped by a thick and unruly mane of dark hair and a pair of eyes whose glare was harsh enough to chill a warm morning.

"We could have met in a five-star restaurant," the man said in a voice stripped of any accent or hint of his background. "Enjoyed a nice meal and finished off several bottles of expensive red wine. And then some champagne once we sealed our deal."

"Sounds to me like you're way too busy to read any newspapers or watch the TV news," Carlos said, his manner relaxed but his body wound tight. "Otherwise, you'd be wise and know eating in one of those high-end restaurants can make you dead in less time it takes to order a scotch and a splash. Take it from the one who knows."

"Dead is dead," the man said, the words spoken slowly. "Faceup in the wet grass or flat down across a backroom table, it's the same page from the same book. In our line of business, it always boils down to one curled finger doing a slow tap on a small hard trigger."

"And if it's your finger wrapped around that trigger, Robles, we need to know whose head it's going to be aimed at," Hector said. "That's the only reason we called you to this little picnic in the park."

Robles nodded. "My finger has always belonged to the hand that puts the most money in my back pocket. That could be yours or it can belong to that cash-heavy poisoned padre cutting into your lines—all the same load of wash to me."

"We bankrolled your first big play," Freddie said, making no effort to disguise his anger. "We put you in motion. Without the G-Men, you'd be washing cars on Bruckner Boulevard or, worse, doing a full roll of dimes up at Attica. And now here you come, all slick and sprayed, ready to piss on my shoes for the fresh breath in town."

"It's not about loyalty, it's about making the most by doing the least and trusting no one," Robles said, eyes locked on Freddie. "Those were your own words I'm throwing back your way. Told me I'd be a fool if I didn't take what you said and shove it deep to my heart. Now here you are, standing out in the rain like you're James Bond with a green card and telling me what? To forget all that you said back when I was a fresh piece of fruit? Am I hearing you right?"

"No, you got it right, player," Hector said. "And there's nobody here asking you to do a flip on that class project. But I am going to ask you to remember what *I* laid on you that very same day. You still got it tacked to the back of your brain, or did that shit get brushed off with a fresh coat of memory paint?"

"Hard to forget that," Robles said with a slow nod. "You were using a loaded gun as a blackboard pointer."

"And even knowing I will plant you six feet down, fancy suit and all, and shit on your grave, knowing all that you still walk up to my face and talk to me about playing for another team?" Hector said, his words closer to shouts now.

"I'm not eager to do a flip, and I don't have a 411 out on the street looking for stray cash to be sent my way," Robles said. "But I put my truth out in the open for you to touch. If an offer to move against you comes in, then I have to give it the weight it deserves. That's the plain and the cold of it. And I know that any one of you would step the same way. I'm for sale, and so are you. It all comes down to the question of price."

"And yours is what?" Carlos asked.

"Depends on the who and the when," Robles said. "Once I get that out of you, then you get a number out of me."

Hector and Freddie exchanged a quick but noticeable glance. Then both gave a nod of their head to Carlos. "A million five," Carlos said without any hesitation. "We do it as per the same breakdown as usual. You get a chunk down, a second chunk when the target's potted, and a final third when you make it out clean. That work for you?"

"That half does," Robles said. "I'll let you know the rest when *I* know the rest."

"The ex-priest," Carlos said. "Angel Cortez."

"How soon?" Robles asked.

"He's moving in fast," Hector said. "Be good if you could do the same."

"And there's no think time on this one," Freddie said, taking two steps forward, the first small plane of the night crossing just off to his right, half drowning his words. "We will know before you leave us tonight which way your balloon floats. With us or with the ex-priest."

"And if I take a pass?" Robles asked. "What then? You let me walk back through the wet grass to my car, no hard feelings, all of us still asshole buddies? Then you just sit back and wait for the bullets to come out of my gun somewhere down the line?"

"Only way to get educated on that is for you to blow off our offer," Hector said with a shrug.

Robles took a step back and raised his face up to the night, cool moisture coating his skin, eyes closed, breathing in the fuel-heavy air. "Two weeks," he said in a low voice. "I need some time to figure his moves and locales. He's new to the town, which makes him new to me. Ten days to learn what I need about the man and four to bring him down. You want it done clear of mistakes, that's the best I can do."

"We can live with that, so long as the deed gets done," Freddie said. "You need to get your eyeballs real close to this padre. He may be new to the city, but he's not in diapers when it comes to moving the goods and tossing a blanket over his trail. He's got a hard-core crew that will lay it down and play it full tilt for their paycheck. Maybe they think if they die protecting his ass they'll get theirs to heaven. No matter. You get in tight and get off the kill shot. That happens, we get what it is we need and you walk free with a couple of suitcases filled with pocket change."

"Is he the only target?" Robles asked. "I don't mind working two jobs side by side. Helps me keep my focus."

"Check the want ads, you looking for more work," Carlos said. "We just tossed out the only one we have to offer."

"You know where it is I bank and how," Robles said. "Soon as that first deposit is there, you can start running down the time on your game clock."

"The cash will be there on time, no worries," Hector said. "The bullet to the priest's head better be, too."

"I never miss a money kill," Robles said with a wide smile.

"Well, then, that's at least one fuckin' thing we all have in common," Freddie said. He glared at Robles for several silent seconds and then held the look as the shooter did a turn and walked off into the mist. They waited until Robles was clear of sight and hearing, their expensive loafers soaked through from the wet grass. Hector pulled out a thin cigar, clicked a lighter, and put the flame to the end. "There's one fucker I wouldn't piss on he was on fire," he said, his teeth clenched around the cigar. "He'll flip us faster than a Big Mac burger."

"My hunch tells me he walked in already on the padre's pad," Freddie said. "Was sent to the meet to see how much money weight we were willing to toss out on the priest. If the vote belongs to me alone, I follow the arrogant fuck right out the gate and make him a piece of the runway."

"You'll take a bite from his apple, no fear there, my brother," Hector said. "But for the here and now let's see how he plays the fresh hand we just spread his way. One five in cash can turn a lot of hungry heads, and if Robles is about anything at all that's real it's the money."

"He does the priest, then he has no other call but to come work for us," Carlos said. "That how you figure he'll map it out?"

"There's two roads he can drive down," Hector said. "That's one of them."

"The other?" Freddie asked.

"He back pockets our up-front money and stays by the padre's side," Carlos said, his glance catching Hector's approving nod. "Takes us for the short ride and partners up solid with Angel's team. It's a bone roll that the priest will end up the winner in any action goes down between us."

"And if he goes that way, then what?" Freddie asked. "What are you going to call from our huddle?"

"Robles is no different than any other gun we squared up against," Hector said. "From day one, they all been cut the same way, and we haven't backed down to one yet. I don't see why this particular fool is going to turn out different."

"He gets tossed like a fresh salad," Carlos said. "Just like the rest."

"If that's the case, then I pray he cubes out and doesn't dirt-nap the priest," Freddie said. "Be a happy day for all when I turn that tough-talking fool into a fuckin' memory."

6

— CHAPTER —

Stephanie Torres had her corner shot lined and ready, upper body leaning against the edge of the wood, right hand holding the thick end of her stick, the fingers of her left hand coiled around the thin base. She gave the stick a hard nudge and watched as the white cue ball slammed the six into a right-corner pocket. "You sure you want to do this for money?" she asked Boomer. "I don't mind playing just for play. Hate to have you walk away empty on account of me."

"It's still your shot," Boomer said, smiling.

Stephanie stared back at Boomer and nodded, thick strands of hair covering the sides of her face, a partially opened curtain. "Nine ball, side pocket," she said. She was dressed in tight black jeans, dark blue denim shirt, and a thin black leather jacket—the standard uniform of the off-duty. Stephanie was one year off the job and six months out of a physical-rehab program, retired now on a three-quarter salary, tax-free disability pension that would last for the rest of her life. The scars from that final fire would last as long as the twice-a-month checks. The skin on the front and right side of her chest was red and scarred, patches as rough and sharp as mountain terrain. The vision in her left eye was damaged, and a section of one of her lungs had been removed. Her throat was always dry and scratchy, and a thin scar ran down the side of her right cheek and ended at the base of her jaw. The fingers of her left hand felt perpetually cold and numb.

Stephanie Torres was not only a disabled cop but a deformed one, the ones the Police Department was always the most concerned about as they prepared for an uninvited retirement. She was considered a high risk, and the department had to do whatever it could to make her less so. "It's only the end of your police career, it's not the end of the road," a therapist assigned to her case by the department said to her during their session. "Your wounds prevent you from being an active arson investigator, nothing more than that."

Stephanie stared back at the therapist, a well-meaning and thoughtful man in his late forties with a choppy manner and a seen-it-all attitude. "Is this just a job to you?" she asked him in a low, barely audible voice. "You know, meeting with cops like me, giving us little pep talks, stamping our papers, and helping us out the front door? Is it only a job, something to fill in your time between nine and five and help you pay your cable bill? Because if it is, then you are one very lucky son of a bitch. And when the day comes for you to pack your desk and walk out that door yourself, you won't really give a flying fuck about any of it and forget you were ever even here your first hour away from the building."

"You'll find a fresh outlet for yourself," the therapist said, ignoring her outburst. "It may take some time, but the opportunity will one day be there for you. You may not believe it right now, but it's very true. And while it won't be easy for you to wade through the initial bouts of depression you'll need to combat and over- come, the notion that there is a way out of your darkness will give you the strength to push on."

"That and the bottle of blue pills you no doubt are going to pre- scribe ought to do the trick," Stephanie said. "You have no idea how much better I feel just knowing that. While we're going at it, let me ask you this. Are you going to mark me down in that little book of yours as a bullet-taker? You know, an emotionally disturbed person with a high-risk potential?"

"Should I?" the therapist asked.

"Only if it helps you keep your job," Stephanie said, before grab- bing her purse, pushing back her chair, and walking out.

Stephanie stood straight up, smiling, as she watched her ball glide slowly into a side pocket. "This is going way too easy," she said. "I figure you're walking me right into the center square of a setup."

"And, remember, we don't take checks, credit cards, or notes," Dead-Eye said, stepping up behind her and handing her a cold bottle of beer. "We deal in cash only, and the older the bills the wider our smiles."

Stephanie took a long swig from the bottle and nodded. "And nothing bigger than a ten," she said. "I bet you'd take your winnings in coins if you could."

"I got a box of leather pouches in the car, if that's how you're looking to pay off," Dead-Eye said with a slow smile and a fast wink. "I can cram twenty-five, maybe thirty dollars easy in each one. All I need is the chance and the change."

"You can lose bus money shooting a few games of pool with your friends," Boomer said, his back against a wood-paneled wall, hands in the front warmers of a hooded sweatshirt. "What made you track us down and pick us for marks?"

Stephanie rested her pool cue against the table and put the bottle of beer next to it. "Next month, on the eighteenth, will be a year since I walked out of the burn unit and took my first steps into civilian life," she said. "And I probably have liked it as much as you two. I guess I needed to be around somebody who understood how I feel and how I cope without the burden of having to talk about it. Anybody fills out that MO to the letter it's you and Dead-Eye."

"That the start and the finish to it?" Boomer asked. "Or did you come looking for more?"

"How about a for instance?" Stephanie said.

"There's no secret to what me, Boom, and a few others pulled together a while back," Dead-Eye said, beer bottle hanging loose between the fingers of his left hand. "Shit, I'd like very much to believe it's a piece of legend by now."

"It's talked about—let me leave it at that," Stephanie said.

"No doubt," Dead-Eye said. "And none more so than by cops facing up to your present situation. Drop-kicked out of a job they love by wounds they do their best to hide. Most are content to know that a bunch of wounded cops like themselves managed to get it up one more time and went out and did the deed, in their hearts believing they could never commit to such an action or be desperate enough to want to make the attempt. Then, there may be one or two out there that need more than that warm thought to get them through a rough patch. Who are looking to go at it for real, with us leading them up the hill."

"And you think I'm one of the ones who fit that bill?" Stephanie asked, looking from Boomer to Dead-Eye.

"You spell it for me another way," Boomer said, stepping away from the wall and walking toward Stephanie. "Convince me you went to all the trouble to arrange to meet us just to find out how good we were at pool."

"I already know how good you are at pool—didn't need to drag my ass over two bridges to find that out," Stephanie said with a downcast shrug and a determined look. "I also knew how great you were as cops, heard the stories just like anyone else that's pinned on a tin last few years. No secret to any of that, either."

"What don't you know?" Dead-Eye asked.

"Whether or not you do have something new that you're planning to move on," she said. "There are more than enough rumors out there that point to a yes, but I never put much weight on bar talk. And if any or all of it is even close to the truth, how much of a chance does someone like me have to get into your game?"

Boomer nodded. "We read your casebook," he said to her after several long, silent seconds. "You were at the top tier—that's clear as a sunrise. Most of those jobs you cracked had cold files written all over the folders, but you worked the evidence and let it lead you to the solve. Now, there are plenty of high-end places for you to take that talent of yours, the kind of companies that will cut you checks with lots of zeros and let you call in your own shots. But you already know that, if you're smart as we figure. To me, that means there's little need for you to come in on a tumble that can end with a flag around your coffin."

"As if neither one of you could pick up a heavy pile working A-list security, either out on your own or for some deep-pocket Fortune 500 company," Stephanie said. "But you didn't. You went back out on the streets, forgot you were off the job, and did what you always did before. You had no choice. It's who you are and what you are. Now, maybe I'm only wasting my time, but I like to think it's part of who and what I am, too."

"You do any narc work while you were on the job?" Dead-Eye asked. "Early on, I mean, before you landed in Arson Investigation."

"I was a Hispanic woman in a mostly Irish and Italian department," Stephanie said with a slight shrug. "I did about eighteen months working drugs—plainclothes, undercover, and decoy. My time in Narcotics booted me up to third grade and helped me get a break into Arson."

"You got any family?" Boomer asked.

"I did," Stephanie said. "I had two, in fact. My mama, papa, and grandpa on the one hand, the PD on the other. They're all gone now. What's left is what you're looking at. Listen, I know I'm probably not the first ex-cop you would think to turn to, probably not even in the top ten, but I'm stepping up here, asking for a chance. You may not have anything in the works. If so, I just wasted some gas money and got to shoot a few games of pool. But if you do I'll be of help to you. And you'd be helping me at the same time."

"How you figure?" Dead-Eye asked.

"You would be saving my life," Stephanie said, doing her best not to shed any tears in front of the two men.

"We could bring it to a fast end, too," Boomer said. "You step in with us, there are no walkaway zones."

"Then I would go out the way I should," Stephanie said, downing her last sliver of beer. "Like a cop."

The pool room was smoke-filled and quiet, Bob Seger's hard-rock voice, coming off a back-room jukebox, filling the void. Boomer moved around the table, preparing to rack up a fresh game. Dead-Eye eased himself up on a stool, rubbed against the pain in his right shoulder, and stared out at the tables spread half a dozen on each side, three rows in all. Boomer walked toward Stephanie and handed her a pool cue.

"I have just one more question," he said to her. "The answer we get back will determine whether we take you in. You good with that?"

Stephanie took the cue from Boomer and nodded. "Let's have it, then," she said.

"Are you afraid of dogs?" Boomer asked.

7

CHAPTER

Theresa sat on the park bench, late spring sun warming her tanned face, her eyes closed, hands folded across her lap. "I knew you were young," she said to the woman sitting next to her. "I am a bit surprised at how young."

"Does it affect your thinking?" the woman asked. She was in her mid-twenties, dark hair flowing straight down the sides of her face. Her eyes were the color of crows, and her short black skirt did little to hide a shapely body.

"No, Natalie, not at all," Theresa said. "If anything, it makes your accomplishments that much more impressive. Back when I carried your years, I would never have been able to manage such a feat."

"You lacked the opportunity, never the talent," Natalie said.

"Perhaps," Theresa said. "But the time has passed and we'll never know the answer for sure."

"Why have you come to me?" Natalie asked. "You have a partner, one from your very own country and someone you have known for many years. But I'm a stranger to you, an unknown and, as such, a danger. A risk. You may not think you can trust your partner, but you will never know for certain whether you can trust me."

"There is no trust in our business," Theresa said, "no matter how long or how little we know the person across the table. Betrayal and deceit are always in the air."

Natalie Robinov sat back against the hard slats of the wood bench and turned to look at the old woman. "Tell me again—why is it I need your help?" she asked. "And why now?"

"I knew your father very well," Theresa said, smiling at the memory, finding no trouble in the harsh tones of Natalie's questions. "We closed several high-end deals down the years, guns coming to me in return for drugs going to him—all of them pretty much going down as planned. He was a man who sensed when a unique opportunity presented itself, and he was never fearful of making the moves necessary to take full advantage of the situation. I have high hopes that his daughter is cut from the same cloth."

Natalie turned from the old woman and stared out across the cobbled walk at a manicured strip of lawn, watching two children make a feeble attempt to get a kite off the ground and up toward the sky. Her face broke into a smile when she saw that the elder of the two, with the help of a soft breeze, had gained some traction and managed to get the kite up slightly over his head. He thrust his small clenched fist into the air in a gesture of triumph.

Natalie took a deep breath and weighed her options. She had a difficult decision to make, and she knew that the old woman would require an answer before she eased herself off the park bench. Forming an allegiance between her branch and Theresa's outfit was the soft part of the equation. It was a business angle Natalie herself had been contemplating for the past several months, and one that offered a number of sizable advantages to the Russians. Theresa had jumped the shark by wrapping her offer with a massive string attached to it, one that called for Natalie to aid and abet the old woman in her betrayal of Angel and his powerful South American drug cartel. It was a move designed to instigate a wide-open battle, forcing her to move sooner than she would have liked into the lucrative but dangerous cocaine market of New York's tri-state area. And it was the weight of just such a decision that Natalie Robinov had been trained and prepped for since back when she was old enough to hide behind the bookcases in her father's large office and listen in on the discussions that took place inside those thick wood-paneled walls that always smelled of stale smoke and fresh vodka.

It was also a move that would put her right in the middle of Boomer's declared war on the SA crews. And she knew how dangerous such a move could be, both professionally and personally. It went against everything she had been taught.

———————

"What is it you want from me in return?" Natalie asked Theresa, turning away from the two children lost at play. "And why?"

"To continue to live and to profit," Theresa said without hesitation. "The same, I don't doubt, as you."

"Has Angel given you any indication that he would prevent you from doing either?" she asked.

"People in positions of power, such as Angel at this moment, never put into words what they carry in their hearts," Theresa said. "Their intentions are never fully revealed until it is too late to alter the outcome."

"And you know this because you are old and therefore wise?" Natalie said, giving the woman a cold smile.

"I know this because I was at one time in such a position myself," Theresa said. "And indifference suited me well."

"I will let you have fifteen percent of the profits I secure from Angel's dealings," Natalie said. "If we make it to a second year, your end will increase slightly."

"In all my dealings with Angel, my cut was never less than a forty-percent share," Theresa said, taken aback by both the proposition and the sudden cold manner in which it was offered. "And we never worked a deal that came in for less than seven figures."

"That may be true," Natalie said. "The two of you complemented each other, and the relationship was good. But on each deal you made Angel needed you. I don't need you or anyone else to complete my deals. On top of that, Angel is preparing to rid himself of you, which makes a forty-percent cut moot, since you won't live to hold any of it in your hands. So a fifteen-percent cut off the top of Angel's cake is as fair an offer as you're likely to get from me or anyone in my position."

Theresa nodded her head slowly, a half-curled smile crossing her thick, scarred lips. "If I live to see it," she said. "I am well aware that I approach the end of my long run. If not by Angel's hand, then by yours. Such is the harsh nature of this life."

"You can walk away from it," Natalie said to the old woman. "Turn your back to it, take your millions, find a quiet place in a warm part of the world, disappear. Not many of us are ever afforded that chance—to walk into a new life and find peace. Even fewer take it, and my guess is you won't. But if you have ever given it any thought, now would be the perfect time. I would even arrange and guarantee your safe passage to any port."

"I was not meant to die in a rocking chair by a fire," Theresa said. "And neither were you. We will do our deal and make our move on Angel and his crew. For now, we share a goal and an enemy. So long as that holds true, our partnership will remain intact."

Natalie stood and looked down at the old woman. "We're partners now," she said. "Until the day when our common enemy is no longer a concern to us. And then we will again be on opposite sides and I will do whatever I have to do to take you down."

"I would have it no other way," Theresa said, her voice resigned but resolute.

Natalie nodded and walked away, disappearing into the crowds of Central Park.

"I don't know, Nunzio," Boomer said, staring across at his friend, a large glass of red wine by his side.

"I *do* know," Nunzio said, slapping at the table with the flat of his hand for emphasis. "You need this kid on your team, sick or not. He won't let you down, and he's got the kind of skills you make good use of, that much I know."

"This is a shit-scary disease," Dead-Eye said from the other end of the table. "How you get it, where you get it, and who can get it— all are questions. All we know for sure is that whoever *does* get it dies fast, and not in a good way."

"How do you connect with him?" Boomer asked, taking a slow sip of his wine.

"I'm a friend of the family," Nunzio said. "I've known Andy since he was old enough to walk in here on his own. He's good people, and he was a great cop. I would never send him your way if he wasn't either one."

"What kind of shape is he in?" Dead-Eye asked. "Once we start our move, we'll need to go at warp speed and we can't make any room for a slow-up."

"Most days you wouldn't even know he's sick," Nunzio said. "He's sharp, alert, on the mark. He can move as fast as you need him to move."

"What about the other days?" Boomer asked. "The ones where he won't be at top speed. What would we be looking at there?"

"I'm in the dark there, as well," Nunzio said. "From what I hear, it's not easy for him, but he can struggle through it if he has to. He's a tough kid, Boom, on a raw break. But this I do know, he would die before he let any one of you down."

"What's he bringing to our table that we can make use of?" Dead-Eye asked. "Most crime-scene guys I worked with only cared about dust and prints. On a job like the one we're going out on, that shit don't even break into our top-ten list."

"You can read his files if you want to know how good he is," Nunzio said. "Besides, let's look at this Delta Force team you're putting together. There's the two of you and Jim. The three of you combined are still missing crucial body parts. You got a burner out of Arson and a wheezer of a dog in need of some serious drug rehab. You ask me, Andy fits your crew like a missing glove."

Boomer set his glass aside and leaned in closer to Nunzio. "The team has one thing in common, the dog included. We all got our wounds doing our job," he said. "It's part of what holds us together. At least it did with the first crew, but I expect the same to be true of this one."

"Andy got his wound on the job, too," Nunzio said. "Only his scars don't come from any bullets or knives. They come from a disease. Look, however you decide about him, that's not my call, it belongs to you. All I'm doing is putting him on the table. But there's no mistake about it—Andy Victorino is as wounded as the rest of you, maybe even more. In his case, you just can't see the scars."

"Where is he now?" Dead-Eye asked.

"You'll meet him tomorrow night," Nunzio said. "You can fill him in on his need to know over some dinner."

Boomer sat back and smiled. "How did you know we wouldn't turn him away?" he said. "That he's not anywhere close to what we're looking to add to the team?"

"I didn't and I don't," Nunzio said, pushing his chair back and casting his look from Boomer to Dead-Eye. "But what I did know was that if you two did take a pass on him it would have nothing to do with his being sick or that he might be gay or that you're too scared of catching whatever the hell it is he's got running through his system. It would be because he wasn't the cop you needed. But he'd get a fair shake, treated no better and no worse than the next guy. And that's the best that anybody can ask."

"Sounds to me like a deal that's done, then," Dead-Eye said, sitting back in his chair, legs stretched out under the table. "And, as far as my money goes, this team is shaping up to be a Super Bowl special. All we're missing is a blind guy and a cop in a wheelchair. Then the photo would be perfect."

"You could take out an ad," Nunzio said as he turned and walked back toward the front of the restaurant. "See what comes out of that."

"That wouldn't be of much help," Boomer said, raising a bottle and pouring out a fresh glass of wine for Dead-Eye as he rested a hand on his friend's shoulder. "At least not so far as it concerns the blind guy."

They both sat and drank their wine in silence, watching as a series of couples and small groups came into the restaurant, eager for a long night of food and fun. Boomer had been a back-table regular at Nunzio's since it first opened its doors, his safe haven away from the hard turns of an outside world he had long ago learned to distrust. The wine list was first-rate, the food Southern Italian and prime, and he could sit alone in a crowded room without feeling uncomfortable about it. And while Nunzio was probably more crook than cop, he was also a man Boomer trusted and loved, one of those rare friends who would always offer his help a click or two before you even realized you needed it.

"Putting the jokes aside," Boomer said, looking away from the other tables and across at Dead-Eye, "what do you think of this team?"

"Way too early to make a final play call on them," Dead-Eye said. "We know how good Rev. Jim is under the heat, seen it ourselves three years back. The dog is, for my money, too fucked-up *not* to be dangerous. I just hope with all that dope that went up his nose he'll be together enough to know to bite the other guys and not us."

"What about Stephanie?" Boomer asked.

"She's at the head of the class with the burn squad, there's no denying," Dead-Eye said. "But we're looking up to a whole different kind of fire with these hard-ass crews, and she hasn't spent many of her days or nights inside that homeroom. How she handles the heat is something we won't really know until we're snap in the middle of it."

"And we know a little less than zero about this new face from the crime unit Nunzio just dropped on our dinner plates," Boomer said. "I figure he was top-tier on the job; no point in Nunzio bringing him to our attention if he wasn't. What I don't know is how much his illness is going to slow him down. And having someone on the team not at full speed is not an option."

"And we're not talking about a couple of bullet wounds with him, either," Dead-Eye said. "He's landed on a disease that the guys in white coats know nothing about, let alone you and me. If it's going to be an issue, we're going to have to deal with it from the get-go."

"Way I see it, Nunzio's right: everybody on this team has wounds they need to deal with," Boomer said. "Maybe his didn't come out of any shoot-outs or from a wacko at a fire scene, but came to him they did, and he was wearing a badge and carrying a gun when it happened. That makes him as much of a cop as any of us. I figure you feel pretty much as me or you would have raised your hand about it by now."

Dead-Eye nodded and glanced across the table at Boomer, pouring out a fresh glass of wine for each of them. "My only question as regards that kid has to do with the why," he said. "He's facing a ticking clock, anywhere from six months on the short side to three years if he rides along with some luck on his end. There are a lot better ways to pass the last pages of his calendar than doing a head butt against a pack of mad-dog SA crews who will be more than eager to waste his ass faster than any disease."

"He doesn't know any other way out," Boomer said. "Same goes for you, me, and everyone that's on this team and was on the last. We're chasers, Dead-Eye, and were from that very first day we hit the streets wearing a uniform that probably didn't look as good as it felt. We chase the targets and stay on them until we nail their ass with either a cuff and convict or a bullet pattern to the chest. And we'll stay chasers up till the very end, when those bullets coming back our way bring us to a final stop. It's who we are and how we go—that's the plain and the simple of it all, and it always has been. To deny it is to turn your back on who it is we really are and what it is we were meant to be."

"That's not something I ever want to do," Dead-Eye said, pushing his wineglass off to the side. "Not back in the day and not in any of the days I have left."

"Which leaves only one door for us to go in," Boomer said. "And it might well be the last one we walk through together."

"Best that we get our asses in gear, then," Dead-Eye said. "Get our team of chasers in place and find out first taste if these drug dealers really came to town looking to play it hard."

Boomer pushed his chair back and stood up, his right hand instinctively rubbing against the gun resting in its shoulder holster. "Die or let die," he said to Dead-Eye as the two walked out of the restaurant, their heads down, footsteps light, bodies tense and poised for action.

———————————

Nunzio sat on a leather-covered stool, his back to the wall, a flat-screen TV hanging just above his head tuned to a sports recap, and watched as his friends disappeared around a tight corner. He sipped from a tall glass of Fernet Branca coated with ice and took in a slow, deep breath. He checked the time on his watch and signaled the bartender to pass him a black phone resting under the central cash register. He slowly punched in the seven digits and waited through five rings before he heard a click and a voice. "It's a go," he said. "For them and for us." He paused briefly before he pulled the phone from his ear and rested it back in its cradle.

His friends were about to start a street war.

The white van was parked in front of a loading area, its back doors swung open and wide, two men standing in the hold leaning against stacks of thick wooden crates. They were wearing long white smocks, hands jammed inside the pockets, the thin barrels of submachine guns sneaking through the open slots. They each wore an earpiece, and their eyes were doing quick scans of both the pedestrian and the street traffic. It was ten minutes past noon, a light rain falling and dark clouds hovering, on an otherwise peaceful morning in a slow-moving section of Long Island City in the borough of Queens.

"They may be aces with those guns they're holding," Rev. Jim said. "But these Boy Scouts could use a blend-in crash course, that's for certain."

"They're nothing but black crows set out to scare the field mice," Dead-Eye said. "The big birds are lying in wait in a darker place, hanging back to take out any city rats that may come their way."

"And you know this how, Obi-Wan?" Rev. Jim asked with a smile.

"For the very same reason you should know it, Rev.," Dead-Eye said. "This ain't our first time at the barbecue pit."

The three Apaches were sitting in a Chevy Impala parked on a side street across from an abandoned parking lot and in front of a gated two-family house whose aluminum siding had seen better decades. The white van was up the block from them, partially obscured by a double-parked UPS truck, its red taillights flashing. "You figure we can say the same about our three new friends?" Rev. Jim asked. "That this isn't the first time they came to chow down on a pull-pork hero?"

"We'll find out soon enough," Boomer said.

Stephanie was walking with Buttercup, the thick leash latched to the collar wrapped around the dog's neck hanging loose in her right hand. She was fifty feet away from the parked white van and shielded her eyes from the raindrops as she inched closer. The dog kept her head down, her breath slow and dragged low by a heavy wheeze as she sniffed and pawed at the filthy street and mutilated gutter. Stephanie looked over at the UPS truck and saw Andy struggling with several oversized boxes he was loading onto his cart. "Be great to see how Ash reacts if that dog takes a major shit right in front of the van," Rev. Jim said with a short laugh.

"Whose ass did you pull *Ash* out of?" Dead-Eye asked, turning in the front passenger seat of the car.

"I put a call in to a friend of mine works in the Fire Department, did a few joint cases with her when she was on the job," Rev. Jim said. "It's the nickname some of the other cops toe-tagged on her."

"He give you a why to go along with it?" Boomer asked.

"Not really," Rev. Jim said. "But mostly she worked her arsons harder than any other cop on the squad, almost as if she took each one as a personal attack. It seems she spent so much time at the burn scene that she would invariably get some of the dust, soot, and ash on her clothes or hair. And I don't have to sell anyone in this piece of shit car on how cops are when it comes to nicknames."

"She okay with it?" Dead-Eye asked.

"Seems to be," Rev. Jim said with a shrug. "She answers to it, most of the time at any rate, and if she's ever coldcocked anybody who called her that I haven't caught wind of it."

"That may well be true," Dead-Eye said. "But if it is, it's only because she hasn't spent all that much time around you as yet."

Boomer sat up straight in his seat. Dead-Eye turned away from Rev. Jim and pulled his service revolver from its holster and jammed it into the right front pocket of his thin black leather jacket. Rev. Jim crouched closer to the front seat and peered through the windshield.

"Let it all play out," Boomer said in a low voice. "We only move when Quincy gives us the signal, remember that."

"I know *we* will," Rev. Jim said. "We just have to hope he does."

"He'll be good. He's never pulled a panic attack before, no reason he should start working on one now."

"He's only gone up against dead people before," Rev. Jim said. "These zombies walk, talk, and shoot. This is his first big-league at bat inside a big ballpark and anything can happen, most of it bad."

"I'm guessing you're probably one of those the-glass-is-half-empty kind of guys," Dead-Eye said.

"I'm one of those glass-is-*empty* kind of guys," Rev. Jim said. "I go in expecting it to be the worst, and most of the time the worst is what I manage to get."

"You hands down missed your calling, Rev.," Dead-Eye said, checking the ammo clip in his gun. "You would have made one great motivational speaker. Or you could have taken a few spins at being the warm, soothing voice working the other end of a late-night suicide jumper's call."

"If you come into a situation looking to die, don't come to me and expect to hear a lie," Rev. Jim said. "That's all I'm saying on the subject."

Boomer snapped open the car door and rested one foot on the sidewalk, his eyes on the van and the UPS truck. "If only your aim is as good as your timing, we might well walk away from this one," he said. "Lock them up. It's just about showtime."

———————————

The two men with the hidden guns jumped down from the back of the van as soon as they spotted Andy walking toward them. Stephanie was on the other side of the street, Buttercup's leash folded in her back pocket, sitting with the dog on the top step of a brown cement stoop.

Andy was walking slowly, rolling a two-wheeled cart filled with large UPS packages along the rickety street. "Hey there, fellas," he said to them with a smile, taking a couple of seconds to wipe a line of sweat from his brow with the sleeve of his uniform shirt, his eyes doing a quick check on Boomer's unmarked car and on Stephanie and Buttercup. "You wouldn't happen to know where the hell Forty-seventh Avenue is, would you? Can you believe this shit? My first day alone working the big truck and here they go sending me out to a place in Queens I didn't even know *was* in Queens."

"You go two blocks up and then make your first quick right," the younger of the men said, his words garbled by a Latin accent. "Near PS 1 and across from a gas station."

"If you can't read a sign, you'll miss it," the second man said, his words less coated with any hints of his background. "Otherwise, shouldn't be a problem to find."

"Looks like you've got some big deliveries yourselves," Andy said, resting the handcart and nodding up toward the back of the van. "There must be about thirty crates crammed inside there, maybe more. What are you moving?"

"You asked about Forty-seventh Avenue and we told you where the fuck it was," the second man said, his minuscule fuse nearly burned through. "And that's the end of it. Worry about your boxes and let us worry about ours."

"I didn't mean anything by it," Andy said, stepping in closer to the two men and leaving the handcart standing at his back. "Was just curious, is all."

"Don't be," the first man said.

"It's just that you don't look like deliverymen," Andy said. "And you sure as shit don't dress the job. Which means you either got a couple of off-the-books heading your way set to unload or you're waiting to start and finish a handoff. You know the drill, I'm sure. You toss a strange face keys to the van, and in return he leaves behind a suitcase loaded with tens and twenties for you to bring back to the pound and hand over to the master of the house."

The two men turned and traded confused looks, not sure quite what to make of the UPS man, who was now standing close enough for them to shake hands. "Finish your deliveries," the second man said to Andy. "And forget that you were here and you ever saw us. This way, you get to go home alive."

"That's exactly what I plan to do," Andy said to them, his hands spread out, a wide smile spread across his face. "Especially since I only have one delivery left to make and the rest of the day and night will belong to me."

"You won't finish it standing here," the first man said. "That's for damn sure."

"I'm on it, believe you me," Andy said. "Don't you let it worry you one bit. But to be totally up front with you, I could use a little help. No heavy lifting—nothing like that. Just a little favor."

"What the fuck are you talking about?" the first man asked, his face flushed red, his upper lip beaded with sudden sweat, his pocket hand wrapped around the trigger of the semi dangling under his white coat. "You are going to die on this street, mister, you don't step off."

"That's a good line," Andy said with a nod. "Now let's get serious, we're all busy men. Just hand over the keys to your van and then you can be off and on your way. I'll give you some heads-up time so you can come up with a cool excuse for Angel as to why you left the drop point with no cash in hand and no drugs."

The two men lifted their guns toward Andy, thin barrels pointed at his chest. They froze in place when they felt two guns jammed against their spines.

"Your hands move another inch and my finger dances with the trigger," Boomer said, talking to both men, Dead-Eye by his side, gun pressed under the edge of the Kevlar vest worn by the taller of the two hitters. "Be smart and live. Let the UPS man do what he came here to do."

"Time to face the facts," Dead-Eye said. "He's better with deliveries than either one of you, so let him at it."

"You'll all be dead before any of you ever get to see what's inside those crates," the younger of the two men said, his confidence and swagger not at all diminished by the gun barrel resting on his spine. "And if I have any luck the bullets that bring your sad life to an end will come from my weapon."

"Now, if you had any luck at all you wouldn't have found your-selves on the nasty end of our bad," Dead-Eye said. "So start your move the fuck away from the van and let those semis slide down slow and loose off your shoulders, to the ground. Don't go any faster than I can blink, otherwise those expensive coats you're wearing are going to be filled with pockets."

"You should do what he tells you," Boomer said, pushing his gun barrel harder against his target's spine. "Before the UPS guy loses his cool and wipes the street with all of us."

Andy waited until the two men slipped the semis off their shoulders and let them fall to the sidewalk. He bent over, picked up both weapons, and jumped in behind the wheel of the unlocked van, spotted the keys still in the ignition, turned over the engine, and kicked the vehicle into gear. Dead-Eye slammed the rear doors shut and stood back and watched the van pull away.

"How soon before the drop car gets here?" Boomer asked the two men, his gun resting at his side now.

"Go fuck yourself, the both of you," one of the men said. "Kill us if it makes you feel like men. What difference does it make now? Angel is going to chop and pop us both for screwing up, and he's going to do a whole lot worse to you two for screwing him. And what that all totals out to is we don't need to tell you or your spook friend shit."

"Black Caddy doing a crawl over by the gas station," Dead-Eye said, gazing over the two men's shoulders. "They pulled in but didn't stop for gas or to use the shitter. Driver and his co-pilot making eyes only for us."

"You going to kill them, too?" one of the men asked. "That the great Brink's job idea you woke up with today? Leave four dead bodies in the middle of Jackson Avenue and bank on no eyeballs looking your way? That true, then you two old pistols are way past dumb town."

"There's no reason we can think of that would make us want to kill them," Boomer said, smiling and snapping his gun back into his hip holster. "I mean, why the hell would we? Those two guys in that car are going to hand over all their money to a friend of ours and—this is my favorite part of the whole episode—one of them, not sure yet which, is even going to take our dog for a walk. Why would we want to shoot anybody who does all that for us, just for the asking?"

The two hitters looked at Boomer and Dead-Eye and then turned toward the far corner of Jackson Avenue, their eyes on the late-model black Cadillac doing an idle spin in the middle lane of a Mobil gas station. "If they do end up doing even a thin slice of that," the taller man said, "you won't need to shoot me or my partner. Just hand over your gun and let us pump the bullets into each other. Better to go out that way than with Angel having at us."

"Why die if you can lie?" Dead-Eye said.

"I don't follow," the taller man said.

"There's a shocker," Boomer said.

"Let me A, B, and C it for you," Dead-Eye said. "But first I need one or two answers to one or two questions, and I need them heart-attack fast, before that Caddy moves away from that station and that lady and her dog make their play."

The two men gave each other a quick glance and an even quicker nod. "What do you need to know?" the taller man asked, looking from Boomer to Dead-Eye.

"The duo in the Caddy," Boomer said. "You laid eyeballs on them before, or they on you?"

"Wouldn't know them if they died in my arms," the taller man said. "We were supposed to hand the keys to the van over to two dudes in a black Caddy and they would toss out a loaded suitcase. That's all we were told, and that's the full run of what we were going to do."

"Either one of you deals with Angel face-to-face, or is it all worked through the ranks?" Dead-Eye asked.

The taller man pointed to the young man standing several feet to his right. "Manuel has met him," he said. "I saw him once, from a distance. I like it better that way."

"How good a liar would you say you are, Manuel?" Dead-Eye asked. "And tell *me* the truth."

"I can bullshit better than most, but if you're asking about Angel, then that's a whole other religion," Manuel said. "You try a line on him and he can smell it out even before the words get past your teeth."

"This his first deal with the two in the Caddy?" Boomer asked. "Or he trade powder for cash with them before?"

"First one I been a part of, that much I can sell you," Manuel said. "But from the way they acting, and the way this was all set to go down, it has that blind-date feel to it."

"Then Angel has more reason to trust you and not them," Boomer said. "Now, it's what you two do with that level of trust that will be the difference between a forgive-and-forget and your bodies ending up under the expressway."

"You want us to tell Angel they double-dealt us—that the ride you want me and Manuel to get on?" the taller man asked.

"That's it, hard on the head," Dead-Eye said. "They got the drop on you, kept the cash, and took the van and all the goodies inside. If you're guilty of anything, it's of not being in gear for a betray move. Now, Angel might well be pissed about that, no doubt. But not as steam angry as he will be at being taken off by a crew he trusted. You two flowing with this, or am I moving at warp speed?"

"We hear you," Manuel said. "You two are invisible. You take the dope and the cash and walk from it clean. Let Angel and the other crew have a dustup about it, each calling out the other."

"It's all one big fucking lie festival," Dead-Eye said. "There won't be a word of truth passing across anybody's lips."

"The big question is still left to hang out there," Manuel said.

"Why the fuck should we lift finger one to let you walk, leaving us with empty hands looking up at an out-for-blood-and-bone Angel?"

"If it were just about that, then that's a question with a slam-dunk answer," Boomer said. "But what we're putting out for you to grab has everything to do with keeping you alive. Because no matter what else happens, we're going to get clean away with it, cash and dope in our back pockets. And if we find ourselves with a little extra time, we might even cash out the van."

"If Angel don't bite down on what we have to tell him, if we get off on poor feet from the first step, then we're looking at the inside of a meat grinder for sure," the younger man said, sweat now forming on his forehead and his upper lip. "And I don't know if I got it in me to sell a man like him a box of wolf tickets."

"Then you'll both die," Boomer said. "Which was going to happen anyway, however you decide to turn the wheel. I figure if you follow our map, you might be able to buy yourself a little bit of time."

"We're not giving you any late-breaking news here," Dead-Eye said. "You walked into a line of work that doesn't come with any pension plans or golden parachutes. The only way out for you is with a cold bullet on a warm night. You want to live to see grandkids, go sell life insurance or old cars."

"The same holds true for the two of you?" Manuel asked.

"Everybody dies in this game, player," Boomer said. "There are no survivors."

Stephanie walked up to the black Cadillac, approaching the driver's side, Buttercup walking leash-free beside her. She smiled at the heavyset man sitting behind the wheel of the car, which was parked next to the gas-station entrance. "Why does a sweet flower like you keep time with a big, ugly dog like that?" he asked, his smile showing a thick line of crooked brown teeth. "You should have a poodle or one of those little shits look like rats."

"She's my partner," Stephanie said. "We split it all down the middle, fifty-fifty."

"Give me a for instance," the man behind the wheel said.

"All you need to do is name it—from Mama's meat loaf to the mortgage, we slice it up and share," Stephanie said, looking from the heavyset man to Buttercup and nodding at the dog as she circled toward the passenger side of the Caddy, which was still idling. "In point of fact, there's nothing that comes to mind that we don't do a fair share on. And that includes any money that might cross our path, whether earned or lifted."

The heavyset man sat up in his thick leather seat, his left hand instinctively reaching for the semi that was holstered against his rib cage. The man sitting in the passenger seat had a handgun resting loose across his lap, the fingers of his right hand gently tapping the thick barrel. He was looking up at Stephanie, her figure half shielded by the light rain, and ignoring Buttercup, who had by now inched toward his side of the car. "Thanks for sharing your shit with us, girlfriend," the heavyset man said, the smile now gone. "But I heard all I want to hear. So no need to let us stop you and your fat, ugly friend from getting to where you need to get."

"Buttercup doesn't like to be called fat, and I can't imagine she'd wrap her paws around ugly, either," Stephanie said. "I don't know any lady that would."

"I give a fuck what your dog likes or doesn't like to be called," the heavyset man said, his voice rising a few decibels. "Now you both get the fuck away from the car, this gas station, and this street. And the faster you do it the better I'll feel about it."

Stephanie leaned in closer to the car. "That's not a problem," she said, her eyes hard on the heavyset man. "Just as soon as you hand over that black bag in the back seat we'll be on our way. No fuss, no muss."

The man on the passenger side had braced his back against the car door, the gun now in his right hand and pointed at Stephanie. The heavyset man stared at Stephanie, watching her curl her fingers across the edge of the car panel, her body relaxed and at ease. "Gas station is no place for a pretty woman to die," he said to her with a slow shake of his head. "And die you will if you don't fucking move away from my car."

"I can't leave without the money," Stephanie said. "After all, a girl and a dog need to eat."

Stephanie and the heavyset man held their look for several long seconds. The man on the passenger side slid his body closer, his leather jacket making a squeaking sound as it brushed against the thick upholstery. At the other end of the car, Buttercup braced her body for a jump, her muscles silent and still, spring-coiled and ready for the action she had learned to crave.

Stephanie dived to the ground as soon as she heard the click of the gun, hammer moving against the cylinder. A bullet zoomed past her and blew a small hole in a large black garbage bin. A second shot rattled off a block of cement, inches from the base of a high-test gas pump. The latch on the driver's side snapped open and the heavyset man put one foot to the ground. Stephanie pulled a switchblade from a leather band wrapped around her right wrist, snapped it open, and jumped to her feet, six-inch blade poised to penetrate skin.

"Will you stop pumping out bullets like a blind fuckin' sniper, Malo?" the heavyset man shouted to the man in the passenger seat. "Do you fuckin' see me here or no, you retarded bastard?"

"I thought you wanted me to take her out, you fat fool," Malo said. "And you know I was keeping an eye out for you, which is why I missed her ass twice. You were twenty-five pounds lighter, bitch be bleeding."

"Let me worry about this bitch," the heavyset man said, stepping out of the car. "You just make sure you take care of the foamy-mouth bitch she came in with."

Malo swung the passenger door open and eased his legs out, gun still in his right hand, feet firm on the grease-stained ground. Buttercup caught him at chest level, pushing him back inside the car, her massive paws fast-squeezing the air out of his lungs, her hot, arid breath heavy on the man's face. Malo struggled to lift his gun hand up and put the barrel against Buttercup's side. The dog pressed her weight down on him even harder and then opened her jaw and clamped down hard on his neck, causing thick lines of blood to gush out of his wild-pulsing veins. Malo's eyes locked onto Buttercup's, filled with both fright and a maddening frenzy, as he felt the warm blood flow. The gun fell from his fingers, and his legs turned light as feather dust without any sense of feel. Buttercup held her position, waiting for her latest prey to surrender the quick.

The heavyset man was lighter on his feet than he appeared, doing a catlike pounce from the car to behind one of the gas-station pumps, knees bent, gun at the ready. He didn't flinch or turn when he heard the turmoil in the front seat of the car between Buttercup and his gunman, Malo. "Fuckin' loser," he muttered to himself. "Can't even take out a fuckin' dog bigger than a billboard. If that bowser doesn't finish his ass off, I sure as shit will."

He clenched when he heard a sneakered foot touch a thick spot of grease and he did a full circle around, his trigger finger ready for a pump-and-dump.

He never got off a round.

The knife blade caught him at chest level and penetrated bone, muscle, tissue, veins, arteries. He couldn't speak and let the gun fall to his feet. His eyes bulged, white spittle mixed with blood rushed down both sides of his mouth. He leaned against one of the gas pumps, his breath coming in slow bursts, his body sliding down the edge of the greasy tank, his elbows knocking aside the black rubber hose and nozzle. "You won't live to wear anything you spend that money on," he rasped.

"Not a problem," Stephanie said to him, turning her back. "I'm not planning on spending one cent of it."

"What, then?" the heavyset man asked.

"I'm going to burn it," Stephanie said.

She snapped her fingers and waited as Buttercup ran to her side. She went over to the car, checked the bleeder in the front seat, opened the rear door, and looked into the thick black bag, stuffed with hundred-dollar bills. She pulled a red cylinder out of the rear pocket of her jeans, snapped down on a black button, and tossed it into the car. Then she and Buttercup turned and crossed Jackson Avenue, leaving two dying men in their wake.

They were two corners down when an explosion tore the car to shreds, sent the gas pumps hurtling into the air, and transformed the area into an inferno. "Lesson to be learned there?" Stephanie said to Buttercup. "Don't ever play with fire."

10

Angel slammed his fist down on the hand-carved desk. "What the fuck am I running here?" he shouted to the group of six men, one from each of his respective crews. "A van filled with high-end dope disappears and cash meant for my pockets is left in the back of a car, burning like wood on a winter night. And the doers, so far as any genius in this room can ascertain, belong to no gang we've ever heard of. And not even the two bright bulbs who survived the take-and-bake can finger them. Did I ace that quiz?"

"We'll find out who they are and where they are, don't worry," one of the men, the youngest of the six, finally said. "All we need is a little more time. The job just happened a day ago; we have to get people in place to get the answers we need."

Angel stared silently at the young man for a few moments. "Your name is what again?" he asked.

"Ramon," the young man said. "I used to run for you in the old country. I was an altar boy back in the day. Remember?"

Angel reached under his desk and came up with a black semiautomatic clutched in his right hand. He pumped three bullets into Ramon, sending the young man reeling to the floor, then let a moment pass as a thick pool of dark blood blended into the room's antique Persian rug. Angel pushed his chair back, stood, leaned across his desk, and fired two more slugs into Ramon's silent body. He then sat back down and looked up at each of the five men standing quietly around their dead partner. "Do you all need more time or was it just him?" He waited for a few moments, letting the silence answer his question. "In that case," he said, "how about I hear what we do know about these fuckers?"

"There are a lot of rumors out on the street," one of the men said. He was tall, with a solid gym build and dark bangs partially hiding the upper half of his handsome face. He spoke with a Latin accent. "Not a lot of facts, which is no surprise given the way they pulled the job. I don't think they're hooked up with any of the other crews, especially not the Italians."

"And what's the why for that?" Angel asked.

"No crew—and I mean not a one—is going to go out and hire a team to take us off and have them come back in the house with only half the haul," the man said. "There are no deal points to be made by burning up a half million dollars."

"It sure as shit got our attention, Eduardo," Angel said. "And let's do a for instance and say that's what they wanted to get out of this whole game from the get-go. Throw down a flag and let us know they're out there and put us in their scope. What if that's their deal? What if they don't give a fuck about the dope or the money, any of it? What if they're just coming in for us?"

"To take over our turf?" Eduardo asked.

"No," Angel said with a slow shake of his head. "To come in and take back what used to be their ground."

"Which dealers are we talking about here?" Eduardo asked. "Any turf left that has anybody else's name stamped on it has either us or the G-Men hovering over it. All the other crews have either stepped back or signed on."

"What if they're not dealers," Angel said. "What if they work the other end of the wide avenue?"

"We got every squad and unit working the drug trade on our radar," Eduardo said. "It was the first step we took when we walked out onto the field. We know all the badges, good ones and bad. If this was pulled off by cops, it would have hit our ears in less than an hour's time."

"Not these cops," Angel said. "They don't cut across anybody's radar. They work on their own timetable and for their own reasons."

"Which are what?" asked a thin young man standing with his back against the mahogany wall.

"They don't want a piece of our business," Angel said as he looked from one face to the next. "They only want a piece of us."

"You know where they crib?" Eduardo asked.

"I know someone who can find out," Angel said.

"What do you need us to do?" Eduardo asked.

Angel stood and rested the flat of his hands against his hips, the crease on his hand-tailored slacks butcher-blade sharp, his shirt crisp as a late-autumn morning. He bent his upper body a few inches forward and stared down at Ramon, a thick pool of blood forming around his back and waist, and then looked up at the men in the room. "You tell me," he said.

11

CHAPTER

The Apaches sat around a wood table in the basement of an abandoned building that once housed the busiest pizzeria on the West Side. The front windows were painted black and boarded up with thick planks of plywood. Boomer sat at the head of the table, a large blackboard hanging on the wall at his back. Rev. Jim looked around the room and took a slow sip from a large cup filled with iced espresso. "I figure the Batcave was booked," he said.

Boomer nodded. "Once we get it set up the way we need it to be, it'll look a lot better than it does now. And it's a solid bet that no one will look for us in here, which means we can work and plan clean and free."

"How'd we come to be in possession of such a palace?" Andy asked.

"Ash found it for us," Dead-Eye said, pointing a finger at Stephanie. "She worked the arson investigation that gutted the place a few years back."

"No one's going to come looking, because no one really cares,"

Ash said. "The case is still going through the courthouse turnstiles and will be for a few years more, at the very least. By then, we should be clear out of here."

"Are we going to live here?" Rev. Jim asked. "I mean, through the run of this?"

"I was thinking that, yes," Boomer said. "We'll clean it up some, maybe even paint it in spots, then bring in all the equipment we'll need, or as much of it as we can get, and stock it with enough food and drink to keep us content for as long as the job lasts."

"Why the quick change?" Rev. Jim asked. "We didn't do that the last time. What makes this one so different that we all have to become frat brothers?"

"Each job goes its own way," Boomer said. "The last time, we had one crew out to kill us. This time, we have two that we know of and whoever else wants to take a shot once they catch wind we're back on the dime. And, while we're on the subject, it might not just be us that will have a gun pointed our way. If any of you have family you want covered, now would be the time to come across with that gift vacation you promised but never delivered on. Just to play it all-the-way safe."

"Besides, we worked out of a squad room when we were on the job or, in Quincy's case, the morgue room," Dead-Eye said. "This is no different."

"Who bunks with the dog?" Quincy asked, pointing at the slumbering body of Buttercup.

"I think we'll make the lady herself make that call," Dead-Eye said. "She's earned at least that much."

"I'll follow your lead, Boom," Rev. Jim said. "I have in the past, and see no reason to point my compass in another direction now."

"Let me hear the 'but' that follows all that," Boomer said,

looking away from the others and squaring down eye to eye with Rev. Jim.

"Just want to make sure you've thought all this through with a clear view," Rev. Jim said. "Having us all in one place like this could be as much of a risk as it is a reward. It's not like we haven't each been on high-end jobs before. We should all know how to work as a team without the need to turn it into Camp Apache."

Boomer stared down at his folded hands for several long, silent seconds and then did a slow nod. "You've slept in worse places in your life, that I know," he finally said. "So how about we make a move past that and get to what this really is all about. There always comes a time when the air needs to be cleared, and for us, every one of us, now is that time."

"Fair enough," Rev. Jim said. "Clear air's always better to breathe. I need to ask Quincy here a few questions before I can roll with this."

"Ask away," Quincy said, sitting up straight in his hard-back chair. "I didn't come in looking to hide anything."

"I know this disease you have is a killer," Rev. Jim said. "I wish I could change that, but it's not in my hands. Now, I don't care how you got it or where. But what I do need to know—in fact, I think we all do—is how much and how often it can slow you up. Because we're going to be fighting in thick growth, and all we'll have going in are the guns in our hands and the partner by our side."

"Most days are good," Quincy said, not backing away from the hard line. "So good there are times when I forget I even have it."

"What about the days that aren't so good?" Rev. Jim asked.

"You mean the days when you just want to curl up in a corner and jam a loaded gun in your mouth because the pain is so bad?" Quincy asked.

"Yes," Rev. Jim said.

"They come on sudden and stay as long as unwanted company," Quincy said. "Mix the worst flu you've ever had with the pain of a knife wound and maybe you'll have half a clue of how bad it is. It's in those hours, lying in a bed soaked through with sweat, that you know the time you have left is short and it doesn't matter. You *want* to die. You *want* that pain to go away. You *want* to be at peace."

"Do you get a heads-up?" Dead-Eye asked.

"Sometimes, but not always," Quincy said. "You might feel a little weaker the day before or you might start to feel your body drag a bit, but most times it hits like a heart attack: hard, fast, relentless."

"So it could happen out on the field?" Boomer asked.

"Yes," Quincy said. "And that's something for each of you to think about before we take another step. Rev. Jim is right to ask the questions. This is a serious business, and I never want to be the one to put another life in jeopardy. I guess this is as good a time as any to see if you want me dealt out of the game. However it is you decide that, it's your call to make."

"You're not alone," Rev. Jim said. "I just asked because I needed to know what to look for, to be able to see it coming before it landed. I can't help you, none of us can, if we don't know at least that. And on the flip side, you each should know about us. You're not the only cripple in this room. Boomer's lung could give out at any time, same as Dead-Eye's bad leg. And I don't know Ash well, but I don't need to be the Amazing Kreskin to know she's got her dark spots like the rest of us. And me, I'm held up by glue and pins. I can fold at any time and will look to you to help bail me out. The dog does give me pause, but shit, she's just as fucked-up as the rest of this crew."

"I guess that just leaves me," Ash said. "There anything any of you need to know about me that you already don't?"

"You single or married?" Rev. Jim asked.

"Single," Ash said.

"Anybody special in your movie line?" Rev. Jim asked. "You know, somebody makes your heart jump a few beats?"

"No, there isn't," Ash said.

"Are you looking?" Rev. Jim asked.

"Always," Ash said. "Just not your way."

Rev. Jim smiled and turned toward Buttercup, leaning down to rest a hand on her massive head. "I guess that leaves just you, sweetheart," he said.

Buttercup slowly opened her large eyes and let out a low growl. Rev. Jim eased up and pulled his hand away.

"It's good to know you haven't lost your touch with the ladies," Dead-Eye said. "They still flock to you like flies to rancid meat."

"What can I say?" Rev. Jim said, his arms held out, a wide smile on his face. "I was cursed with the gift."

"When you get a minute," Boomer said, returning the smile, "you might consider giving it back."

The loud laughter of the group echoed off the walls of the shuttered pizzeria.

12

—— CHAPTER ——

Natalie Robinov watched Tony Rigs toss a baseball into the air and take a hard swing at it with an aluminum baseball bat. The ball flew skyward at the sound of the ping, coming down at an arc toward a young boy in a clean uniform and a worn glove. He was standing on the edge of the infield dirt when the ball landed with a thud inside his open mitt. "Nice way to grab, Joey," Tony Rigs shouted out to the boy, pointing the head of the bat in his direction. "You see, all that practice time does come with a payoff." The boy smiled, nodded, and tossed the ball back.

The fenced-in Little League field was crammed full with teams in full practice, four squads stationed in each corner of the well-cared-for Nassau County grounds. Tony Rigs looked out at his squad, a dozen preteen boys and girls each outfitted in a crisp uniform with "Calhoun Construction Company" stenciled across the front, and turned to Natalie. "You should have seen them two weeks ago, when they first took to the field," he said. "A couple of them had never even caught a ball before, if you could imagine. Now, they're rounding out pretty good, starting to get the feel of a team, which is what you need before that first game is even played."

"If you're looking for an assistant coach, look in some other direction," Natalie said, standing on the other side of the mesh fence, her arms at her sides, her short skirt and tanned legs getting the desired effect. "I know less than nothing about the game, and what little I do know bores me."

"That's too bad," Tony Rigs said, tossing her a smile and getting ready to lift another ball toward the short end of the outfield. "Knowing this game could help make you even better at your job. I mean, the lessons you take from one field can carry over with ease to the next."

"I'm very good at my job," Natalie said. "I'm even better when I'm allowed to do it. Now, since I *did* drag my ass all the way out here as per your request, it would be a solid move for you to step up and tell me why."

"Way I see it," Tony Rigs said, handing the bat off to one of his players, "our league is down to three top-tier teams—my crew, yours, and the South Americans. The rest of the bunch are nothing better than second division, if that. So that leaves the open question of who grabs the top prize and—this I know from baseball—it's not always the best team on paper that wins it all. It's the one that makes it a goal to work together and pulls in place the best and the smartest moves. With me so far?"

"On every word," Natalie said. "And if I understand the direction your conversation will soon be heading down, then the smart move would call for me to do a hookup with you at the expense of the South Americans. I hit that ball out of the place?"

"Out of the *park*," he said, impressed as much with her wit as with her legs. "If that were to happen, how bothered would you be by it?"

"Not one bit," Natalie said. "Just as long as my end of the action tallied up to be as big as yours. I *know* the kind of deal I can get out of the South Americans. I just don't know if I can trust them to hold to it."

"But you trust me to hold to mine?" Tony Rigs said.

"I don't trust anyone," Natalie said. "But I believe it's in your best interest to stay on our good side. On top of which, the Italians have always let others get a cut of the action, often reaching out to groups other crews wouldn't go near. The same doesn't hold true for the South Americans. They want to rule the business, and would very much prefer to do it alone. And if killing either one of us guarantees them that, then they would let fly the bullets and the blood flow. So, while I don't trust you one iota, it can safely be argued that I have a better understanding of your motives."

"We stand on common ground, then," Tony Rigs said, his eyes doing a roll from the field to Natalie. "And that ground will only get firmer and a lot richer if you stay on the sidelines and let what's going to play out over the next week or so go the full run."

"So long as none of my action gets touched, you won't hear from anyone that connects to me," Natalie said. "But if any hand touches profit, those hands will be cut off. No hesitation."

"Can't guarantee that won't happen, but I'll do my best to see you're not bothered," Tony Rigs said. "But a lot of what's going to go down I'll only catch ear of after the fact, same as you."

"If it's not your crew moving on the SAs, then who?" Natalie asked. "And no bullshit, this is one part of the story I need to know, and there's no deal between us until I do."

"You got a Russian name, but an Italian temper and body to boot," Tony Rigs said, tossing out a smile and waiting for one in return.

"Save the sweet for your weekend side dish," Natalie said, not playing along. "Your boring game is going to start soon, and I still haven't heard anything of interest."

"Cops," Tony Rigs said with a resigned shrug. "Ex-cops, you want the full facts. A small team of hard chargers looking for a taste of the get-even. They're outnumbered and outgunned, but if they play it smart—and more often than not they do—they stand a puncher's chance of drawing blood."

"And what are they looking to clear?" Natalie asked, digging deeper. "They want the money? The dope? The turf? All three?"

"It's not even close to something like that," Tony Rigs said. "Least not with these guys. They were as stain-free as Mister Clean on the job, even more so once they were shot and stabbed off it."

"Which leaves them what?" Natalie asked, looking off into the distance.

"Not everybody out there's like us, always looking to bite off a piece and steal it away," he said. "Sometimes the good guys are really just that."

"How well do you know these cops?" she asked.

"I don't know the whole team, just the two who call the shots," Tony Rigs said. "With them I got a history. They stayed on the up-and-up with me, and I did my best to steer any business away from their sectors. If any lines were crossed, they did what they had to do and I did what I needed to do. We each knew the street rules and we followed them."

"And what about now?" Natalie said. "They're not cops any-more. They can't make arrests, can't authorize wires, can't even ask a question and expect to get an answer in return. Which makes them what?"

"Dangerous," Tony Rigs said. "You're right, they can't run any of that pull-over-and-give-me-your-license bullshit. But they also don't have to follow any by-the-book fucking procedures, either. They pinpoint their targets and go after them until one of the two sides does a death drop."

"And what are we supposed to do while all this is going on?"

"Give them what little help we can, for starters," Tony Rigs said. "But, for the most part, the best thing we can do is just stay out of their fucking way."

"Is this a cause for them, or is it personal?" Natalie asked.

"Does it matter?" he asked.

"Just curious," Natalie said. "And, for the record, personal is always better."

"If that's the case, then this job is the fucking lotto of personal," Tony Rigs said. "The priest sent a top-tier team of shooters into a restaurant a while back, no doubt you caught wind of the details. They dropped their targets and got credit for the job. But they also left some mind-your-own-business bystanders dead in the bullet storm. One of them was a blood relative to the lead cop. She was a good kid. Now, they're going to give it all they got left to make the padre wish he'd never put in his order."

"And you think they can pull this off?" Natalie asked, eager to get insights into Boomer's plans. "Angel has wiped out entire police *departments* in his home turf; he's not going to be off running for the Depends when he gets wind of a small team of retired badges on his ass. And if they toss the G-Men and the rest of the SAs in their scope, then they best put in an early order for one of those big-time funerals cops like to give each other."

"Take them all down—not much of a chance on that," Tony Rigs said with a shake of his head. "But they'll put a dent in them, guaranteed. These guys don't work by any cop rules and never did, even when they *were* cops. They'll play one against the other, hit them fast and hard, cause all sorts of shit to slap against the fan belt. Even if they only take down fifteen percent of the SAs, let's just say, then we still walk away from this with a lead. There's no downside for either one of us. We wait for the dust to settle and the blood to dry and grab what we can of what there is to call our own. Be just like taking candy from a crackhead."

"You their only contact?" Natalie asked.

"We'd like to keep it low," Tony Rigs said. "Not make it a finger-walk through the Yellow Pages. The SAs get even a sniff of my involvement in the cause, they'll be looking to spill and splatter my crew. Not to mention how eager they'll be to do a head butt with your team."

"I don't like watching from the sidelines," Natalie said. "It never has worked to my benefit, having others do my dirty deeds. Right now, I've got no problems with the South Americans, and they seem to be staying away from my coastline. That will change over time, I'm aware, but why should I go looking to shake their cabanas when they haven't given me cause?"

"Save the bullshit for a stranger," he said, a wide smile across his face. "You've had eyes for their turf since you first took control of the steering wheel. Same as me—no different, no better."

"If that's true, then I probably have my eyes on yours as well," Natalie said, returning the smile.

"Bet your pretty Russian ass you do," Tony Rigs said. "But that's a battle for another day. Right now, let's eat what we got in front of us. Let's let these guys put a dent in the SA action, much as they can. Once the cocaine powder settles, we'll see where we're at."

"And until then?" Natalie asked. "What?"

"All you need to do is just sit back, put your face up to the warm sun, and enjoy the game," Tony Rigs said. "Sometimes this business is just as simple as that."

Natalie nodded. Maybe it won't be so simple this time, she thought.

13

"You don't know what you're asking of me here," Sean Valentine said. "Passing some classified folders over to your side of the table is one thing. Helping to waste a cop is a whole other pot of soup. Not at all what I signed on to do."

"You signed up to do what you were told," Talbot said, flaunting his lack of patience, channeling his anger. "We didn't rent you, Mr. Valentine. We bought you, and we own you and your services until we determine otherwise."

"I'm *not* going to off another cop," Valentine said, pounding a hard fist on the Formica countertop. "That's the plain and the simple of the equation."

"First of all, he's a former policeman, long retired," Talbot said. "And second and more important to your concerns is you won't be the one killing him. I wouldn't ask that of even you. All I require is that you place him in a position where it becomes an easy job for one of my shooters."

"From what I know and heard, you don't need me to do any of

that," Valentine said, sitting back in his chair and reaching a vein-rich hand out for a near-empty tumbler of Jack Daniel's. "You'll find him and his crew real easy. That's because they'll be either right in front of you or right up your ass. Either way, it's a no-miss."

"Which should make your task all the easier," Talbot said, his words hot with the contempt he always reserved for those who sell off their honor for cash but still insist on maintaining a certain degree of respect. "You'll track their activities and then alert me as to the most opportune time to strike. That is, after all, part and parcel of why your esteemed and dangerous benefactor doles out such a hefty cash-filled envelope each and every month."

"And if I refuse?" Valentine asked, a hint of a step-back creeping into his voice. "What then?"

Talbot sat back, smiled, and stared at the corrupt cop in the designer suit. "I really don't think that's a question you want me to answer," he said. "Though I doubt it would be much of a stretch for you to imagine the inevitable reality. Suffice it to say you're not the only stained cop eager to own a larger home or impress both an older wife and a younger mistress."

Sean Valentine took a deep breath and let his gaze drift away from Talbot, taking in the dark wood furnishings of the old-school club the mob middlemen always chose as their meet-and-greet place. Valentine was now in his mid-forties, a respected member of the police commissioner's hand-selected inner circle, his career marked by a well-timed series of promotional leaps that were accomplished less by his street actions than by his ability to procure the right favor for the right official at the most appropriate time. It was a skill he had mastered in the years since he graduated from an all-boys Catholic high school in Queens, back when the prospect of a career in civil service seemed the fastest and easiest avenue for him to secure a weekly paycheck that brought with it the potential for a number of side benefits. Valentine viewed the Police Department as a stepping-stone to greater riches, knowing full well that the only way to achieve such a goal was to work the corrupt side of the ledger.

He began his climb up the greased pole with short-change shakedowns and pocket-cash handouts, rousting local merchants into doling out weekly payments in return for the extra spin of a cruiser around the street. He upped the ante soon after locking in an assignment to an élite and eventually disgraced anti-crime unit working the rooftops and hallways of the troubled Hastings housing projects in the Bronx. In his eighteen months of running buy-and-bust operations against the Rain Reynolds crack crew, Valentine proved adept at racking up impressive arrests with minimum work while stripping high-end dealers of both drugs and large sums of cash. Covered by the large shadows of a four-member team of hard chargers, he averaged a low-five-figure graft income each month while still managing to catch the roving eye of police brass impressed with his tactical abilities and polished manner. A bogus arrest highlighted by a tainted shooting did little to damage a reputation he helped fuel by utilizing prearranged testimony from a string of street players whose pockets he helped line. It took Valentine all of seven years to bring to fruition his plan of plunder while working under the guise of a respected member of the NYPD. By the time he put on his captain's jacket and walked into his first precinct command in Brooklyn, Sean Valentine was a fully purchased and paid for cop, earning a high-six-figure illicit income and at the beck and call of any crime boss with access to a phone.

In all his years of reaching for bribes and functioning successfully in a tight and well-constructed web of corruption, Valentine had never butted heads with a buyer quite as cunning and ruthless as Jonas Talbot. And more than any drug dealer or crew leader, he had solid reasons to fear Talbot, convinced that the fixer would have his hide wasted as easily as he poured himself a fresh tumbler of bourbon.

"I'll work to set it up," Valentine said. "I would just as soon not be there when it goes down, if it's all the same to you."

"Your reluctance will be duly noted and brought to the attention of all parties concerned," Talbot said. "And I'm sure it won't be a cause for alarm for anyone involved, so long as the target is within the shooter's scope."

"How soon you looking to get this all done?" Valentine asked.

"They've already begun pecking at our seed," Talbot said, "which has ruffled feathers. Using that as an accurate gauge, I would say no more than a week at the most."

"What makes you so convinced that with one of their own out of the way the other five in the group won't keep up the fight?" Valentine asked.

"The one they refer to as Boomer is who leads their charge," Talbot said. "He is also the one who sustained the personal loss. He has more at stake than the others. Minus his hand at the helm, the rest will soon enough lose their desire for the big fight and scatter back to their previous posts. Perhaps not right away, but soon enough for it to matter."

"And if they don't?" Valentine asked. "If you're wrong and Boomer going down turns out to be a rallying cry for them and others out there who want to be them? What happens then?"

"Then you will be one very busy individual, Mr. Valentine," Talbot said. "And, I might add, an even richer one—which is, I presume, your overall intent."

"That and living long enough to spend all of the cash, right down to the very last buffalo nickel," Valentine said. "In my book, the two go hand in glove."

"Then it's best we get ourselves to the starting gate," Talbot said with a wave of his right hand. "And bear in mind, do your utmost to place the target in a situation that makes allowances for only a minimum of distractions. We would prefer, at all costs, not to live through a repeat of our recent restaurant adventure."

"I wasn't anywhere near that job," Valentine said as he eased his chair back, stood, and adjusted the jacket of his blue suit. "The fault there is on the triggers. The setup and timing were all spot on."

"I was merely using it as an illustration and not as an outlet to cast blame," Talbot said. "It is the type of incident that we must all strive to avoid, even if it does send a loud and rather effective signal to our enemies as to the seriousness of our intent."

"I could use some spread money," Valentine said. "I'll need to coat a lot of palms if I'm going to get this job done the way you want."

"First the dead cop," Talbot said, turning his gaze away from Valentine and concluding the conversation. "Then the dead presidents."

The drug dealer with the thin, long scar running down the left side of his face, from his forehead to his jawline, stood with his back firmly against a chipped blue wall, his eyes opened wide enough to pop, sweat running off his light frame like water off the edge of a cliff. His upper body was trembling, and he had soiled a new pair of off-the-rack dark gray cargo pants. His legs were spread wide apart and held in place by Buttercup's head, the police dog's large mouth firmly locked around the dealer's crotch, teeth separated from skin by only a verbal command.

"Motherfucker, you don't need to go and fuckin' do what you lookin' to do," the dealer said to her. "Somebody give this bitch something to eat!"

Buttercup had sauntered into the small empty bar on East 117th Street, moving past empty stools and cheap leather booths as if she were a long-running regular. She looked around, her eyes moist from the dual hit of stale beer and old smoke, her paws sticky and set to slip from the wet spots of booze that filled pockets of the dented and rusted fake-tile floor. The dealer spotted her when he came out the back room, a lit cigarette dangling from his thin lips, his arms hauling a case of warm Coronas. "You either piss or shit in here and I will fuckin' waste your big sorry ass," he said to Buttercup. "Cut you up and toss you to the rats in the basement. Let them feast on your hide."

Buttercup held her place, watching as the dealer tossed the Coronas into a back booth, flicked open a red-handled switchblade, and walked toward her. She locked her rear paws and waited for the dealer to stand close enough to jab the sharp point of the blade against the soft part of her right shoulder. The quick flick stung and drew blood, which did a slow roll down her hide and onto a set of grimy black tiles. "I'm telling you to turn and walk the fuck out," the dealer said, tossing a hard kick Buttercup's way. The blow, softened a bit by the man's bare foot, caught her on the flat end of her stomach, a few inches from one of her many battle scars. "I'm not the kind of fucker bitch like you needs to be handing out grief tickets to, hear me? I don't like dogs and I especially hate big dogs, and you are, hands down, the biggest fucker I ever laid my momma's eyes on, hand to Jesus."

The dealer held the knife at eye level and smiled down at Buttercup. He steadied his feet and crouched down a bit, giving him both leverage and position to plunge the blade deep into the dog's rib cage. Buttercup held her hard stance and timed what would be her first and only move, no growl or sound giving any indication that she was anything more than a large, tired-eye stray who had casually wandered into the wrong bar at the worst time, leaving herself open to the death-rattle intentions of a dealer floating high on his own merchandise.

As the knife flew through the dank air, earmarked for a plunge into her right side, the wounded police dog made her leap, catching the dealer in center square, her strong, rigid jaw locked down on the man's crotch, her eyes open, her body relaxed. She waited out the dealer's panic-fueled attempts to dislodge her teeth from his body, the knife long gone from his hand, released in that first surprised rush of pain and now replaced by closed-fist punches that rained down on Buttercup from both sides. Each blow grew weaker in intensity, and she clamped down tighter.

The dealer turned his head when he heard the front door swing wide open and saw Rev. Jim walk in and nod in his direction. "This your dog?" he managed to ask.

Rev. Jim ignored the question and instead stepped behind the bar and reached down into a sink full of ice chips and water and pulled up a cold bottle of Dr. Brown's root beer. "I used to drink this shit all the time when I was a kid," he said, more to himself than to either the dealer or the dog. "Could never get enough of it. I tell you true, this is *exactly* what I needed after the day I just had for myself."

Rev. Jim used the edge of the wood to snap off the bottle top and took a long swig of the cold drink. He closed his eyes and let a wide smile spread across his face as he leaned his arms on top of the bar. "That more than hit the spot, let me tell you," he said to the dealer, glancing at the thin man shivering across from him, the dog wedged in between his legs. "Bet you could use one right about now. Am I right on that or not?"

"Fuck you and fuck the drink," the dealer said, red-zone anger sidestepping the pain and the fear. "Don't need or want any of that shit from you. What I do *want* is for you to get your hound away from my balls. Right now that's the only business you and me got that's worth even close to two shits."

"I can't help you there, Little Jack," Rev. Jim said. "I wish I could, dealer, really do. But my hands are cuffed on that particular request."

"Why the fuck not?" Jack said. "One word from you and I bet this dog would roll over and lick her own ass. Don't fuck with me. Now's not the time."

"Buttercup's not my dog," Rev. Jim said, lifting the bottle of root beer and bringing it to his lips. "And I can't control what doesn't belong to me."

"The bitch ain't yours, then how come you know her name?" Jack asked. "Answer me that, fuckhead."

"We work together, me and the lady," Rev. Jim said. "Haven't been together long, truth be told. In fact, this is our first time out as partners."

"What the fuck kind of Starsky and Hutch bullshit scam you looking to peddle my way?" Jack asked, his body so heavy with sweat it gleamed in the early-afternoon sunlight. "What the fuck kind of a cop has himself a dog as a partner?"

"You don't even know close to the half of it," Rev. Jim said. "Get yourself ready for this one. That dog not only outranks me, she earns a bigger take-home pension—tax-free to boot, I would like to add."

"You shittin' on me," Jack said, his suspicion coated with a small dose of grudging respect for the dog whose snout was wedged between his thighs.

"If only," Rev. Jim said. "Sad truth of it is if old Buttercup there wants to rip your balls off and turn them into a set of doggie chews, there isn't a damn thing I can do about it, other than stand and watch you scream like a man on fire. It's her call all the way, is what I'm trying to tell you here. I'm nothing to her but a trusty backup."

"I don't fuckin' believe any of this," Jack howled. "If you can't get my ass out of this situation, then who the fuck can?"

"Nobody I know," Rev. Jim said with a shrug. "But I *can* try to reason with her. She is, after all, a lady and might listen if a reasonable request was put in front of her wet nose."

"Like what?" Jack asked.

"Well, let's say—and we're just talking here now—you gave me a heads-up as to where the G-Men brothers crib out," Rev. Jim said. "You know, the real place—not that club in Spanish Harlem that they drink and eat in most nights. I hear something solid like that and maybe I can start to do a little whisper work in Buttercup's ear."

"I do that and it's not just my balls I got to do a wonder worry about losing," Jack said. "Those crazy fuckers get wind of me moving my lips in their direction, they'd turn my ass into a Big Mac with cheese before the morning sun kicks up. Sorry, badge, that's one question that comes with a no-can-do label attached."

"It's your call," Rev. Jim said with a slight shrug. "I just threw it out there to save you some grief and heavy-duty explaining down at the emergency room. But—and these are the last words about your balls that will ever pass my lips—the dog is here now and she has no intention of letting you leave without your care package locked in her jaw. The G-Men, on the other hand, won't know you dropped a dime for a while still, and there's a chance—not a good chance, I'll give you, but a slight one—that they may never find out. I were you, other than wanting to put a bullet in my forehead I would never turn my back on that little bird in the fist."

"You don't know them, man," Jack said, his voice cracking from the strain. "You did, you wouldn't be talking the way you are."

"That may well be so," Rev. Jim said, stepping out from behind the bar and heading for the front door, easing past Buttercup and Jack. "But I do know that dog. All the drugs went up her nose, God only knows what she *thinks* she's got her teeth wrapped around."

"Where the fuck you think you going?" Jack asked, practically shouting out the question.

"Thought I'd go and wait outside," Rev. Jim said. "My lead partner here seems to have it all well in hand. Besides, I'm not the kind of somebody you want around when there's lots of blood flow going on. You toss in a heavy handful of screaming, and all that goes with it, and I'm like an old lady at her son's funeral. I know my place, and it's for sure not here. You need anything, just give a shout-out."

Rev. Jim opened the door and walked out into the harsh sun and cool breeze of a late New York City morning. He stepped across the empty avenue and stopped in front of the driver's side of the dark sedan, engine running, front and rear windows all down.

"How much longer?" Boomer asked, sitting behind the wheel, sipping from a takeout cup of cold coffee.

"Any minute now, be my guess," Rev. Jim said. "Have to hand it to that dog—she held her position and didn't move for as long as I was in there. I've had partners with two legs I couldn't count on to do the same."

"Buttercup's a pro," Dead-Eye said from the passenger side. "I don't give a shit how much dope went up her nose, she's still prime-beef cop."

"Let's hope the same is true for us," Rev. Jim said.

The scream that came out of the shuttered bar was loud enough to shatter glass.

It echoed off the slits of the abandoned buildings where windows once stood and roared with the strength of a winter storm down the wide avenue. Rev. Jim looked at Boomer and Dead-Eye and then did a slow nod. "If Little Jack's ever in the mood to talk, I figure now's the time," Rev. Jim said.

"He's going to be giving out information he didn't even know he had," Dead-Eye said. "Unless he goes into shock and bleeds to death first. That would be the only luck he's going to catch on this day."

"Just in time, too," Rev. Jim said, turning away from the car and walking back toward the bar. "I'm ready for another root beer."

Boomer and Dead-Eye watched Rev. Jim dodge a passing van and do a short run into the bar, slowly opening and then closing the front door. "He going to be okay, you think?" Dead-Eye asked.

"Okay enough to tell us what we came here looking to know," Boomer said in a matter-of-fact tone.

"Not talking about the dealer," Dead-Eye said. "I meant Rev. Jim."

Boomer turned his head away from the street and gazed across the front seat at Dead-Eye, making sure that the concern in his words matched the look on his face. "You have a reason why he wouldn't be okay?"

"Nothing I would pin down as solid evidence," Dead-Eye said. "It's just a stomach feel, is all."

"Tell me, anyway," Boomer said. "Since right now a stomach feel is the best we have to work on."

"I don't think he's up for another round," Dead-Eye said. "He seems slower, and off his game. Now, it could be because we've been away for a few years and he's still in spring-training mode. He'll kick it soon as the first bullets land across his bow. That the case, then I just wasted nothing more than a few hours of worry time."

"And if it's more than that?" Boomer asked.

"Then we have ourselves one serious problem," Dead-Eye said. "We both know this current team is nowhere near as good as the last one we put together, at least on the paper side of it. Ash is a solid cop, courage with a capital K, but she didn't log a lot of hours cracking heads and doesn't sniff out problems before they hit. Quincy is a plus at least until his mind steps up and starts to betray his ass, and then he turns into a liability. And it's no secret

Buttercup is one cool breeze away from a cocaine flashback, and who the fuck knows where that shit leads once it hits the roof?"

"Which leaves you and me," Boomer said.

"Yes, it does, old friend," Dead-Eye said with a smile. "Now, we both still have the taste and the stomach for the fight, but we always had that and probably will until we take the dirt nap. Truth is, though, we're not close to being as good as we were three years ago and, shit, we weren't all that good even then. We just don't have any quit in us, and that often can make up for a lot of other negatives."

"Rev. Jim's always played it close," Boomer said. "Even when he was on the job and at full strength, he always stood out as a loner, kept it low-key until the heat got up to a boil and then he went off. He was there for us packed and heavy when we needed him the last time, and if there was anyone back then who had the doubts about him it was me, as you might recall."

"He's missing that look," Dead-Eye said. "I know he likes to go his own way—that's his style and it suits him, even helps make him the great cop. But that hard-ass look brings with it the hunger for a fight, the need to be found dead rather than get the taste of being on the losing side of the field. And that's not there now, least not so as I can see."

"He could have said no, Dead-Eye, without any worries about being judged," Boomer said, looking back out across the avenue toward the bar. "I didn't pull a gun on him or kidnap his cat, force him to sign up for the second tour. He came in feetfirst and hands raised high. Nobody pushed him in the pool—he jumped."

"Rev. Jim's a sucker for a hopeless cause," Dead-Eye said. "If you stepped back to give it a look, you'd find that's true of most cops. It's not by any accident that Saint Jude's our patron saint. And at the moment there's no more hopeless cause out there than our little merry band of brothers."

"I'll talk to him, feel it out, see if you're anywhere close to being on the mark with this one," Boomer said. "But if you're right and Rev. Jim is on shaky turf, then we'll be down one cop just as the kickoff whistle blows. And that's not good for anybody's health."

"I can go that one better," Dead-Eye said.

"How so?"

"I'm the one with the doubts," Dead-Eye said. "Only holds then I should be the one who sits across from Rev. Jim and asks the question. I'm the one that needs to hear the right answer."

Boomer looked at Dead-Eye and nodded. "There's more to this than what you just put out there," he said. "Why don't you share it so we can both lose some sleep over it?"

"I'm not ready for that yet, Boomer," Dead-Eye said. "Right now all I've got is a puzzle missing a few pieces. Until I get the full picture, there's nothing else to say."

"It's your play, then," Boomer said. "But we don't have much time for diplomacy, so the sooner you get this done, the better we'll all feel. Good news or bad, we're on a need to know right now."

"Tomorrow morning good enough?" Dead-Eye asked.

"Better than good," Boomer said.

He popped open the driver's-side door and stepped out of the sedan. Dead-Eye did the same from his end, and the two walked slowly across the double-lane avenue. "You think Buttercup ate his balls or just ripped them off and spit them out?" Dead-Eye asked.

"From what I hear," said Boomer, "Buttercup never swallows."

15

The Boiler Man sat in the back row of the movie theater, hands resting flat on the fat of his legs, eyes scanning the scattered few in attendance. His red velvet seat was sliced and torn, thick shards of tape holding the remains in place. The movie house had seen better decades, reduced now to highlighting second-run features a few weeks shy of a straight-to-video release. The one showing now was a Western filled with unknown faces and a plot he didn't bother to follow. Instead, he kept his focus on the old woman in the third row, sitting alone, her full attention riveted to the dusty screen above. She was one of seven people in the house, all sitting alone.

The Boiler Man hated movies and had never quite come to a clear decision as to most of the world's fascination with them. Even as an orphan boy who was raised for longer than he cared to be in an ivy-shrouded building in the middle of the Canadian wilderness, he dreaded the Tuesday-night screenings that served as the entertainment menu for the week. He didn't see any of the action onscreen, whether animated or real, as a momentary escape from his horrid existence but, rather, as an extension of his forced imprisonment. He made it through the harsh treatment he and others suffered at the hands of the Christian organization whose uniform he was forced to wear during his years there by the sheer strength of his will and a determination, rare in a boy so young and so vulnerable, that he would not surrender to their desire to chisel him in their mold and coerce him to bend to their beliefs.

Saint Francis the Divine was the official name given to the orphanage situated some three hundred miles north of the Toronto, Ontario, suburbs, and the thirty-two-acre site was his official home practically since the day of his birth. The boys there gave it a name of their own, one that had been passed down through generations of beaten and degraded graduates.

They called it Hell Town.

The Boiler Man allowed his mind to drift as the movie droned on before him, the voices of Italian actors dubbed by American ones, the dialogue making little sense, regardless of the language. He was a bright student and excelled in all his classes. He had a sharp and analytical mind, a great ear for music, and a keen interest in history, especially when it came to military campaigns. As much as the Boiler Man enjoyed his time in the classroom, he truly thrived once out on the athletic field, mastering any sport he turned his attention to—from fencing to swimming to martial arts to ice hockey. He was a sharp enough skater, with a steady shot and a taste for the hard check into corner boards that caught the attention of local area scouts, who were always eager to bring a name out of their schools and into the ranks of the pros.

He further supplemented all the on-and-off-the-field activity with massive doses of reading, carting armloads of books each night into his cramped quarters—a small room, locked only from the outside, situated under the back stairwell of Quigley Hall. He devoured adventure novels, always seeking out the most violent of the lot, and found that in mind and spirit he was linked more with the villains of such works than with the ones who were deemed the heroes. The Boiler Man read through the biographies of controversial world leaders and technical books on weapons and tactics, learning and absorbing valuable lessons in the pages of each one. The combination of the various aspects of his academic and athletic lives helped him to cope with the late-night visits from the Squad.

They were a cluster of in-dorm instructors equipped with whips and rods who believed that inflicting punishment on the flesh served only to strengthen a youthful mind. The beatings were numerous and painful, given that the select members of the Squad were expert on the multiple variety of torture methods that were the practice of the day, often experimenting late into the night on new techniques that had just been brought to their attention. The Boiler Man soon enough became their favorite target, due to his ability to withstand vast amounts of punishment with a strength seldom seen in a student so young and so visibly fragile.

The leader of the Squad was a middle-aged, overweight English scholar who preached Shakespeare by day and doled out beatings under the shroud of darkness. His name was Charles S. Pennington. "He was a repulsive man in all respects," the Boiler Man once confided to one of the few friends he allowed himself. "He only smiled when he had a whip in one hand and flesh to snap it against. I detested his very presence and lived for the moment when I would be able to release my well of pain in his direction. I wanted to show him that his brutal lessons had not been wasted."

Charles S. Pennington was the Boiler Man's first kill.

He waited until two weeks after his official release from Saint

Francis the Divine to exact his revenge on the Squad's leader. He left equipped only with a high school diploma, a certificate of academic excellence, a printout listing the college courses for which he had accumulated credit, and six letters of recommendation presentable to any would-be employer. The Boiler Man was a month past his eighteenth birthday when he walked that final time down the wide, expansive front hall of the only place he had ever lived. He never once looked back at the walls of the institute, allowing himself a small smile as the thick double doors slammed shut behind him, sending him out to an unknown and uncharted world filled with cities and countries he knew only from books and magazines. He ventured out without fear or trepidation, convinced that he was about to embark on an adventure that would not only be justified but might prove to be financially rewarding as well. The Boiler Man's goal was to put all that he had learned in his years at Saint Francis the Divine to full use and then add to it until there would be no one better at the art of murder than the institute's most gifted and valued student. He marked as his first target in that quest the man who took such pleasure in inflicting pain on others, the respected Charles S. Pennington.

He chose his location with care, a local bookstore less than a mile from the school grounds. He wanted a method that would not only be noticed and commented on by the surviving members of the Squad and the student body as well but appreciated by the master of pain himself. It had to be a death of classic proportions, one that would propel the Boiler Man toward his chosen path and help to establish for him a reputation that would soon be etched in the blood of countless victims.

The very instant Pennington spotted the Boiler Man heading his way in the rear of the bookstore, he knew his moment of truth had finally arrived and that the student he had beaten and tortured for so many years was now about to take a giant step forward and surpass the teacher. He didn't put up a struggle or say a word as the Boiler Man quietly led him out of the small store, down a grimy and narrow alley, and into the open mouth of a basement stairwell. And it was there, inside that dark, dank chamber of torture, that the young orphan who had been weaned behind the walls of Saint Francis the Divine vanished off the map and the Boiler Man was brought to life.

It took three long days for Charles S. Pennington to die.

The body was never found, despite an active and fairly intense investigation. None of the officers involved in the case ever bothered to tap into one of the thick oak wine barrels that lined the far walls of the basement. If they had taken the time to open the dozen containers at the back, they would have found the fermented body parts that would eventually make up the human puzzle that had once been Charles S. Pennington.

The movie was in its final moments, and the Boiler Man was ready to strike.

He stood up, eased out of his empty row, and walked down the center aisle of the theater, moving with an eerie silence. When he reached the fourth aisle from the front, he stopped and looked down at the old woman gazing up at the screen. The old woman sat still as stone, her eyes focused on the movie. "You need something from me it had better wait until this is over," Theresa said.

"I didn't come here out of any need," the Boiler Man said, his voice barely audible above the sounds onscreen.

"And you didn't come here to see a Lee Van Cleef movie," Theresa said. "So whatever it is, let it rest until the end of this one."

"Fair enough," the Boiler Man said, slipping into the seat next to

Theresa. "I'm always more interested in endings than beginnings."

Theresa gently moved her left hand down against the side pocket of her housedress, her fingers feeling for the .38 Special. The Boiler Man smiled up at the screen, absorbed in the final climactic shoot-out. "Don't," he said to Theresa. "You'll be dead before you can grasp the handle, and you'll miss the best part of the movie."

"I have people in the lobby," Theresa said, "three of them to your one. Be aware of that fact."

"I've met them," the Boiler Man said. "And they won't interfere with our business. Because they're dead, I mean. It's only the two of us. I figured it would be much cozier that way. I'm not one for crowds."

"What do you want from me?" Theresa hissed, glaring at him with hateful eyes.

"I thought you wanted to see how the movie ended," the Boiler Man said.

"Fuck the movie," Theresa said, practically shouting out the words in the near-empty theater. "And tell me what you want here?"

The Boiler Man did a slow head turn and looked at the old woman, a player in the drug game since she was in her early teens, and smiled. "I come to give you a gift," he said. "From an angel."

16

Boomer stood waist-deep in the cool waters of the Sound, walking a wicker basket filled with fresh-caught clams back toward the moored rowboat. He dropped the basket over the side of the boat, resting it under one of the seating planks. "Two more bushels and we should be set," he said.

"We've caught enough to fill the needs of three restaurants already," Natalie said. "What do you plan to do with all these clams?"

"Half the catch I give to my sister," Boomer said, looking up at her through the sharp glare of the midmorning sun. "She makes the best stuffed clams on the planet, and makes sure I get more than my share. What's left I give to the elderly in my old neighborhood, folks my parents knew and would spend mornings like this with when they were young."

"Do you come out here a lot?" she asked. She was wearing a large black T-shirt over a bikini bottom, her back resting against the side of the boat, her long legs stretched out under the open planks.

"Not as much as I should," Boomer said. "Used to come here every week in the spring and summer like clockwork. Back when my dad was alive. It was our time to spend together, get to talk or just be in each other's company."

"How did he die?" Natalie asked.

Boomer paused. "Like a lot of people," he said. "For no reason."

"Would you have been a cop had he lived?"

"I can't answer that," Boomer said. "I was a kid when he was killed, and all I can remember is wanting to go out and somehow try to make that right. Get the guy who took my father from me. And if I couldn't do that, then go and get the ones who took other kids' fathers. Getting back and getting even was all I thought of. Back then and now."

"Our choices are made for us, more often than we like to think," Natalie said. "It's as if it were all planned out even before we arrived on the scene. Look at the two of us. Your whole life has been built on revenge. And mine has been designed to avoid the clutches of someone like you."

"What if you had decided against going into the life?" Boomer asked. He was leaning against the boat now, his arms folded and at rest on the bow. "Would your father have allowed you to make that call?"

"You not only met him, you went up against him," Natalie said, a hint of sadness creeping into her voice. "What do *you* think he would have done?"

"Could you get out now?" Boomer asked. "If you wanted to?"

Natalie smiled at him. "You *are* out, and you can't stay away," she said. "What makes you think I'm any different? We're both in, Boomer, because we both want to stay in. It's the only life we've known, and the only one we're ever going to know."

"It's crazy for us to be here like this," Boomer said. "You know it, and so do I." He let a moment go by. "But even knowing that," he said, "I'm glad we're here, just the two of us."

"Have you ever come close to having someone in your life?" she asked.

"Once, a lot of years ago," Boomer said. "I was in love. I thought she was. And she was—but with me, not with what I did. She came to see me one day when I was in the hospital, banged up, shot up, and I caught that look in her eyes and I knew. She couldn't handle the danger end, and I didn't want to make her a young widow. It was safer just to let her go."

"I'm not afraid of the danger end, Boomer," Natalie said.

Boomer hoisted himself into the boat, knelt down in front of Natalie, and reached for her hand. "You know," he said, "I've never kissed a crime boss before. At least not on the lips."

"And I've never kissed a cop," she said.

He reached up, took her in his arms, and held her, their bodies warmed by the sun, their eyes locked. Holding her tight against his damaged chest, he leaned down, put his lips to hers, and stepped over a line he never thought he'd cross.

17

CHAPTER

The Cessna rolled to a stop on the tarmac, engine droning, landing lights blinking. The white side-panel door opened and two men stepped out and walked down the narrow steps, one of them hand-blocking the glare of the sun from his eyes. They stood on the tarmac and gave the immediate area a quick scan, both facing the wide-berth hangar, their jackets flapping in the cool breeze of a late-spring day.

"I told those fuckers not to be late, did I not?" one of the men said. "Or was it just me that heard that?"

"Relax, Junior," the second man said. "We got plenty of time. Nobody checks out shit at these private airports. We could be dumping a line of bodies from out the back of the fuel tank, wouldn't even get a second look. Besides all that, our crew has never once missed a delivery, and there's no reason for you to give any thought that they will today."

"I'll relax all right, soon as all that cocaine is moved off my damn plane and into their damn truck," Junior said. "Until then,

I'm going to just stand here and fuckin' worry like some sorry-ass skycap."

"You're a stress machine," the other man said. "No wonder you need to pop all those pills all day. You worry worse than some soft-tit old lady."

"Put a knife to your line of shit and cut it, Raul," Junior said, pulling a thin cigar from his inside jacket pocket and holding it in his right hand, where it would add mileage to his anger meter. "Like you're not standing there with bubbles coming out of your tight ass. If these fuckers are a no-show, we have to make good. And that's bad, cousin. That's top-of-the-tier bad."

They turned when they heard the truck engine and watched as a heavy-duty four-wheeled full-load came out of the hangar with a roar and headed straight for where they were standing. "They may be a few ticks late," Raul said, "but they are for sure hauling ass like they looking to make up for the lost minutes."

"Get away from the plane," Junior said, his senses on high-tension alert, eyes darting from the oncoming truck to the empty lounge to his right and up to the roof of the two-story building that housed the mini-terminal. "Get the fuck away from the plane now!" Junior grabbed Raul by the back of his jacket and the two skirted toward the double doors of the lounge, pulling out semi-automatics as they ran. They slammed open the doors and rushed into the lounge, diving in just as the truck rammed into the parked private jet, the loud explosion rocking the afternoon air and sending flames thick as tree stumps hurtling skyward, brick, glass, and rubber flying in all directions. A wave of brown smoke rushed through the lounge, now littered with debris, and covered the fallen bodies of Junior and Raul like a blanket. Sirens wailed in the distance as fire engines and an ambulance rushed to the site of the explosion.

Boomer, Dead-Eye, and Ash stood a half mile away, their backs against the warm side of an empty hangar, where an overhead awning shielded them from the sun's glare. "It's a little scary what you can learn working in the arson unit," said Boomer, arms folded across his chest, eyes on the smoke and flames in the distance. "I might ask you for the recipe sometime down the road, if that's good with you."

"Wouldn't take you long to figure it out, trust me," Ash said. "It's not rocket science, it only looks like it."

"It still doesn't explain how you got that truck to roll out of there like that," Dead-Eye said, visibly impressed. "The bomb part, I get. You been around it long enough, you pick shit like that up. But you don't learn how to jack a truck, kick the engine over, and have it move on down the road like it's manned by a Formula One driver glued behind the wheel on the arson shift. That much I do know. That's a class you take in a whole other school."

"The name Earl Stanlislaw sound familiar?" Ash asked.

"Earl the Pearl," Boomer said. "A mad bomber worked the city about four, maybe five years back. You the one nailed him?"

"Not directly, but I was part of the team," Ash said. "And then I was assigned to study him, profile him for the department. To do it right, I had to get to know him a bit. I'd go up to Comstock on his visiting day each month, sit across the glass, and listen to him talk about bombs. He was mad, no doubt on that, but not exactly crazy. He might also have been a finger touch away from a genius, at least when it came to explosives and the best ways to use them. I read dozens of bomb books, just so I wouldn't come off as a total moron when I started with my pop-quiz questions."

"Did he show you any other tricks besides the truck one you just pulled off?" Dead-Eye asked.

"I've got one or two more picture cards palmed up my sleeve,"

Ash said. "I'm a rookie next to Earl the Pearl, but I picked up enough to do some damage to the dealers. Nothing all that technical, but I learned how easy it is to blow shit up."

"He's the guy tore apart a downtown department store during a snowstorm," Boomer said. "Or am I thinking of someone else?"

"No, that was Earl's work," Ash said. "It was one of his best jobs, for my money. He planted the device in a perfume display on the second floor, one of those pit stops where a lady gets a free whiff of some new smell. It was timed to go off when the bottle hit the halfway point—which, in this case, was around lunchtime."

"Did he have a beef with the store?" Dead-Eye asked. "Or maybe with the perfume company?"

"That's the madness of Earl," Ash said, shaking her head. "He didn't have a beef with anybody. He just liked to set off bombs and be there to see the end result. That's where we part company. At least, I like to think we do. We only go after the ones who caused us some level of pain."

"How did the drug dealers touch you?" Boomer said. "And I don't need to know if you don't feel like giving it a say. I just wondered, that's all, and we seem to be on the subject."

"They touch everyone, not just you or Dead-Eye or me," Ash said. "Every arson fire that's set in this city can be finger-traced back to drugs. It's true now, and it was true back when I was a kid. They either do the torch jobs themselves or they farm them out to some kid eager to hook up with their crew. Any way you burn it, their torch prints are on every piece of soot in this town, and the poorer the neighborhood the truer that proves out. To tag along with the gas and the flames, you can add a long list of wasted innocent lives that went down in the smoke because of those heartless bastards. That's why I went into the arson unit, and that's why I'm here standing next to the two of you."

"I wish we could get them all," Boomer said to her, "but there's always going to be a hundred of them to one of us. So it turns into a long night at a bowling alley. We just look to knock down as many pins as we can before the lights go off and they send us on our way."

"This is the second haul of Angel's we've hit in less than three days," Ash said. "How soon you think it will be before he hits back?"

"Depends on how fast he figures out who it is that's pulling at his drug chain," Dead-Eye said. "If I had to guess it, I'd say no more than another day or two, four on the outside."

"How will he get to the two-and-two?" Ash asked.

"He's not top-tier because of his looks," Boomer said. "He's taken the years to set his domain up like a small country—complete with connections, legal and not. He's got the money and the names to piece together who we are, and some of those names come to the table wearing a cop's tin. We just need to be smart enough not to let him get close to where he can slice together *where* we are. If we can manage that, then we'll make a dent."

"And if we can't?" Ash asked.

"Then we get tossed out with the wash," Dead-Eye said. He began to walk away from the hangar, the plumes of brown smoke behind him thinning out and covering the length of the tarmac. "But he's always been a cautious man, careful not to rush to a judgment on business matters. Right now, he's still not sure who's playing him: is it us or is it the G-Men? Until he's sure, he'll need to hold his hand."

"Or even better for us if he gets the bug in his ear that the G-Men are fronting us the dough to run our operation," Boomer said. "Then that's an even bigger headache thrown his way."

"We can't beat either crew full-out, take them down head-on," Dead-Eye said. "So we need help from their side. They work and play in a world without trust, and we have to use that to our advantage best we can."

"Who's fronting us the money for our operation?" Ash asked. "I saw enough carpenters and electricians in that burnt-out pizzeria the other day, I thought we were going condo. They can't all be ex-cops out on a favor run."

"More like a half dozen ex-cons tacking the hours on to some developer's tab," Boomer said, reaching the driver's side of his car, which was parked behind the hangar. "Angel and the G-Men go down, let's say. Somebody has to step into that void, fill the demand hole. Now, that's one somebody who would look to help a group of somebodies like us."

"That's crossing a line, if nothing else," Ash said, holding open a rear door. "You have to admit to that, at least."

Boomer looked at Dead-Eye for a few moments and then turned to Ash. "We've never looked at any line," he said. "We only saw who was standing on the other side of it and we went after them, both on the job and off. Far as I can see, there's no other way to get it done."

"There anything you *won't* do?" Ash said. "To get what you want done?"

Boomer looked away from Ash and gazed at the smoke and flames down the tarmac at his back and shook his head. "Nothing that comes to mind," he said. Then he got behind the wheel, kicked over the engine, and drove down the smoldering tarmac toward the rear exit.

18

CHAPTER

Andy Victorino was walking down a side street in lower Manhattan when he saw the dark blue sedan turn the corner and come to a quick stop next to a fire hydrant. Buttercup was by his side, seemingly indifferent to her surroundings, her eyes glazed and droopy. Andy slowed his walk, watching the four men jump from the sedan and head his way, moving at a clip that was much too fast to fit such a quiet morning. They were well dressed and determined, weighed down by guns and the hungry look of up-and-comers eager to make that rush move on the crime ladder. Andy eased Buttercup closer to the curb, standing between a parked car and a dented meat truck, open back doors exposing rows of hanging hindquarters. The street was lined with storefronts and wholesale outlets, one of those downtown streets with a cobbled roadway that seemed locked and sealed from an era when pushcarts and peddlers sold their goods to an array of newly arrived immigrants. The soot-stained tenements directly above the stores had either been converted into office space for the shops beneath them or remained as rent-controlled housing for tenants who had lived there since birth.

The four men broke off into pairs. The two leading the charge toward Andy hit the curb and crossed over to the sidewalk on his right. The other two came down the center of the street, dodging the occasional passing truck or car, hands jammed inside the open flaps of their jackets.

"Ready when you are," Andy said, looking down at the drowsy Buttercup and giving her a gentle tap on the head. "And if you get a flashback, remember, I'm the one that's on your side."

Buttercup moved away from Andy and walked down the center of the street with a slow and confident strut, like an old gunslinger ready for the next drawdown, heading directly for the two men in her path. Andy turned and jumped up into the meat truck and braced himself against the side of a 250-pound hindquarter, fresh drops of blood soiling the sawdust floor at his feet. He eased two .44s from the back of his tight blue jeans and checked his watch.

It was twenty minutes past six on a chilly Thursday morning in late April, and Andy Victorino, a forensic specialist with a deadly disease working its wretched madness through his young body, had not yet had his first cup of coffee.

The two men on the sidewalk were the first to pull their weapons and aim them up at the truck. They waited until they were within ten feet of the meat truck, gave a quick glance to the curious faces looking back out at them from inside the safety of the stores, and aimed their guns in Andy's direction.

"Pull on that trigger and you'll drop like a bad stock," Dead-Eye said to them, locking the men in their place.

He was right above them, standing on a rusty fire escape, his feet spread and wedged against the thin red bars for support. From inside the truck, Andy whirled and turned to face the other two men. They were now frozen in place in the middle of the empty street, with Buttercup herding them as if they were lost sheep, her teeth exposed, a heavy and low growl coming from deep inside her throat. "Try not to look scared," Andy shouted at them. "It turns her on, and then there's no stopping her from ripping out the bones in your legs."

At the other end of the street, Boomer walked out of a pork store and stepped in behind the two men. "There's a diner just around the corner on Little West Twelfth," he said to them. "We can all of us head over there, pocket our weapons, and sit and talk it out. Or we can play Cowboys and Indians out here in the morning light. It's too early for me to make any decisions, so I'll leave it to you and your friends. And while you're tossing it around, add this in. There are two high-powered rifles with two very itchy fingers locked onto their triggers, aimed at each of your heads."

"They sent four of us this time," the oldest of the group said. He was a middle-aged man with a connect-the-dots face. "You waste us and next time they'll send forty and wipe the streets with your fuck-ing blood."

"That may well be true," Boomer said. "But what do you give a shit? You won't be alive to hear the story."

"What you got to say inside a diner can't be said out here on the street?" he asked. "You hard up for eating company?"

"Hookers talk business on the street," Boomer said. "Not me. And besides, Buttercup hasn't had her first meal of the day yet. She doesn't see a chow bowl real soon, she's going to have to revert to Plan B. Which is to say you."

The pockmarked man looked down at Buttercup, who stood inches away, blocking his path, thick white foam edging down the corners of her mouth. He turned to the man next to him and nodded. "There's no need for all of us to go in," he said. "How about we leave it to just you and me? Have everybody else take a chill pill and kick it back while we talk. Work for you?"

"It does only if you're the one in the group carries the most weight with the Gonzalez boys," Boomer said. "Otherwise, I'll take a Pasadena on the meeting."

"I'm the one you want," he said.

"That leaves just one last thing for me to know, then," Boomer said.

"What?"

"Eggs or pancakes?" Boomer asked.

———————————

Rev. Jim had made his way down from the tenement rooftop and stood next to Dead-Eye on the fire escape, each with a full-chamber weapon in hand, the early-morning sun drenching the now busy street two stories below them. "I have a funny feeling that you and me need to have ourselves a little chitchat," Rev. Jim said. "And it does appear that we have a few minutes of kill time coming to us."

Dead-Eye turned his back to the street and holstered his weapon. "That does seem to be the case," he said. "But this might only be part one of the conversation. Once we're done, you might have to move it on to the next badge in the line."

"You got a name in mind?" Rev. Jim asked. "Or will just any old badge make the magic happen?"

"Sean Valentine," Dead-Eye said, staring hard across the fire escape at Rev. Jim. "He's a captain now, working out of the Plaza. Back in the day, two of you worked undercover decoy and saw some narc action to boot, were in steady tandem for about eight months, give or take."

"I remember, though I've spent a lot of useless time trying to wash the taste out," Rev. Jim said. "He was knee-deep in dirty deeds when we worked together. Doubt he has any reason to change course now that he's down in headquarters. There any special request you want me to pass his way?"

"He's on our tail, working for Angel through some highbrow middleman," Dead-Eye said. "And the only link between us and him is you."

"You think I feed him about the team?" Rev. Jim asked. "Is that what all your Dick Tracy bullshit is about?"

"It's a starting point," Dead-Eye said. "You seem out of sorts, especially this early in the game. That Q&A crap you cranked up at the dinner table the other night with Quincy was just one of the red flags."

"Those questions needed to be asked," Rev. Jim said. "There was a time you would have been the one asking them. But since you didn't grab a bat and make a move toward home plate, it was left to me to do it."

"Maybe so," Dead-Eye said. "Or maybe that's the kind of talk you reserve for a one-on-one, much like you and me are doing now. There was no need to call him out about it in front of the team."

"What he has affects the *whole* team," Rev. Jim said. "Not just me."

"So does you having a history with a prime-time dirt badge," Dead-Eye said. "I get some clear answers, then I can move forward with a clear head."

"And if you don't like what you hear?" Rev. Jim asked.

"I hope I don't have to reach out that far," Dead-Eye said. "You're an important member of this team, and I want to keep it that way. But there's too many high-calibers aimed at our heads as it is. We don't need one at our backs, too."

"I'm not dirty, Dead-Eye, and I never was," Rev. Jim said. "And fuck you for thinking it. I worked in the same unit with Valentine, that part is true, but I stayed as clear away from his end of the water as he did from mine. I knew he took, and he knew I didn't. That's the plain and the simple of it all."

"Did he know about you being hooked up with us the first time around?" Dead-Eye asked.

"He did if he read a newspaper or listened to the cop talk in the locker rooms," Rev. Jim said. "We didn't exactly succeed at keeping it on the low and down."

"Which means he would figure you to be in the next card game as well," Dead-Eye said. "And that makes you the hand he reaches out for when he feels a need."

"Well, he hasn't felt it yet or I would have been the first to hear," Rev. Jim said. "Either way, it won't do him much good, since him and me have nothing to share."

"That's where you're wrong, Rev.," Dead-Eye said with a smile. "Off-the-charts wrong."

"I just told you I'm not dirty, and that's the last I want to hear of this shit," Rev. Jim said, his anger reaching full-volume pitch. "You want me off this team, just say the fucking words and I'm gone like a ghost. I'm not here for an ego boost, but I'm not here to take a kick to the nuts, either. Especially from you."

"I know you're clean, that wasn't my concern," Dead-Eye said. "I just needed to make sure you were up for another go-around on the hard turf. Our little head-to-head here gave me the answer to that."

"Good to know," Rev. Jim said. "Now I can die with a smile on my face. You got anything else to throw at me or you through playing judge and jury for the day?"

"Just one more question—I mean, while we're talking up here and all," Dead-Eye said. "I mean, shit, Boomer never leaves a diner unless he's had three cups of coffee and he's old-lady slow drinking it."

"Let me hear it, then," Rev. Jim said. "But I warn you, if it goes to a place that makes me twitch, you and me are going to go at it right here and right now on this piece-of-shit fire escape."

"Fair enough," Dead-Eye said, stepping in closer to Rev. Jim. "Here it is, then. What if Valentine did reach out, and what if you acted as if you were interested? Not a quick yes, mind you. That might cause him to raise his antennas a bit. But a slow and easy dance that would lead him to think you're open to the idea. You game for a little something along those lines?"

"If it has a sound purpose," Rev. Jim said, "it's not something I would toss a wad of spit on."

"He's sure to be driving up our asses, sooner than later," Dead-Eye said. "We could slow him up a bit if we had a pair of hands on his steering wheel. Make him think he went and made himself a trustable friend from among our group. Give him a couple of head fakes on what we got working against the dealers."

"That will only work once, twice maybe if I go in with the luck of a lotto winner," Rev. Jim said. "If the goods don't match the sales pitch, Valentine will bark louder than crazy old Buttercup."

"You'll give him some of the wine, just not a full glass," Dead-Eye said. "Play it like I brought it to you here. Plans are made by only me and Boomer; rest of the group is kept out of the decision loop. You're working under a cloud, batteries are low on your trust meter. Shit along those lines. He's been there himself ever since he slapped on a tin, so you'll be walking with a fellow traveler."

"Might be good to get something back from him we could use," Rev. Jim said. "If we're going in this deep, let's take it as far as it'll go."

"We can't wire you up, he'll go in looking for that," Dead-Eye said. "But if he lets you decide on the meeting sites, then maybe we can set it up that way. I know a guy can drop a wire not even Clark Kent could see if he were staring right at it."

"It'll be harder if we end up with our meetings held outside," Rev. Jim said. "Which is more than likely where he'll want them. I'll try and make sure if that's the case we get together at night. Try and give your guy as much room to work as I can."

"Us nailing Valentine is the second limb on the tree," Dead-Eye said. "The top branch is making sure he doesn't nail *us*."

"You seem pretty confident he'll make a reach-out for me," Rev. Jim said. "That more of your gut, or do you have some intel to back up the words?"

"A skunk can take a three-hour shower," Dead-Eye said. "But when he towels off he's still a skunk. Connect the dots is all I did. He's on Angel's payroll, and he's a cop. We're out to fuck up Angel and we used to be cops. And the two of you shared a workspace. He'll come looking to take you out on a date soon enough."

"My history with dates is not exactly stellar," Rev. Jim said. "The only time I ever get fucked is when I pick up a tab in a restaurant I can't afford."

"I got a strong feeling your luck's about to change for the better," Dead-Eye said. "It goes the way it should and a break or two falls your way, then you for sure will fuck Sean Valentine, dinner or no. Just don't expect him to send you a dozen roses in the morning."

"That's okay," Rev. Jim said. "I hate flowers."

"And I hate Sean Valentine," Dead-Eye said.

———

"You're not going to finish your pie?" Boomer asked the pockmarked man. "They bake it fresh here every day. It's not that trucked-in shit you get in diners."

"Fuck the pie and spill your piece," the pockmarked man said. "I didn't come here to eat. I came to listen."

Boomer took a long sip of coffee and nodded. "There's no reason for the G-Men to come gunning for us," he said. "That's something you should put on a plate and run under your bosses' noses before we go back out on that street and draw down on each other."

"And let you keep fuckin' with as many cash and coke deals you feel like bustin' up?" he said. "We got off our immigrant boat at night, but not *last* night, understand?"

"Yeah," Boomer said. "But here's what doesn't come across my radar. The deals that have been busted don't touch your crew. They belong to Angel, and the last time I looked his picture up the G-Men had a bull's-eye painted on it."

"It's pain management, my friend," the pockmarked man said. "The G-Men have been top guns through two different mayors in this town. One way of doing that is to always be aware of the situation. So, yes, whoever burnt those recent deals put a deep dent in Angel's wallet, not in ours. But that ex-padre is going to be looking for a get-even bite, and it is toward us that he will eventually turn."

"But why do it now?" Boomer asked. "So long as we're in the movie, all his attention is going to be wide-screen on us. I can't sit here right now and tell you we'll win this fight by a knockout, but for sure we'll put that bastard on his knees. Which, by the by, will make him a very easy takedown for the two brothers who pay your salary."

"Are you telling me that you have no plans to hit G-Men business?" he asked. "That you got eyes only for Angel?"

"Angel is our primary," Boomer said. "If we hit any of your works, it's by accident and not design. We got our share of street eyes and ears out there, but not enough to pick up who's on both ends of a deal. You toss us a heads-up now and then, I'll make it a point to stay clear."

"And what's the game plan after you squeeze out Angel?" he asked. "Say, as a for instance, you and the other Crips get a bite of lucky and beat back his holy ass. That's high-seven turf you'll be stepping into—shit that will make you richer than the Beverly Hillbillies. There ain't a lot of people taking in air, on either side of the table, be willing and able to walk from a top-of-the-ladder score big as that."

"That's not my style and never has been," Boomer said. "If I wanted to cop some real money, I would have done it a long time ago—and in a way that wouldn't have put a floodlight on my ass. I don't want Angel's money or his domain, and I could give a rat's dick which crew, yours or some other Wild Bunch, ends up with it."

"So it's only personal, then," he said, "if my lips are reading you the right way."

"Very," Boomer said. "Personal is the only road I take these days. I have no time for anything else."

The pockmarked man sat quietly for a few minutes and then smiled across at Boomer, exposing a bottom rung of tobacco-stained teeth. "I go in wrong on this, I'll be the first to get iced," he said. "I know you may not give a flying fuck, but it is something that gives me pause."

"And you could sit there, sell me a line of cheap shit, and slide out of the booth with the full intent of dropping me in a waste disposal," Boomer said. "We take chances every day, more of them in this line than in most, but if you don't make a move then you got nothing to prove."

"How good is that pie you been munching on?" the pockmarked man asked.

"The best you'll ever have this side of a mother's kitchen," Boomer said. "Toss in a fresh cup of brew and you got yourself a deal that's sealed in the heavens. Or, in your case, in hell."

19
CHAPTER

The interior of the shuttered pizzeria and the condemned tenement had undergone a radical makeover in less than a week's time. A double coat of Benjamin Moore and some crisp two-by-four planks gave the walls a fresh new feel. Office equipment filled the center of the two large rooms, computer screens, printers, and fax machines eating up large chunks of the open floor space. A map of the city with pushpins dominated the wall closest to the still func-tioning pizza oven, and police reports, BOLO requests, case files, and rap sheets were spread out across four oak tables situated in the center of the room. A multiline phone bank covered the front counter. "The top two floors should be ready in a day or so," Boomer said to the rest of the team. "And that should give us all we need to work out of here twenty-four-seven until this is at an end."

"So what happened?" Quincy asked. "You guys hit a Home Depot and didn't clue me in?"

"We got friends on the construction end of the ledger," Dead-Eye said. "And they have a few friends who know where to get computers and printers. Put it all together and we end up making chicken salad out of chicken shit."

"I hope we have a friend who's an exterminator," Rev. Jim said. "I just checked out the basement and stepped into the middle of a rat convention."

"I got a cousin coming in early next week," Dead-Eye said. "The guy's killed so many rats they had wanted posters made up of the little bastard."

Boomer pulled back a chair and sat at one of the oak tables, large coffee mug in his right hand, Buttercup fast on his heel. Quincy and Ash followed the lead and sat across from him. Dead-Eye and Rev. Jim leaned against the wall closest to the group. Boomer took a long sip of his coffee and gazed up at the faces around him. "We've put it all out there now," he said. "We're juggling more balls than a circus act, but it's the only way I can figure for us to at least make Angel flinch the second he hears our names."

"We're giving out trust to a lot of people who probably shouldn't be trusted at all," Quincy said. "I mean, okay, the G-Men pit boss claims they'll fly around us in circles, let us do our damage. It doesn't mean that they'll hold to that position."

"And it also doesn't mean they're right now not sitting across a table from Angel halfway to working a sellout," Ash said. "We butted heads with these crews while we were on the job, even put some of them behind bars for long runs. Now, all of a sudden, we're Lucy to their Ricky. It's a risk with plenty of damage potential to it."

"You're right on target with that shot," Dead-Eye said. "But none of us are on the job at the moment and won't ever be again, unless the department puts out the word and sets up a disabled unit. We have to deal with the real of the here and now, which means we reach out to any hands, clean or marked, that help put our asses in the end zone."

"All the while happily ignoring the clear fact that we can't trust any of the people we're standing next to?" Quincy asked. "That any one of these bastards would cut our fucking necks as easy as they'd carve a late-night roast?"

"You jump into a vat of oil, you're bound to catch a few splatter stains," Boomer said. "We're playing on a hard surface here, pitting one group against another, all the while trying to make it look like we're holding up our end of a devil's bargain. We're going to catch a bite in the ass somewhere on the trail, no doubt, but it's the only way I can figure to make any of this work. Any one of you have a better road map, now's the time to spread it out and share it. Otherwise, this is what we know and this is how we go."

"Best-case scenario is we bought ourselves a little time and I suggest we put it to the utmost use," Dead-Eye said. "Angel will send his boys out gunning for us, you can bet your pensions on that. But until that dark cloud crosses our path, we need to reach in and slap at them heavy and hard. Put a fender bender in their cash flow and put a hole in their drug bag, leave them in a place where they're running in circles just to catch up and not know whether to shit or wind their fucking watch."

"We're going to split our little crew here into three teams of two," Boomer said, reaching for one of the thick folders stacked to his left. "Not on every job, but on enough of them to cause Angel a second of pause. Let him wonder if there are more of us lined up against him than he's been led to believe. And in every case, whenever possible, we make sure the drugs are destroyed and the cash goes missing."

"We'll mix and match, depending on the operation, look to blend whatever's left of our skills into as much of a Pearl Harbor scenario as we can muster," Dead-Eye said. "The goal is simple: disrupt and disarm, and get away with it enough times that the evil bastard loses his cool and his focus. That happens, we will have his ass on the run."

"And if none of that happens?" Ash asked, skimming through a DEA folder. "What's the lay of the land look like, then?"

"Then game, set, match will go to Angel," Boomer said. "And we lose both the game and probably our lives."

"You certainly do know how to charge up a room, Boomer," Rev. Jim said, moving away from the wall and toward one of the large PCs. "Now, I don't know about the rest of you guys, but I am more than ready to begin my *Mission: Impossible* turn at the wheel."

"What's Tony Rigs bring to our team?" Quincy asked. "Other than supplying the lumber and hardware around us here in central HQ. Should we only look his way as a quiet and noble sideline benefactor? Or is he another reach-out by us to the dark side?"

"He's an organized-crime boss, somebody me and Dead-Eye did a rumble and a tumble with for a lot of years," Boomer said, tossing aside the folder. "Sometimes we got the better of it and sometimes he did. And maybe down the road we might resume that battle and see where it takes us. But for now, for this particular war against this particular foe, Tony Rigs should be considered a friend. And one we can trust."

"He'll step into the void when and if Angel takes the fall, whether it's at our hands or not," Dead-Eye said. "It's what Tony does and who he is, and no one here is preaching a different tale. But to get to that place where he stands tall on SA turf, he will go the extra yards to ensure that we have a few helping hands at our backs."

"He's a gangster, but he flows with the street rules," Rev. Jim said. "He stepped into it in a big way for me back in my narc days. I was butting heads with a low-life dealer with some solid Upper East Side money backing his play. The guy had more connections than I had buttons on my shirts, even some high rankers down at central command."

"That song gets a lot of play on the jukebox," Ash said. "It would be nice to run up someday against one of these top-tier guys who *don't* have a hook deep inside the department."

"How did Tony come into it for you?" Dead-Eye asked. "Was the dealer moving in on his ground?"

"Not directly," Rev. Jim said. "He was his own best customer, it turned out, and, like a lot of these clowns who toss a large chunk of their profits up their nose, his ugly side rose to the surface. He was into masks, chains, and whip sex, regardless of whether the lady on the receiving end was so inclined."

"Did he touch one of the young ladies in Tony's stable?" Boomer said. "Or did he cross the line?"

"He *erased* the line," Rev. Jim said. "He tossed a few free bags of Special K coke to a group of kids winding down on their prom night in some Chelsea club. Not too many hours later, the party had ventured into the dealer's loft a few blocks away. By the time the sun came up, we had ourselves a full-blown crime scene. There was one blood-soaked overdose, two rapes, and a beating severe enough to land one of the ladies in an emergency room, where it was more touch than go for a few hours."

"That should have been enough to jam him for a double-decade stretch upstate easy," Ash said. "Or am I thinking like a Girl Scout here?"

"Spot on, Nancy Drew," Rev. Jim said. "Maybe in the real world that would happen, but none of us are lucky enough to live there. The scumbag got boned out by his friends with three names and a Tiffany coke box with their initials stenciled across the top. He was let off free and easy even before the ADA on the case had read either the folder or the DD-5 report. Let off by the powers that be, that is. He wasn't counting on Tony Rigs's heavy shadows stepping across his front door."

"Which one of the kids belonged to Tony Rigs?" Dead-Eye asked.

"The girl who landed in the emergency room was his goddaughter, and you don't need the Pope to spell out how serious Italian guys, on the legal end of the ledger or not, take that kind of shit," Rev. Jim said. "And there's no amount of Upper East Side bling-bling that can pull your ass out of that particular fire."

"Which put your dealer where?" Ash asked.

"Depends on which body part you went looking for," Rev. Jim said. "His head was nailed to the front door of an Upper East Side brownstone belonging to the deep-pocket dude that had paid for his lawyer. And—this has always been my favorite part of the tale—his hands were express-mailed to the dealer's business partner. I saw it as a not-too-subtle way to imply he get his ass the fuck out of town."

"I have to admit," Ash said, "I'm a sucker for happy endings."

Boomer shoved his chair back and walked toward a corkboard that was hanging to the right of the oak tables. There were a series of different-colored index cards pushpinned in a straight line on the board. "For the last few years, Angel has had three large shipments of coke brought into the country, each crossing the border at different entry points," he said. "He's no innovator when it comes to this end of the business—standard transport methods, all of which we've come across in our time. He prefers mules, car rocker panels, pets, dummy liners on suitcases, and double-wrapped kilos buried deep inside shipping and trucking supplies."

"Does he send the money back the same way?" Quincy asked.

"Half of it, yes," Boomer said. "The other half he has transported to a series of banks for deposit and safe houses for expenses.

The entire operation, from the packing of the drugs to the return of the cash, is always done in under twenty-four hours. He likes to come in fast and go out faster."

"How many of his deliveries manage to get through?" Dead-Eye asked.

"He's at a ninety-one-percent completion ratio," Boomer said. "Which puts him on the high side of the ledger. Some of it you can write off to luck and skill, and some to cracks in the INS and DEA stop-and-seize wall. But let's give the credit where the credit should be given. Angel *never* uses the same mule more than three times. The transport cars he chooses are always owned by people with Mister Clean police files and young children they want to see stay alive. The trucks and vans are rented out by third parties or stolen from pump-and-dump operations whose owners would rather have a stroke than call in a lifted piece of equipment. Add it up and it totals out to a guy who is crazy smart but not stupid."

"How much does each of the hauls bring in?" Rev. Jim asked. "The ballpark on his cut—what's it come out to be?"

"Depends on who you believe," Boomer said. "DEA has him running at a six-hundred-thousand-a-month profit margin. Some of the street narcs I've reached out to tell me the number is double that, easy. And Tony Rigs puts it at a million per, not a nickel more or less."

"Either way, the guy's working off a hefty take-home," Dead-Eye said. "And he's not going to crack a smile if those numbers quick-sand into five-digit land. Now, we flecked a few jabs his way and come away neat and clean. That's mostly due to him not expecting to be swung at from our end. On the next beach assault, he'll be locked in and waiting to haul us in."

"He figures our group to be small and underfinanced," Boomer said. "That's why he's not too worried about sustaining multiple losses for too long a period. These next few days will change his thinking on that approach. And then he'll not only look for us but try to put the puzzle pieces together and get a picture of who it is might be feeding us and run their ass through a meat grinder as well."

"Where is it we want him to turn his eye?" Ash asked.

"The logical look will be toward the G-Men," Boomer said. "He's already getting red-flagged for encroaching on their turf, and so far he's brought himself a little peace and quiet by dropping a few coins in their weekly collection plate. But if we pull off a few heavy-target hits these next couple of days, the padre's going to be eager to dole out last rites to the two brothers and their crew."

"How do you know when the drugs are coming in? Not even DEA has wind of that," Ash said. "Or INS, for that matter. If they did, I would be tossing out a guess and figure they'd do something about crashing that party."

"Most times, cops, especially on the federal level, are a lot like the open-eyed husband," Boomer said. "Always the last to know. Not everybody's happy to see the SAs walk into town and treat it as a suburb of their home turf. The unhappiest ones like to point and sometimes talk. If I'm lucky, I'm there to offer a degree of comfort."

"There are a solid half-dozen crews in the city want them out of the way," Dead-Eye said. "And I'm talking about balls-to-the-floor unforgiving bastards with the men and the guns to back up their talk. One reason they haven't moved to this point is that it can be to their advantage not to do anything, at least for the foreseeable."

"How's that work in their favor?" Ash asked.

"All cop attention—city, state, and federal—is pointed down South American way," Dead-Eye said. "That leaves the Italians, Russians, and the blacks and Hispanics to work their magic under the radar, so long as they stay clear of the drug trade. They rake in their profits and don't have to do a duck-and-wince every time they hear a police siren."

"But while that makes sound and sensible business sense, it would be insane to think it would last," Boomer said. "Gangsters are, if nothing else, greedy sons of bitches, and the very thought of someone making bigger illegal scores than they are night in and night out is enough for them to pull their pieces and go out looking to cut into that pie."

"And that's where we step in," Dead-Eye said. "The more we can get these different crews to square off against Angel and his wild eyes, the easier it will be to work our way through his army of dealers. Look, it's not like they trust or even like each other from the tip-off. All we're doing is putting a light to the fuse and taking a step back when it goes off."

"And what happens if they sit pat and none of this help comes flowing down our way?" Quincy asked.

"Even if they do and every imaginable break falls to our side, there's still no win in this war for us," Boomer said, his voice hard and direct, his eyes moving from one Apache to the next. "Now, if any of you are even close to thinking that, it's best to erase the thought right away. And if we do end up with no help, or so little we won't even notice it, the end of our trail will arrive all that much sooner. That's why we have to hit Angel so hard and so heavy and make him guess where the hell it's all coming from and why. Take as many of them down as we can before we start our fall."

"Well, shit, I don't know how the rest of the group feels, but speaking for myself, I just can't wait to go out there and get wasted by a whacked-on-high-test coke dealer," Rev. Jim said, slapping his hands together. "Now which of you lucky bastards gets to team with me on the way down to Death Street?"

"On this next one, you go with Ash," Boomer said. "Dead-Eye matches up with Quincy. And Buttercup rolls with me."

"And for you newbies in the group, you remember all the rules and regs hammered into you while you were in the PD?" Dead-Eye asked. "Like, never shoot at a fleeing suspect, search-and-seizure procedures, don't pull your weapon on an unarmed suspect. Shit like that?"

"Sure we do," Ash said, throwing a look toward Quincy. "How could we forget them? We would get tossed out on our ass, faces plastered in the tabs and on the six o'clock news we forgot even one of them."

"Forget them all," Dead-Eye said. "And forget them *now*. If you don't, sure as there's a rat in every sewer, you won't ever live to *see* the six o'clock news."

"Grab your folders," Boomer said, pushing his chair back and heading for one of the upstairs rooms. "And read up on your assignments. It's time for us to get Angel's party started."

20

CHAPTER

Nunzio Goldman hung from a meat hook in the back of the empty meat locker, arms and chest red and bruised, face dripping blood, right eye swollen shut. His head hung to one side, his breaths becoming white clouds in the ice-cold room. He looked down at the ground that was filled with gold sawdust and saw the small circle of blood forming at his bare feet. He shook his head slowly and for the first time in his life felt old and foolish.

He was walking on a downtown street, crisscrossing the main square off Fourteenth, his back to the Old Homestead Steakhouse, when he was grabbed by two men with thick hands and thicker accents. He felt their guns in his rib cage and let them lead him across the avenue toward the parked sedan with the engine running. He was tossed headfirst into the back seat and taken for a two-block ride toward the rear entrance of what had once been Murray Baker's old slaughterhouse and had now morphed into a high-end wholesale meat distributor. He was pulled out of the car, dragged down a flight of steep steps, and shoved through thick aluminum-tinted double doors, doing a hard landing on the concrete floor, his mouth and eyes feeling the tinge of sawdust. The two men stripped him of his jacket, shirt, shoes and socks, tossing them all in a rumpled heap in a corner of the well-lit room. They wrapped and locked a bicycle chain around his neck and hoisted him onto a meat-locker hook, the sharp edge jabbing into his neck. And in that moment Nunzio Goldman and Angel put eyes on each other for the first time.

"This will be a very painful last day for you, regardless of what you do or do not tell me," Angel said to him, stepping away from under the glare of the sharp overhead lights toward Nunzio. He was wearing a long white butcher's smock that only partially covered a pair of razor-creased slacks and matching polo shirt. His black shoes were so shiny they glared like headlights. "I thought it only fitting for you to die in a meat locker. The childhood memories such a place brings to light might prove to be of some comfort to you during these next hours of agony."

"I would tell you to go fuck yourself ten ways till sundown," Nunzio said. "But I was taught never to curse in front of a priest. Low-life scumbag or not."

Angel smiled, thin lips barely exposing any teeth, and nodded toward the two men standing on either side of Nunzio. "I'll be back in an hour," he said to them. "He's yours until I return." Angel stepped up closer to Nunzio and wrapped his fingers around his face, their eyes separated by lashes. "You will beg me to give you your last rites," he said.

The two men removed their jackets, rolled up their sleeves, and went to work on Nunzio Goldman. Both in their mid-thirties now, they had mastered their torture rituals at a young age and were proficient in the pain trade. Throughout the entire brutal and ceaseless ordeal, Nunzio never uttered a sound or made a plea for them to stop. He had spent his life in the company of hard men on both sides of the law and had learned well the lessons they passed his way.

The greatest of all those lessons was to know when death was at hand and to accept its arrival.

———————————

Nunzio opened his one good eye and stared at Angel, back now, standing in front of him, a thin lit cigar in his mouth. "Give me their names," Angel said, "and I will put an end to your pain with a bullet. You have my word."

Nunzio smiled, his upper row of teeth loose, a warm stream of blood running from his mouth down to his chin. "What they say about you is spot-on true," he said to Angel. "I didn't buy into it wholesale at first. But then I got a look at you and there's no doubt about it."

"Humor me," Angel said.

"You never get your hands dirty," Nunzio said. "Most hair balls work up to that, but you can always look back to a time when they were bone breakers. But you're not them, padre. You got manicured hands in a callous business."

"Interesting," Angel said, blowing a thin line of smoke into Nunzio's face. "And I wish you and I could have enough time to give such a topic the attention it so demands. But we must get to the important question of the moment. What are their names?"

"You know the other mistake you made?" Nunzio asked, sharp bolts of pain coursing through his upper body, his head light and his vision blurry from the heavy loss of blood. "I'd ask you to guess, but you sound like you're a little pressed."

Angel grabbed one of the men and tossed him against Nunzio. "Take one finger off each hand," he said to him, his eyes on Boomer and Dead-Eye's best friend. "Perhaps that will help him better understand my question."

Nunzio's screams echoed through the empty meat locker, his eyes bulging, his body shaking without control, sweat flowing in torrents. Angel stepped into the large puddles of blood at Nunzio's feet and leaned into his wet and bloody face. "I want their names," he whispered.

Nunzio was taking heavy breaths, his mind light as a rain cloud, his eyes rimmed with hot tears. He looked at Angel and nodded. "I don't know them all," he gasped, "but I think they call the bald one Curly."

Angel took a step back and his face hardened. "Torch his restaurant, along with anything and anyone in it," he said to the two men. "And have him watch until it goes down. Then torch him and leave his body where it can easily be found."

Nunzio looked at Angel, his body weak but his heart still gangster strong. "You don't need their names," he said. "And you don't need to go looking for them. They'll come find you. And when they do, my name will be the one you hear just before you die."

21

CHAPTER

Natalie and Boomer were sitting in the back row of an empty movie theater in the East Bronx, the wide screen in front of them covered by a thick velvet curtain. "Do they still show movies in here?" she asked. "Or is it as abandoned as it looks?"

"In her time, she was one of the greats, gave even a horrible movie a shot at looking good," Boomer said. "She's older now, but she can still kick it. The owner runs retrospectives during the week and Spanish-only movies on weekends."

Natalie rested her head against the back of the battered old theater chair, then lifted her legs and crossed them over the top of the seat in front of her. She was dressed in a thin black leather jacket that partially hid a black cotton shirt, blue jeans sharp, and crisp black leather boots that reached just above her ankles. Her full black hair shielded her face, rich dark eyes shining like a cat's under the theater lights. She was the most lethal woman Boomer had ever met, and the most beautiful.

"I love movies," she said to him. "So did my father. We would watch as many as three a week. That was our time together—like you and your father and the fishing boat."

"I don't know much about Russian movies," Boomer said. "They any good?"

"A few are great," she said, "but there isn't much in the way of money to get many of them made. So I grew up watching mostly American and British movies."

"You see them on television, you mean?"

"There are only two channels worth watching in Russia, and neither one shows movies," Natalie said, giving Boomer a warm smile and clutching his hand in hers. "No, we got our movies the way we get everything else in my country—on the black market. We lead the planet in bootleg movies, and my father earned quite a bit of money feeding the demand on the street for American product."

"A crime boss *and* a studio boss," Boomer said.

"Something along those lines," Natalie said. She sat up in her chair and eased in closer to Boomer. "Let me see how compatible we really are. If you had to pick, which would you choose and why? Bogart or Cagney?"

"Cagney," Boomer said. "He not only acted it, he lived it, too. Bogart was great, don't read me wrong, but he was only *pretending* to be tough. Cagney was the real."

"The Beatles or the Rolling Stones?" she asked.

"You got them over there, too?" he asked.

"You make it, we steal it," Natalie said. "Now pick."

"The Stones," Boomer said. "I like their music and their style. The only Beatle I ever cared for was Lennon. He seemed to have a core, even if it was a bit skewered when he hooked up with the screamer."

"No one seems to like Yoko," Natalie said with a warm smile. "Not here and not in my country. Some women just hit you a certain way and it sticks forever."

"John seemed to like her," Boomer said. "And he was the only one she really needed to impress."

"Now here it comes," Natalie said, "the true test. Frank Sinatra or Dean Martin?"

"The Rat Pack, too," Boomer said. "Now stealing them from us, *that's* a crime."

"If anyone would appreciate it," Natalie said, "they would. So which of the two sits in your corner?"

"There's no splitting those two up," Boomer said. "In my mind, they come at you as a package. Frank runs the pack, but they're both sitting on the top shelf, by themselves. Still, there is a time when Frank does take a little bit of a lead."

"Which is when?" Natalie asked.

"I got my head down, a dark day behind me and a dark night ahead, it's Sinatra's voice I want coming off my radio," Boomer said. "Nobody—and I mean *nobody*—deals with the hook and jab of pain and loneliness the way he does. Those are the only moments I give Sinatra the edge. Other than that, they come in as one and one-A in my little book." Natalie stood, shoved her hands in the slit pockets of her leather jacket, and looked down at Boomer.

"So," he said, gazing up at her, "did I pass the pop quiz or do I need to sign up for a refresher course?"

"There was no right or wrong," Natalie said. "There were only answers."

"And what story did those answers tell you?" he asked.

"You're stubborn, like to go your own way, and don't want to be told what to do by anybody," she said.

"Are those good traits or bad, you figure?" Boomer asked.

"Excellent, at least from where I stand," Natalie said, stepping out into the aisle and turning up toward an exit sign partially hidden by a low-hanging curtain. "Tells me all it is I need to know."

"Which is what, exactly?" Boomer asked.

"We are more alike than either of us would want to think," Natalie said. "And you *will* need my help against the crews you're going to fight. And when you do come to me and ask for it, that help will be there."

"And what if I never ask?" Boomer said. "What do you take away from that?"

"That I overestimated Angel and the G-Men and their ability to take out a band of rogues," Natalie said with a shrug. "And I also underestimated the damage a man like you could do."

"Would you be disappointed if that were to happen?"

"No," Natalie said as she moved toward the exit sign, wrapping an arm around Boomer's back. "I would be impressed."

"If we leave now, we'll miss the movie," Boomer said. "They got a good one today. Cagney in *White Heat*."

Natalie looked at Boomer, her sleek body sheathed in shadow. "He dies at the end of that, am I right?" she asked.

"Dies big-time," Boomer said.

"I hate sad endings," Natalie said. "I always like the movie so much better when the bad guys walk away with a win."

"I always root for the cops, myself," Boomer said. "From when I was a kid to now. It seemed the right way to go."

"Well," she said, "I'm rooting for a cop now."

22

Rev. Jim brought the dark blue sedan to a stop at the red light, the harsh rays of a setting sun hitting his windshield, the rattle of the elevated subway drowning out a Bob Dylan song playing on the radio. He glanced in the rearview mirror and then turned to Ash, sitting shotgun. "There are four of them in the lead car," he said. "The white van behind them with the goods should have two in the front and two more in the rear. That means, if nothing else, you better be as good with a gun in your hand as I think I am."

"Okay if I ask you a stupid question?" Ash asked.

"If this is the part where I'm supposed to say there's no such thing as a stupid question, then you're in the wrong car," Rev. Jim said, inching the car forward on White Plains Road as the overhead light shifted to green. "But ask anyway."

"I'll keep it short," Ash said. "We're supposed to take their van—which, if our intel is on the money, is jammed tight with the hottest high-grade street coke on the market. Am I right, so far?"

"Perfect score," Rev. Jim said. "Just as an FYI, though, the street calls the new brand of coke Terminator. A couple of sleigh-ride hits on the pipe and you'll be back for more."

"If that's the case, then why are we in the lead car?" Ash said. "I realize I'm one of the new kids on the Apache block, but wouldn't it make just a little bit more sense if we were the ones chasing *them*?"

"We *are* chasing them, Ash," Rev. Jim said, doing a quick eye check on the slow-moving traffic that was working both sides of the wide avenue. "We're just riding the pace car for now. We're about three blocks away from the next light, and that's when I'll make a quick right-hand that will put us smack in the heart of Gasoline Alley—and that's when all the fun should start."

"That's where the money end of the deal is supposed to be waiting," Ash said. "Which should put four more guns, at the very least, aimed right at us. And here I sit, up front and all smiles, stuck in the middle with you."

"Can't ask for much more than that out of any one day," Rev. Jim said. "Best seats in the house, action ready to rain on us from both ends of the street, good against bad, and a small bushel of lives on the line."

Ash looked in the side-view mirror and then turned back to Rev. Jim. "They're riding so close to the bumper they might as well be in *our* back seat," she said. "That could mean they've already fingered us for trouble or they just drive like shit."

"Little bit of both is where I would toss my five-dollar chip," Rev. Jim said. "Not that it matters all that much what the hell they think. In less than a minute, we will remove any trace of the unknown."

Rev. Jim turned a sharp right at the corner of East 241st Street and White Plains Road and gunned the eight-cylinder engine to full throttle. Overhead, the IRT number 2 train screeched to a halt, making the last stop on the East Bronx line before its return trip to Manhattan. Ash pulled two .38 Specials from her shoulder holster and took a deep breath. "Don't worry about keeping the wheel steady, which will be hard enough to do on these streets, especially as you rev it up," she said to Rev. Jim. "I'll get a clear shot at the driver, and I'll get it no matter how much you swerve."

"Good to know, Batgirl," Rev. Jim said, bouncing from one large crater-size pothole to another. "But keep your head down all the same, because aim won't mean much once we get in tighter quarters. They'll be pegging eight shots to your two."

Rev. Jim shifted gears and turned the car onto a dead-end street, veering toward a double-gated open-air chop shop, three sedans parked in a semicircle two hundred yards beyond the chain-link fence. The two cars and a battered white van were several feet away from his tailpipe, thin clouds of smoke coming off their rear tires, two men holding semis in both hands doing a half-hang outside the back windows and taking shake-and-bake aim at the hard-chugging unmarked just ahead of them. "This isn't the Indy 500, Ash," Rev. Jim said to her, "so don't be waiting for anybody to come out swinging a checkered flag giving you the go sign."

A stream of bullets sprayed the street close to the car, two of them pinging off the trunk of the unmarked. "Stay cool, Rev.," Ash said, her voice as calm as her outward demeanor. "Just keep your eyes on the road and give me a shout a couple of ticks before you blast through that chain-link."

"Where are you going to be while I'm doing all the heavy lifting?" he asked. "Or you one of those Annie Oakley cops likes to put on a blindfold before she shoots off a few rounds? Just to show me how much better your aim is than mine."

"It's a little stuffy in here, with your Taco Bell smell," she said. "So I thought I'd go out and get myself some air."

Ash jammed the .38 Specials into her waistband and lifted the door handle, using her right foot to swing it out wide. She eased herself out of the car, stepped on the rocker panels, and then propped her feet on the open windowsill. Three bullets rang past her as she bent her knees and hoisted herself onto the roof of the car, resting flat on the curved surface, fingers stretched out and wrapped around the thin edges of the beat-up Chevy's upper body. The lead chase vehicle was close enough for her to see the faces of the men sitting up front and the two in the rear hanging out through the open window slots, their semis pointed in her direction. "How's the weather up there?" Rev. Jim shouted, slicing close to a parked car and avoiding a pothole the size of a moon crater.

"Cut the cute and jam on that horn before you ram the fence," Ash shouted back, releasing one hand from the upper lip of the car and pulling a .38 Special from her waistband. The harsh wind whipped her hair across her eyes, partially blocking her view. Two-story dump warehouses, with their graffiti-riddled doors rolled open, mingled in working-class discomfort with aluminum-sided mom-and-pops, but they all became blurs as the two ex-cops zoomed past at a hurried clip. "Get ready," Rev. Jim shouted. "You're looking at less than a ten-second count."

Ash closed her eyes and released her other hand from the side of the roof, using her sneakers as leverage to steady her body, the car swinging and swerving down the carved-up street, aimed dead straight for the gates of the chop shop. She pulled the second gun from her waistband and pointed them out toward the chase car. She opened her eyes and pressed her fingers to the triggers.

The car smashed through the gates, sending pieces of lock and links flying, front tires and bumper landing hard against a three-foot break in the ground and setting off a series of sparks as it rose back up. Ash's legs swung to the right and dangled off the front side of the car, partially blocking Rev. Jim's view as he kept a hard grip on the steering wheel. Ash had fired off ten rounds and three had found their mark, wounding the driver of the chase car with one and killing the shooter in the front seat with the other two. The chase car veered to the right, slowing its pace, the two men in the back popping open the doors and joining the hunt on foot, semis clutched in their hands. The van came up along-side the unmarked, its back doors open wide, two men with shotguns bracing their bodies against the rusty walls, waiting for a chance to pump out a stream of bullets against the two Apaches.

The unmarked was a few hundred yards away from the three sedans parked in a tight cluster next to one another, their doors open, six men with machine guns standing next to their respective cars. A second chase car was now closing in on Rev. Jim and Ash, the four men inside firing off rounds as if on a clay shoot. "Drop your guns and hang on," he shouted up to Ash.

"What are you going to do now?" Ash shouted back down, shov-ing her guns into her waistband.

"You really don't want to know," Rev. Jim said.

Rev. Jim slammed on the brake, turned the steering wheel hard to the left, and then gunned the engine, doing a full turn, kicking up rocks and debris, his front end nicking the side of the white van and sending one of the shooters flying out the open rear. He landed headfirst against a row of rusty pilings. Ash hung tight, fingers and the edge of her sneakers wedged into the door sockets, her body bouncing up and down against the roof of the car like a flattened handball, upper body coated in dust, right wrist nicked by a sharp piece of rock and bleeding.

Rev. Jim drove straight for the second crash car, the driver fran-tically weaving in reverse, doing all he could to avoid the inevitable collision. The other three men in the car continued to rain bullets down on the unmarked, one shot hitting Rev. Jim on his left arm. As blood streamed down the right side of his face from a glass cut to his cheek, Rev. Jim pulled a .44 from his waist and fired off a series of rounds as he inched closer to the chase car.

Ash reached for a .38 she kept in an ankle holster and did a slow crawl off the roof of the car, slithering down toward the windshield, her hands sliced and diced from the maneuver. Rev. Jim watched as she eased herself down the front of the bullet-riddled glass, smearing it with her blood, the front end of his car following the chase vehicle as it revved in reverse, looking to steer it against a pile of cars resting on the back end of the chop shop. Bullets were coming at them from all directions, and the front seat was riddled with holes, the engine block smoking and hissing, a rear tire running flat and on its rim. Rev. Jim tossed aside the .44, reached under his seat for a double-pump sawed-off, and aimed it out his window. He and Ash did a quick eye exchange and both nodded as Rev. Jim came nose to nose with the chase car, both doing about forty and moving fast and steady toward a small mountain of smashed cars.

Ash fired first, getting off two rounds and clipping the driver in the shoulder, causing him to lose control of the wheel. Rev. Jim unloaded his shots and blew out the right side of the windshield, killing the shooter on the passenger side. He eased his foot over to the brake and slowed the unmarked down, watching as the chase vehicle, now with a badly wounded man behind the wheel, slammed into the shaky mound of rusty hulks. A half dozen of them collapsed on top of the crash car, pinning the surviving passengers deep inside.

Ash threw herself to the ground and slowly rose to her feet, her head and body thick with soot and smeared with blood. Rev. Jim put the car into park and left it running, stepping out of the glass-and-blood-strewn front seat and walking over to where Ash stood. "I have to figure you feel a lot better than you look," he said to her. "Am I right on that?"

"There is just no end to your charm," she said. "I'm fine, for now. But I'm down in bullets and we still have that van to worry about."

"Don't lose any sleep over it," Rev. Jim said. "Or blood." He turned, looking past the glare of the sun at the white van, now surrounded by the shooters from the three parked sedans. "Especially since that van is of no concern to us."

"Is there a part of this plan you didn't share?" Ash asked. She looked back and saw the men from the sedan tossing bodies out of the van and stepping inside to pop open a few of the stacked crates to check on the merchandise.

"What's a party without a surprise?" Rev. Jim said. "The hired guns in the sedans were supposed to be G-Men holding the cash to transfer to Angel's crew in return for the stash of drugs inside that van. That would have been the start and the finish of a mid-six-figure transaction. In other words, a nice paycheck for one side and a big street score for the other."

"Looks like the Donner Party beat them to it," Ash said. "How about I take a guess?"

"I *always* let a lady go first," Rev. Jim said. "And if you put the last piece to the puzzle the right way, then dinner will be my treat—soon as you shower and get all that glass out of your hair."

"You tipped off Tony Rigs as to the where and the when of the give-and-take," Ash said with a smile, wiping blood off her lips with the sleeve of her jean jacket.

"Ready for the Double Jeopardy round," Rev. Jim said, doing a quick return on the smile.

"And he arranged for the G-Men to fade while we were leading the chase cars and the van his way," Ash said. "Now, for my money there's no better spot anywhere in this city than a chop shop if you're looking to rid yourself of a few dead drug dealers."

"It's a low-end risk for a high-end score," Rev. Jim said. "The kind of deal Tony Rigs wouldn't turn down if his own mother was driving one of the crash cars."

"And none of the heat flows his way," Ash said. "Angel and the G-Men aren't going to cast blame on anyone but us. Meanwhile, Tony Rigs takes a walk with both the drugs and the cash."

"The drugs, yes," Rev. Jim said. "We don't touch that end of it. But the money comes to us. We're not Mobil Oil, baby. We have to pay for this little party of ours somehow, and who better than Angel to cough up into our empty pot?"

"Then we're done here," Ash said. "You okay with me doing the driving on the way back?"

Rev. Jim turned and started walking toward the shattered fence and out to the East Bronx streets. "If we had a ride, I would be all-for-one on it," he said to Ash. "But we need to leave the cars and the cash behind. Rigs will have the money delivered our way when the time is right, along with a fresh set of wheels. Which means it's the subway for us."

"A cab might be a better way to go," Ash said. "We get on the number two looking like this, caked with dirt and blood with glass sprinkled on our heads and shoulders, it might catch a curious eye."

Rev. Jim laughed, rested a hand on the small of her back, and pulled out his detective's shield, which was hanging from a chain under his pullover. "You and me were anywhere else, that might present itself as a problem," he said. "But we're in New York City. In this town, the insane and the cops ride free of charge."

23

CHAPTER

Hector Gonzalez and his main muscle man, Robles, stood over the bloody man, his upper body hanging over the side of a grime-filled sidewalk, his legs half wrapped around a dripping fire hydrant. Robles held a small black iron pipe in his left hand and had a lit cigarette hanging from the corner of his mouth. He leaned against a parked Ford Taurus and looked over at Gonzalez. "This the third straight week he's been behind on his payouts and the third straight week he's caught a beating," Robles said. "We're running on a reverse track with this loser, getting nowhere in a hurry."

"Maybe it's not him we should be touching," Gonzalez said. "Man's got a chubby wife and two fresh daughters. We retool them up a bit, then maybe he would be a lot quicker to cough up the cash he owes."

"Are you hearing any of this?" Robles asked the bleeding man, whose lips were kissing the street. "You don't come across with the pesos, we're going to have to head in there, pull out our muscle tool, and bump bellies with your wife and *chicas*. We do that, then maybe we slice about fifteen percent off of what you owe. If we make you watch, then maybe we shave off another five."

The man fought to lift his head off the sidewalk and rest it on the rear bumper of a late-model Suburban. "Doing that won't get you your money," he said. "Nothing will until I can get my business in the shape it once was, and that's not going to happen until you get that fucking priest off my back."

Hector Gonzalez gave a head nod to Robles. "Stand him up and pull him closer," he said. "I want to make sure I hear all his words."

Robles grabbed the front of the man's floral print shirt, thick splotches of fresh blood smeared across his chest and shoulders, and yanked him to his feet, tossing him against the hood of a Chevy Impala. "There, now that's better," Robles said. "You feeling comfy now, Quinto?"

"How much a week are you shaving to the priest?" Gonzalez asked, his dark, soulless eyes giving the street around them a quick look. He stood close enough to Quinto to see the blood pour off his wounds and smell the sweat running down his body. "And how long have you been feeding him?"

"He takes the skim," Quinto said, his lower lip shaking like a faulty brake pedal. "Leaves enough for me to stay even on a good week, fall back some on a slow. Been coming in steady for about a month now, give or take a day."

"And why you wait till now to pass it on to me?" Gonzalez asked. "He tell you not to say, or did you find that street on your own?"

"He said he would kill me and my family if I put even word one in front of you," Quinto said.

"And what do you think *I* will do?" Gonzalez asked, grabbing the cheeks of Quinto's chunky face in his right hand and pressing them together hard.

"Sounds like he wets his pants a lot more when he hears from that ex-priest than he does when the words come at him from our side, Papi," Robles said, standing now right next to Gonzalez. "We need to change the color of that shit, and fast, before it spreads to the rest of the neighborhood."

Hector Gonzalez looked over at the shivering Quinto and shook his head. "You know I can't have that happen," he said. "It doesn't take a lot for word to get out that the G-Men lost their grip and let any low-ride pussy with a gun and a posse come in and piss on their land. This starts with you, Quinto, and it's going to end with you."

"I won't let it happen again," Quinto said. "I won't give the priest any more of the money. I'll stand up to him, make him turn away with empty hands. I swear to it."

"If you had any balls, Quinto, you would have done that the first time he stepped into your place," Gonzalez said. "Spit in his face and tell him he was one shit shy of a pot of luck. But you covered yourself, made the priest a blanket for you and your family, in case he made a move our way and it paid off."

"Give me one more chance, Hector," Quinto said, his hands clasped, his body close to doing a full crumple. "I beg you to please do that, for all the years I have worked for you. I will do anything. Please."

"Fair enough," Gonzalez said. "You been with us from day one, Quinto, so it's only right for me to give your rope less of a tug. Go back inside your shop and bring your two girls out here to see me. I'll take it from there."

"This is between *us*," Quinto said, the panic in his voice taking a back seat to the rising anger. "My family has nothing to do with what goes on out here."

"We're all one family, no?" Gonzalez asked. "Me, you, Robles, your wife, your daughters. To make it work, we *all* need to work. And that's what the girls will do. They will work off the money you owe us, and if they taste anywhere near as good as they look, then you'll be in the red chips in no time. You should be happy, not upset."

"I can't let you do this," Quinto said. "No father could."

"I understand," Gonzalez said, stepping closer to Quinto. "Believe me, I hear what you're trying to say. You just didn't grasp what it is *I've* been running off at the mouth about. But that's okay, it's not the first time I've run into this situation. My man Robles here is right. He's always telling me I don't make myself easy to understand."

The long blade slid down the side of Gonzalez's jacket and slipped into the palm of his right hand, fingers quick to curl around the thick wood handle. Gonzalez didn't flinch as he jammed the knife hard and deep into Quinto's stomach and held him in place with his other hand, watching as he crumpled from the biting pain, his eyes bulging, warm blood oozing onto his hand and jacket, choking on the blood rushing up into his throat. With surgical skill, Gonzalez twisted the blade and pushed it up through artery, fat, and muscle, carving a slow and bloody arc. He held Quinto in check all the way through the death rattle and then stepped away, releasing his grip on the blade handle and watching as the man fell to the ground in a dead heap. "Go inside and bring those two bitches out here," he said to Robles. "Show them their father and then tell them what they need to do unless they want to find their fat-ass mother the same way."

"How soon you want them to start?" Robles asked.

"They're on the clock as of now," Gonzalez said. "They need to make up the money this piece of shit owed me before I sit down to dinner."

"Okay if I break them in?" Robles asked, walking toward the store. "Show them what they'll be expected to do?"

"As long as the money's on my table before I cut into my steak," Gonzalez said. He moved toward his parked sedan, the dead man's blood running down his right arm and hand, dripping onto the sidewalk.

"You want me to save one for you?" Robles asked. "Or bring her out to your car?"

"Not this time," Gonzalez said. "I got a date of my own, and this is one I don't want to be late on."

"You might want to stop and wash that blood off first," Robles said. "That shit could be a big turnoff for a chick."

"Not with this Russian," Gonzalez said, swinging open the door of his black Cadillac. "She's got the hunger for blood. The two of us together, it's a marriage made in hell."

24

The cross-town bus came to a slow stop in the middle of the street in front of Madison Green. The front doors swished open and two men in leather coats, carrying duffel bags, stepped in and paid their fares. They walked down the aisle and sat across from each other six rows deep. There was one other passenger on the bus, a man hunkered down in the corner seat of the last row, hat covering his face, the lip of his jacket serving as a blanket as he looked to sleep off a long night of heavy drink.

The doors closed and the bus slipped out, moving like a tired snake toward Madison Avenue, then taking a left turn uptown. One of the men stared out at the passing street action, his neck arched to catch a glimpse of the next scheduled stop. He smiled when he spotted a man in a white raincoat and a blue baseball cap holding a large gift-wrapped package in his arms. He turned away and gave the man sitting across from him a quick nod. "So far," he whispered with a slight smile.

The smile disappeared when the bus moved past the stop and

ran through a yellow light and kept sliding up Madison, the driver oblivious to the error. "Hey," the man shouted up to the driver. "You just missed a stop. Weren't you watching?"

"Too late for that now, chief," the driver said. "You can get off the next time I stop, not to worry."

"There was a passenger at that other stop," the man said, his voice barely under a shout. "You're *supposed* to pick him up. It's your fucking job."

"Maybe so," the driver said with a chuckle. "But this is only my second day behind the wheel and a man can only learn to do so much so fast, you understand. I think I got the driving part of it down, but the rest of it may take me a little time."

The bus stopped at a red light, riding in the center of three lanes, far removed from any shelters where small groups of passengers were gathered. The other man, silent until now, leaped to his feet, pulled a heavy-caliber handgun from his jacket pocket, and took several steps toward the driver. "Pull this fuckin' bus over to the side and do it now," he said to the driver.

The driver looked in the rearview mirror and glanced at the man with the gun standing less than five feet away. "Tell you what," the driver, Dead-Eye, said. "I'll cook you a deal. And I promise I'll make it one that's on the fair and square for all four of us."

"What the fuck are you running off at the mouth about?" the man with the gun said. "There's no deal and there's no four of anything in this shit, it's just the two of us and you."

"I knew I should have RSVP'd," Quincy, the man at the back of the bus, said with a shrug. He was standing halfway down the aisle, two .38 Specials in his hands, feet braced against the steel base of the seats. "I always suck at that kind of shit. Chalk it up to bad manners."

"You guys are on the salary end of the business, not the profit end," Dead-Eye said, easing the bus forward, careful not to veer too close to an off-duty taxi shifting lanes. "Same holds for the fool lugging that heavy gift box of cocaine a few stops back. So play it smart and give yourself a chance to live and breathe a few more days. I drop you off at a safe and cozy spot on my route and you walk off free and with a breeze to your back."

"Just so long as you leave the two duffel bags behind," Quincy said. "You have to throw that into the mix as well."

"Oh, right," Dead-Eye said. "I forgot to mention that one tiny little detail. What the money boys like to call the deal breaker."

"We can't leave the bags," the man with the gun said. "And we won't."

"Take a second," Dead-Eye said, letting go of the steering wheel, his eyes off the road and on the two men, the bus parked in the middle of a busy avenue, his voice as serious as an illness. "Take a long, hard second before you make that your final call."

The man sitting, the duffel bag resting against his left leg, made the first move. With his left hand he threw the bag toward Quincy, pulled a .44 bulldog out of his jacket with his right, and started firing shots at Dead-Eye. The man standing whirled and fired off two quick rounds at Quincy.

Dead-Eye did a quick duck behind the driver's barrier, heard the bullets ping against the front end of the bus and then lunged out of his seat, guns in both hands, firing at the two men. Quincy jumped into the rear stairwell and shot off rounds from both his guns at the sitting man. The inside of the bus was now a hot and shuttered fire zone, as a dozen bullets flew in four different directions. The four men held their ground, each prepared to die.

The man standing in the middle of the bus, his back to Quincy and pegging rapid-fire shots at Dead-Eye, was the first to go down. The gun slipped away from his hand and he fell slowly to his knees, a large dark hole in his cheek holding the fatal slug. He rocked back and forth for several seconds, bringing the action around him to a halt, then dropped flat on his face, a blood mass forming around his neck.

Quincy did a quick clip reload, and Dead-Eye moved away from the driver's side and down the aisle, their guns aimed at the remaining man, sitting now with his back pressed against a cracked window. "You don't need to die," Dead-Eye said to him. "You only need to drop your piece and get your ass off this bus."

Police sirens exploded around them, traffic and crowds swarmed and stalled around the bus, locking it in place. "He's not the only one," Quincy said. "We got less than two minutes to get lost before we're pinned in for good."

Dead-Eye walked down the aisle, stepped over the body of the first shooter, and rested the barrel of his gun on the man's chest. "If I'm going to get arrested on this bus, it's going to be for *two* murders," he said to the man, his voice low and direct. "It's your call to make, but you need to make it now."

The man nodded and slowly slid his weapon back inside the front flap of his jacket. "You win, at least for today," he said, watching as Dead-Eye backed away, moving to the rear doors next to Quincy. "We'll be back for our money. Only next time, you'll be facing more than two of us."

"Good," Quincy said. "I'm always up for a party."

The shooter stood and ran toward the front doors, his left hand reaching for the lever that slid them open. He jumped off the bus, gave one final look to his fallen partner, and ran out into the crowd and the traffic.

Dead-Eye grabbed one of the duffel bags and tossed it to Quincy. He picked up the other and together they pushed open the rear rubber doors and stepped out onto the crowded street. "Is there any plan if one of us gets nabbed?" Quincy asked.

"You're holding two hundred thousand in neatly bundled bills in a duffel bag," Dead-Eye said. "That should be more than enough to buy you a sweet-talking lawyer and still have some left over to skim a few held-out palms."

"Is that the best you can offer?" Quincy asked.

"You can always float your way over to Plan B," Dead-Eye said, making his way around a blocked cab and three stalled pedestrians.

"Which is what?" Quincy asked, stepping over the bumper of a UPS truck landlocked alongside a battered Chrysler Cordoba.

"Bust your way out of Rikers," Dead-Eye said. "You may not make it, but we would be more than impressed by the attempt."

Quincy laughed, waved, and disappeared into the thick fog of cars and people, black-and-whites and fire engines flooding the outskirts of the area. Dead-Eye watched him fade away as he slowly made his way east toward Lexington Avenue. He looked back, smiled, and shook his head. He stopped at a corner, waited for a red light to turn green, and gave a nod to two uniformed patrolmen heading toward the chaos at his back. The duffel bag in his right hand, he walked away with another dent in Angel's daily cash flow.

25

————— CHAPTER —————

Boomer and Buttercup ran together, moving at their briskest clip, breath escaping in painful spurts from two sets of damaged lungs. They turned a sharp corner and veered down a tight alley, thick black garbage bags lining both sides, hot blasts of steam shooting from the rusty mouths of aluminum chutes. Four gunmen were fast on them, semis held low, shoes and boots stepping into small mounds of waste and thick puddles of oil mixed with stagnant water. Boomer looked down the long alley, past the low-hanging clothesline crammed with stained napkins and sheets, at the street-lights half a block away and came to a quick stop. Buttercup came to an equally rapid halt, her tongue hanging out one side of her mouth, white foam dripping from her jowls, and cast a steady gaze up at Boomer. A thick rain washed over them both, mixing with the hot sweat pouring off their bodies. Boomer ran a wet hand across the police dog's soggy head. "It's not like you to run from a fight," he said to her. "Not like me, either. If you're up to taking one down, I'll make on the other three."

Buttercup turned away from Boomer and stepped in front of him, her eyes focused now on the four gunmen making their way toward them down the alleyway, her rear paws digging into the mud and soot of the wet ground, looking for traction, her muscular torso coiled and tight, her mouth open and small, warm puffs of white air forming around her nostrils. Boomer pulled two guns from his waistband and moved to his left, using the hanging wet sheets as cover. Buttercup stood her ground, waiting for the first of the gunmen to get close enough for her to pounce, aware of the loaded weapon in his hand and the crazed look in his eyes.

The lead gunman wiped the rain from his face, searching out Boomer through the heavy rainfall. The loud noise of half a dozen crammed restaurant kitchens, minimum-wage workers washing and rinsing dishes, echoed through the alley. Added to the noisy mix were radios blaring songs from three different continents. Every so often, a pail of dirty dishwater tossed out of an open doorway would splash across the black stones of the alley.

The lead gunman never saw Buttercup.

The police dog waited until he was only a short leap away and made her move. The first bite was quick and meant to bring him down, a fast, sharp snap to the left ankle. The jolt of pain brought the gunman to the ground, his weapon sliding out of his hand and landing against a half-filled crate of pearl onions. He landed face forward, the blow causing his nose and chin to bleed, the bone in his left leg snapped beyond fixing.

Buttercup turned and hovered over her fallen foe. The man lifted his right hand and made a feeble attempt to slap the dog away, his other hand reaching for the gun several feet beyond his grasp. Boomer stepped in from out of the shadows, raised one of his guns, and put two heavy blows to the face side of the man's head, leaving him stiff and cold. He then dropped to both knees, straddling the unconscious man. He pointed his two arms out and opened fire, the sparks, smoke, and pop from his guns adding to the noise and confusion of the bustling alleyway. He pulled on the two triggers until all he heard was empty clicks.

Boomer then rolled over toward a grimy wall and jumped up, reaching for the bottom rung of a fire-escape ladder. He pulled it down and hoisted himself up. He reached the first landing, raced to the far edge, and looked down through the rain, smoke, and dust. One of the gunmen was down, and it looked as if he would need more than time to get back up. The other two had their guns out and were silently inching forward, not sure from which direction the next rounds would come. Boomer waited until the one to his right was close to the fire escape. He lifted himself up on the rusty edge, checked to see where Buttercup had positioned herself, and then made his jump.

He landed on the gunman's back and both did a hard-and-fast roll on the soiled turf, their hands, heads, and clothes drenched in soot and rain. Boomer reached around and clasped a forearm across the man's throat, using a three-deep mountain of black garbage bags as leverage, his boots digging into the dark cobblestones, his back arched, the full force of his strength sapping the gunman of what was left of his. Boomer leaned away from the wall and lifted the man's head up, then gave it a final and vicious twist, snapping his neck bone and windpipe. He moved his arm off the man and eased his head down onto one of the garbage bags, turning away to make a grab for the semiautomatic that had fallen from his hand.

He never heard the fourth gunman.

He came up behind Boomer and pressed his gun hard against the back of his neck. "If you're smart as they say, throw a signal to that fuckin' sixteen-wheel dog of yours to stay wherever the fuck it is," the man said.

"Forget the dog," Boomer said, "and tell me what it is you think I need to hear."

"What makes you think I got anything to say to you?" the man asked.

"You were sent after me, the four of you, to deliver a message," Boomer said. "The other three aren't in any kind of shoot-the-shit mood. That just leaves you. So let's hear it."

"Five million," the man said. "That's how much you, the dog, and the other gimps in your crew can take home just by stepping the fuck out of this and let the business go on without you."

"That's a lot of cash for a priest to be hauling around," Boomer said. "Don't you think?"

"Better in your pockets than in his, is how I would look at it," the man said. "Either way, I need to walk from here with an answer, good or bad."

"And if it's not an answer you want to hear?" Boomer said. "What then?"

"I kill you and the mutt," the man said.

"You really don't like dogs, do you?" Boomer said.

"Five million in cash or one bullet to the head," the man said.

"Do you have the money with you?" Boomer asked. "Or do they only trust you with the bullets?"

"Decide now," the man said, moving the gun from the base of Boomer's neck to the back of his head.

Boomer lowered his head, his hands resting flat on the wet ground, and nodded. "I've never been any good with money," he said. Boomer pressed down on both hands, lifted his feet off the ground, and pushed them hard against the trigger man's ankles. The force of the push, coupled with the slippery wet turf, threw the man off balance, the gun pointing up at the sky, his body arching at an angle toward a pile of crushed cardboard boxes. Boomer turned and reached a hand behind him, his fingers searching through the mud and grime for the rain-soaked semiautomatic. The trigger man rolled off the cardboard boxes, jumped to his feet, and raised his gun in Boomer's direction, his finger wrapped around the trigger. Boomer, his back to the gunman, placed his right hand and fingers on the semi and did a fast ground roll, quick to avoid the first stream of bullets. The blasts skimmed the ground around him, sending thick specks of wet dirt and rock slapping against a far wall.

The gunman was now on his feet and looking down at Boomer, still fighting to get a grip on the slippery semi. "You could have walked away a very rich man," he said to Boomer. "Instead, you're going to die a poor man in a shithole of an alley. Just like any other loser of a cop."

The pointed end of the knife went into the gunman's back hard and with precision, and he dropped to the ground with a muted thud, his clear eyes opened wide and a stream of blood flowing from his mouth as his teeth jammed down on his tongue. The gunman teetered back and forth, his body in the throes of a death tremble, his face drained of color and life. He landed flush against the wall, his dying body propped up by a thick pile of garbage bags.

Boomer stood and walked past the gunman and toward the young man standing in the lit entryway to a restaurant's hot and smoky kitchen. "You always stick a knife in somebody who's blocking your doorway?" he asked him.

"I do if he's aiming to kill a friend," the young man said, stepping deeper into the doorway and away from the heavy raindrops.

"We're a dozen miles away from calling each other friend,"

Boomer said, looking down as Buttercup stepped up next to him. "I don't even know your name."

"There's no need for you to know it," the young man said. "It was just important that I knew yours, and that I picked up earlier today."

"Who passed it on?" Boomer asked.

"My friend," the young man said, turning away and disappearing into the heat of his kitchen. "Tony Rigs."

26

CHAPTER

Boomer stood in the middle of Nunzio's ruined restaurant, the outside shell dark and smoking, the interior smoldering and destroyed. In the center of what had been a bustling dining room, less than a dozen feet from where the bar had stood, the charred remains of Nunzio Goldman were nailed to a beam that had managed to withstand the worst of the blaze. Rev. Jim sat by himself in a corner of the restaurant, his black jacket pressed against a still warm wall. Quincy paced in a tight circle, his hands at his sides, his head lowered, lost in deep thought. Buttercup sat next to Nunzio's body, her front paws folded one over the other, her large eyes tired and worn, her brown coat darkened by the layers of soot on the ground. Ash was hunched over a series of burnt wires, her fingers gently easing their way from the burnt cords to the wall unit, the search for the cause of the fire not requiring any of her skills.

Dead-Eye stared at Nunzio, losing the battle against his tears. "He didn't have a part in this," Dead-Eye said. "If that was one of us up there, I would feel the hurt but I would understand the why. But Nunzio had earned a better way out."

"They got to him because they knew it would get to us," Boomer said. "That's who they are and it's what they do. If we didn't know that before today, we better know that now."

"They didn't do anything to hide their intentions," Ash said. "If I did a scan of this place, I bet I'd find everything—from prints to DNA. It's all here except for a paper trail."

"We knew who it was *before* we walked in here," Quincy said. "Question now is where do we take it?"

"First we need to bury our friend," Rev. Jim said.

"And after we do that?" Ash asked. "Do we still keep to the current plan, or do we take it a step higher?"

Boomer turned to face the other Apaches, his back to Nunzio's remains. "It's not enough anymore just to put a dent in their operations," he said. "We need to take them out. We need to take them *all* out. Angel and his crew, the G-Men, and anyone else eager to line up on their side have got to go down."

"How's that plan play out?" Rev. Jim said. "I'm willing to shoot until I die, but there's a shitload more of them than there are of us. The numbers don't stack to our side."

"Up until now, we've been bending the rules," Boomer said. "Making side deals with Tony Rigs, asking some of the other crews to step back or lend a hand, knowing they would profit in the long run if we found any success."

"And not everybody in here was comfortable with those alliances," Dead-Eye said. "Myself included. That's because we were still thinking like cops—retired, disabled, or not. We can't think like that anymore. Ever again. We're not cops, and we haven't been for a long time."

"If we're going to get these bastards, we need to forget the badge and the bag of rules that comes with it," Boomer said. "Because this isn't a job for cops, never was. We only kidded ourselves into thinking that way."

"And if we're not cops, what are we?" Ash asked.

Boomer tugged on the question for a moment. Turning away from them all, he said, "We're killers."

3

BOOK

Will you partake of that last offered cup
Or disappear into the potter's ground?

—JOHNNY CASH
"THE MAN COMES AROUND"

1

Dead-Eye stood staring out across the empty racetrack, the early-morning mist fading fast with the arrival of the postdawn sun. Boomer stood next to him, back to the quarter-horse racetrack, long since abandoned to decay and indecision by executives low on cash and lacking in incentive. He gazed up at the grandstand, the once clean white seats and ornate poles coated now with a harsh tint of rust. "It's a shame to see what's happened to this place," Boomer said. "I remember when the gates first opened; it was as beautiful and elegant as any palace you could imagine. Now, it just sits back and waits for the wrecking ball."

"You know what's even more of a shame?" Dead-Eye said. "At least to me?"

Boomer looked over and shook his head. "Tell me," he said.

"A great cop, maybe the best ever, tossing all the good he ever did away for a woman he has no business being near," Dead-Eye said, anger seething through every word. "To me, that's a lot worse than any racetrack on its last legs."

Boomer stayed silent for several moments. "I know what I'm doing, Dead-Eye," he finally said. "I don't need you to tell me otherwise."

"You think so?" Dead-Eye asked, stepping away from the railing. "Well, then, let me clue you in, partner. You are so knee-deep with this broad, you can't see more than five feet in front of you. Shit, man, this isn't a fucking prom queen we're talking about here; this is a top-of-the-line crime boss. And she will fucking waste you soon as look at you, no matter how much in love you think she is. Which, by the way, she isn't. People like her *never* fall in love, and if they do, it's *never* with someone like you."

"I've been seeing her—that part is true," Boomer said. "But I'm not in love with her. I know what's at stake here, and I know what's real and what isn't. And I would never mix up the two."

"Look, we've crossed every line a cop can cross and still, at the end of the day, we could hang on to our shields, knowing we did right by them," Dead-Eye said. "But this is one line, Boomer, that you *cannot* cross. There is no way back. I'm not telling you this to break your heart. I'm telling you this because there's still time to save it. We can never help who we fall in love with. But in this case you have to turn and walk away from it."

"We need her help," Boomer said, "and she'll give it because I'll ask for it. After this is done, and if we're still around, she goes her way and I go mine. And that's how it's going to play."

Dead-Eye leaned back and took a deep breath, letting the coolness of the morning wash over his face. "There's no need for the others to know about this," he said, his voice lower, calmer. "This should stay where it belongs—and that's between the two of you."

"You spotted it, why not one of the others?" Boomer asked.

"They don't know the signs, least not the way I do," Dead-Eye said. "Shit, we've been together so long, when you inhale I exhale."

"Well, then, let's hope that between the two of us we got enough breath left to take out these bastards," Boomer said.

Natalie cradled the warm cup of tea between her fingers and looked over at Boomer, the lines around her dark eyes weighed down with concern. "I'm very sorry about what happened to your friend," she said. "They went after what they thought would hurt you the most."

"Would you have done it the same way if you and me were sitting on opposite sides?" Boomer asked.

"We *are* on opposite sides," Natalie said. "But to answer your question, yes, I would have done it the same way."

"Why?" Boomer asked.

"To show you the level of my anger," Natalie said. "And to illustrate how far I would be willing to go to rid myself of such a pain in my side. It also would force you to turn to desperate means in order to achieve a victory that on your own you cannot ever hope to attain."

"Is that what you think I'm doing now?" Boomer asked, leaning closer to Natalie. "Reaching out to you—is that how you see it, a desperate measure?"

"A detective seeking my help in wiping out two crews of drug dealers?" Natalie said. "I think that answer presents itself."

"You put it on the table before and I turned away," Boomer said. "It was a mistake, and a friend of mine died because of it."

"Before this is over, with or without my help, you stand to lose many more of your friends," Natalie said, taking a sip of her tea. "And the same is true of your enemies. It's what the two sides in any war have in common."

They were in the back room of a small Upper West Side tea-and-biscuit shop with a cozy feel and an old-world design, the walls around them crowded with large framed photos of European settings from earlier eras. Natalie was wearing a floral print skirt with a blue jacket and black pumps with low-cut tops, looking more like a banker on her day off than the ruthless leader of a criminal enterprise.

"What kind of help can I expect to get?" he asked, reaching over to pour her a fresh cup of herbal tea.

"That depends on what you expect to accomplish," she said, her spend-the-night eyes sparkling under the chandelier's soft glare. "On what it is you want to see happen to the two crews on the other end."

"A wipeout," Boomer said. "A total dismantling of their operation and elimination of the players at their table."

Natalie shook her head. "That's not what you want, and it's certainly not what I do," she said. "That's just your anger talking."

"Then you tell me," Boomer said. "But know this, with or without you, we're going in against these crews and we'll stay in until they carry us out."

"There are six on your team if you include the dog," Natalie said. "And you've done quite a bit of damage with that small a group in a short period of time, but you've accomplished nothing.

You've been flies buzzing around. You need to be quite a bit more than that."

"Can you get me to Angel?" Boomer asked. "And the Gonzalez brothers, too, as well as the people in their tight circle?"

"Yes," she said. "These guerrilla tactics you use are very effective on the street, especially if the dealers on the other end are working blind to any trouble. You can do the same on a higher level, you just need access."

"And what is it you want in return for that access?" Boomer asked.

"I move in, once the blood settles, and take over their operations," Natalie said. "It's as clean as that."

Boomer sat back and stayed silent for several moments. "You know, there's a thin line you need to navigate when you're on the job, a cop like I was," he said. "To get it done—and more often than not to get it done right—I needed to step over that line. And believe me, I stepped over it more times than I ever want to admit, but I always justified it by the results. I knew the rules and was well aware of when I was breaking them."

"And now?" she asked.

"Now?" he said. "All those rules, the ones I broke and the ones I followed, mean shit to me right now. I don't know what that makes me. I know I can't call myself a cop anymore—that tugboat took off a long time ago. I was kidding myself into believing otherwise. It was easier than thinking what I was out there doing was criminal."

"Then why do it at all?" Natalie asked. "You can turn around and walk away from it, even now. No one would come after you if you went that route. I would see to that."

"With you," Boomer asked, "or without?"

"I would like to think with," Natalie said. "I just can't think of how we could ever make it work."

"Neither can I," Boomer said to her. "So how about we just keep it to business for now until at least one of us can?"

Natalie nodded, her eyes locked on Boomer, who sat across from her now clear of the warmth he had shown earlier, resembling more a fighter ready to get into the ring for one last, vicious battle. "The odds are stacked against you, regardless of how much help you get from me," she said. "You go in with the numbers heavy in their favor and face two crews who give no thought to any lines being blurred. You've seen how they conduct their business, the coldness with which they dispatch an enemy. There is no collateral damage where they are concerned. If you and your team bring the fight to their turf, they will consider anyone you know and like a target equal to one of you and they will make a move against them."

"Same true for you?" Boomer asked her. "Is that how you come in ready to do battle?"

"Yes, only more so," Natalie said, wiping loose strands of hair from her eyes. "It is not enough to beat your opponent. Victory is accomplished only when he is destroyed. Are you prepared to do that?"

"I wouldn't be in a tea room if I wasn't," Boomer said. "And if you come in with us it makes us more than friends. It makes us partners."

"I've never had a partner," Natalie said. "And I don't have friends. I can't afford the risk either brings."

"Then what is it you and me do have?" Boomer asked.

"Something we can both embrace," Natalie said, "and which I find to be stronger than either a friend or a partner."

"And that's what, exactly?" Boomer asked.

"Mutual enemies," Natalie said.

3

Jonas Talbot stepped off the elevator on the second floor and made a sharp right-hand turn, heading down a carpeted hallway for the wood-paneled library at the far end of the five-story town house. He was holding an unlit Delmonico cigar in his right hand and cradling a leather-bound copy of *Zorba the Greek,* by Nikos Kazantzakis, in his left. He was, as usual, meticulously dressed and groomed, and appeared eager to embark on his late-afternoon respite of a few hours of quiet reading mixed in with the enjoyment of a fine cigar. It was the only leisure break he ever allowed himself in the course of an otherwise crammed schedule, preferring to do the bulk of his work in the quiet hours of the New York nights and early mornings. Talbot suffered from dual jolts of blinding migraine headaches and chronic bouts of insomnia, and found his only relief from both demons in the sanctuary of a three-thousand-book library collection and the aroma of swirling cigar smoke. Only then was he a man at peace with both himself and his surroundings.

He had read six pages deeper into the novel before resting it open against his chest, his body sunk and snug inside the contours of a thick and rich brown leather wing chair, and reaching for the wide cigar and a gold lighter dominated by the open mouth of a lion. He snapped the tip of the lighter with his right thumb and watched with one eye closed as the long, thin flame scorched the brown tobacco. He took in a deep drag and then flinched when he heard the unfamiliar voice come at him from behind. "I never lose my sense of amazement at how sweet a life some of you rich fuck-ers have," Boomer said. "And all of it built on the backs, good, bad, or nasty, of a handful of poor fucks who would kill you in a tick if they knew how good a ride you coasted in on."

"Am I to suppose, based on your initial statement, that I'm in the middle of some sort of shakedown?" Talbot asked. "Or did you venture in here out of mere curiosity?"

"They pay you extra to talk like that?" Boomer asked, stepping around the wing chair and looking down at Talbot. "If that's the case, you're better off saving the store-bought vocab for the easily impressed."

"Now that we can safely rule out conversation," Talbot said, "what is it you came in here expecting to walk out with?"

"Details, mostly," Boomer said, stepping back and looking around the thick wooden bookcases, which reached up to the very base of the fourteen-foot ceiling.

"Concerning what, if I may ask?" Talbot said.

"We're going to start our little journey with Sean Valentine and work our way through his grease-stained pad," Boomer said. "From there, you're going to tell me what you know about the Boiler Man and where and how I can reach out his way."

"Is there anything else?" Talbot asked, taking a long and deep drag on his cigar, his face surrounded by puffs of white smoke.

"Assuming you get that far and are still alive, we'll move on to

Angel," Boomer said. "I always figured he kept a fleshy mound of jelly as his bitch, him being an ex-priest and all, but I never banked on it being someone with pockets deep as yours."

"Do you mind if I ask how you managed to get in here?" Talbot asked. "Just to appease my curiosity, nothing more."

"I let myself in," Boomer said with a smile and a shrug. "The front door was open. All I had to do was sidestep the two guys curled and bleeding in your foyer. It wasn't like I had to concern myself with an alarm going off or anything like that, especially since they don't usually work without their wires attached. Now, do you have all the background info you need for us to get started or you want to know how it is I figured I'd find you in here, sitting all nice and cozy-like?"

"I can save you a great deal of time and trouble," Talbot said. "I never give any information about my clients to anyone, regardless of the threat level directed toward me. There is very little you can do, short of murder, to change that course of action, and you don't seem like the cold-blooded type, despite the harsh talk."

Boomer had his hands in his pockets, his head down, pacing in a tight circle several feet from Talbot's chair. "You collect art as well as books," he said. "I read that about you in one of the file reports. Expensive art—worth millions, some of the pieces. In fact, if what I read was accurate, you put all your money into books and works of art. That right, would you say?"

"Get to the point, policeman," Talbot said, his soft face no match for the harsh voice. "You've already cost me the privilege of a relaxing afternoon."

"You like bonfires?" Boomer said. "Me? I can take them or leave them. But my friend Ash, she lives for that shit. So trust me when I tell you, your afternoon is just about to start."

The paintings were stacked one on top of the other in two piles, six to each. Rev. Jim and Quincy had brought them into the library, scouring the rooms of the town house to take down the designated works. Ash stood next to the paintings, a tin of gas resting between her and Buttercup. Dead-Eye was in one corner of the library looking through a row of books. "This guy has all the works of Alexandre Dumas," he shouted out to Boomer. "He was always my favorite, ever since I was a kid. I used to read his books in the library next to our building every day after school, stayed until my eyes burned. But they didn't have copies this good, not with all this leather and shit."

"Take them, every last one," Boomer said. "They're yours. I am certain that Mr. Talbot here would want you to have them."

"My mother used to say there are four things you should never lend out and expect to have returned to you," Talbot said, his eyes focused on the stacked paintings.

"My mom used to say the same thing," Dead-Eye said, walking toward Boomer and Talbot, his arms weighed down with a thick stack of leather-bound books. "And I bet the two ladies were of one mind. You never lend books, umbrellas, money, or your wife."

"That's correct," Talbot said.

"Well, you can stay free of worries on that score," Boomer said. "You're not lending him those books; you're giving them to him. And don't think for one quick second that none of us are grateful."

"If this is how you expect to get any information from me, you're so sadly mistaken," Talbot said. "I can have every one of those books replaced by morning."

"No kidding, Sheerluck," Boomer said. "But not any of those paintings, you can't. They're one of a kind. Am I right?"

"I brought down a Degas and a Picasso," Rev. Jim said. "And I think I might have seen a Monet somewhere in one of the batches.

But since I don't know shit from sunshine about art, I can only guess they're worth a few loose coins to somebody."

"I'd ballpark the whole lot to run between forty and sixty million," Quincy said. "Give or take a million on either side."

"That's some ballpark to be in," Ash said. "I hope Buttercup doesn't get the urge to take one of her five-minute bladder drains on any of them. I can't get urine stains off a couch, so I can only imagine how much damage it would do to canvas."

"Not to mention the gasoline in that canister," Dead-Eye said. "Shit, that whole batch, top to bottom, would go up faster than a winter sneeze."

"That's enough," Talbot said. "Your juvenile humor is wasted on me, as is your time and mine. As ignorant as I'm sure each one of you surely is, I doubt very much that even low-rent Neanderthals such as the lot of you would venture to destroy great works of art."

"Really?" Boomer said. "And what's the why not to that theory?"

"There's neither profit nor pleasure in it for you," Talbot said with calm assurance. "And it won't help get you one inch closer to your intended targets. It would be a fruitless and pointless gesture."

"He might be onto something there," Dead-Eye said. "I mean, let's face it. We don't know shit from squid about any kind of art, other than that paint-by-numbers stuff my kid likes to work on."

"Don't knock it," Rev. Jim said. "That's nowhere near as easy as it looks. Takes a lot of hand-to-eye skill to stay within those dotted lines."

Boomer turned away from the Apaches and looked down at Talbot, the lit cigar still clutched in his right hand, the smug look returning. "You know, there's a lot of weight to what they're saying and you're probably right. Burning them would be nothing more than a waste of time. Except for Ash, none of us would really get any kind of a kick out of it."

"I'm glad to see you curtail your initial anger and return to a sensible position," Talbot said.

"So how about we do this, then?" Boomer said. "And I do think you'll like this idea a lot better than the first one."

"I'm still your prisoner," Talbot said. "And even if I weren't, I would still be eager to listen to any solution you can cleverly devise."

"We'll just give them away," Boomer said, the smile fading. "All of them. The ones stacked behind me and the ones still left hanging on the walls. Every fucking painting in your collection, gone. And I have to believe that doing something like that to a guy like you will hit you harder than any bullet I can pin your way."

"And who is it you could possibly know that would have the knowledge and the know-how to fence and move such valuable and well-documented works of art?" Talbot asked, each word filled with a syrup drip of sarcasm. "Tony Rigs would be a poor choice indeed. The man is dumb as a tree stump, thinks Degas is a shortstop for the Mets. Stay to your strengths, cop, and don't risk the drive onto unfamiliar terrain. Works of art do not fall under your skill set."

"Would they fall under mine?" Natalie Robinov asked, stepping up behind Talbot, a leather-backed copy of *Crime and Punishment* cradled against her chest. "Or do I need a degree in art history to move your paintings on the black market?"

Talbot responded to the sound of her voice with a sudden jolt and turned to face her, the cigar slipping from his fingers and onto the thick carpet by his feet. "What are you doing here?" he managed to stammer. "It's not like you to be seen in the company of lawmen, retired or otherwise."

"I'm a sucker for a bargain," Natalie said. "So when I heard the whispers that your vast collection might be coming on the market, I just had to come and see for myself. And, sure enough, it's available—and at such an affordable price."

Talbot stared at Natalie for several moments and then eased himself out of his wing chair and walked over to her. "I will tell them anything they need to know," he said, his words more a plea than a statement. "Just please, leave me my collection. I've poured my life and my fortune into the possession of these works. You can't take them from me, I beg you."

"Give them all the information they require," Natalie said to him. "The full details, and leave nothing out. Whatever questions you are asked, give them a complete and total response."

"And what will come my way in return?" Talbot said.

"I will allow you to keep one of your paintings," she said, her smile as cold as a late-winter storm. "And it will be your choice as to which of the works stays behind. Think it over with great care."

"I would rather die than live without my paintings," Talbot said, using up his final doses of defiance. "That you must believe to be true."

"You will die, Talbot," Natalie said. "That is why the decision behind which painting you choose is so critical. It must be your very favorite, the one that holds the greatest meaning. For it is that painting that will be placed over your body and buried with you."

Talbot turned away from Natalie and looked over at Boomer and the rest of the Apaches. "I misjudged you," he said. "I felt you would veer from the rules of your previous profession, but never abandon them completely. It was foolish of me to read a situation so completely wrong."

"You were the one that broke the rules, Talbot," Boomer said, "not me. You went out and touched my family, and then you reached down and touched my friend. That was what led you to wrong. And, in your case, that meant dead wrong."

4

The Boiler Man was in the center of the bed, his pants undone, his shirt and jacket hanging across the back end of a wooden chair in the corner of the dimly lit room. He had his hands folded and tucked under his neck, a glass of bourbon resting on the small end table to his right, eyes closed, body in full relax mode. It was late in the afternoon of a windswept spring day, overhead clouds bordering on menace, heavy rains taking a long, slow path from the Midwest skies toward the tristate area.

The knock on the hotel-room door was soft and quick, knuckles barely making contact with the thick mahogany. The Boiler Man didn't flinch, the gun jammed under his pillow still in place, the switchblade strapped to his right ankle within easy reach. "Use the key," he said.

The lock snapped open and the young woman walked into the room, stopping only to latch the door shut, deadbolt firmly in place. She turned and stepped farther into the room, her head down, her slender body partially hidden by heavy shadows. The Boiler Man, his eyes still shut, manner calm and controlled, spread out his arms and rotated his shoulder muscles, easing out any tension that might lay hidden. "There's bourbon and gin in the mini," he said. "Help yourself to whatever you like, short of calling room service."

The woman swung open the door of the small fridge, bent down, and picked up a dwarf-size bottle of vodka. She snapped open the top, letting the red lid fall to the carpeted floor. She took the drink in one swallow, rested the empty bottle next to a Zenith flattop, and walked over toward the right side of the bed.

The Boiler Man opened his eyes and looked into the woman's face. He smiled. "I knew we would eventually meet," he said to her.

"I'm surprised you recognize me," said Ash, her mind flashing on the fire that killed her mother and her grandfather. On the man who set the blaze. And she felt grateful once more for Natalie Robinov's tip on the Boiler Man's whereabouts. "I was a kid back when it happened, and a lot has changed since then."

"Yes," the Boiler Man said, "and I'm aware of most of it. I've kept tabs on you best I could all these years. It was all new to me back then. My timing was off. You were meant to die that day as well."

"It didn't need to happen," Ash said. "They didn't need to die the way they did."

"It had nothing to do with them," the Boiler Man said. "It was about a building that someone felt had to be burned to the ground and was willing to pay for that to happen. Besides, some good came of it all. You found a profession in which you excelled, until the flames of another fire brought that to an end."

"It was your only fire," Ash said. "So why?"

"The money was more than enough for my time and efforts, but I found the method to be too impersonal," the Boiler Man said, reaching his right hand out for his glass of bourbon. He took several swigs, his eyes on the woman a quick reach away from his bedside.

"I prefer the more direct approach when it applies to my victims. I found a great deal more satisfaction in being an assassin than in being an arsonist. And greater financial rewards as well."

"Do you ever think of them?" Ash asked. "Your victims? Are they anything more to you than a paycheck?"

"I thought of you," the Boiler Man said. "But you were a victim of a different stripe. I obviously didn't kill you. Instead, you must live with the memory of those who did die."

"Did you know I would come after you?" she asked.

"In my line of work, you are not allowed the luxury of surprises," the Boiler Man said. "I figured you would one day make a move against me."

"Did you give any thought to trying to stop me?" Ash asked.

"No," the Boiler Man said. "I felt the first move in our little lethal dance belonged to you. I assume this is it. Unless, of course, you do indeed work as a high-end Upper East Side call girl."

Ash shook her head slowly. "Not too many men would be willing to pony up two thousand an hour for a woman with burn scars," she said.

"I'm sorry for what happened to you back then," the Boiler Man said. "I want you to know that before I kill you."

"Take your apology with you to hell," Ash said.

The Boiler Man sat up in the bed, the .44 pulled from under his pillow and in his right hand, cocked and ready to fire. Ash did a roll-and-tumble toward the door, snapped open the deadbolt, and came up with a .38 in one hand and a small detonator switch box in the other. She caught the surprised look in the Boiler Man's eyes and smiled. "The device is in the fridge," she said, the anger in her voice audible. "Take it as a lesson: Never offer a lady a drink until you know her true intentions."

Ash took advantage of the slight pause and got off the first rounds, popping three slugs in the Boiler Man's direction. Two dented the headboard and sent a thick cloud of old wood chips into the dry air. The third nicked the Boiler Man in the muscle end of his shoulder. Ash swung open the door and leaned against it, one foot in the hall, one finger on the detonator button, her eyes on her enemy. "You should have killed me," she said to him. "You should have hunted me down and killed me."

"It's never too late," the Boiler Man said.

He jumped off the bed, his feet flat on the carpeted floor, arms held out, gun aimed in Ash's direction, and pulled off three quick rounds. Ash dived into the empty hallway and landed with her back to the flower-print wall, her gun by her feet, both hands holding on to the small detonator. She pressed down on the button and threw herself to the floor, face rubbing against the thick carpet, eyes closed, images of her mother and her grandfather clear in her mind.

The Boiler Man lowered his weapon and waited for the truth that each man who devotes his life to murder must eventually face.

His own demise.

The blast shattered the windows that looked out onto Fifth Avenue and crumpled the bed and the chairs. The walls folded in from the heat, and both the television and the fridge melted from the intense explosion. A ball of flame followed by a thick wave of smoke flew out of the room and raced down through the hall, rushing over Ash's still body, her hands masking her eyes and mouth.

The Boiler Man was no longer a ghost for her to hunt down.

5

—— CHAPTER ——

Angel leaned against a yellow wall next to the blackboard of a third-floor classroom in an empty public school. It was a sunny Sunday morning, and the street outside was lined with the silent elderly, loud children, and tired couples making their way to the nine o'clock Mass at the Catholic church across the way. Taped to the blackboard, starting on the left with Boomer and ending on the far right with Buttercup, were head shots of the Apaches. Angel looked down the rows of chipped and stained desks, set in a line of four, six to each, and glared over at the Gonzalez brothers, each one jammed inside a seat meant for a twelve-year-old. "This situation has to be brought to an end and fast," he said to them. "You know it and I know it. Our differences aside, this is one we should handle working as one."

"They've only picked our pockets," Hector Gonzalez said. "Meantime, they cleaned out your bank account. Doesn't speak well of your street talent."

"It only *started* with me," Angel said, ignoring the slight. "But you're in their scope just as much as my crew. We're linked together in this, like it or not."

"For that they need to have found themselves some heavyweight help," Freddie Gonzalez said. "I don't give a virgin fuck how Hall of Fame good these six badges are, they don't have the manpower to deal with one crew, let alone two."

"Before they made move one, they lined up with Tony Rigs," Angel said. "He fronted them some seed money and helped them set up shop. Far as I can tell, that's where his deal started and ended, no men of his own thrown into the deal."

"They would have needed more than Tony Rigs to reach Jonas Talbot," Freddie said. "That fucker was covered tighter than a mummy, and they walked right up to him like he worked in an out-side parking lot. Got rid of him nasty, and wiped out his art collection in no time flat. Now, Rigs has a good crew, but they ain't nowhere near that fuckin' good. Besides, the only painting that old Guido knows about involves Benjamin Moore and a roller."

"Then who do you think it is?" Angel asked. "Who not only could get to Talbot but has the talent and the connections to move anywhere from forty to eighty million worth of art on both the open and the black markets? I can swear on a stack of dead bodies I don't have those worldwide hookups and I know that the two of you don't, either."

"The Russian," Hector said without hesitation, looking first to his brother and then up to Angel.

"Good answer," Angel said. "She has the necessary means and the required motives to come in, clean house, and walk away with the proceeds from Talbot's stash. On top of which, any damage or delay to our operations done to us by this group of piss-poor cops, no matter how inconsequential, is sure to put a warm smile on such a pretty face."

"We had a meet with her not too long ago," Hector said, stretching out his legs and folding his arms across his chest. "Told me she was in New York only to strengthen the Russian beachhead and keep the profit flow from their porn operations running at full tilt."

"And did you believe her?" Angel asked.

"Had no reason not to," Freddie said. "Her people never stepped on our toes before this, and they always do a back turn when it comes to our line. I'm not saying they don't move shit, but they stick to pills—Triple Ex, Up and Downs, Speed Racer, like that. They like the money our action brings in, but not the natural-life prison run comes with it you get caught with your pants down and a couple hundred kilos inside a leather."

"We're not a threat to her end and she's no threat to ours," Hector said. "This city is one big fuckin' hot pie, and there's more than enough for us all to dig in and get fat. I don't see her hungry for a tangle with the G-Men."

"Perhaps you were too busy listening to the woman talk to hone in on what the gangster was thinking," Angel said. "Which is exactly what she wanted you to do."

"If we have to go into a hand-to-hand with the Russians, then we got ourselves a bigger problem than five gimpy cops and a dog with a limp," Freddie said. "You toss Tony Rigs on top of her pile and we're staring out at a two-out-of-three-falls-drive-the-loser-to-the-morgue death match."

"That's the inevitable we face and the final results won't bode well for us, not unless we unite and move into this battle as one," Angel said. "And we head up the ladder one step at a time, starting with these flies-on-shit cops."

"Why them?" Freddie said.

"It sends out a signal," Angel said. "We know they're linked to Tony Rigs, and we have strong suspicions that the Russian is helping guide their actions. And there's our ladder. We start with the cops and then move to Rigs and then, finally, to the Russian. We need to make some noise, show these crews that we're not here just to move in coke and cut up the cash. Let them know without any doubt that we will kill anybody who won't make room for us at their table. And that starts with those fuckin' cops. They need to die."

Angel turned toward the blackboard and pulled down the pictures of the Apaches that were taped there. He stacked them in a neat pile and tossed them into a brown wastebasket. He then tore a sheet of yellow paper from a notebook resting on a teacher's desk. He pulled out a lighter, snapped on the flame, and put it to the paper. He held the burning paper for a few seconds, looking up at Hector and Freddie, then tossed the sheet into the wastebasket. He watched the fire smolder for a few seconds, flames burning through the photos and sending a line of smoke up toward his face and over to the open window at his back.

"Those cops need to die *now*," he said.

CHAPTER

Dead-Eye stood on the subway platform, a creased and folded newspaper in his hands, halfway through a back-of-the-book story about the newest player to wear a Yankees uniform. The Upper West Side station was well lit and filled with an assortment of lunchtime commuters, many heading back to their cubicles to finish off a day's work, a few students and a handful with nowhere to go, really, and all the time to get there. He heard the rumble of the downtown IRT chugging through the tunnel and into the station, tossed the newspaper into a bin, and walked closer to the edge of the platform, hands at his sides.

He had spotted the three men on his tail as soon as he stepped out of the coffee shop on Amsterdam. He had spent most of his adult life needing to be aware of any activity that took place around him, the faces that belonged and those that didn't, the fast movements of the suspicious, the hard glares of those on the prowl for prey. It was all very much second nature to Dead-Eye, as much a part of him as the guns in his holsters and the tin in his pocket.

He led the men across Amsterdam, forcing them to cross against oncoming traffic, and made his way to the Seventy-second Street subway station and the ride downtown. He took them to be more than a set of rover's eyes sent to report back on his daily activities—they looked too hard and seasoned to be relegated to such a mundane chore. These were hitters with a mandate to bring him down.

Dead-Eye waited as a small array of passengers stepped off the train, brushing against one another as they shoved their way to their next destination. He then stepped into the third car of the ten-car train and walked across to the other side, standing with his back to the shuttered doors. The three men tailing him were the last to get on, seconds before the doors rolled to a close. Dead-Eye rested his hands at the base of his spine, fingers feeling for the gun he kept in a waist holster, his head down but his eyes catching the huskier of the three men as he ran a hand along the right side of his jacket, making sure his piece was in place.

The train inched forward and the three men started to move in his direction, breaking off and locking in on Dead-Eye from three sides of the car. The train picked up speed and rumbled through the darkened tunnel, interior lights flashing on and off, casting all in an eerie glow. Dead-Eye pushed himself from the door, wrapped a hand around a pole, and moved toward the rear of the car, head down, body poised. He paused in front of the back door, peered through the glass into the next car, snapped open the handle, and stepped into the rattling void outside the train, lights speeding past, blue volts popping off the skidding rails, red and yellow signals rushing by him in a blur. The train was about thirty seconds away from the Fifty-ninth Street stop when he pulled two guns out of their shoulder holsters and held them down low and against his legs. The three men behind him in the car had inched closer to the rear door, the cocked and loaded Lugers in their hands half hidden by the folds of their jackets.

Dead-Eye jumped off the subway car and onto the platform, his momentum taking him toward the white-brick wall at the station's edge. He streaked to a fast halt and turned, the three men off the train now and coming at him with guns visible, passengers running past them, heading up the stairs or onto the train before the doors closed. The husky man raised his gun hand, aimed it at Dead-Eye, and let off two rounds, each chipping pieces of brick. Dead-Eye turned a tight corner, kicked open a men's-room door, and disappeared inside, the three gunners fast on his heels.

They stepped into the men's room, two inches of old water coating the tiled floors, three stalls with their doors shut on one side, two urinals rusty and running, and a set of ivory sinks, one half hanging off its cracked base. The sharp odor that filled the tight space was enough to make breathing a chore. There were no windows and no other way in or out.

The three stepped deeper into the room, their guns and eyes focused on the stall closest to the far wall. They moved in tight, tossing quick glances at one another, the husky man working off hand signals and placing them in the best positions to take out Dead-Eye. They were seconds removed from turning the wreck of a subway-station restroom into a high-intensity shooting gallery.

The door leading into the room swung open with a violent thud. The three shooters turned, weapons focused now on a drunk standing on shaky footing in the narrow entryway. The drunk looked down at the small water well soaking through a pair of torn and tattered sneakers and then back up at the three gunmen. "You're *supposed* to piss *in* the bowl," he hissed, the words a series of slow slurs. "I'm fucking drunk and I know shit like that. Bad enough my pants are soiled, now my fucking shoes, too?"

"Get the hell out of here," the husky man said, waving his gun at the drunk. "Go look for another bathroom. Or go piss against a wall. I don't give a fuck what, just get out of here and do it now."

"This is *my* bathroom, little brother," the drunk said, walking into the room, getting in closer to the husky man with the gun. "And besides, I didn't come in here to piss. Came in to wash up."

The husky man was now inches away from the drunk. "I'm not going to tell you again," he said, speaking through clenched teeth. "Get the fuck out."

The drunk lowered his head and dropped his arms to his sides. "I'm what the doctors call an EDP, and you need to be very careful how you talk to somebody's got something like that."

"What the fuck is an EDP?" one of the other gunmen asked.

The drunk moved with lightning speed, one hand on the husky man's gun, the other grabbing his free arm and whirling him in a circle, turning him so that he was facing the other two shooters. In less time than it would take to turn a light switch on and off, the drunk had the gun in his right hand, pressed against the husky man's temple, and his left arm was wrapped tight around his neck. The drunk leaned his head on the husky man's wide shoulder and looked across at the two shooters. "EDP is an emotionally disturbed person," Rev. Jim said. "But don't worry—the doctors *think* I'm cured!"

A small closet door swung open and Dead-Eye stepped out, two guns still in his hands. "I have never been inside one of these subway shitters and *not* seen them flooded," he said, waving for the two shooters to drop their weapons. "More water on the ground than in the toilets, that's for damn sure."

"As long as there aren't any rats," Rev. Jim said. "I can deal with anything but that shit. I see a rat and I scream like an old lady getting mugged."

"Then it would be best for you to stay away from that closet," Dead-Eye said, walking toward the two shooters. "And for me to stay away from you in the event you don't."

"Let's just deal with the Three Musketeers here and then hit the damn prairie," Rev. Jim said. "How in hell did you figure on this shithouse as the drop zone?"

"My cousin Big Ernie has been working MTA going on thirty-five years now," Dead-Eye said. "He knows every bathroom on every stop in the city, and the best place to hide in each one."

"That's the kind of knowledge that's earned," Rev. Jim said, "not bought."

Dead-Eye kicked the gunmen's two dropped weapons under a closed stall and then turned to face the husky man. "Let me hear your name," he said.

"Phil," the husky man said, his eyes as hard as his body was soft.

"Did he just say Phil?" Rev. Jim asked, easing the weapon from the man's temple. "Line of work you put yourself in, you have got to get yourself a much tougher name. Or add a little something to it. Like Big Phil. Then maybe you got a chance at pulling off the tough-guy stance. But Phil alone doesn't cut it, trust me."

"I'm sorry me and motor mouth here fucked up your chance at leaving me dead inside some rotted-out stall," Dead-Eye said. "Now we could reverse the coin, pop you a few shots, and then flip you, one on top of the other, in one corner. Or we could work it out to where we all walk out of here, wet but still alive."

"I'm listening," Phil said, shrugging away from Rev. Jim's grip and waving the other two shooters closer. "Put some words to what you got in mind."

"That's a Big Phil talking there," Rev. Jim said with a smile, giving him a firm slap on the back.

"You part of Robles's team—am I right on that?" Dead-Eye said.

Phil nodded. "I captain his downtown crew," he said. "Or did until I stepped into this fuckin' disaster."

"Captain Phil," Rev. Jim said. "Shit, that's even better than Big Phil."

"Captain or not, you're still a street soldier," Dead-Eye said. "And our beef is with your bosses, not with you. You've been around it long enough to know the real—that if you fall by the wayside, facedown or faceup, they'll forget your name between the cocktail and the first course."

"Which puts you and me where, exactly?" Phil asked.

"Washing each other's backs," Dead-Eye said. "We can shoot it out, here or in some other rat hole, if that's the way you want it to go. But you and me both know that doesn't help push either one of our agendas."

"What does?" Phil asked.

"We want a head-to-head with your boss," Dead-Eye said. "You can set it up from street level, using an outside pay phone. Lay it out clean and neat for him if you want, or lie like a married man in a pickup bar—your call. Just get us in with him and walk away."

"And then?"

"If it goes our way and Robles ends up on a slab with a ME trying to ID his ass with a cavity search, you get to stand on his watch and call his turf your own," Dead-Eye said. "And not worry about getting any heat coming your way from us."

"And what if it's Robles who wins the battle?" Phil asked. "Where does that put us then?"

"Right where you are now," Dead-Eye said. "Only in drier clothes. Me and Robles are the ones looking at a fifty-fifty. You and your boys here are standing at the win-win window."

Phil glanced over at his two men and down at the still water that reached up to the cuffs of his creased trousers. "He'll want the meet to be in a public place," he said after minutes of quiet thought. "He's a cautious guy and feels safer out in the open. If you're okay with that, then I think I can get him to agree to stand across from you."

"You got the name, Big Phil," Rev. Jim said, smiling across at him. "And if this goes right, soon enough you'll have the fame. And we'll have one of our targets. What more can any bum ask for?"

"A pair of dry shoes," Dead-Eye said.

7

CHAPTER

Captain Sean Valentine aimed his .38 Special at the stationary target and fired off two rounds, hitting the mark both times. He repositioned himself to the left of the shooting area, braced his left shoulder against a wood beam, and rapid-fired four more rounds, all on the mark. He placed his gun on a counter and removed the protective gear around his ears, then stared out at the results of his marksmanship.

Valentine loved the shooting range, his one recreational hobby. He made a point of coming up to the five-acre park every Sunday, just before sunup, letting himself in with a set of keys given him by one of the borough commanders who shared a similar passion. He ran the gauntlet of skill sets that the range offered, from the operational sequences where he would be placed in kill-or-be-kill situations to the standard field tests to determine which targets should be shot at and which shouldn't. He always ended his routine with an hour out in the fields, shooting an assortment of weapons at various distances from a variety of set positions.

Valentine picked up a container of lukewarm coffee, holstered his weapon, and then walked down a grassy slope toward the targets, eager to check out his score. His hands were always steady, his gaze unflinching, his marks always hovering near the full bull's-eye range. Behind him, an early-morning sun began to peek above the tree coverage, the dew and mist that came with dawn starting to dissipate.

"You're pretty deadly with paper targets, bales of hay, and empty Coke cans," the voice at his back said, startling him for a brief moment. "How good are you when the targets can move and fire back, I wonder?"

Valentine stopped, tossed his coffee container into a thick pile of leaves, and turned to face Boomer. "Who let you in here?" he asked.

"You did," Boomer said, stepping up beside Valentine. Valentine hesitated for a moment and then flashed Boomer a smile and offered his hand. Boomer ignored both and, instead, walked past Valentine and headed toward the target area. "My bet is that you score pretty high on the contests, too," Boomer said to him without glancing back. "Would I be right on that?"

"I never lose," Valentine said, trailing Boomer down the hill.

Boomer turned and looked at Valentine. "You don't rig those scores, too, do you?" he asked. "I mean, you don't pour dirt on *everything* you do as a cop—or do you?"

"Why are you here, Boomer?" Valentine asked. "If you want something, just spill it and then get the fuck out. Otherwise, hit the bricks and go back to your pretend to still be on the job life."

"You know, me and Dead-Eye worked Narcotics together for a year or so," Boomer said, gazing out at the lush scenery and then turning back to Valentine. "We started to land pretty heavy on this team of dealers from Flushing, over by the stadium. They had been pulling in about three, four hundred thousand a week, but within two months we had them down to pay-the-rent scores."

"Save it for the retirement parties," Valentine said. "I don't really give a shit."

"The top dog in the crew—guy called himself FM—figures if he couldn't bury us, then maybe he could buy us," Boomer said, ignoring Valentine's remark. "Or at least rent us. So he passed the word to me and Dead-Eye through a street stool that if we stepped back from his operation he would set aside a hundred and fifty thousand a month in cash for the two of us—each and every first, just like Social Security."

"Let me take a wild guess here," Valentine said. "You passed on the offer. And why wouldn't you, kind of cops you and your pal were? Walked into the job poor and limped out poorer."

"We did more than pass," Boomer said. "We got serious. We went in after FM and his team that same night, and we wiped them out—brought the whole operation to a close, and put down as many as we could for the dirt nap."

"And the point to this memory-lane trip is what?" Valentine asked.

Boomer stepped up closer to Valentine, puffs of mist coming out of his mouth when he spoke. "It's time for you and me to get serious," he said.

"You may get away with that shit you pull on the street," Valentine said, his words spiked with venom. "Cops turn their heads and act as if they don't know you and your crippled crew are nothing but a band of vigilantes out breaking the law. But you even come close to pulling a weapon on me, I'll have your ass hauled in for attempted assault on a police officer. Is that serious enough for you?"

"I wouldn't be pulling my weapon on a police officer," Boomer said. "I'd be pulling it on a crooked piece of shit that treats his badge like a license to steal."

"While you, Double-Fucking-Oh-Seven, have made yours a license to kill," Valentine said with a smirk. "Look, you and me, we both aim for the same results, and that's to get what we want. We just choose to come at it from different directions. We're a lot more alike than you may want to believe."

"True or not," Boomer said, "that little theory of yours comes to a hard end after today."

"How do you figure?" Valentine asked.

"Well, I figure one of us will be dead," Boomer said.

Sean Valentine rested his back against the center of a thick tree, using shade and low-hanging branches for coverage, his .38 Special clutched to his chest. He was breathing heavy, and his upper body was coated with sweat. Blood from an open gash ran down the side of his right leg, a tear in his black sweatpants exposing the wound. He moved his head from the tree and gazed out at the wooded terrain around him, knowing Boomer was still out there, not sure if any of his half a dozen shots had found their mark.

"We're both too old for this kind of shit," Valentine shouted. "Let's bring the fun to an end, Boomer, and I promise to forget this ever happened."

"I'm not your problem," Boomer said, stepping out from behind the shadow of a large boulder up the hill from where Valentine stood. Buttercup was by his side, a detective's gold shield hanging on a chain around her neck. "Your beef is with my partner here." Boomer and Buttercup walked slowly down the hill, a .44 hanging loose in his right hand, the dog's paws swishing and swaying over the thick wet leaves and twigs, her eyes on the corrupt cop less than a dozen feet away.

Valentine moved away from the tree and took several steps toward them, wiping at his sweaty brow with his gun arm. "That's good for me to know," he said, "because I fucking hate dogs."

"Not as much as she hates you," Boomer said. "You see, unlike you, this dog here is a real cop—and straight-up honest to boot. Wouldn't even take a Milk-Bone from the hand of a drug dealer. And you know one of the things all real cops have in common? Well, in your case, you'd have to take a guess. But go ahead."

"I don't know and I don't give a fuck," Valentine said, moving in closer to Boomer and Buttercup, looking for the leverage and the footing to get off a kill shot.

"They never forget a face," Boomer said. "And this gold-shield lady has yours burned to her memory."

"Now I know you've taken too many fucking bullets," Valentine said. "Your mind's gone. I've never laid eyes on that drooling piece of shit in my life."

"Maybe not so you'd notice," Boomer said. "But she's seen you, and she knows who you are and will never forget what you did."

"Educate me, asshole," Valentine said.

"A few years back, you were padded up with a dealer named Paco," Boomer said. "He mostly moved cheap coke and cheaper heroin out of the projects, and you were more than eager to supply him with some cover for whatever your I'm-for-sale rate was in those days. Am I coming across on your radar yet?"

"Keep talking, Boomer," Valentine said. "It's what you've always been good at."

"My friend was partnered up with a hard charger named Steve Ramoni, and he made it his business to put Santos out of business," Boomer said. "The takedown didn't go exactly according to the script and Buttercup here took a few slugs, which is how she eventually made it onto my team. But, even worse, she had to watch her partner go down, and that's something else a good cop never forgets."

"And I give a fuck about all this because?" Valentine said.

"Because you were there," Boomer said. "The dealer who brought her in and saved her life fingered you as one of the shooters. Nobody really believed him, didn't think an on-the-rise golden boy would be down in a sewer, waist-deep in shit, stuffing his pockets with a cop killer's money. But there were some who knew better; they just didn't have the pull or the muscle to bring it down your way."

"They didn't have it then, they sure as shit won't have it now," Valentine said.

"That might be true down at One Police Plaza," Boomer said. "But you're standing in a different court now. I know that you were one of the shooters that day. You came in to pick up your cash and stayed for the fireworks, pumping bullets into men with badges. It was your bullets that killed Steve Ramoni. And it was two of your slugs that made their way into Buttercup."

"And so what happens now?" Valentine asked. "You want me to say sorry to the mutt, maybe even throw in a little pat on the head?"

"Your verdict is in, Valentine," Boomer said. "Buttercup didn't run her ass all the way up here to grab a cheap apology. She came here to even it up for Steve Ramoni. I told you that you were going to die today. Now I'm telling you who it is that's going to put you down."

"It's going to take more than an old shot-up dog to make that happen," Valentine said.

"Then you were right before," Boomer said. "You don't know this dog."

Buttercup came at Valentine from the side, the upper part of her body landing with a hard thud against the cop's left side, sending them both sprawling to the ground. She was fully unleashed now, her police instincts and training bursting out in a vicious assault of bites and snaps, drawing fresh blood with each move. Valentine, his gun well out of reach, rained a barrage of closed-fist hits to Buttercup's head and rib cage but to little effect. She was in another zone, her eyes focused on the target, her massive girth and power crushing the air from Valentine's body. Her head was now over his, blocking his breathing passage, her jaw open and wrapped around the veins of his exposed neck. She held the position, waiting for the next command.

Boomer came up behind them, a cocked gun in his right hand, his eyes glaring hard at Valentine, quick to catch the frightened look that now ruled over the corrupt cop's sweat-and-blood-streaked face. Steve Ramoni's gold shield, hanging from Buttercup's neck, rested on his right shoulder. Boomer uncocked his gun and shoved it back into his shoulder holster. He wiped the blood from a small gash on his forehead and brought his hands to his sides.

"Don't do anything crazy," Valentine said, the confidence gone from his voice, replaced by a cornered fear. "There's no reason to take this to a place it shouldn't go. Your point's been made."

"I didn't come here to make a point, Valentine," Boomer said. "Neither did Buttercup."

"Don't do this, Boomer," Valentine pleaded. "You're too good a cop to go and pull shit like this."

"I'm not a cop anymore, remember?" Boomer said. "And neither are you."

"Please, Boomer," Valentine said. "Please, not this way."

Boomer stared at Valentine for several long and silent seconds, the tight grip Buttercup held on his neck drawing blood and causing him to lose air.

"Memory him, Buttercup," Boomer said. He then turned away, walking back down the hill, blood from a twig cut running down his forehead and into his eyes, not bothering to wait for the snap of bones and muscle that came from the powerful snap of the dog's jaw. Not waiting for the death rattle that gurgled through the throat of a corrupt cop. Not interrupting as Buttercup savored the warm taste of revenge.

8

Quincy and Rev. Jim were standing on the scaffold, twelve stories up, cleaning the thick floor-to-ceiling office windows. They were dressed in blue coveralls and each had on a matching cap, their hands covered with workmen's gloves, surgical masks hanging loose around their necks. Quincy took a deep breath and ventured a look down. "This is not a job for anyone with a fear of heights," he said.

"Then let's not talk about it," Rev. Jim said. "Let's just do it and hope these losers show up for their meeting before one of us slips and ends up kissing the pavement."

"We're latched to the building," Quincy said, pointing to the two clips attached to the belts around his waist. "The only way we drop is if the building collapses."

"There was a cop working in the two-seven back when I was a rookie," Rev. Jim said. "He had a moonlight business doing this kind of work. Made more money from the second job than he did from the police work, overtime included."

"I can believe that," Quincy said. "It's probably a union job, and they have to overpay to find anyone crazy enough to do this sort of work full-time. Did your cop friend eventually leave the department?"

"He eventually left the planet," Rev. Jim said. "Took a full header off the middle tier of a downtown office tower. They found his work boots three blocks away from where he fell. And he had on *two* of these latches!"

"I wonder what goes through your mind during those few seconds before you hit the ground," Quincy said. "Who do you think of, what's the last image that flashes across your eyes?"

"I know what it would be for me," Rev. Jim said. "Fucking Boomer and Dead-Eye talking us both into doing something this insane. If I was so eager to commit suicide, I would have picked a much less painful escape route."

"I've picked mine already," Quincy said. "You know, for when the time comes."

Rev. Jim turned to Quincy and locked eyes with him, tossing aside his fear of heights. "It may not come to that," he said. "You've been with us for a while now and you seem to be getting stronger, not weaker. Maybe it's not a death sentence for everybody that has it."

"I joined a small support group a few months after I was diagnosed," Quincy said. "Early on, I kept up that cop ruse we all use—the one that allows us to make-believe nothing gets to us. But I found I needed to talk to somebody, and who better than a group of men with the same disease?"

"Was it a help?" Rev. Jim asked.

"Very much," Quincy said. "If for no other reason than knowing you're not the only one thinking the thoughts and feeling the pain and dreading the next day or the next month. Point is, though, there were fifteen original members in that group when I first signed on about three months ago. We're down to six. It *is* a death sentence, Jim. The only unknown is the where and the when."

"If you have to die, it won't be alone," Rev. Jim said. "If I'm still breathing, I'll be there right next to you, for whatever the hell that's worth."

"You may want to rethink that," Quincy said. "I appreciate it, don't get me wrong. But watching someone waste away during the last stages of this isn't something you would wish on any friend."

Rev. Jim worked his side of the window in silence and then rested the brush in a wide bucket of water by his feet. "So what plan did you work up?" he asked. "How do you figure booking that final checkout?"

"I ruled out eating a gun from the get-go," Quincy said.

"Good call," Rev. Jim said. "That way is so cop."

"Besides which, I don't think I'd be able to pull the trigger," Quincy said. "So I thought I'd charge a very expensive bottle of wine to my Amex and down that while listening to a Sinatra album."

"What kind of wine?" Rev. Jim asked.

"A Brunello," Quincy said. "I was always told it was a wine to die for. This is my chance to prove that theory."

"Then what, wash a few pills down with it?" he asked.

"No, that takes too long," Quincy said, "and I don't have that kind of patience. I'm going to wrap a plastic bag over my head, tie it up nice and tight with some thick cord, lie down on a soft bed, and let it all play out."

Rev. Jim held on to one side of the scaffold, stared across at Quincy, and then smiled.

"It's just too bad we didn't know each other back in the days I was hooked on drugs," he said. "We would have made one helluva fucking team, let me just tell you that."

"What about you?" Quincy asked. "You ever give any thought to ending it? I always thought every cop did at one time or another."

"I used to think about it," Rev. Jim said with a shrug. "Especially after I got wounded and couldn't work anymore. I didn't see much point in going on with what would be left of my life. So, yeah, I ran a few different death dances across my mind, but I never did come close enough to act on any of them."

"What changed it for you?" Quincy asked.

"I hooked up with Boomer and Dead-Eye," Rev. Jim said. "Once you line up on their end of the field, you can forget all about the need to waste yourself. Those two bastards will come up with ways to end a life all by themselves."

———

Freddie Gonzalez walked into the large office, a long, wide conference table sucking up most of the free space in the room. He walked over to a corner, past the two men on the scaffold scrubbing the windows, swung open the door to a small fridge, and pulled out a cold can of beer. Three other men followed him in, each holding large leather satchels, and sat around the table, resting the bags by their feet. A woman in a designer business suit was the last one in the room, closing the thick oak door behind her. She walked over toward Freddie and stood next to him near the head of the table, both facing the two men on the scaffold.

"Why all the mystery?" he asked. "We usually handle these trade-offs out in the open and without me anywhere near them. What's changed?"

"Hector thought this would be safer, given all that's going on," said one of the men, the one sitting close to the center of the conference table. "We make the exchange, you sign off on it, and we all go our separate ways not having to worry about either the Russians or those fuckin' cops causing us any grief."

"Has the room been scanned for bugs?" the young woman asked.

"We had a crew check it out less than an hour ago, Isabel," one of the men said. "It's as clean as it looks."

"What's here when we're not?" Freddie asked.

"An insurance company," one of the men said, lifting his leather satchel from the floor and resting it on the table. "They use this room for video conferences."

"How'd we end up with it?" he asked.

"Their legal counsel is one of our biggest and most dependable customers," the man said. "I put a little extra in his weekly sniff-and-smell package, and he gave us weekend security clearance."

"You tell me, Richie," Freddie said, "where the fuck would our business be without those high-rise white-bread fuckers with a taste for the thin line? You think we would haul in the kind of cash is in one of those bags regular if we had to depend on street skells and nickel baggers? Tell me straight?"

"We would barely make rent most months," Richie said. "That's the down and true."

"You bet that skinny little ass of yours," Freddie said. "It's the Wonder bread wonders who land us the cars, the houses, the booze, the pussy. The rest of the trade is Christmas tip money for the doorman, not even."

"There four hundred heavy in your bag?" Isabel asked one of the men.

"Washed and ready to wear," the man said, sliding the satchel over to Richie. "Count it if you like, but it's there down to the penny."

"We don't need to count shit," Freddie said. "If it's short even one dirty dime, I know where to find you. And, believe me, you won't want to be found if that happens."

"I'm expecting to have ten kilos in return," the man said. "I figure that's in the two bags not holding the cash. Once they make their way into my hands, we'll be done here."

"You got your powder and we got our green," Freddie said. "Which means we conclude one of these with smiles all around, which will be a nice fuckin' change from what's been going on around here the last week or—"

The harsh breeze from the two open windows forced them all to look up. Rev. Jim and Quincy stood on the black lacquered ledge inside the office, the scaffold at their back.

"What the fuck do you two windshield wipers want in here?" Richie asked, the wind gusts forcing open the front of his jacket, exposing the edge of a gun jammed inside his waistband.

"Me and my buddy here were just curious about something," Rev. Jim said. "I know it's a weekend and all, but you think we could apply for an insurance policy?"

"I've heard you have a special discount on one," Quincy said. "Just for people in your line of work, and ours."

"You know the one," Rev. Jim said. "It comes with a two-bullet deductible."

Richie was the first to pull his weapon and fire, moving fast and pegging two shots toward the window ledge. Rev. Jim and Quincy both dived forward, yanked off the guns that were taped to the backs of their uniforms, and came up firing, each on one side of the conference room. They were braced on one knee, their arms out, throwing heavy heat at the four men and one woman less than a dozen feet away.

Freddie and one of the men dived behind a set of leather chairs in a far corner and started to peg shots at the two Apaches. The third man fired away, using a table leg and the base of a chair as cover. Isabel reached under the conference table and came up with a semiautomatic. She stood her ground without fear, letting loose a wild fusillade of high-caliber artillery, a cloud of white gun smoke floating up to partially cover her face.

"I hope you came in here with a Plan B," Quincy shouted across the room to Rev. Jim. "If not, I wasted a lot of man-hours planning a suicide I'll never need to pull off."

"Fire all your rounds and then get your ass back on that scaffold," Rev. Jim shouted back. "The second you pop on, kick it in gear and start to lower it down fast as you can get it to go."

"And how do you plan on getting out?" Quincy asked. He swung his handgun toward Richie, emptying three rounds in his direction. The first two caught and chipped the rich wood paneling, the third crash-landed through flesh and sent the drug dealer facedown and feet spread onto the carpeted floor.

"I'm going to jump," Rev. Jim said.

"If anyone's going to jump, it should be me," Quincy yelled. "Remember?"

"Don't be so sure," Rev. Jim said, using the wall to lift himself up to his feet and firing in a left-to-right arc, making sure to keep everyone's head down. "Are you on empty yet?"

Quincy fired the final two bullets in his chamber and got one grunt and a wild volley in return, then turned and did a fast jump-and-roll out the window and onto the scaffold. "I am now," he said. He pushed free the release lever and unwrapped two thick cords of rope wedged on either side of the structure. "I pray you know what the fuck you're doing."

Rev. Jim's eyes lit up. "Me, too!"

A heavy stream of bullets came at Rev. Jim from every possible direction, shattering glass and landing with loud thumps in the wood, lamps, and imported tile. He kept his head down and snapped open the front of his blue uniform, reached into his belt buckle, and pulled free two hand grenades he kept lodged on a clip around his belt. He undid the pins on both before the first bullet landed against the small of his back, followed by a second that nicked his right shoulder, forcing him to twirl and face the shooters bearing down his way. A third bullet hit him just below the chest and sent him halfway out the window. Rev. Jim, blood rushing out of his mouth, did an underhand flip and sent the grenades floating into the room, sending the shooters scattering for cover. "Eat it, you fuckers," he said.

He lifted his legs off the floor and floated out the open windows.

Rev. Jim landed with a violent thud three stories down, on the middle of three wooden planks of the scaffold, shaking it loose. Quincy was fighting with all his strength to hold it in place, hands suddenly cut through, upper body trembling from the struggle. He managed to steady the scaffold just as the loud explosion came at them from three floors above, shaking and rocking the very foundation of the forty-story building. A large fireball flew out the open windows above and burned through one end of the thick cord, causing the structure to tilt to one side as it moved with dangerous speed down the damaged high-rise.

Quincy bent down on both knees and lifted Rev. Jim in his arms, cradling his dying body. "You crazy bastard," Quincy said to him, his voice cracking, both their bodies coated in blood. "Hang on to me, just hang on. We'll be on the ground in a few minutes."

"Do me a favor, would you, Quincy?" Rev. Jim said, each word a struggle.

"Name it," Quincy said.

"Fight back," Rev. Jim said. "You're too good a cop to end it with a Hefty bag wrapped over your head. And you're too good a man. So skip that, will you? Fight back."

Quincy nodded, eyes burning, the scaffold making its descent. Rev. Jim looked toward the sky at the smoke and the flames filling the air around them and rested his head against Quincy's shoulder. "You take my point," Rev. Jim whispered. "It's better to die with a friend."

And then he did.

The Apaches stood in front of the altar, three rows of flickering votive candles illuminating their faces in an otherwise empty church, their heads bowed in silent prayer.

"He was our heart," Boomer said.

"He deserves more than the minutes we can spare right now," Dead-Eye said.

"He'll get that," said Boomer, "as soon as all of this is behind us."

"And he deserves to be buried proper," Dead-Eye added. "Soon as our dustup is over, whoever's still standing should see to that."

"I'll keep his ashes until then," Quincy said.

"He always used to say he never wanted one of those police funerals," Boomer said. "He would have hated the flags and the guns going off."

"What did he want?" Ash asked.

"A Viking funeral," Dead-Eye said, a smile flashing below his wet eyes. "Put out on a boat, piles of wood all around him, us shooting flaming arrows his way as he floats off to the deep sea."

"Then that's what he'll get," Quincy said, reaching down to pet Buttercup, who was resting under the warm lights of the candles.

Boomer nodded. "I know what else he would have wanted," he said.

"What?" Ash asked.

"For us to finish the job," Boomer said.

10

Dead-Eye stood on the walkway on the Queens side of the Whitestone Bridge, three lanes of cars and trucks zooming past him, the clouds overhead threatening rain, the river below choppy and looking cold. Ash was next to him, her back to the traffic, her hair whipping around her face, eyes taking in the majestic view. "This is what passes as a public place to Robles?" she asked.

"Never expect logic of any kind from a drug dealer," Dead-Eye said. "No matter what happens and what crazy shit he's got up his coke spoon, just remember: if we *stay* cool, we'll *be* cool."

"Thanks for the heads-up, Yoda," Ash said. "But if I had to call this game, I'd be sitting on one of those sailboats down there, glass of wine in hand, heading for no place in particular."

"Somehow, I doubt we'll ever live to see days like that," Dead-Eye said.

"I've never even been on a boat," Ash said, brushing strands of thick hair from her face, tiny drops of cold rain beginning to fall.

"Not even a Circle Line ride up to the Statue of Liberty. But when I was a kid, being out on the water was all I dreamed about. I used to have this image of taking this big boat out in the middle of a wild ocean, sails stretched by the wind, me at the helm, land nowhere in sight."

"Why'd you never do it?" Dead-Eye asked, scanning the traffic around them for any sign of Robles.

"I guess I just turned my back on it and went in the opposite direction," Ash said. "I chose fire over water, not even fighting them but working the pieces to see who it was that started them. I don't regret any of it. I just wonder a bit now and then and think how different it might have all been. Only natural, most people spend their lives wondering what it's like on the other side of the fence."

"Most, maybe, but not all," Dead-Eye said. "It might look a whole lot better on the other side of that fence, but who's to say that it is?"

"You're a world-class pessimist, you know that?" Ash said. "It's not just you, either. Most cops I've crossed paths with come with that mind-set. And the better the cop, the darker the view."

"Every cop's got a good reason for feeling that way," Dead-Eye said.

"What's yours?" Ash asked. "Of course, if you don't want to go near it, not a problem."

"Lucinda Jackson," Dead-Eye said.

"She family or a friend?" Ash asked.

"Never met the young lady," Dead-Eye said. "I was in my first month working homicide, coming off a tour in plainclothes. My attitude had taken a nick here and there, but I still looked with hopeful eyes."

"Until you caught a case," Ash said.

"Not much of one, either," Dead-Eye said. "Lucinda lived, if you want to stretch the word enough, with a crack mother and her cracked pimp. Her real father wasn't much better, doing a stretch upstate for a statutory. She was eighteen months old and weighed about as much as an eight-week puppy. All she knew of life was steady beatings and not much food. Then one night her crying got too loud for the cracker and the pimp, and they did the only thing that seemed logical to their demented minds. They shoved her inside a toaster oven and kicked it to high. Played with the timer like it was a radio dial. I cannot bring myself to ever imagine the pain that innocent child felt before mercy took hold."

"You were the one who found her body?" Ash asked.

"What there was of it," Dead-Eye said. "There was no money to pay for a funeral, and the only family she had were the two who made her life a hell. She deserved better than to be tossed into a hole in an unmarked grave. So I paid to have her buried out in St. Charles on Long Island, headstone and all. We gave her a full service and got the police chaplain to serve Mass and say prayers over her coffin. She even got a police escort out to the cemetery. About a dozen cops made the ride out and stayed with her until she was buried. Boomer was one of them."

"The doers get nailed?" she asked.

"The doers that cross paths with me *always* get nailed," Dead-Eye said. "You know, Lucinda would have turned twelve this coming June had she lived, and not a morning passes that I don't flash on her face. Those people down there, riding on them waves, in those tilted sailboats you used to dream about, are so very lucky. The shit we see stays invisible to them. And it's our job, if we do it right, to keep it that way."

Ash looked over Dead-Eye's shoulder at a black four-door Benz that had slowed to a halt in the right-hand lane, red hazard lights flashing, the engine running on idle. "Speaking of shit," she said, "it looks like our little band of brothers has finally arrived."

Dead-Eye turned just as Robles stepped out of the back seat, followed by one man from the passenger side and a second from behind the wheel. The driver popped the trunk and pulled out three red cones and lined them up behind the Benz, alerting the oncoming traffic to switch lanes. Robles stepped onto the walkway and moved slowly toward Dead-Eye and Ash. He was wearing a pin-striped suit, with shoes shiny enough to help guide a man's shave. He had an expensive brown topcoat slung over his shoulders and a small cigar in the corner of his mouth. He stopped in front of Dead-Eye and leered over at Ash. "I don't know if you're recruiting better," he said to Dead-Eye, "but at least you're recruiting better-looking."

"Nice outfit," Dead-Eye said. "Wait until Julio Iglesias finds out one of his suits is missing."

"Save the smart-ass for the cop bar," Robles said. "You got something you need to say, let me hear it."

"I lost a couple of friends this week," Dead-Eye said. "One of them was a cop, so he knew there might be a chance he'd step on a land mine. But the other one wasn't; he was a civilian and had no play in this fight we're in."

"You waiting for me to cry?" Robles asked.

"Just listen, dealer," Dead-Eye said, his words harsh and his body coiled and ready for any action that might come his way. "You're still fresh in this town, still used to doing business like you did back on the home front. Kill anybody you get the itch for, never worry about any consequences. But this is NYC, and in this city there are *always* going to be consequences."

"A badge here," said Robles, "means the same to me as a badge anywhere else. I either buy it, rent it, or toss it aside. And if there's a woman behind it and I get the urge, I might even fuck it."

"I think that was meant for me," Ash said. "He's such a romantic little prick. And I do mean little."

"You see, that's my point," Dead-Eye said. "It's not just badges you have to worry about. Everybody you touch has somebody out there they can reach. And one of those somebodies is going to be looking to fuck you up."

"Like who?" Robles asked.

"Like Nunzio Goldman."

"I heard about him," Robles said, a smile crossing his bleached teeth. "He ended up on the well-done side of the menu. He must be one of them friends you been running off the mouth about."

"More like family," Dead-Eye said. "But not just to me. He was tight with a lot of cops, that part is true. A few of us got to know him well and came to love his ass. But he was even tighter with some that worked the other side of the street. Your side, you might say. With them he shared a history, and he shared blood. Now, I don't know if any of this applies to the SA crowd you dance with. But to Italians and Jews—and Nunzio was a blend and a shake of both—a shared bloodline is as serious as fucking cancer. And that's what I'm here to tell you. Killing him the way you did and walking away may work fine in your little bodega. But out here you will have to face up to the consequences."

"Which are what?" Robles asked, tossing his cigar over the side of the bridge. "Other than having to listen to your line of shit?"

"I'm a fraction of your concern," Dead-Eye said. "I reached out for your ticket, eager to take you down, but somebody already had their hand out, with a bigger claim to even Nunzio's score than either me or Boomer could muster."

"I read you now," Robles said. "You set up a meet, feed me the name of Nunzio's hook, and I let you and your friends skip out from under my weight. Okay, then. Tell me who he is and where he is, and while I got him next in line for the barbecue pit I'll think about whether or not to go light on you and your cop buddies."

"His name is Tony Rigs," Dead-Eye said. "He's Nunzio's half brother. And I don't mean a fucking midget, either. Same mother, different father. And looking for him should be a snap, even for your dried-up raisin of a brain."

"Why's that, cop?" Robles asked.

"He's right behind you," Dead-Eye said.

Robles did a fast whirl, coat flying off his shoulders, and saw Tony Rigs standing with his back resting on an iron beam, hands inside the pockets of black slacks, a mellow look to his face. Robles glanced over toward the Benz and saw his shooters hovering close to the car, hands open flat and at their sides, surrounded by six men wearing overalls and construction hats, a blue truck with a cherry light flashing on top blocking the sedan's path.

"Tony's crew is doing some repair work on the bridge," Ash said. "Now how lucky would you say that is? Him being here the same time as you?"

"Nothing's going to happen," Robles said, spreading out his arms, the swagger still in his voice and manner. "Not here, broad daylight, with all these cars driving past. You can't take that kind of risk. You may not care about dying, but for cops like you two, ending up in jail is a whole other chapter."

"You see," Tony Rigs said, stepping up next to them. "Told you he couldn't be as stupid as you painted. So you might not want to be here for this, no need to get yourselves jammed up. You were good friends to Nunzio, all of you. He cared for you as much as you cared for him, cried like a baby when any of you went down. And now you've done right by him, and I'll see to it that it gets finished."

"You better do what he tells you," Robles said. "He's got it in him to deal with someone like me, but you don't and you never will. No matter how many colorful names you think up and pin on yourself. A street fighter like me goes down, it can only come from the hard hand of another hood. Never from the hand of a cop. Especially not a nigger or a muchacha."

"Let it wash off you, Dead-Eye," Tony Rigs said. "This isn't your time or your place. It's mine."

"You'll take them all?" Ash asked, nodding toward the three shooters by the sedan.

"Trust me, I'll have a very lush garden this summer," Tony Rigs said. "It won't lack for nutrients."

"You'll always be left to wonder about how it would have ended between you and me," Robles said, his focus on Dead-Eye. "Those are the kinds of questions that can eat at a cop, make him want to reach out for a bottle or a gun. Very often both."

"Not really," Dead-Eye said. "You can kid yourself if you want, but gun to gun, you could never take me. Not only do I know that, but you do, too. And you're going to die knowing it."

Dead-Eye gave a nod to Tony Rigs and reached a hand out for Ash. He stared at Robles for a few moments and then turned and moved down the walkway toward the pay tolls and his parked car. He was about ten feet away when he pushed Ash to the ground and whirled back to face Robles.

The dealer had caught Tony Rigs with a sucker punch to the side of the face, sending him off balance, then turned, pulled a .44 from his waistband, and aimed it straight at Dead-Eye.

He never got off a round.

Dead-Eye walked back toward Robles, two .38 Specials in his hands, firing a series of rounds from each as he moved forward, every bullet finding a mark. Robles dropped his gun and fell to his knees, blood pouring out of his open wounds. Dead-Eye then fired a final shot, square into his forehead.

"Wonder no more, dealer," Dead-Eye said. He holstered his guns, walked over to Ash, and helped her to her feet. Together the two Apaches walked with their heads down, in silence, off the Whitestone Bridge.

11

Hector Gonzalez came out the back door of the Spanish Harlem funeral home and walked down a short flight of steps, two heavily armed G-Men fast on his tail. He stepped into the dark hallway of the tenement next door, navigating his way to a ground-floor apartment just off the foyer. "You sure it's him?" he asked one of the men at his back.

"Hands-down certain," the man said, struggling to keep to the strides. "He matches the photos we got and the background checks that were done. Anything you can name points a finger his fine way."

"And you sure he came in alone?" Hector asked.

"I had the street scanned four times since he walked in," the man said. "He's as alone as a kid on his first day at a new school, nobody out there ready to give him cover."

"He give you any hint as to what he wanted?" Hector asked, his hand reaching for the handle to the wood door of apartment 1-B.

"It was a lot stronger than a hint," the man said. "He told us straight and true why it was he came here."

Hector held the door half open, one foot in the apartment, the other still in the hall. "And that was what?"

"To kill you," the man said.

Hector stood in a small, sparsely decorated living room, a two-seater couch at his back, his reflection playing off an old nineteen-inch Zenith black-and-white on a shaky nightstand. "I have to be truthful," he said. "You got some pair of balls to come in here and ask to see me. A lot more than I would ever give you credit for, even though it don't mean shit so far as where you and me stand."

"You lost your brother and I lost a friend," Quincy said. "That, so far as I can tell, is the only common ground between the two of us."

"So what happens now?" Hector asked. "You want to exchange sympathy cards? I know the intentions you came in with, but you have to know you're standing on my ground. There's no way I ever let you walk out of here. So make your move, player, and make it fast. Because as bad as you want me dead, that's how hungry I am to carve you up for making my brother die."

"You're full of shit," Quincy said. "You didn't care about your brother when he was alive. I don't really see why you would give any care to him now that you need to put him back together with tweezers."

"What the fuck are you talking about, cop?" Hector said. "I *loved* my brother. We started this outfit alone, me and him, and built it up, just the two of us. Who the fuck are you to come in here and sell a line of shit like that?"

"Is that why you sold him out and set him up?" Quincy asked. "There wasn't any need for Freddie to risk being at that drop. You have enough manpower to handle an exchange, especially a mid-tier one. Plus, you had a tip-off that me and Rev. Jim were going to find a way to hit that conference room."

"Where the fuck do you hear shit like that?" Hector asked, flustered. "Your street info is way off target, not that it's any of your fuckin' business. Freddie went to the deal drop because he wanted to make sure this one went down without any hitches. It's no more complicated than that."

"He asked you to go with him, though, didn't he?" Quincy said. "But you begged off, told him you had another meeting to be at—one that was crucial for the two of you and for the G-Men. He bought it, both the lie and then what went down at the site, never once even thinking that his brother was the one sent him in there to die."

"I'm going to fuckin' put you down right here," Hector said, reaching into his waistband and pulling out a .44 semi with a full load. "Make you beg off every one of those words, until you piss blood and die."

"I'm not the only one who thinks it's true," Quincy said. "Word is out, spreading like a California brushfire. The G-Men are working for a traitor, a rat, a man who gives up his own flesh to keep playing his game. You might kill me. Shit, somebody is going to sooner or later—may as well be a banger like you. But how long you think they'll let you keep taking deep breaths knowing what they're thinking?"

Hector looked around the room and then turned to gaze out into the hall. "If you're looking for your men, none of them are here," Quincy said. "They're either in the home next door praying over your brother's body or they're gone—off to work for a new boss, someone they think they can trust more than you."

"Who the fuck has been talking to you?" Hector asked.

"Same person you were talking to," Quincy said. "The only

difference is I know enough not to trust the Russian. But I don't have greed in my eyes, just revenge."

"I don't need any men around me to take out a fag cop," Hector said. "That I can do on my own, and with great pleasure."

"Let's forget the guns, then," Quincy said. "You're supposed to be the best in the drug trade with a blade. Prove it."

Hector whipped off his leather jacket and pulled a switchblade from the rear pocket of his jeans. He snapped it open and crouched down, his left hand held out for body balance.

Quincy let the knife slide gently down from his shirtsleeve to his palm. It was a stiletto with a hand-carved white handle, a gift from an old forensics mentor.

The two men circled each other in the center of the tight quarters, shaded light flashing their shadows across a bare wall. Hector swung first, a controlled jab that barely missed Quincy's chest, forcing him to back away slightly, so that he bumped into a small table lamp and a pot filled with artificial flowers. "You going to dance the night away?" Hector asked. "Or did you come here to fight?"

Quincy snapped open the black belt wrapped around his jeans and pulled it out of its loops. He held the belt, buckle wrapped around his left knuckles, in his left hand, letting it hang low, ready to snap when the need arose. "Where did you pick up that pussy shit?" Hector asked. "From watching *Zorro* movies?"

"*Zorro* didn't wear a belt, moron," Quincy said.

Hector leaped off his feet and jumped out at Quincy, catching him at chest level, both men spiraling against a far wall, knocking down the television and sending it smashing to the linoleum floor. Hector's blade slashed across Quincy's right arm, cutting through jacket and shirt and deep into skin, drawing a heavy flow of blood. A second vicious backswing swiped across Quincy's neck, the sharp cut sending a long spurt of blood over the faded wallpaper and onto Hector's shirt and face.

Quincy's knees buckled and his eyes were moist with tears, the small room around him doing a rinse-and-spin dizzy swirl. Hector's hulking body had closed in and was pounding out a mad series of powerful closed fists across Quincy's waist and chest, weakening him even further. He lowered his head and braced himself against a greasy wall, grappling to catch his breath and ignore the massive flow of blood.

"It's coming, cop," Hector said, huffing. "And I'll do you a big solid. I'll make it happen real quick for you. Save you a handful of pain."

Quincy glanced up at the ceiling and took in a breath. He gathered what was left of his strength and swung the belt up and around Hector's neck, using it as a noose and gripping it tighter as he lifted the stronger man to eye level. He turned away from the wall and shoved Hector against it. The tight belt turned his face crimson red. Quincy then gripped the stiletto's white handle and jammed it deep under the drug dealer's chin. He pushed it in, slashing aside fat, skin, and bone, going through the inside of the mouth and jamming the blade as far up as it would go. He stopped only when the handle wouldn't allow him to go any farther.

Quincy took a step back. He looked at Hector and got only a dead man's stare in return.

The onetime head of the G-Men stood up, his feet wedged against the side of the small couch, his head backed to the wall, his mouth open dentist-visit wide, the thin blade inside, a well of blood pouring out.

Quincy turned out of the room, clutching the walls and the furniture for support and leaving streaks of blood in his wake. He turned right as soon as he hit the foyer, slammed through the entry door, and made his way to the street outside. He leaned against a parked white Ford Tempo and rested his head on the hood, his eyes closed, his body prepared to give up the ghost.

A police car, red lights blaring, streaked to a stop alongside the Tempo. "Hang on, buddy," the young cop on the passenger side said, jumping out of the black-and-white. "I put in a call for an ambulance soon as I saw you come stumbling out of the building. It should be here any second."

"I'm on the job," Quincy said to him.

"We know, sir," the officer said. "Call came into the house about five minutes ago."

"Who?" Quincy asked.

"I didn't get a name, sir," the officer said. "All I know is it was a woman that phoned and gave the heads-up."

Quincy nodded and then let out a low chuckle.

"What's funny, sir?" the officer asked.

"You're too young to know," Quincy said to the young officer. "But you'll pick it up in time."

"Know what, sir?" the officer asked.

"That you should never be around when you're really needed," Quincy said.

12

CHAPTER

Boomer checked his rearview mirror and looked across at Buttercup, sitting up in the front seat. "I suppose it would be a waste of time to ask you to buckle up," he said. Buttercup opened her mouth wide and yawned, then curled her girth into a semicircle and rested her head on her paws and closed her eyes.

Boomer swung his car onto the Seventy-ninth Street entrance to the West Side Highway and eased into the far-left lane. The black shaded-window four-door sedan behind him pulled the same maneuver, its front bumper right up against the rear taillights of the rusty unmarked Chevy. Boomer kicked his engine into high gear, zooming past the Ninety-sixth Street entrance, his speedometer hitting the mid-eighties, the front end shaking, the hood doing a rapid-fire tremble. The northbound traffic around the two cars was midafternoon light, with a heavy spring rain landing hard on the damaged roadway, making the numerous potholes more treacherous to navigate. Boomer kicked his wipers into high gear and gave his side mirror a long look, trying to make out the faces inside the vehicle riding hard on his tail. "Let's take them up to the Bronx," he said to the sleeping Buttercup. "See how they handle those streets. But don't let it worry you none. I think I got it under control."

Boomer went through the winding and curving roads of Riverdale as if he were on the last lap of a NASCAR run, the sedan keeping pace no more than a dozen feet behind. He veered to the left and motored up the two lanes of the Henry Hudson Parkway, a pair of low-riding rails on both sides, heavy tree coverage eating up the view on his right. He drove like a cop, one hand on the wheel, the other gripping the gun in his waistband, swinging the car from one lane to the next, taking full advantage of the lack of traffic, his front end doing a hard bump and scrape over the edge of a small crater, sparks flying off both fender and bumper. The blow lifted Buttercup off her seat, the dog shooting Boomer a tired look. "Don't throw the blame my way," Boomer said. "Toss it to the four shooters on our ass."

Boomer moved the car to the right and then sharp hard to the left, the Benz slow to react to the move. He then slammed on his brakes and brought the car to a bracing and violent halt. Thick puffs of smoke and shards of tire treads quickly filled the air, and the smell of burning rubber and shocks scorched Boomer's nostrils.

The Benz slowed its pace, but not before Boomer had swung his unmarked behind it, his window down, his gun drawn, rapid-firing a series of rounds into the darkened rear windshield. The Benz swung wildly to the right and left, skidding against the railing, a few feet removed from a fatal fall, one of its rear tires blown. Boomer tossed his gun onto the front seat, eased the unmarked alongside the Benz, and jammed it in tight, banging door against door, the tires of the two cars rubbing hard one against the other, sparks and a thin line of flames shooting out from under the Benz.

The sharp turn that led into the entrance to Exit 4 and the Cross County Parkway was now less than a quarter of a mile away. "Hang on," Boomer said to the dog. "And if you want, wave goodbye to our new friends while you still have the chance."

Boomer clicked the unmarked into overdrive, squeezing the hood of his car in front of the Benz, the two tops bending from the speed and pressure, tires smoking and tearing, thick rubber peeling off the wheels like skin off fruit. Boomer swung the steering wheel as far to the right as it would go, only five hundred feet away from the slick curve leading into the exit. "C'mon," he said, his upper body straining as much as his battered car, the sweat running down hard off his chest and arms. "Flip, you bastards, flip."

Boomer was positioned in front of the Benz, still pressing it heavy, the older unmarked chugging hard against the newer and better built model. He tapped on his brakes several times, allowing the back end of the car to swing out and putting it parallel against the Benz, then he slammed his foot hard on the gas. The Benz did a double flip over the low rail and out onto the heavily wooded terrain. It shot like an unguided rocket down the sloping hill, banging against trees and low-hanging limbs until it came to a fiery and smoke-filled stall by the edge of the Bronx River.

Boomer frantically turned his steering wheel to the left, hitting the gas and skimming against the side of the rail, the car shooting into the sharp curve of Exit 4, thick lines of smoke, sparks, and fumes in its wake. He came out of the curve and slowed the car down, easing onto an off-ramp and shoving the gear shift into neutral. He stepped out of the car, the cool breeze feeling good against his sweat-soaked body, leaving the passenger door open for Buttercup to follow. The dog jumped out, waded past the thick clouds of smoke, and stood next to Boomer, who was leaning now against the back end of the damaged vehicle. She rested her front paws on his legs and curled her head against his chest, drool running off her mouth. Boomer reached down and gently patted her thick hide. "I know," he said to her. "I'm glad we made it, too."

Boomer took one last look at his car, and then he and Buttercup turned and sprinted across the highway, going up a short hill and out onto the streets of the nearest exit.

13

Dead-Eye sat with his feet wedged up against the side of the table, case folders and police reports stacked on both ends. Ash leaned on the old school blackboard, taking a sip from a mug of hot coffee. Buttercup prowled from one end of the room to the other, stopping occasionally to lap from her large NYPD water bowl. Boomer stood alone in the center of Apaches HQ, looking out at the remaining members of his team. "I just got off the line with the doctor taking care of Quincy," he told them. "He's going to be laid up for about a week, ten days at the most, but he'll pull through. They need to be cautious, since they're not really sure how the heavy blood loss will affect his condition. Those waters are uncharted."

"We're still not done," Ash said, "and we're down two key players. You going to bring in fresh faces or do we go as is?"

"There's not enough time to work in anybody new," Boomer said. "We go in as we are. But that doesn't mean we're not without any backup. Tony Rigs will send in a team of his shooters to give us some coverage, and the Russians will help as much as they feel the need. But the bulk of the takedowns are on us."

"How many you figure to be covering Angel's end?" Ash asked.

"About twenty spread out inside the brownstone," Boomer said. "And another dozen or so shooters working the street outside. Most of them will either be sitting in parked cars or working the corners, eyes on the lookout for us."

"Trust me, you'll know them when you see them," Dead-Eye said. "And when you do, don't even think. Just shoot. And not to drop—to kill."

Boomer glanced across the room at Ash and waited for her to look his way. "You'll be all right," he told her, looking to offer comfort along with confidence. "You wouldn't be out there with us if we didn't think you could handle this. And besides, now we'll find out if you're as good at setting fires as you were at catching the ones that did."

"Let's all remember one crucial detail beyond the planning," Dead-Eye said. "The wise guys will be there and they'll do their part. The same holds for the Russians. But we only trust each other and look to one or the other for help. The only four that we need to worry about are in this room right now. Clear?"

"You okay with getting there early and laying down your smoke?" Boomer asked Ash. "Or you want one of us to tag along?"

"If I had to pick someone in here to take, it would be Buttercup," Ash said with a smile. "Besides, I don't figure on being alone."

"How's that?" Boomer asked.

Ash opened her jacket and pointed to a detective shield clipped to her waistband. "It's Rev. Jim's tin," she said. "Quincy gave it to me. So I do have someone looking over my shoulder."

"I can't think of anyone better," Boomer said. "But remember that Angel is who we want. He's the last peg on our board. This started with him, and it's with him it's going to end."

Dead-Eye walked over to one of the cabinets and slid the door open. He reached inside and pulled out two .44 handguns and jammed them into his shoulder holsters. He slipped a .38 Special into a third holster and clipped it to his back. A fourth gun went into his ankle strap. He filled the side pockets of his thin black leather jacket with clips and bullets and then grabbed a double-pump shotgun and shoved it inside a brown duffel bag by his feet. He turned and looked across the room at Boomer, Ash, and Buttercup and nodded. "The time is in the here and now," he said to them, "for that fucking ex-priest to be put down for his last rites."

"I love it when you get spiritual," Boomer said.

The night was cool, spring making its last stand. The Upper East Side street was quiet, row upon row of expensive and well-maintained town houses filling both sides, along with the lights and signs of two 24-hour parking garages. A young boy, no more than fourteen, was walking a miniature Aussie on a long leash, the dog moving slowly from parked car to fire hydrant to the side of a tree, sniffing at the damp concrete. A middle-aged couple, both bundled up in sports jackets, scarves, and wool caps, quick-stepped their way toward the front door of their basement apartment.

Angel's town house was in the middle of the block, four stories high, a small gate and a garden off to the right, a dozen steps in the center leading up to the thick white front door, a large overhead light illuminating the entrance. Two men were posted at the bottom step, one of them reading a Spanish-language newspaper. Three other men sat inside a parked Chevy two spots up from the house, the one in the back with his head braced against the window, asleep.

Boomer stood in the slanted entryway of a parking garage, across from the town house, and checked his watch. He leaned his head against a white cement wall and closed his eyes. So many men and women had died for him to get to this moment, and so many more needed to in order for it to pass. And, for the first time in as many years as he could recall, Boomer began to wonder if all the carnage was worth the end result. It wasn't lost on him that more people he cared about and loved were dead than alive, and that more than a handful had ended up that way because of his actions. He didn't know if he still had the courage to bury yet another friend and he prayed that, on this night at least, he wouldn't need to be tested.

The explosion rocked him back to reality.

He turned and felt the blast of heat come at him, the car with the three men inside now nothing more than a burning skeleton of steel. Boomer checked his weapons, scanned the street, and ran from the parking-garage entrance toward Angel's town house, charging his way into yet another battle.

The two men who had been guarding the steps lay on the ground now, wounded and bleeding. Boomer stepped over one of them and made his way up the steps of the town house, taking them two at a clip. He turned when he heard the scattered gunfire coming from up the street, three of Angel's men in a shoot-out with two burly Russians. At the other end of the block, he knew the hitters sent by Tony Rigs were doing their duty, utilizing the darkness, the element of surprise, and their expertise with ropes and knives to full effect. Whatever troubles the Apaches faced on this night would come from inside the town house, not out.

Boomer was in the middle of the foyer, both guns drawn, his right shoulder wedged against thick wood paneling, when he saw the man in a dark outfit flip over a third-floor banister and come crashing down onto the black-and-white tiled floor, blood and brain matter wedged under his head and neck. He looked up and saw Dead-Eye give him a clear-to-move wave. He had made it to the top of the first-floor landing, turned, and then heard a door creak open behind him.

Boomer never hesitated.

He whirled, crouched down in a catcher's position, and fired four rounds through the thick wood. The thump from the other side told him the bullets had found their mark. There were two other doors in the corridor, both closed, one facing him and one at his back. Boomer stood and walked with silent steps on the carpeted floor, full adrenaline rush masked by a calm and confident exterior. Both doors swung open at once and two men armed with semis rushed out of each, Boomer in the middle of their rapid and lethal cross fire. He braced himself against a wall offering a few inches of cover from each side, his arms extended left and right, responding to their salvos. Bullets chipped the sides of the wall extension, sending dust and Sheetrock fragments hurtling through the air. Boomer fired the last rounds in his weapons and leaned his head against the wall, his fingers rummaging through his jacket pockets for fresh bullets. The four shooters, two on either side, eased their fire and closed in for the kill.

Dead-Eye appeared as if from the heavens.

He vaulted off the top of the third-floor landing, his arms extended, feet spread apart, a gun in each hand, bullets ripping through the bodies of the four unsuspecting hitters and sending them sprawling to their death. He landed with a thud and a roll, his back to the thick banister, his face locked in a grimace, a smile creasing across as he looked over at Boomer. "So," Dead-Eye said, "how you been?"

"We clear upstairs?" Boomer asked, shaking his head in wonder at his old friend. "Or are there more surprises in store?"

"Third floor looks good," Dead-Eye said, "at least on a first look. Fourth floor is where our priest is holed up. He had three men on the roof covering him from the top."

"You get to them yet?" Boomer asked.

"Didn't have to," Dead-Eye said. "It could have been Tony Rigs or maybe the Russians. Or just a deep depression set in. Either way, they did snow cones off the roof and into the alley."

"How do you suppose Ash is making out?" Boomer asked.

"We should have our answer any minute now," Dead-Eye said. "If this building lifts off the ground like a NASA space shuttle, we'll know she came through. Why, you worried about her?"

"I'm Italian, Dead-Eye. I worry about everything."

He jumped to his feet and reached out a hand to help ease Dead-Eye back up. They both looked around: the ornate wood-work, old-world lighting fixtures, flowers, the textured wallpaper, the expensive portraits in gilded frames that surrounded them. "It always plays out this way, you know," Dead-Eye said. "These kinds of homes never end up with the owners they deserve."

"Maybe some do," Boomer said. "Just never the ones we get to see from the inside."

"You think it's us, then?" Dead-Eye asked. "That we always gravitate our way to the wrong people?"

"In our case, the wrong people are the ones we want," Boomer said. "That's why we took the badge, and that's why we're still fighting not to give it up."

"Maybe so and probably true," Dead-Eye said. "But I tell you, just for once I'd love to walk into one of these places without having to bring it to the ground."

"Start hanging out in museums," Boomer said.

The blast shook the foundation and tossed them across the room. Boomer landed on top of the body of one of the shooters. Dead-Eye hit shoulder and back against the last row of the stair-well, blood running down the right side of his head from a three-inch gash. Pockets of flames roared through the town house, with thick dust clouds fast in their wake. Glass from the ornate windows on every floor exploded in shards and landed on the street and in the rear courtyard. Through the crackle of the fire and the collapsing façade around them, Boomer and Dead-Eye could hear the distant whine of fire and police sirens. "I have to admit," Dead-Eye said, "that Ash is one scary young lady. But you have to love a woman who can handle dynamite the way she can."

"Let's express-mail our way up the stairs," Boomer said. "We got about five minutes, maybe less, to put the grab on Angel."

Boomer stood in the middle of Angel's room, lined with books and works of art, its windows blown out, thin lines of smoke billowing in from both inside and out. Dead-Eye sat on a dusty sofa chair, a gun on his lap. Angel sat across from them, in the middle of a thick-ply couch, his expensive clothes tinged with a coating of soot, a pair of black rosary beads curled in his right hand. "A little late to reach for the prayer card, wouldn't you say?" Boomer asked.

"It's an old habit," Angel said, his voice low and calm, a sharp contrast to the smoke-filled madness that surrounded them. "And you know what it is they say about old habits?"

"They're tough for others to take," Dead-Eye said.

"I misjudged you," Angel said. "Not your skills, those I was well aware of. It was your determination that surprised me. I had my doubts as to whether or not you possessed the fortitude to get past those I had placed in your path. It appears that while the years and the wounds have slowed your movements, they have not yet put a dent in your courage."

"A lot of people just died because of you, quite a few of them good," Boomer said. "One of them was my niece."

"There are some that have the belief that our next life is the better one," Angel said, his manner as relaxed as it was cold. "Perhaps that can offer you some form of solace."

Boomer lifted his .38 Special and fired a round into Angel's right shoulder. "No, but that just did," he said.

Angel lowered his head, left hand clutching his open wound, blood flowing out between his fingers, down his silk shirt, and onto the couch. "Your police friends will be coming through that door any second now," he said to them both, struggling to squeeze out the words. "If you kill me, as I'm sure you intend to do, you might have a difficult time talking your way out of a murder charge, and that would end up being a horrible stain on records as distinguished as yours."

"They might go for a bribe," Dead-Eye said. "That seems to have worked for you."

"You don't have that kind of money," Angel sneered. "And you never will."

"Anyway, we're not going to kill you," Boomer said, walking toward Angel and lifting him off the couch. "We're going to let you escape. You make it out, then you get out. Free again to deal and steal."

Dead-Eye jumped up from his chair and went over to the door, cracked it open a notch, and glanced down the stairs. He looked back at Boomer. "They're on their way up," he said. "Three uniforms and a plainclothes, guns showing in the lead."

"But don't think we're going to let you leave empty-handed," Boomer said to Angel. "That wouldn't be fair to either you or the cops who will be pegging bullets your way." Boomer grabbed Angel's left hand and put a .38 in it, wrapping the gun around his fingers and palms using a roll of clear tape. He reached over and did the same to the other hand, ripping the rosary beads from Angel's fingers and holding them up in front of his eyes. "You should have used these when you had the chance," he told him. "You never know, it might have helped."

Boomer looked to Dead-Eye, who nodded and swung open the door.

Boomer tossed Angel out into the hall just as the cops were rounding the top stairwell, slamming the door shut behind him. Dead-Eye lifted his gun and fired three rounds into the ceiling.

They held their position and listened as Angel tried to shout out his innocence, the two guns taped to his hands, blood running down his right shoulder. They listened as the cops unleashed a storm of bullets and the former priest howled out his last, brief prayer.

———

Boomer and Dead-Eye walked over to the small staircase in the corner that led to the rooftop garden. Boomer looked to his left and caught a glance of a painting that was hanging between the door and a floor-to-ceiling bookcase. He tapped Dead-Eye on the shoulder and pointed to the painting. "Have we seen that before?" he asked.

"I think so," Dead-Eye said.

"And what does it mean that it's here?" he asked.

"It means we have a problem," Dead-Eye said. "A serious one."

The two Apaches opened the door leading out of the room and stepped into the carpeted hall, Angel's fallen body to their left, resting facedown against a corner wall. The stairwell, from top floor to bottom, was lined with police officers, both uniform and plain-clothes, all with guns drawn. Boomer and Dead-Eye stared out at them and watched as each one silently holstered his weapon. The two Apaches walked down the stairs, flanked by cops on either side, heads down, arms at rest. No one spoke as Boomer and Dead-Eye left the town house and disappeared into the safety of the cold, New York night.

15

—— CHAPTER ——

Boomer rested the fresh basket of flowers against the gray headstone, his moist eyes locked onto the name, Angela Bromardi, chiseled across its front. It was a sun-drenched Sunday morning, two days into the start of another summer, the grass around the grave site freshly mulched, the soil brown and soft. "I wonder how she would have felt about what you, Dead-Eye, and the others went out and did," his sister, Maria, said. She was standing to his right, one arm linked through his. "She was cut from a different cloth than you and me. Getting even wasn't in her blood, it seems."

"I wish none of it had to be done," Boomer said. "I can't imagine she would have been all that happy with any one of us. Most especially me."

"She loved you, John," Maria said, holding him closer. "You always were the one she went to when she needed to talk. Not to me or her dad, only you. She felt she'd get a fair listen, whether you agreed with her or not."

"And I usually didn't," he said, managing a smile. "I think that was part of the fun for her. You guys didn't argue, but I did and she got a big kick out of that end of it. But I was only her uncle. I can get away with crap that a mother and father never could. It's a very unfair advantage."

"I miss her," Maria said. "Every day and in every way. I thought as time passed it would be a little easier. Not that I would forget her—that could never happen. Just that maybe there would be one night when I didn't sit up in bed and cry. The other day, I was in the middle of the supermarket, reaching for a box of tangerines, and I just broke down, remembering how she could never get enough of those. Even as a toddler, she saw a tangerine and it was like she saw gold. I had to be helped out of the store; that's how bad it was."

"That part will get easier," Boomer said to her. "But living with her loss will always be hard. It's like losing a key piece of your own body. You adjust your life to it, but you're always aware that there's something missing."

"Thank you for what you went and did," Maria said, wiping tears from her eyes with the fingers of her right hand. "I tell you, I feel like such a hypocrite sometimes. I go to Mass every day, say the rosary the way Mama taught me, and go to confession each Saturday. And, at the same time, here I am, happy that the people who did this to our Angela are dead. And knowing that it wouldn't have happened if you hadn't taken a hand. What does that make me, John? What kind of person?"

"You're a mother, Maria," Boomer said. "A mother whose daughter was stolen from her for no reason. What you do in that church and those prayers you say every day matter to the ones you say them for, and the scum that took Angela away from us were never to be included in that mix. That's not hypocrisy. That's reality."

"What happens now," she asked, "to you and to Dead-Eye? You two can't keep doing this, not if you expect to live long enough to make collecting that pension of yours worth the time and effort. I know the main reason you both went out after the men that did this was to get payback for Angela. But there was more to it than that. It gave you a reason to throw yourselves back into the action. And that was a piece of it neither one of you could turn your backs on."

"Well, we're both too old and banged up for the Peace Corps," Boomer said. "And we're still a few years removed from a slot in a nursing home, so I don't know what we'll do. But some door will open up. It usually does."

"And standing inside that door will be somebody with a gun in his hand, looking to kill the both of you, mark my money," Maria said. "Good as the two of you are at what you do, eventually you'll run into somebody better."

"We don't talk about it much, me and Dead-Eye, but I think we both have the sense that our run is coming to a close," Boomer said, staring down at his niece's headstone. "We never had to give it a lot of thought before, didn't really need to take the time. I guess being the kind of action-junkie cops we were, we had to figure that we weren't going to get much of a chance to be close friends with old age. So why bother even giving it more weight than it needed."

"Angela always worried about you," Maria said. "She never showed it and didn't want it to be discussed in front of you, but there were times when if we ever got a late-night call she would be convinced it was someone telling us you'd been shot."

"I remember that time you brought her to see me in the hospital," Boomer said. "She couldn't have been more than, what, seven? Maybe eight? Big brown eyes open wide, her head barely reaching the edge of the bed, looking up at me all bandaged up, tubes running into my arms and down my throat. I opened my eyes and put an arm around her and lifted her to the bed. She never said a word, just rested her head on my shoulder and stayed with me most of that afternoon."

"I remember," Maria said, sniffing away a fresh rush of tears. "She told me she stayed there to protect you, make sure no one came in to hurt you anymore."

"And that she did," Boomer said. "But tough cop or not, I couldn't do the same for her when she needed it the most. That's what makes you walk away from it, Maria. It's not the job, the hours, the politics, the bullshit, or the danger. It's the simple truth that no matter how hard you work it, how good you are at it, how many you put away or put down, you still will never be able to protect and keep safe the ones you love the most. I've seen too many people I love die without cause, and I don't think I can deal with that part of it anymore."

"You'll figure it out," Maria said, rubbing a hand across the left side of his face. "It'll just pop one day when you're not even looking for it. Whatever it is you do next, John, I really hope it's something that makes you happy. You deserve that, and you've more than earned it."

"I'll drop a dime and give you a heads-up soon as I find it," Boomer said, smiling over at his sister. "I just hope whatever the next stop is it's not something that requires me to wear a tie."

"I'll go wait for you in the car," Maria said. "We need to head back soon, and I want to give you and Angela a few minutes alone."

Boomer gave her a nod and watched as she walked down the sloping hillside, her steps slowed by both age and the weight of grief. He turned back to the headstone and crouched down, one knee touching the soft dirt. "I'm sorry, kiddo," he whispered, his voice cracking. "For all the times I wasn't there, especially on that last day. But if it means anything to you, we went out and got them all—the ones that put you here. Almost all, anyway. There's still one left. But I give my word, once that's done I'll bring an end to it. Put away the gun and the badge, and this time for good. I promise, and it's one I won't ever break. If I do, you'll never let me hear the end of it. I love you, Angie. I wish I had told you that more when you were alive, but I think you knew. You own my heart, kiddo, and you always will."

Boomer reached into his jacket pocket and pulled out his detective's gold shield, half hidden in a black leather pouch. He rested it against the front of the headstone, then leaned over and planted a soft kiss above the young woman's name. He lowered his head, folded his hands, and whispered a soft prayer, the sun warm on his back, casting its glow across the cold dirt of a crowded cemetery.

16

Quincy sat up in the hospital bed, his thin body covered by an even thinner gown, a starched white sheet folded up to chest level. Ash stood on one side of the bed, pouring cold water from a plastic container into an NYPD coffee mug and handing it over to Quincy along with a smile. Boomer and Dead-Eye stood on the other side, careful not to brush up against any of the tubes and drips that were attached to Quincy's arm. Buttercup sat curled on the edge of the bed, her eyes looking up at Quincy.

"The doctor told me you caught some luck, that the cuts went deep but not deep enough to do serious damage," Dead-Eye said. "They might check you out of here in a day, two at the outside."

"It's nice to have some good luck for a change," Quincy said. "I'm ready to leave, tell you the truth. Grab a good meal somewhere that's not here. Have you seen what they call breakfast?"

"Buttercup did," Ash said. "She took one look at your tray and I thought she was going to hurl. And this from a dog that will eat shit out of a cat-litter box."

"I didn't think they let dogs in hospital rooms," Quincy said, looking down at the K-9 and giving her a wink.

"They don't," Boomer said. "Luckily, she's a cop."

"Which means she can come and go as she pleases so long as she flashes that tin," Dead-Eye said. "And that includes riding for free on buses and subways and getting into ballparks to watch any game she chooses."

"You want to talk about a dog's life," Ash said, "look no further than our fair lady."

"Any fallout from what went down at the town house with Angel?" Quincy asked. "Especially given that Ash, the mad bomber here, nearly took down an entire Manhattan street."

"There would have been if we had just gone out and done it on a whim," Dead-Eye said. "But taking out one of the top drug dealers on two continents does have its perks."

"We threw the full weight of the bust over to NYPD and the Federal Drug Task Force," Boomer said. "We figure we let them fight over who gets final credit, long as they leave us out of it."

"They get to clear most of Angel's team as well as the G-Men off their dockets," Ash said. "That's a heavy load of yellow folders to toss into the case-closed file."

"And Tony Rigs and the Russians cut up and clean up on the leftovers," Quincy said. "It's the revolving door of crime: two crews go out weak and two come back in strong. The best we can do is try and keep as many civilians as we can clear of the traffic."

"Their turn will come sure as sunrise," Boomer said, exchanging a quick look with Dead-Eye. "It's all about when, how, and who comes in to take them down and wash them out."

"You never know," Ash said with a slight shrug. "Down the road, it might even be us."

"I wouldn't bet your tax-free pension on that," Boomer said.

"From here on, when the bad guys topple, it's going to have to be some other cops to tip them over. Not us. We're done. At least I am."

"Count me out of the game as well," Dead-Eye said. "If you guys are eager to keep the Apaches going, you have our full blessings. I wouldn't give it a high recommend, but I'll leave it to you to make the call."

"So the one job was it?" Quincy said. "We now all go our separate ways?"

"We stay friends, always," Boomer said. "And we'll be there for each other, help out in any way we can. Our lives aren't over. Just our Apache days."

"We need to move on with our lives," Dead-Eye said. "Maybe me and Boomer more than you two. But the truth is, we'd only be working on borrowed time, we keep going in the direction we're in now."

"I *am* on borrowed time," Quincy said. "That's the only kind of time I know."

Boomer stepped up closer to Quincy, resting a hand on top of his folded ones. "You won't be alone," he said. "Even if you wanted to be, we won't allow it. We're linked to one another tight as a chain. And nothing can take from that—not our wounds, not old age, and sure as shit not some fucking disease. That's our next fight, and it's one we fight together."

"And you just got the word from the head Wopahoe himself," Dead-Eye said. "There's no step back from friendship. We don't know any other way. But our days doing a duck-and-dodge against a crew of bangers will soon be set in the past."

"Which leaves us where, exactly?" Ash asked.

"On a one-day-at-a-time clip," Boomer said. "And as for the rest of this one, how about you and our sleepy-time pup hang here with Quincy and see if you can score him a high-caliber lunch?"

"Maybe even get somebody with soft eyes and a warm smile to change his bandages," Dead-Eye said. "You know, put to good use that overabundance of charm we all know you secretly possess."

"And where will you two Galahads be off to while Ash and Buttercup are doing their candy-striper routine?" he asked.

"We have a date," Boomer said. "And we can't be late, not with this lady. She's the punctual type."

"A special kind of woman, no doubt," Dead-Eye said, leading the way out of the room. "What my father would call a real killer."

17

Natalie sat back and watched as Boomer poured out three glasses of chilled champagne and handed one each to her and Dead-Eye. She smiled, nodded her thanks, and raised her thin glass toward the two Apaches. "To a job perfectly executed," she said.

Boomer sat back and stared across at Natalie, dressed in a black Karl Lagerfeld dress that was slit at the thigh, her rich dark hair falling over her shoulders, her olive eyes bright and alert.

He would never sit across from a more beautiful woman.

"Yes, it was," Boomer said. "But I have to spread credit to where it needs to be put, and that's square on your well-turned-out lap."

"I helped," Natalie said, holding the smile, her eyes moving from Boomer to Dead-Eye. "But you were the ones who pulled it off. None of it would have worked without your team being in the middle of it all."

"You did more than plan, Natalie," Boomer said. "You played us and we walked right into your game, chess pieces on your big board."

"There was a time," Dead-Eye said, "when we might have smelled it out. Maybe seen the moves sooner, not been as blind to your actions as we were."

They were sitting at the back of a small dining room in a quiet Italian restaurant on the tail end of West Forty-sixth Street. It was an hour past the lunchtime rush, and they were the only diners in the place, most of the waiters heading off to a well-earned break. "Get to your point," Natalie said, the smile gone now, the eyes hard, the Lady Who Lunched quickly replaced by the born-and-bred mob boss. "I came here to celebrate, or thought I did. I didn't come to be lectured or listen to any insane blather."

"I have to hand it to you," Boomer said, his voice tinged with a sad resignation. "You had me going for most of it. Maybe because I wasn't expecting it, or more like I just didn't want to see it."

Natalie finished her glass of champagne, rested the glass on top of the table, leaned back in her chair, crossed her legs, and smiled over at Boomer. "Where did I botch it?" she asked.

"I caught a glimpse of a piece of art hanging in a corner of Angel's room," Boomer said. "It was the same high-end work that we took out of Talbot's brownstone, included in that big batch that was supposed to have been fenced halfway around the world. Yet, miracle of miracles, it somehow found its way into Angel's little cave and that was when it all fell into place."

"You sell it or just hand it over as a gift?" Dead-Eye asked.

"I never give," Natalie said in a voice as harsh as they had ever heard it.

"No, I guess you don't," Boomer said. "And you usually don't make mistakes. At least not ones big enough that even two beat-up cops like us could catch."

"I don't see where you have much to complain about," Natalie said. "You wanted to bring down Angel and do damage to his operation, and that you certainly accomplished. Adding the G-Men to the mix was merely sweet icing to a very delicious cake."

"That may all be true," Boomer said, "but we were used, plain and simple, and that sort of shit doesn't sit well with us."

"You needed help and I offered to supply it," Natalie said. "You made use of my skill set as much as I made use of yours."

"You could have taken Angel and his crew down on your own," Dead-Eye said. "Same holds for the G-Men. You didn't need to bring us into it."

"It was important to me and to my business interests that both groups think we were partners until the very end," Natalie said. "I couldn't very well do that if we were at each other's throats in the middle of a gang war. So that's where you came into my picture, and I colored you into my plans."

"And the only reason we stepped into your picture was because of a restaurant shooting," Boomer said, his words hard and measured. "A shooting that killed my niece. A shooting that wasn't the accident it was so carefully made to look like. Feel free to step in and stop me if you think I'm taking this in the wrong direction."

"It put you in play," Natalie said. "While Angel and eventually the G-Men focused their limited attention on a small band of rogue cops, I not only was able to make my moves under their very gaze but they would even on occasion turn to me for advice. Talk about having your cake."

"So the only collateral damage to come out of that restaurant was the sap in the booth," Dead-Eye said.

"It's not as if Angel ever needed an excuse to rid himself of potential enemies," she said. "But the only real target in that restaurant, as far as I was concerned, was the waitress."

The room swirled slightly, the bile rising in his throat. For the first time in his life, Boomer felt overwhelmed by the horror of a crime. His right hand instinctively moved toward his holster, fingers eager to grip the hard end of a gun. He felt duped and foolish, a washed-up cop taken in by beauty and a beast all rolled into one. "What made you so certain that I would go after them?" he choked out.

"The same that tells me that as much as you want to kill me right now, you won't," Natalie said. "And you never could. I made it my business to get to know you. I studied you. You were my exam and, if I may grade my own results, I passed with flying colors."

"You did more than pass," Boomer said, struggling against the odd sensation of heaviness that was overcoming him. "You won it all. And I lost. I'm walking away as empty as I came in."

Natalie nodded. "And where does that leave us now?" she asked.

"Back where we were before all this started," Boomer said. "You on one side, me on the other. Only this time I won't be putting together a team to come after you. The field is all yours."

"A wise move by a wise man," Natalie said.

"But we *will* stiff you with the tab for the champagne," Dead-Eye said. "And don't be a short arm when it comes to the tip, either."

Boomer slid his chair back and stood, his eyes never moving off Natalie's face. "If luck holds for both of us, we won't ever see each other again," he said. "Not in this life, at any rate."

Boomer turned and walked toward the side exit of the empty restaurant. He reached for the door handle and turned it. He stopped and lowered his head when he heard the three muted gunshots, three bullets firing in rapid succession. He listened for the gasp and the low moan that quickly followed and waited for the thud of a body falling facedown against the hard surface of a thick mahogany table. He opened his eyes, swung the door away from his face, and stepped outside into the light of the warm afternoon air.

18

CHAPTER

Boomer and Dead-Eye sat in the front seat of a parked sedan, facing the Hudson River on the edge of Pier 72, their backs to the southbound lanes of the West Side Highway. A four-story cruise ship was moored to the dock, water gently lapping against the sides of its mammoth hull, its passengers free for the day to explore the streets of the city beyond.

"I'm sorry you had to be the one," Boomer said.

"It had to be somebody," Dead-Eye said. "So why not me? She had to stand for what she did to Angela, and there was only one way for that to happen."

"But I could never have done it," Boomer said. "I could never have pulled the trigger on her. Even after what I knew she did, I still could never have brought myself to the point of raising my gun and pulling that trigger. And that's the first time I could ever say that about anyone."

"That's because you were in love with her," Dead-Eye said. "You denied it, but we both knew it was true. And love clouds your judgment as much as it does your vision. I didn't go in with that particular monkey on my back. Not that it was all that easy for me to do—don't get me wrong on that count. Just that it was *easier*."

"She wasn't surprised by it, was she?" Boomer asked.

"Not so you would see it on her face," Dead-Eye said. "She was smart enough to know I wasn't hanging back to get in a quick hug and a kiss. And she grew up in this rodeo, so she had to have a sense of what was going to happen."

"You think she knew it coming in?" Boomer asked. "That one of us was going to take her out?"

"I think she knew coming in that we were wise to her," Dead-Eye said. "And that you were there to tell her so and I was there to put her down."

"But still she came in," Boomer said. "On her own, empty. No bodyguards anywhere in sight."

"She came to see you, Boomer," Dead-Eye said. "That was the only reason she agreed to the meet. She wanted to see you one last time."

"What are you getting at?" Boomer asked.

"Give it some thought," Dead-Eye said. "A woman that smart, able to run an outfit that big and cold enough to waste an innocent kid just to get you and me back into the game so she can take down two bands of dealers without them catching a whiff, is going to be dumb enough to walk into a restaurant setup that could be put together with scratch paper and Crayolas?"

"You're saying she came in there knowing it was going to end up a hit?" Boomer asked. "Am I reading you right?"

"Finally, the dust is starting to clear," Dead-Eye said.

"Why would somebody that smart do something that stupid?" Boomer said.

"Same reason a cop like you couldn't draw down on a gangster like her," Dead-Eye said. "She fell in love, too."

Boomer put his head back and closed his eyes, the sound of the traffic behind him a blend of white noise. "I was crazy enough to think there might be a way for it to work," he said. "Until I knew she was behind it all, I was looking for a happy ending."

"Don't start getting sobby on yourself," Dead-Eye said. "You're not the only cop to get caught up with someone from the dark side. We all skirt the line at one time or another, and you can't cast blame on us for doing it. Three-quarters of couples out there met their lady or their husband on some job or other. People who work in banks marry bankers. Doctors tend to screw nurses, like that. We look to stay within our world, and in that case our options are fairly confined. On the high end, if we're really lucky—a lawyer maybe, an ADA we worked a case with, or, God forbid, one of those Legal Aid Set 'Em Loose Betty types. Otherwise, a partner or a cop you know from the job. And then, on rare occasions, somebody we should be chasing for reasons other than love."

"Who was it for you?" Boomer asked. "If you don't mind telling me."

"There are no secrets in foxholes and squad cars," Dead-Eye said. "It was a while back, wasn't even married yet. I was in uniform, and let's just say she wasn't. At any rate, I'm banging heads pretty heavy with her crew, even going on the hunt during my off time. I mean, I'm in fifth gear, looking to take them all down and get my ass booted up to plainclothes."

"That was the old Action Jackson crew, am I right?" Boomer asked. "They treated the edge of the Queens-Nassau border like they were left the deed to the land."

"That's them," Dead-Eye said. "Gail was one of the runners in that crew. And, just like you at first, I took one look and fell flat on my face. I was so hooked that I might as well have been jabbing a needle into my arm. It was as close as I ever got to forgetting who I really was—that's how much love I carried for that lady."

"What changed it back?" Boomer asked.

"I saw a kid on the street one morning," Dead-Eye said. "Right after I had done an all-night stakeout. I was heading toward a deli to grab some coffee when I spotted him faceup in a filthy alley. He couldn't have been more than seven, weighed as if he were two years younger, track marks like a fucking Metro-North Westchester route up and down his arms. He was stone-cold dead, and I remember thinking at the time that was probably the luckiest thing that could have happened to him. And in that same moment I realized I could never make a life with someone who moved the shit out onto the streets that put this kid into an early grave. It doesn't take much, Boomer. Most times nothing more than a cold, hard slap of reality."

"How did it end out?" Boomer asked.

"The same as it does for most in that chosen line of work," Dead-Eye said. "She caught a few slugs from someone who wanted to move a lot faster than she did. The last time I saw her, she had her eyes closed and her hands folded, lying faceup in an open coffin. But let me tell you, even with all that shit I think about Gail every once in a while. About what could have been between us. And the answer to your next question is no."

"You read minds now, too?" Boomer said. "Or is that a talent you've been keeping on the down and low from me?"

"Yours is the only mind I can read, because it's so much like mine," Dead-Eye said. "But no, I could not have been the one to put Gail down. I didn't want to be with her and I wanted to put her out of business, but I couldn't do it with a gun in my hand."

"You know the guy who did?" Boomer asked.

"It was one of her own that put her down," Dead-Eye said. "Some delusional dealer accused her of taking too much skim from his daily profits. He waited until she nodded off and then strangled her while she was asleep."

Boomer lifted his head, rubbed his eyes, and looked over at Dead-Eye. "You fall in love with a drug dealer," he said, "and I drop head over toe for some Russian mob queen. I guess it doesn't really say much for either one of us."

"Are you kidding me?" Dead-Eye said. "It shouts out everything you need to know about us. It sums us up all the way to the letter *t* and tells you the kind of men we both truly are."

"Which is what, exactly?" Boomer asked.

"Face up to it, old friend," Dead-Eye said. "The two of us, you and me, we're nothing more than a wasted pair of fucking romantics. Hard-core heartbreakers."

19

CHAPTER

It was a cloudless New York morning, the type of sun-drenched day that made the city streets glimmer and the skyline seem as if it were chiseled by magical hands. The Circle Line cruise boat slipped out of the dock, did a slow turn at the edge of the pier, and wound its way through the cold waves of the Hudson River, engine churning against the ever-present strong currents, up toward the serenity of the open waterway.

The summer crowd was sparse, free of children not yet clear of a daily school schedule and adults who had still not dipped into their valued vacation days. The passengers were a colorful mix of camera-toting tourists, retired couples, college students eager for a morning spent away from the confines of dorm life, and a cluster of middle-aged women—all leaving the demands of city living behind, at least for a few hours.

Boomer leaned on an iron railing on the top tier of the boat, staring out at the city to his left. Buttercup sat up next to him, her head tilted back against the cool river breeze, her gold shield resting on her chest, clipped to a thick chain around her neck. Ash stepped up next to both, handing Boomer a container of coffee, the lid still on firm. "Black, three sugars," she said. "That should toss your heart into high gear."

"If you're going to bother drinking it," he said as he reached for the coffee cup, "might as well drink it right."

"Let me guess," Ash said, looking down at Buttercup, a smile on her face. "She didn't pay for her ride. Am I right?"

"You'd be surprised at how far in life that shield can take you," he said. "Get you into places you never dreamed you'd get in."

"From private clubs to smoke-filled back rooms, the shield is your key," Dead-Eye said, stepping up beside them, Quincy right behind him. "Properly used, a shield can be a much more powerful tool for a cop than even a gun."

"Give me a for instance," Quincy said.

"There was this place on the West Side a few years back, had all sorts of shit going on behind closed doors," Boomer said. "During the day it was an art gallery—anybody, from housewife to homeless, could go in free of search or charge. The minute it turned dark, it became a millionaire's social club, and anything went once that happened. Drugs, S&M—you name it and they tried it. There were no boundaries in that place."

"I tried getting in the undercover way," Dead-Eye said. "I dressed myself up as sharp as any high-end dealer—leather pants, matching top and tie, fedora with a feather, the works. I wasn't just the bomb. I was a ticking bomb."

"How far did that getup take you?" Ash asked, not hiding her laugh.

"He didn't even get through the front door," Boomer said. "There was a guy big as a '57 Chevy blocking the entrance. He towers like a skyscraper over Dead-Eye and asks to see his Gold American Express card, which, oddly enough, he did not possess."

"More than that," Dead-Eye said, "I didn't even know what the fuck he was talking about. I'm standing there and I'm thinking, Shit, you mean American Express makes cards in different shades? Where was I when that memo hit the air?"

Their laughter echoed off the waves, the cruise liner doing a gentle bounce, easing through the water as it made its way up the Hudson. "So did you ever get in?" Quincy asked.

"I walked back to the unmarked and there's Boomer sitting there fuming," Dead-Eye said. "He's not seeing me standing there dressed as Huggy Bear from *Starsky & Hutch*. He only sees a detective treated like a wet mop by some guy built like a semi with half a dozen priors on his sheet. Boomer jumps out of the car, storms right past me, and heads off like a runaway bull for that front door. And damn if he wasn't inside in less time than it takes to boil an egg."

"What did you tell the guy at the door?" Quincy asked.

"I get there and he slams a hand right on my chest," Boomer said. "It felt like he crushed a lung. Looks down at me, smiles, and tells me that his club is a private club for members only. I looked right back, jammed my gold shield right between his eyes, and said to him, 'So is this, asshole. And if I'm not inside in less than a minute I will drag your big ass downtown and put you inside a crowded holding pen. Now, you may have a good lawyer and he may make a call and get you out in five, maybe six hours, but by that time you would have been everybody's woman.'"

"What did he do?" Ash asked.

"The only thing he could do," Boomer said. "He stepped aside, swung the door open, and let me in to do some damage. As it turned out, he was the only player that night me and Dead-Eye *didn't* bust."

The cruise boat veered upriver, swinging slightly to the left, the sun doing a slow rise, warming their faces, its late-morning glare giving the water a glassy look. Quincy leaned his back on the rail and raised his face to the sky. Dead-Eye slowly unwrapped a piece of Bazooka bubble gum and slipped it into his mouth. "You still feeling any pain in your wounds?" he asked Quincy.

"Not really," Quincy said. "They healed up pretty fast, which even caught the doctors off guard, considering my other problem."

"How are you doing with that?" Boomer asked. "It getting any better, any worse, or still the same?"

"A little bit of all three," Quincy said, staring out at the soapy-looking waves. "I never know which myself until I open my eyes and start the day. If you had called yesterday and asked me to make this trip, I wouldn't have had the strength to pick up the phone. Today, I feel strong enough to go for an afternoon run. Tomorrow is anybody's guess."

"Was that doctor I reached out to any help to you?" Boomer asked.

"He knows as much about the disease as most of the white coats, which isn't all that much. But the one thing he doesn't do is bullshit me, and that I really appreciate," Quincy said. "He never feels the need to put a happy face on the truth. That means a lot. So has every minute I've spent with this group, including Rev. Jim."

"Put the thanks in your pocket," Boomer said. "I didn't put you on this team because I felt sorry for you. I chose you and I chose Ash for one reason only. You're both great cops, and without either one of you it wouldn't have gone down anywhere close to the way it did."

"You and Dead-Eye did more than that, and you're probably not even aware of it," Ash said, struggling with her emotions and choosing her words with care. "You showed us we could go on. That our lives didn't have to just wither away and end with scars and injuries or a sickness. That we could still have an impact. I don't know where I'll go from here, but wherever it is and whatever it is, I'll be able to handle anything that comes my way."

"Where would you like it to go?" Dead-Eye asked. "You had your pick of the lot, either one of you, what would it be? I know you both hinted at it a few times in the past, but now would be a good time to hear it said out loud."

Ash and Quincy exchanged a look and then both turned toward Boomer and Dead-Eye, Buttercup sound asleep at their feet. "Before you take it there," Boomer said, "okay if I ask if your boat trip was worth it, even if it's not a sailboat?"

"It was better than any dream I ever had," Ash said, smiling, back in control of her feelings again.

"You could have a lot more days like this one, you know," Boomer said. "It doesn't need to be a onetime thing. Look around and take in what you don't see as much as what you do see. No dealers, no shooters, no bangers, just a hot sun on a warm day. I'm just pointing out what maybe should have been pointed out to me and Dead-Eye way too many years ago."

"I need to *feel* alive, Boomer, for as long as I'll still *be* alive," Quincy said. "And you're right, it is beautiful out here and in many other places neither one of us has ever seen. But the only time I've ever felt alive, truly alive, has been these last few weeks working and banging heads with this group. And I don't want to lose that, at least not until I have to."

"You're not going to lose anybody—toss the worry on that right now," Dead-Eye said. "If that's what it is that you want—that whatever it is we do next, we do it together—then that has my vote, too."

"Does that go for you as well?" Boomer asked Ash. "We keep the team in place and go into the next step as one?"

"I didn't have a family for the longest time," Ash said. "I got so used to being alone, I didn't even think twice about it. But I found a family again, standing right here, right now. And I'll do what it takes and what it needs not to lose it."

"I'm guessing one of you ran this past Buttercup's desk," Dead-Eye said, winning a laugh from the others.

"Well, our team's still in place," Quincy said. "Now all we need is to find us a job."

"We got a job," Boomer said. "One that's going to pay us a boat-load of money, assuming we do it right."

"We signed off on it before we came aboard," Dead-Eye said. "And we signed you two on along with us—Buttercup, too. So we're more than thrilled to hear you express how you're so Boy Scout eager to keep working together. Because if you had said otherwise, me and Boomer would have been big-time screwed."

"But you swore off going gun-to-gun back on those streets," Quincy said. "At least that's what I thought I heard."

"You heard right," Boomer said. "We're not hunting bangers or shooters and not drug dealers, nothing like that."

"What, then?" Ash asked.

"You remember all that art was lifted out of Jonas Talbot's brownstone?" Boomer asked.

"How could we forget?" Quincy said. "Just one of those paintings was worth more than what each of us can probably hope to earn in a lifetime."

"Those are them," Dead-Eye said. "And Natalie and her crew moved them fast as she could, and as many as she could, out into the black market. Now, anybody brings those paintings back and returns them to their proper owner, be they an individual or a museum, they're in store for a pretty hefty reward."

"That's our job?" Ash asked. "Finding stolen art?"

"That's exactly our job," Boomer said. "And we're working legit this time. We're being funded by the NYPD Art Squad. They want all the paintings back, but they lack the manpower to go after them. That's where we step into the frame."

"They could be anywhere in the world by now," Ash said.

"You mean like Europe, the Far East, Latin America?" Dead-Eye asked. "All those places we could never afford to go on our own?"

"I won't always be able to travel with you," Quincy said.

"We took that into consideration," Dead-Eye said. "We still have our main base, and when you can't get yourself on a plane, then you work out of there. Otherwise, you're on the road with us. Square with you?"

"Very," Quincy said.

"What about Buttercup?" Ash asked.

"What about her?" Dead-Eye said.

"She can't just hop on a plane with us and waltz into any country," Ash said. "There are quarantine laws we need to look into."

"Let's worry about the art, educate ourselves on that," Boomer said. "I wouldn't waste much time on any quarantine problems."

"She'll get in when she wants, where she wants," Dead-Eye said. "She's a cop. She's an Apache."

"And so are we," Boomer said. "So just go ahead and try to stop us."

The sun was burning-hot now, the day warming, the cruise liner easing past the Statue of Liberty and making its way back to port. To their left, the city of New York gleamed like polished silver. The Apaches stood in a line, taking in the full view.

"Try and stop any one of us," Boomer said.

ABOUT THE AUTHOR

LORENZO CARCATERRA is the author of *Paradise City, Street Boys, Gangster, A Safe Place,* and the *New York Times* bestsellers *Sleepers* and *Apaches.* He has written scripts for movies and television, and has worked as a writer and producer for *Law & Order.* Learn more about his work at www.LorenzoCarcaterra.com.

ABOUT THE TYPE

This book was set in Fairfield, the first typeface from the hand of the distinguished American artist and engraver Rudolph Ruzicka (1883–1978). Ruzicka was born in Bohemia and came to America in 1894. He set up his own shop, devoted to wood engraving and printing, in New York in 1913 after a varied career working as a wood engraver, in photoengraving and banknote printing plants, and as an art director and freelance artist. He designed and illustrated many books, and was the creator of a considerable list of individual prints—wood engravings, line engravings on copper, and aquatints.